THIS BOOK IS TH[...]
THE NATIONAL CIT[...]
NATIONAL CITY PUBLIC LIE[...]

We would appreciate your returning
this Library item by the due date so that
others in the community may have use
of this material.

NATIONAL CITY PUBLIC LIBRARY
200 E. 12th Street
National City, CA   92050
474-8211

War Comes to Castle Rising

War Comes to Castle Rising

Fanny Cradock

E.P. Dutton · New York

First American edition published 1978 by E.P. Dutton, a Division of Sequoia-Elsevier Publishing Company, Inc., New York

For information contact: E.P. Dutton, 2 Park Avenue, New York, N.Y. 10016

Library of Congress Catalog Card Number: 78-60715

ISBN: 0-525-23009-2

10 9 8 7 6 5 4 3 2 1

TO SARA, PAUL AND JONATHON

With love, because they are our continuation.

FANNY

Acknowledgment

The author wishes to express her very great gratitude to her colleagues in the *Daily Telegraph* Information Offices and to Mr Matthews of the London Library for their infinite patience in researching information for this book during a period of over three years.

Contents

THE
FAMILY
TREE

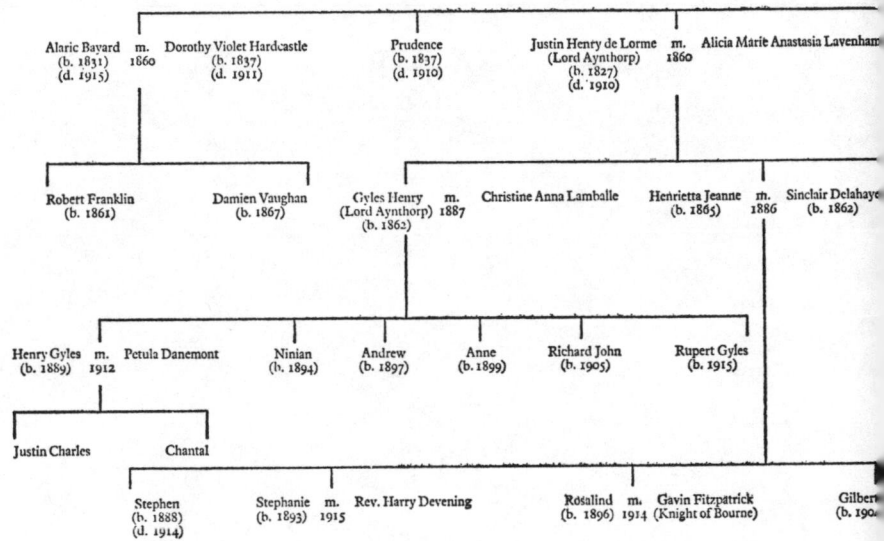

Alaric Bayard   m.   Dorothy Violet Hardcastle
(b. 1831)   1860   (b. 1837)
(d. 1915)   (d. 1911)

Prudence
(b. 1837)
(d. 1910)

Justin Henry de Lorme   m.   Alicia Marie Anastasia Lavenham
(Lord Aynthorp)   1860
(b. 1827)
(d. 1910)

Robert Franklin
(b. 1861)

Damien Vaughan
(b. 1867)

Gyles Henry   m.   Christine Anna Lamballe
(Lord Aynthorp) 1887
(b. 1862)

Henrietta Jeanne   m.   Sinclair Delahaye
(b. 1865)   1886   (b. 1862)

Henry Gyles   m.   Petula Danemont
(b. 1889)   1912

Ninian
(b. 1894)

Andrew
(b. 1897)

Anne
(b. 1899)

Richard John
(b. 1905)

Rupert Gyles
(b. 1915)

Justin Charles

Chantal

Stephen
(b. 1888)
(d. 1914)

Stephanie   m.   Rev. Harry Devening
(b. 1893)   1915

Rosalind   m.   Gavin Fitzpatrick
(b. 1896)   1914   (Knight of Bourne)

Gilbert
(b. 1904)

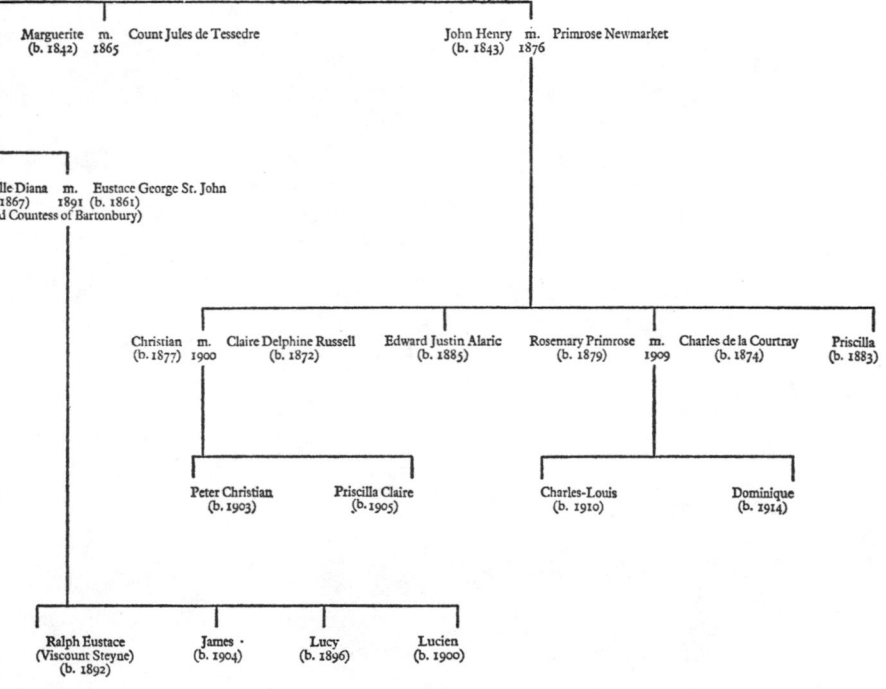

Marguerite　m.　Count Jules de Tessedre
(b. 1842)　1865

John Henry　m.　Primrose Newmarket
(b. 1843)　1876

brielle Diana　m.　Eustace George St. John
(b. 1867)　1891　(b. 1861)
l and Countess of Bartonbury)

Christian　m.　Claire Delphine Russell
(b. 1877)　1900　(b. 1872)

Edward Justin Alaric
(b. 1885)

Rosemary Primrose　m.　Charles de la Courtray
(b. 1879)　1909　(b. 1874)

Priscilla
(b. 1883)

Peter Christian
(b. 1903)

Priscilla Claire
(b. 1905)

Charles-Louis
(b. 1910)

Dominique
(b. 1914)

Ralph Eustace
(Viscount Steyne)
(b. 1892)

James ·
(b. 1904)

Lucy
(b. 1896)

Lucien
(b. 1900)

Author's Foreword

I began Book 1 in 1966. The name I gave to the Lorme castle just walked into my mind. I wrote just over 25,000 words and then set it aside owing to other commitments.

Many months later our friend Miss Alison Leach, who had been our personal assistant for many years, came down to see us and announced, 'I suppose you know there *is* a Castle Rising in Norfolk!' She showed us a little guide book which she had found in which it was mentioned. We subsequently discovered it marked on a modern map, just above North Wootton and a few miles from King's Lynn; but as it is no longer inhabited and is, in fact, a ruin, I decided to retain the name since it had by now become inseparable from my thinking on this book. In the original MS I had sited my Castle Rising on the edge of the Blakeney Marshes because of the Viking Funeral.[1] The original Castle Rising then turned out to be only twenty-six miles from Blakeney!

When I resumed work on Book 1 in the winter of 1972–3 I decided to help myself to my own family history from 1064 in Normandy to the 1800s in England. By then I was in possession of some ancient family data which took me into Essex on numerous explorations which were relevant to records showing that a certain Sir Gilbert de Pêche, Bart.—a Norman—settled in this country in the eleventh century. The records stated 'Pêche was the name of a considerable family who owned many manors hereabouts'. So I resited my Castle Rising on an eminence above one of these.

I then discovered that the dictionary definition of *péché* is 'sin, trespass, transgression'; if, however, this is made plural—*les péchés capitaux*—it becomes in translation 'the deadly sins'. Small wonder then that Sir Gilbert de Pêche is recorded as

[1] See Book 1, *The Lormes of Castle Rising.*

'sometimes called *"Peccatum"* meaning sin in abstract "for he was a verie naughtie fellowe" '!

This settled for me—as any reader who fights his way through these books will appreciate—that from then onwards I would plagiarise certain aspects of my own family for certain Lorme characteristics. Later I gave the Lormes the Pêche crest, an astrolabe,[2] and the arms of our Norman ancestor Sir Gilbert. In fact, the earlier Lorme 'runts' are Pêche 'runts'; but those who come after the 1800s are entirely my own creation and bear no relation whatsoever to any person or persons either living or dead.

FANNY CRADOCK

[2] An old instrument for taking altitudes.

War Comes to
Castle Rising

Petticoat Government

Gyles Aynthorp, eldest son of Justin, inherited the title when he was forty-eight. His flamboyant and rumbustious old father had been killed on the hunting field in his eighty-fourth year. Two months later, in the May of nineteen hundred and ten, Justin Aynthorp's King and friend died too. With the departure of these two roystering and self-indulgent Edwardians the Era ended and a new King and Queen ascended to England's throne.

Four short years and, for the Lormes, innumerable alarums and excursions later, England declared war upon Germany and within weeks Castle Rising became in part a Convalescent Home for Commissioned Ranks under the aegis of the little Dowager Lady Alicia and her irrepressible seventy-two-year-old sister, the widowed Countess Marguerite.

With the immediate exodus of every able-bodied man over eighteen and under thirty to join the armed forces, the Castle, its lands and cottages, lodge houses and stablings, hot houses and pleasure gardens, farms and vast acres suffered an unprecedented volte-face of management; becoming in a few short weeks, and in the rueful summing-up of the Dowager, 'nothin' but a concentrate of petticoat government to which it is our bounden duty to submit!' She added reflectively, 'for so long as we may hope to keep them, we have at least some of our finest old hardy perennials to impart a vestige of sound masculinity to this tedious superfluity of females!'

By this the Countess Marguerite knew full well her sister referred to Gyles, now Lord Aynthorp; to widower Sir Charles Danement whose estates marched with their own and who, on the outbreak of war, had taken on the management of both estates, thus releasing his own and Gyles' land agents to follow the flag; to the Family's inestimable butler, Sawby, to Plumstead, the head coachman, known to all the 'Castle folk' as 'Plum' and to Sawbridge, the crotchety and unpredictable head gardener, who now found himself with 'a passel of silly females' on his work-shabby hands and, as ever, made no bones about speaking his mind.

Each and every one adjusted with predictable rapidity. The women were well-chosen by Lady Constance. She had gleaned them from among her fellow suffragettes, amnesty-blessed and touchingly grateful for posts which enabled them to work like slaves without complaint and win the approbation of everyone concerned.

Even Mrs Parsons, the Lormes' cook, who had no peer—not even Sawbridge—when it came to expressing her opinions with maximum clarity, made her portentious pronouncement after only two weeks of the new regime.

'Ef anyone 'ad arst me wot would 'appen to life in this Castle, turned topsy turvy, badgered from piller ter post and invaded by a horde of young wimmen, most of oo 'as never come in contack with the haristocracy in all their born days, I would 'ave said 'ell pure and simple. But it aint like that at all. Orl I can say, 'aving 'ad time to refleck is, if this is wot Suffragette sufferin' 'as done for 'em they orter be grateful that their 'orrid persecutions 'as turned them into as nice a spoken collekshun of clean and willin' workers as it 'as ever been my lot to meet. They're a blessin' in disguise that's wot they are, even if they does eat like gannets!'

Where the rule of pleasure had run with a luxurious self-indulgence only surpassed in eighteenth-century France, the Castle rooms and endless corridors now resounded with the resolute tread of women and a mere handful of men going about their chosen duties with a resolution and determination which even excelled their past dedication to entertainment. There was too a new unity between employers and employed which stemmed from the former's determination to match the latter's willing service.

It was on this spirit of unity that Gyles' wife Christine reflected as she and her daughter-in-law walked their mares down the long village street of Upper Aynthorp in the growing twilight.

As they rode, lights began to sparkle in the shop windows and cottages. Then, as quickly as they had appeared, deepening in strength as the women who tended them turned the wicks up very slowly, so the same women hurried to the windows to draw the curtains until only fine threads of light remained.

The two horsewomen glanced sadly at the simple notices which were affixed to almost every door—A MAN HAS GONE FROM THIS HOUSE TO FIGHT FOR KING AND COUNTRY.

These poignant statements served to underline Christine's thankfulness that her sons were not 'out there', though the sands were running out for her first-born Henry, Petula's husband who was still home-based and under training.

A few women, gossiping in doorways, bobbed respectfully as they went by, silencing their chatter to take in every detail of the two erect figures in their blue habits, their bowlers held down by close-drawn veils through which Petula's dark curls and Christine's chestnut ones glinted in the little patches of lamplight.

'They do say as she's expectin' again,' whispered one cottager to her neighbour.

'Well, that's as maybe,' the neighbour sounded doubtful, 'she's not showin' noways, even if she be.'

The two women under discussion dismounted from their side saddles, tethered the mares and shook out their riding skirts preparatory to entering Mr Palfrey's Grocery.

The village women watched avidly, little knowing that in fact both were pregnant, Christine with her sixth child, conceived after Lady Mond's May Ball at the beginning of that last brilliant London season which now seemed such light years away and Petula, who had conceived in the early August evening of the day before war was declared.

As they picked up their skirts and walked across the fallen autumn leaves, Christine put up a protective hand for an instant as the child within her womb quickened. Then the pair disappeared inside Mr Palfrey's establishment as his little bell pinged.

Christine had undertaken to give the village grocer two Castle orders written out by Chef André and Mrs Parsons. Only thus could using the telephone be avoided. This was one of the many new measures to which the Castle inmates had become accustomed during the first few weeks of war. There was a notice in the Great Hall and another above every other telephone which warned *Unless absolutely necessary do not impede operators in the vital work of passing on urgent messages.* Each was signed by Gyles in his big, sprawling hand, 'Aynthorp'.

Mr Palfrey's was a very proud establishment. The sawdust floor was swept and sprinkled freshly each morning by the Boy, whose first duty this was when he crawled from his palliasse under the bacon counter and before he, as Mr Palfrey phrased it, 'performed his ablutions at the yard pump, prior to partaking of his porridge'.

Now, scrubbed, pink-cheeked, stuffed with tea and bread and dripping, the child returned to the shop, trussed up like a fowl in his canvas apron with the green tapes sewn on by Mrs Palfrey. As the bell pinged so he shot forward to hold open the door for these very distinguished customers. Then he drew two chairs for them, set these before the dry goods counter and, muttering 'excuse me, my lady' to Christine, dashed around the corner to where Mr Palfrey sat on a high stool just inside the weighing room, sipping at a steaming mug of cocoa.

'It's my lady from the Castle and Mrs Enery,' he announced breathlessly, 'I've set 'em down, Mr Palfrey.'

Down went the white enamel mug with the blue rim. 'Reach me that clean apron,' commanded his employer hastily untying the one he was wearing.

In the shop Christine looked around her reminiscently. 'I remember,' she told Petula, 'when this shop was tiny. Sacks stood about with their tops rolled back displaying the sago, semolina, pearl barley and rice. There was a pair of old blue scales on a tiny counter and little Mr Palfrey weighed out everything, trundling whatever it was into neat twists of blue paper and tucking in the ends. I used to watch, fascinated by his neatness.'

Mr Palfrey appeared behind the counter bowing and smiling. The effect of the smile was completely wasted, for when he bowed his head went over the counter and the smile was unseen. He was a very small man, with sparse black hair which he plastered over his pink pate in a vain attempt to conceal impending baldness. His bright, black, boot-button eyes darted from one to the other as he lifted his head again and displayed himself to the shoulders.

'A privilege, ladies, I'm sure,' he observed happily, 'and what may I have the honour of doing for you?'

Christine explained their mission, provided the lists and

handed them to him over the counter. Mr Palfrey took them, as if receiving the orb and sceptre.

'If, my lady,' he asked, ' I might presume to beg that you wait while I glance through them ... shortages, you know, my lady, have already occurred ... only this morning the carter brought me my autumn delivery of "fancies" from my supplier and when I opened them up I found a letter. It seems that as they are an enemy product there will be no more Karlsbad plums ... for the duration.' He looked anxiously at his customer, 'Most inconvenient I know but ...'

Christine smiled. 'Have you any at present?' she asked kindly.

'Oh yes, my lady. Might I be permitted to include some in your order?'

This exchange was interrupted by Petula who was peering into the long row of lidded biscuit boxes which flanked the wine counter, 'You had better add some biscuits, too, Christine. I see the box of fish pond biscuits is already half emptied. What would Chef André do for the children's parties if he could not make fish pond pudding any more?'

The call developed into a shopping orgy. They bought puff cracknels known to the nursery folk as 'puff and blow biscuits', anent which Richard, Christine's youngest had earned himself more than one spanking, for taking a huge bite and then blowing the puffy crumbs out with distended cheeks. Karlsbad plums were duly added to the list, together with a dozen jars of Patum Peperium in round white china pots with black lettering, Mr Palfrey happily scribbled, '1 doz. gents. relish,' and shouting 'Boy', then gave instructions for samples of crystallised fruits and fat, gilt-clipped china jars of *Le Véritable Foie Gras de Strasbourg* to be produced.

Petula then prompted for 'Brandy Balls and Barley Sugar please, Christine,' who added boxes of crystallised cherries from the Black Forest, and a sack of wine sugar, explaining, 'It looks so charming dangling from our Christmas tree, like icicles.' Eventually they were bowed out by Mr Palfrey who returned to the counter to tot up the, to him, enormous total, over which he rubbed his hands and returned to his now cold cocoa.

Christine and Petula rode home slowly in the deepening twilight, to where Plum awaited them. Indeed he was peering out fussily from the saddle room doorway, the lamplight illuminating his gnarled figure and deeply bowed legs. He came out the instant they crossed the cobblestones, handed Christine down and with the familiarity of a lifetime's service gave tongue.

'You'm no right my lady to be out ridin' after dark, nor Mrs Henry neither. In your condition, ladies, it's a scandal. I said to Mrs Plumstead only this mornin' it's enough to make me go inter a n'ncline and slide away,' he nagged as he lifted Christine down tenderly. 'Now jest you go right in an take a nice ort barf. I'm a good mind to tell Nanny,' he added darkly.

They chuckled. Christine, wickedly and over her shoulder as she turned towards the Castle called back, 'Nanny knows! Good night, Plum, and our compliments to Mrs Plum.'

The old man stood stunned into silence for a moment. Then muttering, he trotted inside again, brought out two horse blankets, flung them over the mares and shouted 'Boy', just like Mr Palfrey, seeming not a whit put out as a breeched young woman strode obediently towards him.

'Them boys,' Plum muttered to himself darkly as he returned to the warmth and familiar smells of old leather and dung in his harness room, 'is gorne ter fight and gawd knows ef we'll ever see any of 'em again,' and he gave a great long drawn-out sigh, after which, as always he found himself in need of consolation, so he began polishing as if his life depended upon it.

Gyles Aynthorp sat in his old office with a sheet of buff writing paper in front of him. His long legs were stretched beneath the refectory table which served him as his desk. The heels of his riding boots rested on the cross beam which Cavaliers' spurs had worn down to a shard. Beside him sat his Borzoi bitch Diana, her long jowl resting on his knee. He leaned back, absently stroking her silky flank, wondering what the devil he must do.

He picked up the buff paper and read it again. It simplified nothing.

Stephen Delahaye, his sister Henrietta's disastrous eldest son, had been killed in action in the Royal Flying Corps on the twenty-fourth of August. Stephen had apparently met his death while displaying courage of a very high order so now, according to the buff paper, His Majesty King George V had graciously approved the award of the Distinguished Service Order to the dead subaltern.

Gyles' problem was a simple one. Whom could he delegate to receive the medal from the King at Buckingham Palace?

Stephen's father was lying upstairs paralysed and showing no signs of recovery after his stroke. His querulous spouse was also laid low—by the appalling behaviour of her daughter Rosalind. From that shattering August night, so soon after the declaration that Britain was at war with Germany, when Sinclair had collapsed at the foot of the great staircase, Gyles had undertaken to handle his brother-in-law's affairs and had done so meticulously; but this letter had come as a complete shock to him—as it would be to all the family, since no one except James and Ninian, who were back at Sandhurst and had elected to keep their own counsel anyway—had even an inkling either that Stephen had been in England, or that he had joined the R.F.C., let alone that he was a qualified pilot who had flown to France in the van of the first reconnaissance aeroplanes.

Gyles glanced at the travelling clock on his table. The hands registered four o'clock. Suddenly a huge nostalgia engulfed him. He experienced an overwhelming desire to re-enter the past, so that at this precise hour he could do as he had always done, quit his office, go to his rooms, change and then come down into the White Drawing Room to take part in the tea-time ritual... find the women of the Family sitting about in tea gowns... the footmen bringing in the gleaming tea equipage... the children being brought in by Nanny and the governesses... all the small change of their daily lives. He scowled at the closed door as if it were the cause of the metamorphosis which now lay beyond it.

There was no White Drawing Room, as he remembered it. It was all shrouded in dust sheets, the priceless bibelots crated and stored with the great paintings in the closed Museum, where a septuagenarian tottered about attending to the stoking of the boilers, testing locks, doing his rounds.

There were no footmen, only the footwomen whom Christine and Sawby had schooled. Tea would be served in the small Blue Drawing Room for those who could spare the time to snatch a cup before dashing back to ward duty; or to checking the despatches of hothouse fruits and vegetables; or to sorting the consignments of books which poured in from generous friends to form a library of light fiction for shell-shocked and wounded young men. If it were dinner time, though admittedly Sawby would still install himself, half hunter in hand for the footwoman who now sounded both dressing and dinner gongs; this too would be served in the unhallowed Breakfast Room so as to lessen the burden on the staff. At least they still dressed for dinner! —save only those who were 'on duty' and so were permitted to dine in their white head-dresses and starched aprons.

He looked up as the door opened quietly and a footwoman came in in her white blouse, black bow and long black skirt, holding out the evening papers on a silver tray.

'Good evening, my lord,' said she, 'the evening papers, my lord.'

'Oh put them down, please.' Gyles rallied sufficiently to say, adding, 'more casualty lists I suppose!'

The woman nodded. 'Yes, my lord, they seem to get longer every day. Do you require anything else, my lord?'

Gyles declined perfunctorily. The woman 'milorded' him too much, he must speak to Christine!

When she had gone he stood up reluctantly. He took out his monocle. He polished it. He replaced it—his gesture indicating inward stress. Then he went across to the maps which now replaced the estate plans across one wall. He made a slight adjustment bringing the positions of the French, British and German armies into line with the morning news and stood staring at the relative positions—finally with one unbearable word hammering in his head—'retreat ... retreat ... retreat'— he opened the door and left the room with Diana at his heels.

CHAPTER 2

An Unexpected Romance

In the few weeks which had elapsed since the outbreak of war the Castle's peace was fractured in a dozen ways and places.

An army of builders and decorators filled the echoing, emptied rooms of the Convalescent Home designate with the sounds of sawing, planing, hammering. They impregnated the air with sawdust and the combined smells of paint and turpentine; but though the work was done with quite exceptional celerity, it imposed further strain upon the servants. They had already seen their ranks denuded in a hitherto unprecedented manner by the enlistment of so many of the younger men. Simultaneously their working quarters were churned into chaos by the invasion of Peak, the remaining carpenter, 'Old Jimmy' from Upper Aynthorp village, who had a club foot but was almost as skilled as Peak and by four seventeen-year-olds impressed by Jimmy and thereafter bullied by Peak who prided himself on being a rigid disciplinarian. This small team ripped out walls, thus gaining access to hitherto unused rooms below stairs. They 'made good', hung paper, painted walls, distempered ceilings and then set to work making tables and chairs in order to furnish these additional eating and working areas for the influx of female labour which was at present distributed around the estate in home farms and cottages.

'Old Jimmy', arch diplomatist amongst the villagers, tactfully explained: ' 'is lordship's plans' to Mrs Parsons and Chef André, applying the soothing ointment of his personal reassurances. 'We'll be out afore you knows it, leaving all ship-shape and Navy fashion, never fear. 'Is lordship was most es-pli-cit that 'is designs was ter make you older ones as comfortable as may be and stop them young wimmen from pilin' up like spilly-kins atop of yer. Yerse,' he added, 'and we'll move sharper abaout it than a pack of rattin' terriers.'

The team was as good as Old Jimmy had pledged. When they

departed they did leave all shipshape even if, as Mrs Parsons complained, 'the 'ole plice smells 'orrible of them paints'; but snowy tables, neat chairs, a roomy bureau with drawers for personal possessions and a simple wooden sideboard were left behind in the pleasant Dining Area for 'them girls', while as Peak and the rest took their leave so Mrs Peace descended, *châtelaine* clanking, her arms and those of Pearson the house-parlour maid, who followed behind, heaped high with red merino cushions for those hard, wood chairs, red merino cloths for the easy-to-scrub tables, and warm red merino curtains for the barred windows, which Boots had cleaned until they shone. When the top of the dresser was fully arranged with 'them girls' ' mugs and plates and dishes, Sawby came in and surveyed all. Having so done he went out again without comment returning with a hammer, one nail and a notice board. When he had affixed this to his satisfaction he proceeded to put up several notices proclaiming: *Times of Meals, Castle Fire Drill* and one special notice *Boots are not Worn Indoors. Slippers may be obtained from the Housekeeper Mrs Peace between the hours of eleven and eleven thirty A.M. only.*

Nor was this all, for Peak and company merely transferred themselves, their paper-hangers' tables, carpentry bench and sundry tool bags to the Dormitory Wing For Female Staff Only. This did not include the footwomen as they merely took over the rooms which had been occupied by the footmen.

All through this 'helter-skelter' Mrs Parsons bore up under the fond delusion that Pansy Appleby as she was still called, although now she was Pansy Sawby the butler's wife, would be loaned to her for the duration to help with the extra cooking. Certainly Pansy helped, but she still had to fulfil her duties as house-parlour maid with the added responsibility of training the new girl Ethel in these duties. Thus a good deal of extra work devolved upon cook. No one in their senses could expect a French chef to concern himself with meals of boiled beef and plum duff for outdoor workers.

When the Convalescent Home was ready and the first contingent arrived André and Pansy between them prepared their meals. There was by now far less culinary strain upon André, for the family meals had been severely curtailed, added to which the fiat had gone forth *'no more entertaining'.*

Even so, by the time the second complement of wounded or

shell-shocked young men were installed, chef and Pansy were stretched to their limits despite the fact that the young V.A.D.s laid, filled, then carried and returned the trays upon huge rubber-wheeled trolleys which Lady Constance had bought in London. The lift was not yet completed, therefore by the end of the day the V.A.D.s too were exhausted by the endless carrying up stairs and down again.

At least four small pots were about to boil over. Mrs Parson's pot was on the seethe already as she became disagreeably aware that—largely due to her efforts—Pansy had already outstripped her in the cooking stakes and would be most unlikely to remain as her willing assistant. Upstairs in the nursery, Rose's pot was coming nicely to the boil. She desired and felt she had earned promotion from mere nursemaid and was chafing more every day at the way in which Nanny sat back in her rocker ordering her about and doing precious little herself. Chef's pot was teetering on the brink of eruption too, for he not only desired help—of his own choosing—but found himself ridden with guilt concerning his '*belle patrie*'. All of which conspired to make him '*complètement bouleversée*', and damnably flare-tempered to boot.

Finally Pansy, the victim of the pull beggar, pull baker bedevilments of both Mrs Parsons and the irascible Frenchman, was working herself into a shadow and teetering upon the brink of collapse.

It fell upon Pearson to be the intervener in all this small coinage of domestic infelicity. Having been elevated from house-parlour maid to personal maid to no less a person than Christine Aynthorp, and adoring both her appointment and her employer, she sought for an opening in one of the many companionable sessions spent attending Christine in her boudoir. Apart from her abilities as a maid, Pearson possessed the invaluable quality of being able to see and hear a very great deal and to hold her tongue concerning any of her gleanings. This, in turn, allowed Christine to indulge in a freedom of conversation before the woman which had hitherto been unthinkable with any servant. All her life she had been indoctrinated '*pas devant les domestiques*'—an iron rule never before broken. For her part, Pearson's drab life was coloured immeasurably by the sippets and snippets she was permitted to glean when in attendance upon her ladyship.

When Christine left the Blue Drawing Room preparatory to

being dressed for dinner, Pearson awaited her as usual. She undressed her, wrapped her in warm towels after bathing, powdered and scented her and finally enfolded her in a foamy pink negligée. Then she cleared up the mess while her mistress settled at her dressing table and began opening and reading the letters which had come in by the afternoon delivery.

Setting aside a small pile of bills, receipts, invitations and appeals, she gave permission to Pearson to brush and dress her hair and began withdrawing from its envelope a letter which bore a Harrow-on-the-Hill postmark. She turned the single page over, glanced at the signature and began reading. Pearson watched her carefully. Seeing the frown replaced by a smile she ventured,

'Good news, my lady?'

Christine nodded at the face reflected in her looking-glass. 'Excellent news, thank you, Pearson,' she confirmed, then looking a little more closely at the woman's reflection, she added, 'but that does not appear to be the case with you if one may judge from your expression.'

'No, my lady,' Pearson answered in a flat voice.

'Do you wish to talk about whatever it is?'

'Yes, if you please, my lady, I think the time has come.'

'Then pray do so, knowing as you do that I should not act upon anything you might tell me until I had so informed you and then only in such a way as to leave you completely unconnected.'

'Yes, my lady, I do indeed know that,' Pearson's expression softened, 'and I am greatly honoured by your confidence in me. It's just that . . .' The floodgates of confidence opened and she poured out her version of the situation both below stairs and in the nursery. When she had done Christine picked up her ivory nail buffer and began polishing her nails. Her first question was,

'Do you think Monsieur André needs assistance at this time?'

Back came the very firm reply, 'I am quite sure, my lady.' She waited, brushing out the long chestnut hair with firm brush strokes, then she added, 'I do know that family luncheons and dinners is simpler now by far and that you have ordered there shall be no entertaining, but, twenty-four trays of delicacies for the young gentlemen, four times every day is quite a lot of work. I know chef does not do the teas, seeing as Mrs Parsons does them with Pansy helping; but you see, my lady, it wasn't as if all them trays was the same, what with some having this and some having that and some being fed six times a day with the Lixer . . .'

Christine looked up in bewilderment, 'Lixer?' she repeated.

'Well,' faltered Pearson, 'all that smashed to pulp prime chicken packed into a big champagne bottle and filled up with special brandy and it having to be what chef calls "an-fu-say" for twenty-four hours non stop.'

She broke off as light dawned and Christine's face cleared. 'Oh, the Elixir you mean don't you?' she asked.

'Yes, miladi, and that's not all. There's meals for the nursing staff as well and meals for all them young women what we've got now. Proper appreciative they are too; Mrs Parsons says they eat like gannets.'

Christine laughed. 'Do they indeed, and who cooks for them?'

'Well, it's like this, with Pansy having to train that young Ethel to take her place and not having really enough time to do her own work she does try her best to help Mrs Parsons; but it isn't enough. And she's proper swamped, Pansy is.'

Christine nodded, thinking deeply, 'Where should we plug the gaps do you think?' she enquired.

'Oh, my lady, it's not for me to presume . . .' Pearson protested, her voice trailing away.

'Fudge,' said her mistress with startling inelegance, 'and likewise fiddle-faddle! I wish to know. You have a direct contact with these dissatisfied members of my staff. While I am mistress here no one is to be driven distracted with overwork; the answer is that we must fill the gaps. It is only how we must fill them which vexes me.'

'If Pansy could have a girl as she could train, say from one of the villages, then she could begin to delly . . . delly . . .'

'Delegate?' supplemented Christine.

'Thank you, my lady, yes delly-gate. Then she could be free to do more with Mrs Parsons; or if Mrs Parsons had a girl as she wouldn't frighten silly . . .' Pearson was happily unaware of the glint this stray revelation sparked in Christine's eyes but just ran on, 'then perhaps it would be better if Pansy spent more time in helping chef. He'll never take to a village girl but he would to Pansy.' Now it was the maid's turn to twinkle momentarily.

'Oh, smitten too, was he?' Christine asked, highly amused.

'Well yes, my lady, a bit I think so, but of course not what anyone could take exception to as you might say.'

'Quite so,' Christine spoke absently. 'Oh and how about Rose? You say she's almost ready to revolt. Supposing I talked to Nanny? She has only little Master Charles-Louis and baby Dominique until, until my little one arrives, so if I began by suggesting that she would obviously need more help in the nursery by the time Mrs Henry's babe arrives too, perhaps then I could talk her into promoting Rose to Under Nanny with the promise of looking around immediately for a new Nursemaid for her to train.'

'Perfect!' exclaimed Pearson happily.

'Good. Then I can kill two birds with one stone by seeing Mrs Peace and instructing her to find the Nursemaid and Mrs Parson's cookery pupil. Then,' she looked up mischievously, 'both those old martinets will have someone to bully a little.'

'Oh, my lady,' gasped Pearson, highly diverted.

Christine sobered, 'but I rely on you to let me know if either of them goes too far.' She glanced at her little gold clock, exclaimed, 'Pearson, the time! I shall be late for dinner, for pity's sake hurry. Get me out that lilac thing with all the flounces. It will help to conceal my vanishing waistline. You must lace me in tightly first though, for there is no need for me to look a sight before it is necessary. Now leave the rest to me,' she added, rising hurriedly, 'and when you go to your room take that brown walking suit of mine with you. It's already too tight for me and I know you have always admired it. Call it a thank-you present for your invaluable help and discretion.'

When she swept from her boudoir to Gyles' dressing room, carrying her fan, reticule and the Harrow letter, Pearson executed a little dance in the disordered room as she had done on the occasion when Christine told her that she was to be her future lady's maid. Then she went to the great armoire, took down the walking suit and pranced over to the cheval glass holding it in front of her and singing, 'Ro ho hoses are bloo oo oo ming in Picardy ...'

Christine went into Gyles' dressing room and spoke pleasantly to Pine, who was brushing invisible specks from his master's dress clothes; Gyles then dismissed the valet. When they were alone Christine waved her letter triumphantly.

'Read this,' she said, 'it is good news for a change. I would say that it really does look as if we have heard the end of that unpleasant business over Stephen's child.'[1]

'Really, my love?' Gyles registered vague astonishment, 'well first permit me to tell you that you look ravishin'.'

'Carefully disguised around the waistline,' she twinkled.

He put his arms round her and drew her close. 'Possibly,' he acknowledged, 'but still it is absurd to think that you have borne me five children already, let alone are carryin' a sixth.'

She lifted her face. 'Be serious, Gyles. What shall we call this one, if it is a girl?'

Gyles studied the upturned face. 'You know,' he told her, 'you do not look a day older than when I married you. Oh, let's call her Christine.'

'No,' she pushed him away, 'I do not think so. Would you mind dreadfully if we called her after that naughty beauty on your French side? I think Chantal de Lorme sounds so very pretty.'

Gyles drew her back and kissed her mouth lingeringly. Standing thus he murmured, 'Call her whatever you like. I believe you have already made up your mind anyway. Supposin' it's a boy, what then?'

'Oh Rupert Justin Charles I think. Then we could ask our Charles to stand godparent.' She pulled herself away again, 'Gyles, darling, please read my letter.'

For answer he drew her down on to a wine red conversation piece. 'You read it to me instead,' he suggested, 'then I can look at you while you do so.'

'Oh, very well.' She gave him a little coquettish glance, then said more severely, 'now listen carefully. It is from Andrew.'

'How much?' he sounded resigned.

'Only tuck. Now, Gyles, will you please listen,' and to achieve her object she laid one hand across his mouth. He promptly turned the palm over and began kissing it.

She read aloud, '*Dearest Mama, term has started very well and so far I have had enough to eat, but the food here is getting worse every day. Mrs Parsons' tuck helps out but without it I should starve. Ask her to be sure to send me some more of that ripping pâté. I do get some grub from Gillett, but he is so expensive . . .*'

'Always was,' Gyles grunted.

[1] See Book 2, *Shadows Over Castle Rising*.

Christine read on: '*I wonder if you and Pater remember that boy I mentioned to you that I wanted to bring back for the hols as his parents live in Australia?...*'

Gyles snorted inelegantly. 'Remember!' he exclaimed with feeling.

'*Well anyway I can't because he isn't here any more. Someone came over and took him back. My housemaster tells me the poor little devil will have to go to some crummy Australian school which he will loathe after Harrow.*'

This time Gyles interjected, 'Shockin' little snob!' Christine frowned at him and again read on: '*I expect you have forgotten all about it anyway by now. What I want to do is to bring back a chap called Acrington, so please Mama will you write and invite him for Christmas? Otherwise he will have to spend it with his grandma which he says will be pretty crummy. You see his Pater is a general—he's in France and his Mama is going out there to drive an ambulance so their place is being closed up altogether. "Akkie" says that Pater was with the General when they were both in Africa as subalterns. Don't forget the tuck, your loving son, Andrew.*'

'A masterpiece in more ways than one,' said Gyles thankfully. 'Lorme Luck does not seem to have wholly vanished after all! I am bound to admit I have had more than one sleepless night wonderin' what the devil we were goin' to do about that child of Stephen's. Now it seems we may forget about it...' he rose and held out his hands, 'come, my beauty. If I am not mistaken there goes the dinner gong.'

Unfortunately Gyles' not inconsiderable prescience did not extend quite far enough over this intensely personal problem, or he might have seen fit to apply to 'the Stephen affair' a more fitting title, and file the matter away temporarily under the heading, unfinished business.

Sawby's humour had also improved. He had evidence that at last 'things' were settling down.

The family went into dinner 'properly dressed' which further contributed to his content. Even Lady Constance, who had every excuse for not dressing since her last rounds of the Home, in uniform naturally, were not made before eleven p.m., but even she rustled in wearing a most becoming pale lemon gown, her hair swept high in a style hastily contrived by Pearson who rushed to her after tidying Christine's boudoir.

Sawby watched, outwardly imperturable as ever, inwardly smiling benevolent approval as everyone was seated. At a tiny nod from him the footwomen served the soup. Admittedly, ran Sawby's thoughts, the menu had been shockingly truncated. Only six courses and no alternatives for any of them! Admittedly the Family was 'camping out' in the Morning Room. Seemingly he overlooked the fact that such 'camping' was being done in a room panelled in linenfold and furnished with pieces wrought by master craftsmen during the reign of the first Charles of England. He began reflecting upon the dreadful straits to which the war had brought this distinguished family and so doing, he went round with the sherry which had been laid down by the late Justin Aynthorp.

The silver glistened, the crystal sparkled, the damask shone. Sawby was forced to acknowledge that the Leeds dinner service looked well enough too in such a setting, with family portraits looking down upon the assembled company. The little Countess had also done well with the flowers. This he only acknowledged to himself very grudgingly for it had long been a secret bone of contention to him that she did the flowers at all—at her age! He was convinced he could do just as well himself. However, against the black and white and silver Marguerite had chosen to dress the damask with green. She had robbed the last green seed heads from a south wall's *Cobea Scandens* and let their curiously curved green stems droop through the marbled leaves of Italian Arum lilies found growing wild against the warmth of a stove house. With these she had clustered small *Euphorbias,* used the fat black-eyed seed heads of *Euphorbia Wulfenii* between and pierced them with pale sharp green of *Hellebores.* Spilling down upon the white cloth were bunches of pale green and purple grapes. Gyles shook out his napkin and eyed the arrangement approvingly. Sawby was compelled to recognise the originality and dramatic effect as set off by the two great silver candelabras, his spirit lightened by even these small tokens of civilised dining in a castle which had for so long been acclaimed for the splendour of its table settings in the now dust-sheeted dining room. An infinitesimal sigh of nostalgia escaped him as he replaced his decanter in its coaster.

After the soup would come trout because Sir Charles had

made a providential catch. Christine had thus decreed that these should provide the material for chef's *Truite Farcie à ma Façon* which would be paired with a modest *Pouilly Fuisée 1909*. A dish of sweetbreads *Marechale* would comprise the only *entrée* accompanied by a *Grands Echezeaux 1902*. The beef which would follow had come from their own beast since Gyles had insisted that chef would have to 'make do' with what the Lorme estate yielded. It had become more than his place was worth to order anything from London, or anywhere else. Sawby poured the *Pouilly* with his mind on those recent days when food had flowed into the Castle from Paris, Rome and London. Memory presented him with a litany of foodstuffs: oysters from the Grand Duchy and the bay of Cork; white truffles from Bologna; black ones from the Perigord; tiny pink shrimps from Scarborough; lobsters from the North coast of Devon; ormers from the Minquiers and Ardennes Hams from the smokehouse which had despatched them by mule pack to Rome since the hey day of the Caesars. He supposed gloomily that even Mr Henry's favourite—Haggis—would come under the same embargo now. Frustration growing again, the Lormes' butler stalked through the service of dinner examining the *Filet de Boeuf Feuilleté* with its garnish of beef marrow on tiny toasts, watching the handing of the *entrée* dishes of *haricots verts, Gâteau Rothschild, Pommes Soufflés*, brightening only when chef, easing his frustrations with the creation of a new dish, sent up, for the cheese course, individual cheese soufflés baked in leaf-opened artichokes; the *croustillant*, bubbling cheese tops nestling in the centres. Then, 'No puddings indeed!' he thought indignantly, watching as the footwomen withdrew the covers, set the port at Gyles' elbow, moved the Countess's green centrepiece and placed the tazzas of hot-house fruits. Then he dismissed the women, murmured his customary, 'Will that be all, my lady?' at Christine's shoulder, received his *congé* and left, closing the doors behind him.

'I am bound to confess,' observed the Dowager as she selected a nectarine, 'this is the first time I have ever appreciated what splendid fruit Sawbridge grows for us. I cannot speak for you younger ones, naturally; but with my lessening appetite I find these truncated dinners much to my liking.'

Gyles lifted his glass to her. 'Thank you Mama,' he smiled, so declaring an end to their previous brush with one another.

Charles Danement looked up from his peach, 'Has anyone had news from Doctor Jamieson yet?' he enquired.

Constance answered, 'He came back of course, I waited for him, but no sooner had he arrived than I was summonsed so did not have the chance to speak with him. I do understand, however, that he intends returning after dinner. We have one or two problems with our young men which require discussion. He will undoubtedly report to me then.'

'After which,' sighed Claire languishing and bored in the absence of her husband Christian, 'I suppose we shall have to decide who tackles the difficult task of telling Henrietta.'

'That will not be necessary,' Constance said serenely.

This swivelled all eyes in her direction. She wiped her fingers on her napkin, set it down and continued calmly, 'I am happy to report that she is now sitting up in bed drinking a rather large bowlful of André's admirable *bouillon*. It had occurred to me that it might be better for someone who was not personally involved to perform this task. So, I elected myself and did so this afternoon.' She looked around, 'I do trust that no one thinks I have taken too much upon myself? I have done very little really and have only just touched upon the fringes of the facts. May I explain?'

She looked first at Christine, then to the Dowager and finally to Gyles. No one replied so it was left to Gyles to say, 'Pray continue.'

'I talked to Mrs Delahaye at some length in a purely general way about the urgent need for her to take herself in hand; but this brought absolutely no response. Here I should explain that in my opinion, for what it is worth, but also in that of Doctor Jamieson which is inestimable, Mrs Delahaye had come perilously close to the schizophrenic condition in her persistent withdrawals. When I realised that I was making no headway whatever, failing in fact to fix her attention in any way at all, I became extremely anxious. *So I told her.* I said that I had news for her if she would please be so good as to give me her attention. She made a slight movement at this but still remained silent. I went on, "I have such wonderful news for you, I know it will delight you above anything else," still she merely twitched a little and then turned over on to her back. I went on, speaking very slowly and carefully, "Your son Stephen" and I repeated this three times, "has become an officer in the Royal Flying Corps. He has

been flying on reconnaissance over the front line in France, for
we are at war with Germany. One day Stephen sought out and
exterminated a nest of manned machine guns which was
menacing the British forward line. He dropped bombs on them
from his aeroplane and simply wiped them out. We have just
received the news that he has been awarded the Distinguished
Service Order for his gallantry."

'After that I waited. Very slowly Mrs Delahaye pulled herself
into a sitting position. Then she buried her face in her hands. I
slipped some pillows behind her to support her back. That was
when, through her fingers she spoke at last. She said "The . . .
Distinguished Service Order! . . . Stephen! My son". Then she
removed her hands. The tears were raining down her terribly
sunken cheeks; but when she opened her eyes it was evident that
she was in full possession of her faculties—that she was *there*.
Presently she let me wipe the tears away. I gave her a clean
handkerchief. I rearranged her pillows. That was when she
clutched at me and begged me to tell her all over again. So I
repeated what I have told you. She listened in silence. After
quite a long while she spoke again, more to herself I think than
to me. She said, as if the words were being wrung from her; "but
you know even so it will all begin again . . . some day . . . that . . .
is . . . inevitable".'

Constance drew a wisp of handkerchief from her reticule and
put it to her eyes. Then in a low voice she concluded. 'That was
when I told her that her son had lost his life for King and
Country in heroism, and fearless of the consequences.'

Charles Danement watched her throughout as did the rest;
but it was fortunate for him that all their attentions were upon
what Constance said or they could not have failed to see what
he was in no way ready for anyone to see, as yet.

The Dowager was the first to break the silence.

'She is now sitting up sipping *bouillon* did you say my dear?'

Constance nodded, managed a little unsteady laugh, then
apologised, saying, 'I must be a very bad nurse to allow emotion
to overcome me in this way; but she was so utterly pathetic . . .'

'I always knew you were a very remarkable young woman,' the
Dowager retorted, 'now you place us all even more deeply in
your debt my dear and I know no way of expressin' my profound
gratitude for what you have once again done for this remarkably
tryin' family.'

Her old eyes swung to her daughter-in-law, 'Christine my love,' she said with some emphasis, 'do you not think we should now withdraw and leave our three remainin' males to their port?'

Christine rose immediately. The Bishop had dropped off again so Sir Charles went to the door and held it open until they had passed through. Then he closed it behind them. In the great hall Christine put her arms around Constance. 'Thank you, my dear,' she said softly, 'we are all indeed most deeply in your debt, a seemingly constant state of affairs between us now.'

Somewhat shakily Constance replied,

'Please, you must permit me to say I happen to hold your er, trying family in rather high esteem. Therefore what I can do becomes very easy,' and so saying, she pulled herself away, turned round and incontinently fled.

Later that night, while Christine, the Dowager, Marguerite and Petula alternated between Sinclair's room and Henrietta; while Lady Constance made her nightly rounds; Gyles, Petula's father and Dr Jamieson sat in the library sipping brandy and talking quietly. The benign aura of good cigar smoke and old brandy filled the air.

'It is a curiously interesting case,' Dr Jamieson reflected. 'Lord Aynthorp, I must say how greatly I am enjoying my cigar —now where was I? oh yes, well undoubtedly Mr Delahaye would have been dead long ago if we had not fed him intravenously. As it is, he had a bleed into the brain and the blood clot— to put the matter within laymen's comprehension—has been pressing upon the speech area. What is occurring now is that the blood clot is shrinking fast, thereby diminishing the pressure, and as it appears to me after examining the patient tonight, it is likely that the shrunken blood clot will eventually diminish sufficiently to enable it to ease off altogether. I am not for a moment denying that some speech therapy will be required. I think I can put you in the way of the right person for this when the time comes. He is something of a pioneer in the field but one in whom I have the greatest confidence. As to the paralysis, we shall just have to wait and see. It may be that Mr Delahaye will be left with no more than a slight limp. That I think is the best for which we may hope. What I do find quite remarkable is Mrs Delahaye's recovery.'

Gyles had been watching the doctor keenly, but not solely for the words he spoke.

Now he said, 'What I find astonishin' after watchin' you in action over a span of years is why the devil you chose to immure yourself in this country practice when you could have swept into Harley Street wealth and fame long ago.'

It was the doctor's turn to listen. He did so with a faint smile on his lips.

'No time for parlour pranks or unctuous flatteries,' he answered, 'nor for all the jiggery-pokery of flattering the rich and famous. I am only interested in sick people. Thanks to you I have considerably widened my scope since this war began. I am well satisfied.' At this point he appeared to brush the question aside as if it were of scant importance. When he spoke again it appeared he was reflecting, aloud.

'The older I become,' he told them, 'the more convinced I am that the medical profession has not as yet even nibbled at the fringes of what may prove at some future time to be the greatest advance in the history of mankind in effecting cures where at present few are regarded as even possible.'

'Meanin' precisely what?' asked Gyles. 'Havin' not the faintest notion of your theories we do find ourselves a bit fogged, old chap.'

Dr Jamieson stared at the glowing logs under the chimney piece. 'I'm not at all sure I can really clarify my meaning,' he regretted, 'at least not to my satisfaction.' He transferred his gaze to his cigar tip as if it were a particularly interesting patient, 'but I'll have a shot at it if it won't bore you. I have long held the somewhat disquieting view that bodies and minds are indissolubly linked, and that is not a truism from where I stand. Look how wide a gulf separates the two at present. A man has a broken leg. My colleagues mend it and consider the job completed! Yet supposing *how* that leg healed depended upon the state of mind of the patient to such a degree that the healing of two broken ends of bone were inseparable from untangling any pressures which beset the owner's mind . . . and spirit. Supposing that there was such a degree of rapport between both mind and body that when the balance of the mind is profoundly disturbed the body is unlikely to respond properly to any physical reparation. No,' he corrected himself, 'rather that the treatment of the mental condition could, in part if not in whole bring about

the curing of the physical condition.' He smiled at them both.
'As you can see, I am still groping, so let me strike off at a
tangent for a moment and speak of what I know but, because
of the times in which we live and the shibboleths and strictures
which surround the limited view of the medical moguls, I could
imperil my very right to practise if I propounded any of it to all
and sundry. Take women,' he broke off to smile again, adding,
'the ultimate imponderables I admit; but take them as I have
seen and worked among them. Can you imagine the cat I would
put among my eminent colleague pigeons if I spoke out and said
that the root cause of the vast majority of potty women is mal-
adjusted sex and, in particular, the lack of sexual fulfilment.'

'Yes,' said the two men quickly.

Charles added, 'The French concept, in fact, is what you are
advocating for the remnants of Victoria's England?'

Dr Jamieson nodded. 'Now come away from that fascinating
red herring and let me get back to the fundamental.'

'One question first,' Gyles leaned forward in his chair, 'it's
a fascinatin' idea. Does it, could it work in reverse too?'

'Give me an example of what you mean,' Dr Jamieson seemed
puzzled.

Gyles attempted, 'well if the body is sick should the cause
first be sought for in the mind?'

The doctor nodded, as if he were thinking out and then
affirming as thought clarified.

'Let us take Mrs Delahaye as an example,' Gyles suggested,
'if only because we all know about her. Accordin' to what you
say, her mind had withdrawn from its normal involvement due,
er, due to . . . well you tell us if you will.'

'Due to excessive tensions brought on by accumulative shocks
and naturally deep distress, plus subsequent anticipatory terrors
that there would be more and more to come. So, again in layman's terms, *her mind withdrew because it decided that it could
endure no more*. It has to be so. The news of her son's decoration for gallantry merely tempted that withdrawn mind to return.
What rooted it back securely was the fact that there could be no
more as her son was removed from her irrevocably.' He started
up in his chair. 'By heaven that reminds me—there must be no
mention of Rosalind's name or we might lose her again! At present her mind is wholly fixed upon her son. If the awful reminder
of what Rosalind has done came back to her before she was

strong enough to handle it, she might, she could and very probably would revert, unless my entire theory is at variance with reality!'

'How do we handle that one pray?' asked Gyles.

Dr Jamieson frowned, 'I think,' he decided 'we must try to fabricate something, anything, which could seem to be good news concerning that disastrous young woman. Have you heard anything by the way?'

'Nothin',' said Gyles shortly, 'nor do I expect to. I, er, wrote a pretty strong letter to that flamin' Knight of hers. I told him in so many words,'—he grinned a little ruefully—'never to darken our doors again. I also stressed most emphatically that these same doors would always remain open to Rosalind who could feel absolutely free to return whenever she wished.'

'I see. Well then we must, I feel, consult Lady Constance without delay. If that ingenious lady cannot devise something I shall be very surprised. I will speak to her first thing tomorrow morning.' Dr Jamieson nodded. 'It would be cruel to worry her at this late hour. She would only worry at the problem until she found a solution and thus deny herself her much needed sleep and rest.'

'Quite so,' said Gyles. 'And now I think it is high time I replenished your glasses. Charles?' he said rising, and taking Dr Jamieson's glass.

'Thank you,' said Charles absently.

Gyles smiled. 'We're all at it,' he said wryly, setting the glasses on the central table and lifting the decanter. 'My trouble is I want to start another hare.'

'Then by all means do so.' Dr Jamieson smiled. 'First let me say this. I was about to say it when I thought of your niece. I think this proposition of mine has another parallel of which we all three may well have had some experience. You see I have long held the conviction that the mind is our master—*the* ruling force above all other. Some might even want to link it with the soul but I'll stay with the mind if you don't mind—for a while at least.'

They waited expectantly. Then:

'Let me put it to you as a question. Do you not think that there is such a thing as a threshold of pain?'

'I'm afraid that will need explanation too,' said Charles regretfully.

'Well let's use women again. The threshold of pain in a

European woman's labour is manifestly different from that of a native woman working in the fields who suddenly has her first pangs. She merely goes behind a convenient palm tree, gives birth, severs her own umbilical cord, clears herself up (I won't be tooo explicit about thát) and then goes back with the new-born babe strapped to her back to finish the row she was hoeing. Her pain threshold is somewhat different to that of a gently-nurtured, cosseted woman who experiences her first birth pangs. It must be so. Environment either toughens or softens as is the case with a woman like, well, Lady Aynthorp.'

'Point taken,' grunted Gyles.

'Well then, let us progress to the peaks of pain. I have long believed that while a peak for one may not be a peak for another, when that peak *is* reached the mind takes over and cries "enough" and then oblivion follows.'

'Would you say that of torture?' asked Gyles curiously.

'Particularly of torture.' The doctor looked at his questioner, and was rewarded by a fleeting expression in Gyles' eyes which once again reminded him of the hidden depths he felt were at work under Gyles' urbane exterior. 'But why Lord Aynthorp?' he felt compelled to add.

'Because,' Gyles looked away as if unwilling to disclose too much, 'I find myself wholly responsive to what you have already said and would therefore wish to ask you another question.' He reached to the cigar case for a fresh cigar, first proffered the box to the doctor who refused, then busied himself with the usual ritual. When he had gathered his thoughts into the desired shape he asked his question.

'*If* you had unlimited millions at your disposal; *if* with them you could build and run what you chose, then what would you envisage as the perfect centre for treatment of the sick—for any and every form of disability—would you envisage such a Utopian project being staffed by only the finest medical practitioners in every field? Or would you rather divide your staff between an equal proportion of physical experts and mental experts, plus, it goes without saying, the most up-to-date medical and surgical equipment?'

'Of course,' said Dr Jamieson, 'there would be no other way but,' he smiled wryly, 'I must point out that if I had the means and opportunity and were to put such a proposal to the British Medical Council, let alone embark upon such an enterprise, I would without the slightest shadow of doubt be adjudged mentally unsound myself and I should most certainly find myself subsequently struck off the medical register. That is the measure of the distance to be covered in such a matter. This, remember, is nineteen fourteen not nineteen ninety-four!'

Gyles nodded again. 'Let us talk more of this another time,' he said dismissively. 'We are well reminded that we are tiltin' at windmills.' He glanced at the clock on the mantelshelf. 'It is now half-past one in the mornin' so I will have done, I have only one more thing to add if I may.'

Both his listeners waited.

'In respect of both the Delahayes, I want you to understand, Jamieson, that however you elect to treat them, in conjunction with Lady Constance, you have my fullest consent and acquiescence. Take yer own line. There is no one who will gainsay the pair of you; I for one consider Lady Constance to be a most remarkable young woman.'

'You understate the case,' Sir Charles rose, yawning. Then he tossed back over his shoulder, 'come to that, you're a pretty remarkable feller yourself, Jamieson. G'night, Gyles, good night to both of you.'

When he had gone the two men sat on by the dying fire. Hesitantly the doctor enquired, 'might I ask what on the face of it is a very impertinent question?'

Gyles shook his head. 'No need to ask,' he said, 'I fancy we are of one mind. Some day, when all this is over I have a strong feelin' m'y self that there may well be yet another weddin' in the old Castle. I might add that if I am right it would have my unqualified blessin'.'

'Despite the considerable difference in their ages?'

'Oh yes. The breed is lusty, like m'y own. Charles may be into about fifty-three, anyway the early fifties. His father was in the saddle even later than mine, rode to hounds and was up with the kill when he was past eighty-five. As to these two I should conjecture that there's close on twenty years dividin' them; but with such longevity in the Danement line ... well, as I see it,' he paused and then began to quote, smiling as he did so, "Let me not to the marriage of true minds admit impediments ...". Now come, Jamieson, it's long past your bed time. Your wife will doubtless begin worrying if you are any later so let me see you to your carriage.'

CHAPTER 3

The Power of Lady Mathilde's Bequest

In spite of the many duties which the little Countess had undertaken since she and the Dowager achieved the Convalescent Home for which the naughty pair had plotted, Gyles saw with appreciation that she still found time to 'do' the Castle flowers in the rooms still left open for the Family's use.

As he crossed the Great Hall he looked appreciatively at her latest arrangement which flowed out from an old Copeland urn on to the green and gold central table; then hearing a slight sound he turned to see her trotting towards him carrying yet another, this time contained in an old Bible box.

'Tante Meg!' he exclaimed, 'that is far too heavy for you, pray let me take it and what may I ask are the footwomen doin'?'

Breathlessly Marquerite relinquished her burden. 'Thank you, my dear, this is for Sinclair's room . . . the footwomen were all occupied . . . you see I always put flowers where he can see them, so that when he does return to,' she selected the word carefully after a moment's hesitation 'to, er, sensibility, they will be there to greet him.'

'Exactly so,' Gyles nodded, 'I am going there anyway so you need only to tell me where you wish them placed.'

'On the pedestal by the west window dear, and if you will also be good enough to put the container of tired ones just outside I will arrange to have them collected later.'

The master of Castle Rising mounted the wide staircase carrying his aunt's arrangement, realising as he did so that it was almost certainly the first time he had ever performed such an office for anyone. Negotiating the sharp turn leftwards he vanished with Diana at his heels. When he opened Sinclair's door he found Christine sitting by the fire.

'I thought I would find you here,' he said softly, 'I brought these for Tante Meg, she was carrying them herself!'

Christine chuckled, 'It's even funnier to see you doing so,' she smiled, watching her husband's progress with amusement. She also put out one hand to Diana who arranged herself across her feet and composed her nose and paws for sleep.

'Any change?' Gyles asked, dusting his hands together having completed his dual chore.

Christine sighed. 'None I fear. Oh Gyles, sometimes I wonder . . .' she broke off, unwilling to speak her fears.

He drew a chair alongside and held out his hands to the blaze.

'More than ever now,' he agreed heavily, 'I have such need of him.'

Christine's eyes became anxious, 'What now, my darling?'

'Just this.' Gyles drew the buff paper from his pocket and saying, 'You had better read it,' he handed it over.

For some unaccountable reason she read the stark announcement aloud. The lamp-light from a nearby pedestal conspired with the flames from the logs to make an aureole of her chestnut hair. Tears sprang to her eyes.

'Oh Gyles,' she explained, 'How glad I am for Sinclair . . . Who would have thought? . . . Well, perhaps such things really are possible."

He took her thought immediately. 'Meanin' "out of evil cometh good?" ' he made the quote a question.

'Yes indeed. How glad Sinclair would be if he could know of this. Oh if only we could tell him!'

'But we cannot,' said Gyles heavily, 'and y'know I have sat in my office for I do not know how long tryin' to enter into his mind in order to discern what he would have decided . . . and I still do not know what I should do.'

'Do?'

'Well, yes,' Gyles so far forgot himself as to raise his voice, so that his words rang out very clearly. 'Whom would Sinclair have chosen to represent him at the Palace to receive Stephen's posthumous decoration? Do you suppose that in these circumstances he would want Stephanie? After all, they have been very close recently.'

They pondered the question together with the great bitch sleeping beside them. A log shifted in the fire basket, it set up a stream of tiny orange stars. The Lundstrom clock on the mantelshelf ticked loudly. Then suddenly they both heard a slight movement from the bed. Instantly they swung round, awakening Diana who came up on her forepaws and now turned her lovely head in the same direction. Into the silence they both heard a halting voice speaking thickly and with difficulty.

'I ... will ... go ... myself ... of ... course,' said Sinclair.

In an instant they were at the bedside and bending over the sick man. Sinclair's eyes were open. Tear drops were rolling down his emaciated cheeks.

'My ... son,' he managed, then after another pause, 'so ... proud ...'

Gyles flung a questioning glance at Christine who mimed, 'It's all right.'

Then once again with greater clarity Sinclair said, 'My ... son ...' and then after another silence, 'so very ... very ... proud. ...'

They both waited, scarcely daring to breathe. Slowly the lids folded over the unnaturally bright eyes and Gyles looked up in anguish.

Christine shook her head reassuringly, 'I think he has fallen asleep,' she whispered. 'Go darling, see if you can find Constance. Then we can telephone to Dr Jamieson for I fancy he is at home at this hour taking a short break, poor man.'

Any unease which remained with Gyles and Christine was quickly dispelled by Lady Constance. This remarkable young woman, head of the Convalescent Home—by the Dowager's own intervention—one time militant Suffragette, had become perilously close to an oracle for all the Lormes. Petula's father joined the ranks of her admirers after a mere few days of acquaintanceship and of late the two had fallen into the habit of taking a walk together each afternoon in the Castle grounds or on Sir Charles' adjacent estate. The gradual ripening of this friendship was described by the Dowager in the idiom of her day as a 'companionship between May and September'. It was accelerated by the fact that Sir Charles had moved in and taken up quarters in the Castle 'for the duration' in order to combine the offices of agent in chief and general supervisor of both estates. In this he was partnered by his daughter Petula who flung herself eagerly into all and every activity available. She was feeling totally adrift without her Henry, so any inactive hours dragged interminably.

In the evenings, while she worked at the estate books her father played chess with Constance, as he now called her. While they were so occupied, significant glances passed between the women of the family over the two heads, the one silver, the other like spun gold both bent intently over the beautiful old ivory chessmen.

Constance, coming in a trifle breathlessly in her outdoor uniform, pulled off her cap, unfastened her cloak and shooing the others out, bent over Sinclair.

That evening she reported that he had slept for quite a while had then woken and taken a few teaspoonfuls of the Dowager's Elixir. All else remained unjudged until after Dr Jamieson had seen him.

Sitting, peering through her lorgnette at the pages of the listed book titles which comprised the contents of the Home's library—contributed by generous friends—the Dowager lifted them towards her eldest son and spoke.

'If I were you, Gyles,' she informed him, 'I should compose a nicely pompous, naturally deferential letter. Use our writin' paper for it will undoubtedly add weight. Set out the case quite plainly. Enquire if His Majesty might see fit in such unusual circumstances to be so graciously benevolent as to postpone the posthumous investiture until such time as Sinclair is sufficiently well to receive the decoration himself on his dead son's behalf.' The familiar twinkle then appeared as she added, 'if that fails my dear I can always set about a little string-pulling of my own.'

Gyles grinned back. 'Mama, you are incorrigible,' he informed her, which in no way ruffled her. In fact she preened a little.

'In any event,' Gyles added, 'that *is* sound advice and I will do what you suggest.' He rose, teacup in hand, gave it to his Tante Meg who was as usual installed behind the tea equipage and then wandered over to the windows. Thus he missed the tiny but significant nod which passed between tea pourer and lorgnette wielder.

Gyles turned at length, collected his cup and saucer and went back to his chair. When he had settled himself once more,

'Gyles, my dear, I have been thinking . . .' said the Dowager.

He looked at her in alarm, 'Oh no, Mama!' he protested, 'pray not another of your ideas! I have enough to handle for the moment without any of your Machiavellian mischiefs to contend with.'

'Nevertheless,' the Dowager continued, relentlessly, 'there are certain matters which I,' she paused, then corrected herself, 'to which *we* feel bound to draw your attention if you will just be good enough to listen for a moment.'

Gyles drank his tea, put down the cup, sat back and said resignedly, 'Very well, Mama, as you wish of course,' implying by these compliant words that hell fires would not persuade him into anything more no matter what it might be.

'Well then, dear, we shall begin with Christine'—thus she produced her trump card first, 'and with your Tante Meg, Claire, me and of course our little Petula. We have been discussin' memorials, fittin' I would conjecture since we have already experienced one loss in this family. Therefore we feel confident that you will agree with us that it is only right, proper and befittin' our standin' in the county, for us to put up a roll of honour in our chapel. No, dear,' she wagged her lorgnette at him, 'pray let me conclude. If you so wish you shall annihilate us all when I have done, should you be so disposed.' She drew breath and then swept on. 'No one in their senses could still be of the opinion that this war will be over by Christmas. That we shall ultimately win is not in dispute, of course; but I believe I speak for us all in sayin' that victory is a long way off.

'In consequence, not only this Christmas but also any forthcomin' ones while we are in a state of war will represent increasin'ly sad times for everyone, ourselves, the tenants, villagers, alike. Nothin',' she added hastily, 'could be further from our thoughts than any lavish diversions. The times are quite out of tune; but we do feel very strongly that anythin' we can do to stiffen determination, strengthen morale and, at the same time, provide some measure of consolation to the separated and indeed the bereaved should and indeed must be done.'

During this peroration some of the younger petticoat members of the family drifted into the small Blue Drawing Room. These were now seated, almost all of them in most unsuitable dress for the afternoon tea hour, at least by any previous standards. They perched on the richly embroidered chairs eating with a voracity which could at best be termed indelicate for young women of their birth, background and upbringing. Cucumber sandwiches vanished at an alarming rate, buttered scones were swept from the silver dishes, cakes plum, seed and sand were munched at a great rate and Marguerite was in constant demand for 'more tea please, Aunt Marguerite'.

For an example, Stephanie, Sinclair's erstwhile 'hair shirt', the problem daughter of a problem family, embracer of many 'unfortunate' causes and now dedicated recruit to the Women's Voluntary Aid Detachment, a V.A.D., was stuffing food in with one hand and pushing back escaping hair with the other into a cap which appeared to be long past its first, pristine freshness. Then she proceeded to brush crumbs on to the Bokhara from an apron which appeared to have been a crumb basket for some considerable time.

Rosemary de la Coutray, John and Primrose's girl, had also slipped in while her grandmother was talking. She merely flopped down in the Holland pinafore she had wore all day while working in the tomato houses. Once sufficiently sated she dipped one hand into a capacious pocket, from which protruded a strand of bass and a pair of sécateurs. She withdrew a silver cigarette case. Then she caught Gyles' eye and hastily returned it, settling with a sigh for yet another piece of buttered gingerbread. In consequence of much stopping and tying, picking and packing under Sawbridge's eagle eye, Rosemary's fingers had turned a most peculiar yellowy green which on its own account would have earned her dismissal from the room at any other time, married woman and mother though she was.

Nearby sat little Lucy St John, soberly dressed in plain dark blue with simple touches of white at throat and wrists. The simplicity only served to enhance her delicate prettiness, but it was distinctly out of character. She had hastily created a niche for herself in this working hierarchy by proving to Lady Constance that she was more than capable of keeping the books, checking and recording the accounts and attending to all the filing for the Convalescent Home. What she also had done, with the utmost speed and secrecy was to enlist the help of the tutor, Sissingham. Thanks to him Lucy had executed her test work with both neatness and precision, thus winning praise from the highly critical Constance.

Lucy had seen that she must indeed do something which made her indispensable if she were to be sure of staying undisturbed in the Castle with her brother Lucien. In all this she was ably assisted by Lucien himself, in a manner equally secret and predictable. Somehow this devious fourteen-year-old was managing to fulfil his tutor's requirements as laid down by the Dowager and Gyles and still finding time to spend with his precious 'Lucy Lou' as he called her when they were alone. Now they sat, very close together like two small, beautiful love-birds-without-perches, listening intently to everything, saying nothing, just following their agreed course of drawing the absolute minimum of attention to themselves yet missing nothing!

Near to them, occasionally smiling affectionately at the pair, sat Petula wearing a riding habit. The rest of the young were at their respective schools; except those who were still fed and watered in the now communal nursery/schoolroom, including Gilbert who was home for his half-term holidays only.

Among this motley assembly sat Bishop Alaric, widower, with fingertips joined to fingertips—just—across his enormous belly. On his face was an expression of combined piety and wariness as he too listened and cat-napped alternately.

Only Claire among them all sat wearing the uneasy expression of one who is perfectly aware of shoals ahead and merely wonders when the lord of Castle Rising will erupt.

Even she, the superlatively elegant Claire, now wore a V.A.D. uniform. She had offered herself and had been accepted as personal aide to Constance and at this moment was only snatching a few minutes' respite before going to hold a watching brief over the convalescents in the big Rest Room during their pre-dinner hour. Thus there remained only two women who were still dressed in the manner to which they had all been accustomed—Christine's fondly-named 'two old naughties'. Even she sipped her tea as did Petula, in riding dress, a display of bad taste which would have drawn thunder a little more than a month ago.

The 'naughties' were disarmingly frank as to their reasons for as they put it 'maintainin'' standards'. The young men, they defended themselves, appreciated their gowns, their jewels, their coiffures. It reminded them of their own womenfolk; though whether when they returned home they would find the women of their families in such array was certainly a matter for conjecture.

Collectively the Lormes at tea on this early October afternoon might well have sat for a Conversation Piece entitled 'Afternoon Tea at Castle Rising, October, 1914'.

Gyles was on the point of saying as much when his mother stopped speaking. So he changed instead to 'Well, Mama?' and waited.

'Well indeed,' she replied a trifle tartly, '*if* you will bring your attention back to me, we might just manage to postpone a discussion on the advisability of such a paintin' as I realise you have just envisaged until a more appropriate occasion.'

This did cause her son to start and to speculate once more upon his redoubtable parent's clairvoyant powers.

'Just how did you arrive at that deduction?' the question slipped out under his guard.

'Obvious!' she brushed the matter aside. 'Let us please return to our *moutons*. We feel that we should put up two rolls of honour in the chapel, one for the family and one for the villagers, staff and tenants. Then, in our sorely curtailed leisure we can bend our minds to the devisin' of a suitable permanent memorial.

'As a matter of more immediate concern we also feel it incumbent upon us to devise some special Christmas services which Alaric can conduct in his inimitable fashion . . .' She broke off as her brother-in-law roused himself from his latest cat-nap and emitted a single, startled grunt; but she swept on, leaving the Bishop no time for comment.

'We should throw open the chapel at Christmas to our dependents. They should worship with us. If we could cram the numbers in which we did for Henry and Petula's wedding,[1] we can surely do the same in this cause dear to the hearts of all of us? I admit we may be forced to duplicate the services. I would like to see two special nine carol, nine lesson services *by candlelight*; for which your aunt Marguerite, assisted by Sawby, whom Christine has discovered has particular leanings towards expressing himself in floral and evergreen decorations, will beautify the chapel. In addition Alaric'—her fat brother-in-law opened one drowsy eye again, regarded the speaker balefully and then closed both in resignation—'should conduct two separate services of prayer and intercession for our fighting men; with our vicars to assist. We should also have a Midnight Communion service on Christmas Eve. The late hour will I fancy decimate attendance sufficiently for all to be encompassed at one session. We should likewise arrange for hot drinks to be served to every-

[1] See Book 2, *Shadows Over Castle Rising*.

one afterwards before they set out, possibly through deep snow, on their homeward journeys. In addition you, Gyles, should donate one of these new-fangled gramophones to the village hall. Such an instrument would form an added inducement to woo lonely women to informal meetings. These could easily be made extensions into evening time from our regular afternoon meetings for bandage rollings, parcel packing, knitting and sewing. It will all form a nucleus for the formation of those Women's Institutes in which Stephanie has so great an interest.'

This last bit of deliberate vote-catching brought vigorous nods of approval and enthusiasm from Stephanie which in turn caused more wisps of hair to escape from her white head-dress.

'Added to which,' the Dowager forged on relentlessly, 'we should give much more consideration to the presents we give this year. Petula, bless her, has volunteered to help us despite all she has on her hands already. She will canvass the women, find out each one's particular desire and then place orders—through Christine of course—for knitting needles and wool, also ingredients for each woman to make things for their menfolk's food parcels, and include in the gifts, cigarettes and tobacco for the parcels. Oh, I cannot enumerate all the things now but Pet agrees with me that they are legion and it would make our gifts far more personalised.

'Finally, there is the matter of Puck's Hill.[2] By tradition all the poor things can do until victory is won is to carry more brands to the summit bonfire. None can be lit of course, and hauling up brands is poor work for heartening the spirits. So I propose that we erect a really huge Christmas tree—do not worry, I have already found such a one—we can plant it temporarily outside this Castle where hounds meet, also by tradition, every Boxing Day. Then we will light our tree with a multitude of fairy lights so that it may constitute a beacon to our total confidence in ultimate victory, and also to gladden the eyes and heart of every child in the neighbourhood.'

Gyles looked up—thinking she had done; but there was more to come.

'Naturally,' she continued, 'you will wish to have the usual present-giving and supper thereafter, but this too should be adapted a little to suit the circumstances. There will be so many women! Therefore something slightly different should be

[2] See Book 1, *The Lormes of Castle Rising.*

planned and Sawby and Plum should entertain the men for us separately. There!' she said contentedly, 'I have done. What say you, Gyles?'

First she flung down her gauntlet, then she looked about her and quite deliberately forced a murmur of approval from her audience.

Gyles seethed inwardly. She had done it again! She had taken his assent for granted as she had always done with him, as with his father before him. She had suborned the others, at God alone knew how many private discussions at which it had all been worked out! Now she sat 'lookin' deuced pleased with herself' because only a curmudgeon or a Scrooge could gainsay any of such proposals. 'Dammit,' he thought furiously, 'she treats me like a schoolboy . . .'

He knew well enough that he was cornered, but did not intend giving in without handing her a *mauvais quatre d'heure*.

He rose slowly, well aware that all eyes were upon him and longing to administer a good sound slap. 'Thank you, Mama,' he said courteously, 'I am much obliged to you for such a lucid exposition and now if you will excuse me, I have some urgent matters which demand my attention before dinner, you will be comin' down?'

'I am not decrepit yet,' she retorted, 'of course I will be comin' down?' While we are on *that* subject may I say'—she was definitely ruffled now—'that I shall expect everyone not actively engaged in nursin' duties to do me the honour of dressin' properly so that we may at least enjoy one comparatively civilised meal.'

Gyles nodded, 'Quite so, Mama.' He then walked out of the room. The soft sound of the doors closing might have been an explosion, so great was the astonishment which followed.

Charles Danement, a fascinated witness to these exchanges now exclaimed, 'And not a flamin' word one way or t'other! well he is piqued if I may say so!'

The little Countess was laughing. She mopped her streaming eyes. She looked around her and abruptly became aware of the round-eyed attention of Lucien.

'Oh dear!' she exclaimed, 'we quite forgot you were still here. How remiss. Christine my dear, is it not time that child went upstairs to Nanny? I'm sure he has spent much longer than usual with us. Nanny might be gettin' worried.' This was ignoring the obvious—that if Nanny were anxious she would have come down and said so in no uncertain terms.

Christine took her cue obediently, saying, 'Yes, say goodnight to everyone dear and I will take you up. Indeed I must go up myself or I shall never be dressed in time for dinner and that would never do. Are you coming, Pet?'

Petula rose. Gradually the room emptied. At length the two schemers were alone save only for the Bishop who was now deep in slumber and snoring like a muted saw-mill.

The conspirators exchanged glances.

'Has he bitten Alicia?' the Countess asked, evincing a distinct tendency to slip back into another spate of giggles.

'He certainly was in a biting mood,' the Dowager answered trenchantly, 'yet I think he will come round all right. He is rather cross at present. The chief damage is to his *amour propre.*' Her lips quivered. 'He was so taken aback by my being practical for once. He obviously expected one of my old, scatter-brained extravagant proposals. So, he is just puttin' on his little performance to save face. In the meantime I think we can tell Sawby to telegraph for that Christmas tree; and now my dear Marguerite let us too dress for dinner.'

Gyles had always been predictable. In his father's day outbursts of temper from him were unknown. Only those closest to him knew that he was capable of them but merely held them in check. When Justin Aynthorp died, and the Castle ceased to be rocked by those volcanic eruptions which made Justin's reign so highly colourful, his eldest son shed his perennial calm overnight. From the moment Justin departed to bully the archangels, Gyles showed that sweet reason and total lack of intransigence were no longer to be expected. As Christine commented to her mother-in-law, 'it was only to be expected'.

Autocratic behaviour was as much a part of the Lorme inheritance as their Norman tradition, their recurring 'runts' and their flaming copper hair. In youth this had matched highly burnished copper. As they matured so it ripened until it exactly matched the colour of the leaves on a mature copper beech tree.

Hence the legend of 'Restoration Rupert' that excessively runtish Lorme, the disgraceful henchman to King Charles II. Whether or not His Majesty knew the depths of Rupert's wickednesses, he certainly kept him close to him throughout his reign. He had done so from the time when Rupert had first presented himself with a purseful of gold to the impoverished fugitive, in Holland. After King Charles returned, Rupert could seem to many infuriated courtiers to do no wrong in the King's eyes. The tale ran that this randy buccaneer at length laid himself across one too many of the Court beauties and was discovered *in flagrante delecto* by the lady's spouse who, not surprisingly was murderously incensed. Before the door to my lady's chamber had been broken down Rupert had prudently flung himself through the casement, narrowly missing a broken neck as he plunged into the moat. He had scrambled ashore, mounted his horse and fled incontinent. On discovering that he was hotly pursued by the cuckolded husband and a posse of vengeful 'family', Rupert galloped through the surrounding forest, espied a giant copper beech tree and at full thundering pelt grasped an overhanging bough and drew himself up into the concealing branches. Here he hastily reversed his cloak and thus enveloped in brown hid his tell-tale hair amid the matching leaves. He stayed crouching undetected while his pursuers scoured the area. When they ultimately called off the hunt and the lady's spouse returned to his castle unfastening his belt as he mounted the steep stairs to my lady's chamber, Rupert merely slid down the tree, no more than a trifle cramped from his concealment.

The lewd rhyme which he subsequently penned for the amusement of his monarch, ' 'Twas M'y Hair Which Saved Me Sire', was even now in Gyles' custody; although, so far, he had flatly refused to allow his favourite Tante Meg to include it among the memorabilia in the Museum.

In youth, the unhelmeted hair had been a banner to companions in many a battlefield from Pevensey to Spion Kop and now had already left its first tribute on the ravaged soil of little Belgium.

More potent by far in the minds of contemporary Lormes, Gyles thought, as with temper rising he walked back towards his office, was the influence of the family's Talisman, the Lady Mathilde's somewhat wry bequest to the first Henri de Lorme, founder of the English line. As he walked into his office it was this, far more than his Mama's actions, which occupied his thoughts.

In a nutshell, the men of the family who had been present

at the opening of that ancient, rusted 'treasure'[3] felt that the act of opening up the Talisman after so many centuries, had loosed some powerfully destructive forces upon the famous Lorme luck, which heretofore had always brought them round in times of stress and difficulty. Lorne luck had enabled them, time and again, to repair the depletions to property and means wrought by those recurring 'runts'. Lorme luck had also enabled them to expend vast sums in the concealment of every trace of runt-behaviour so that the name remained untarnished to the world at large.

Even so their greatest troubles dated from the opening of that treasure. The culmination was the outbreak of this present war which in itself constituted a sharp reminder to the older members of the family at least that England's history and their own were of identical age. Ergo, reasoned men like Gyles, if England went down, then down too would go the house of Lorme and all it represented. Though such thoughts were unthinkable, Gyles could not hold them back.

Nor was this the first time. He remembered very vividly that night just before Henry's wedding[4] when he had walked across the great saddle back of his own lands and let the tide of prescience break over him. So now, his forward vision confirmed the accuracy of the Dowager's statement: 'victory *is a long way off*'.

Sitting at his desk table, Gyles also remembered some lines which he had read in a women's magazine which one of the girls had left lying with other periodicals on a table in the Blue Drawing Room. He had picked it up idly, leafed it through and in so doing had seen an editorial which startled him. He recalled the words very clearly: '*How*,' asked the writer, '*Shall we fare in the new world that is being built for us before our eyes? . . . for it can hardly be doubted that in place of the old world familiar to us, something in many ways new and strange will arise with the ending of this war. . . .*'

He shivered, staring blankly ahead of him. Then he was reminded of Lord Kitchener's warning, that it would take at least three years to defeat the Hun and he began to think of the costs of such a war. They would be astronomical, not only to the country as a whole; but also to every single rate-payer who owned land. Income tax was already under threat of increase to a staggering six shillings in the pound. Soon now, food would

---

[3] See Book 1, *The Lormes of Castle Rising*.
[4] See Book 2, *Shadows Over Castle Rising*.

become scarce, with sea trade reduced and farming affected by lack of men to work the land. Women he knew were flocking to fill the gaps. There was already talk of women making munitions, following the plough; but assuredly efficiency would be diminished, at best until these women gained experience and even then he doubted whether their stamina would enable them to be anything like as productive as the men had been. A country run by old men and women! That is what it would come to before long. The casualties were appalling already. Over twenty thousand of the flower of England and the Empire's men lay dead upon the battlefields of Belgium already. Supposing, just supposing this carnage continued for the four years Gyles was so sure it would take for Britain and her allies to win, then over a million in the army alone would pay the price of victory.

For the young women of the generation there could therefore be no hope. They would form a huge majority condemned to loneliness and single life. Nor could such frightful depredations be made good in one generation alone.

Gyles moved restlessly, trying to stem the thoughts which beset him. If this lay ahead for England what then for the Lormes?

Should Henry go, then, if Petula bore a son, the title would pass to him; but if not the line would break at last and the title go to Ninian; but Ninian was already at the front, so what if he fell too? And if he did, would not Andrew, already seventeen, fling himself into the breach and insist on fighting?

The little travelling clock received the full benefit of Gyles' sombre stare. Diana, a seismograph to her master's feelings, thrust her muzzle into the curve of his elbow and nuzzled him consolingly. The man put one hand out to gentle her. He was speculating now on what his father would have done.

'Why damme! fight of course ... fight taxes ... fight everythin' and anythin', not sit about like a moonstruck calf inventin' tragedies, aint that the proper thing to do?' As clearly as if he had heard the old man's voice, the imagined words chivvied him back to reality.

'And it will not happen,' said Gyles aloud, 'if you're on the other side stravaiging around and makin' things hell for everyone except yerself.' He rose abruptly. 'All right, sir,' he said to his father's imagined shade, 'I'll stravaig around here too!' And so saying he hurried from the room to dress for dinner.

CHAPTER 4

November Eighteenth, Nineteen Fourteen

The north wind, already enraged by the time it flayed its way down from Iceland, worked itself into a frenzy as it reached the Wash. Here, like a demented giant it scooped up the waves and flung them on to the shore in a welter of stones, seaweed and small craft.

As it rampaged on into the Anglian marshes, scouring the shore, the broads, rivers, and mud-flats so the birds fled.

Bitterns sank deep into the reed-beds where the white-collared bunting, water-rails and gadwall were already in sanctuary with the tiny dunlop, who scuttered away like minute, white smoke puffs before the sweeping vengeance. Even the heron, trailing their legs in gale-tossed flight, sought shelter under the over-hanging growth along the inner reaches of the estuary, while shovellers scuttled into dead tree hollows where, in springtime, they made their nests.

Only the bittern's booming, the heron's 'kronk', the moorhen's 'kurruk' and the dolorous 'tonk' of the wild geese sounded inter-mittently as the wind paused to draw breath for further onslaughts.

All through the night it growled and howled about the Castle walls, screaming through the chimneys and shaking the casements in a frenzy of frustration.

With the dawn its mischief was plain to see. The home park was strewn with savaged branches. Young trees, wrenched from the soil lay scattered about, their torn roots forlornly exposed, while a litter of twigs, leaves and thatch ripped from cottage roofs and pulled into shards by the wind's destructive fingers disfigured the grass.

Further afield the same sorry ravishings were plain to see; fences torn down, tiles wrenched out of roofing and flung upon the cobblestones, hen houses in tipsy ruin. Then the wind dropped and the rains came. It fell from the heavens as though God's reservoirs were being emptied upon the earth beneath. Presently the river levels rose perilously.

At seven thirty, half an hour beyond his appointed time, a drenched Sam Groby, the 'newsboy', a mere stripling of sixty-seven, struggled into the yard, rain pouring from his sou-wester, cascading over the sacking shawl he had drawn close about his shoulders and running in rivulets into his wellington boots.

As Mabel, the older of the two kitchen maids opened the yard door just sufficiently to peer through, Groby croaked to her hoarsely, 'Tree's down acrorst the drive. Carnt bring cart up nohow. Ever so sorry I'm late.' So saying he withdrew from beneath innumerable layers of clothing an oilskin sack which he held out to the girl.

' 'Ere's papers an' all, git them along inside quick afore they'm wet like me.'

Mrs Parsons could be heard shouting from the Servants' Hall, 'Ef that's Groby bring 'im in for a drop of summink 'ot afore 'ee tries ter git back, Mabel.'

Groby nodded to the girl. 'Take 'em along to Mr Sawby, my lass. Tell Mrs P thank you kindly an' I'll be along jest as soon as I stop puddlin'.'

Mabel obeyed, thankful to escape the whistling chill and return to the warmth of the hall.

'Mr Groby's drippin' orf first,' she announced, holding out the sack. ' 'Is wellies is chock-a-block with water. 'Ees 'ad to walk the larst bit. There'm a tree down right acrorst the drive 'ee says and cart won't come through.'

Mrs Parsons now issued orders from her rocking chair which she had drawn close to the roaring stove.

'Run along then, fetch them old carpet slippers from the broom cupboard, take 'em to Mr Groby and make 'im give you them rubber things. Then you and Agnes can dry 'em out inside afore 'ee goes back.'

Sawby stood at the end of the huge scrubbed table which was now covered by the early morning tea trays. Here he received the letters and papers, set the latter to one side for the moment and sorted the letters on to their respective trays saying, half to himself as he did so, 'His lordship ... m'ilady ... Mrs Petula ... that's nice! there's one for her from Mr Henry ... Mrs

John ...' he broke off to eye Raikes over the top of his steel rimmed spectacles, which had a tendency towards sliding down his nose. 'Pst! iron those newspapers, Raikes, look sharp now, quick as you can we're behind time already...' He gave an irritable prod to the spectacles as he returned to his sorting.

Raikes' ironing board was already set between the back of a windsor chair and the other end of the table. A flat iron stood on the hob. Now she took up the red flannel iron holder, spat on it exclaimed, 'Drat the thing,' as the bubble seethed and rolled off, added 'too hot!' and hurried off in search of brown paper and cold water.

Mrs Parsons directed the reception of Groby with some haste. She knew she barely had time in which to greet, shoe, feed and settle him before it would be urgent for her to direct her attention elsewhere.

Groby shuffled in—the slippers three sizes too large for him. He apologised, saying, 'Thankee kindly, Mrs P, I look a rare sight and no mistake but I'm mighty glad of your kindness, ma'am.'

It was plain to see that at some time in the past Mrs Groby had, as she would have phrased it, 'come in the way of' an unwanted scarlet, emerald and black plaid rug. It was equally plain that she had seen in it the potential for an immensely protective garment for her spouse to assume in inclement weather. She had cut a hole in the rug at centre, added two slits at left and right and dropped the arrangement over her husband's bullet head. His arms stuck out of the gaudy stuff. A piece of strong twine drew the folds in amidships—roughly where his waist would have been if he had possessed one. Thus he resembled a plaid-covered cottage loaf.

He was 'sat down' and was given a huge white enamel, blue-rimmed mug of steaming cocoa and a plate piled high with crusty slices of dripping toast.

When all was done Mrs Parsons just managed to return to her chair, place her over-white cook's hands on her stout knees and fix her gaze upon the butler as he took what he described as 'certain precautions'.

As Raikes ironed the daily newspapers, so she handed them to Sawby. He searched among them for copies of *The Times*, opened one out and began running one finger down the casualty columns watched unwaveringly by Mrs Parsons who closely resembled a stout terrier at a particularly small rathole.

The rest of the servants tip-toed about glancing back at Sawby with nervous frequency, for they were all involved. There was not a single one of them, like their employers who did not know someone, whether relative or friend, who just might have reached those battlefields by now and therefore could well be missing, wounded or even dead.

Sawby possessed a royal memory. He also kept a book in which for the past fifteen years he had pasted the records of all table placings for luncheons and dinners, all guest lists for what he called 'functions', all room plans for house parties. For the rest, anyone connected with Lormes, St Johns, Delahayes, Tessedres, Coutrays, or, on the distaff side with Hardcastles, Lavenhams, Newmarkets, Lamballes, Russells or Danements he knew down to the last third cousin twice removed.

He searched on. Then suddenly he straightened his back, took off his glasses and began polishing them as if they were a piece of the family gold plate or he Lord Aynthorp with his monocle. Perhaps unconsciously he had caught the trick from his employer whose hand flew to his monocle whenever he met what his son Henry called 'a facer'. Finally Sawby laid them down, met Mrs Parsons' horrified gaze and nodded grimly. Then he took a pencil from the pocket of his alpaca coat and traced a ring round one name.

Mrs Parsons raised her voice. 'Yer all lingerin!' she shouted.

'Wilkins, Spurling, Raikes, get them trays up this instant. Mabel, Ethel, get our breakfus things tergether in the pantry and just as soon as this table's cleared *lay up*! Look sharp now and no more dawdlin' and footwomen can leave *ALL* them papers 'ere—and jest take the letters.'

When they had all gone, ' 'Ooo is it?' she demanded hoarsely, ' 'Ooo in God's name is it?'

Silently Sawby handed her the newspaper.

'I 'aven't got me glasses!' she wailed, ' 'ere chef, read it fer me, quick.'

Chef André took the paper, read the marked entry and then read aloud, '*2nd Lieut. George John Newmarket. 60th Rifles. Died of Wounds . . .*'

Up like a white flag went Mrs Parsons' apron as she buried her head in it. Through this screen came the muffled sounds of weeping and, 'Oh that pore boy . . . wot could only 'ave bin there a few days . . . oh, whatever will Mrs John say . . . 'er lovely nephew . . . Oh this wicked, wicked war!'

Pansy came running down the stairs. She took in the scene, glanced at her husband who said, quite steady now, 'It's Mr George, love. He's gone!'

She burst into tears but ran across to the apron-canopied mourner and put her arms around the starchy protection. 'There, there now dear, there, there,' she soothed, 'don't take on so, quiet down do, you've a real hard day's work before you. Just you let Pansy pour you a nice hot cup of tea then try to come out from behind that dratted apron and drink it.'

Sawby jerked his head in the direction of the Steward's room, turned towards it, chef followed and little Sam, who despite his horror went with the other two men holding a half eaten slab of dripping toast in one hand and a half-finished mug of cocoa in the other. The door closed behind them.

'We'll give them a few minutes, then we must move. I shall put all the papers into his lordship's office, he never goes there before his breakfast and,' Sawby added grimly, '*I* will take the responsibility of holding back the news, at least until they have eaten their breakfast.'

Presently, with a leaden heart and wearing a formidable expression Sawby rallied his staff. Somehow Pansy had wheedled Mrs Parsons into some semblance of control. Somehow Sawby had managed to stem the noisy sobs of the kitchen maids; but he let the stream of invective which chef loosed upon *Les Sales Boches* flow uninterrupted.

Pausing only to pat Mrs Parsons gently on the shoulder, Sawby turned to go upstairs saying, 'I'll put these papers in his lordship's office and then I'll get into the breakfast room.'

All the while he thought about the young man who would never return, whom he had known since he was a little boy in his first knickerbockers when he first came to spend a holiday from 'prep' school with his Aunt Primrose, his father's sister. Sometimes Master George had gone to the John de Lormes' Newmarket house but, Sawby remembered, it didn't matter to him really where he went just so long as there were horses. This brought Sawby up with a jerk. Someone would have to tell Plum. Master George had been the old man's pet and many's the time that Sawby, taking a 'turn' in the grounds before dinner had come upon the pair of them in the harness room. At first he would find them munching sweets which Mrs Plum had made. Later George would produce two bottles of beer from the pocket of his hacking jacket. There they would be sipping and talking in a companionship which knew no class distinctions. Plum would take this hard. But then wouldn't they all? They missed him even when he returned to New Zealand. When he came back again he always brought gifts with him, a tankard for Plum with his name inscribed on it, and once, one of those boomerangs. A fine set-to there had been when he showed Plum how to throw the thing and nearly beheaded his lordship who was cantering home. Mister George had brought Sawby a tie pin with a turquoise in the head and turquoises for every lady in the Castle, a right generous, happy young man he had been. Always happy. Last of all he had shared the London season with the family ... 'At least,' thought Sawby gratefully, 'he had a good life, such as there was of it!' So thinking he completed his breakfast room inspection and came out to station himself in the hall as usual for gong duty. Wilkins was already there, neat as a pin, gong in hand. Sawby pulled on the white gloves she handed him, dipped for and sprang open his old gun metal half-hunter and as the clocks began to chime the hour of nine he gave the signal.

The Dowager and the little Countess came down together as if they too had been waiting for their cue. Behind them were Primrose and John then Christine and Gyles with the younger members of the family following behind.

When everyone had helped themselves from the laden sideboard and the footwomen had placed their tea, tisane or coffee cups beside them, Primrose looked up from her *Oeufs Jeanette*, 'I forgot to tell you all yesterday,' she said smilingly, 'I had such a sweet note from George and he enclosed a photograph. I thought you might like to see both.' And so saying, she passed the opened envelope to her sister-in-law.

There was a chorus of assent. Wilkins' hand shook slightly as she handed croissants but this went unremarked, as did the horrified expression which flashed across Sawby's face.

The Dowager was studying the photograph through her lorgnette.

'Very nice,' she pronounced, 'charmin' boy. His uniform becomes him.' She passed it on and withdrew the letter.

John de Lorme was now studying the photograph. 'Very

much aware of his new status as a commissioned officer, dontcher think?' he said twinkling.

Gyles grunted, taking the picture and studying it with Christine at his side. 'Dear boy,' Christine said affectionately, 'you know, Aunt Prim, he's really very like you. The family resemblance is most marked, I think even more so than when he was a boy.'

'Almost as marked,' Sir Charles interpolated, 'as the joint families' predilection for horses I would say.'

The Dowager had by now read the letter. 'Most endearin',' she remarked, 'would you all like me to read it to you?'

A murmur of assent ran round the table. 'Then,' said she, 'pray listen. He writes, "*Dearest Aunt, Please excuse this hurried scrawl but we embark at noon. I have just snatched time to have a photograph taken for Mama. I thought you might like to have one too. My comission came . . .*" ' she broke off. 'Are there not two m's in commission? yes I thought so, now where was I? oh yes . . . "*in the knick of time . . .*" ' again she broke off, 'really this boy's spelling. Someone must tell him nick is not spelled knick . . . "*in the nick of time for me to go to the front with my battalion. I will have a proper studio portrait taken on my very first leave. This is just something to be going on with. Please give my love to everyone and my regards to Plum. Tell him to take care of the gees. Your loving nephew George.*" '

When she had done, Gyles said crossly, 'I miss my *Times*. What did happen, Sawby?'

The butler turned, 'I can only suppose, my lord, that Groby could not get through,' he replied. 'The drive is strewn with fallen trees.' He glanced significantly at the windows outside where the rain was still sheeting down. 'Wilkes has offered to take the trap to the village just as soon as she can get through.'

'No need for that,'' Gyles put down his empty cup. 'I shall be ridin' with Sir Charles, we can call in at the post office on our circuit.'

Thus he forced poor Sawby's hand.

Seeing what lay in store Sawby replied, 'Just so, my lord,' then spoke his usual, 'will there be anything else, my lady?' received his quittance and left the room.

As he told his wife, 'I felt sick when I heard who they were all talking about. It made it even harder. There was Mrs Henry saying, "George is such a darling", she added, "I must write to him at once" and then asked "should we not all say a little prayer for him in the chapel?" His Grace took this up of course. There he sat on to his third helping of devilled kidneys. Still, he said ever so kind and benevolent, "a beautiful thought my dear, of course we should, I shall be glad to accompany you".

'As if that wasn't enough, Lady Constance came in, explained why she was late and then off they all went again telling her and showing that poor young man's picture. I tell you, Pansy, I couldn't get out of that room fast enough. Before I could escape his lordship asked me about the papers. I stuck to my story but now he says he and Sir Charles will collect them.'

Pansy made little clucking sounds of comfort and then Sawby said wearily,

'Now I shall have to go and ask his lordship to please go into his office before he leaves the Castle.' He got up, patted her hand, added, 'Better tell the others.'

Gyles, without the added inducement of his *Times* left the breakfast room shortly after Sawby. In fact as he closed the breakfast room door behind him he came face to face with his butler.

'If you please, my lord,' Sawby said haltingly.

'Yes, Sawby?'

'Would you please be so kind as to accompany me to your office, my lord?'

Gyles frowned. 'What the devil for?'

Sawby glanced round him nervously. 'Not here, my lord, please.'

Gyles looked a little closer. He then noticed the unmistakable signs of strain and suppressed emotion. He sighed, said, 'Oh very well,' then turned on his heel with Sawby and Diana trailing behind him.

Sawby closed the door. He stood just inside. Gyles crossed to his table, saw the pile of letters neatly set out, and atop them all that opened copy of *The Times*.

'It's all there, my lord,' he stammered, 'I, we, that is, we held them back.'

Gyles stared incredulously, 'You ... held ... them ... back?'

'I make it my business to examine the casualty lists every morning,' said Sawby falteringly.

At the mention of these Gyles stiffened. Then, like his butler with his glasses, he took out his monocle and began polishing it.

'Who?' the word snapped out.

'It is in there,' Sawby countered, 'we thought . . . we felt . . . we er . . . wished that the Family might have a proper breakfast in peace before . . . before . . .' his voice trailed off.

Gyles bent over the opened paper. He saw the pencilled ring. He read. He remained bent over the page in silence for what seemed to the waiting man like hours.

At length two words escaped: 'I . . . see.' Then his head came up. 'I believe,' he said looking ruefully at his butler, 'I am considerably in your debt for a remarkably thoughtful and kindly act. Please accept my apologies for my behaviour. I never thought, I never imagined . . .' from somewhere Gyles achieved a kindly little smile, then added 'well you have gained your remarkably tactful objective. The Family *has* breakfasted in tranquillity.'

Sawby made a great effort to reply. All he achieved was a strangled sound. 'Quite so,' said Gyles, 'no need to say any more. I suppose the servants all know?' Sawby nodded.

'We really are most splendidly served by you all. I find myself at this sad time much blessed by your joint conspiracy of kindness. Do you think you could possibly convey my gratitude for me? Say that of course I will thank them all personally later; but first I must see her ladyship. Someone will have to tell Mrs John, too. Do you not suppose it would come more gently from another woman?' He was, of course, only voicing his thoughts in order to give Sawby time to recover.

While Gyles and Sawby were engrossed in the office, Christine hurried up the stairs on her way to a conference in the Housekeeper's room, always a lengthy business, for Mrs Peace, in Christine's opinion, had been born stately. She had never been seen to move with haste in all her long years of service with the Family. Now, primly correct, not a hair of her whipped-cream-walnut arrangement out of place, the inevitable hair brooch at the throat of her plain black dress, her *châtelaine* dangling from the hard black leather waistbelt in which she confined her still narrow waist, she rose, bobbed, drew out a chair, waited until her employer was seated then sat down herself and pulled a pair of paper cuffs over her wrists. Only then did she open the topmost of an intimidating pile of household books, take up her pen and say respectfully, 'Indeed, my lady, I am grateful for this visit. There are so many matters which require your ladyship's attention . . .'

Christine sighed inwardly. Clearly this was to be a particularly protracted discussion.

Primrose and John made their way back to their own suite preparatory to their morning ride, while those two arch schemers, the Dowager and the little Countess, trotted towards the Dowager's boudoir. There was still an hour before they were needed in the Home. They were about to hatch yet another of their little plots and were anxious to make the best of their brief leisure.

'As I see it, Meg,' the Dowager opened the proceedings, 'it is our duty to provide some sort of entertainment for our young.'

Her sister-in-law's eyes sparkled. 'All work and no play makes Jack and Jill dull . . .' she affirmed sententiously.

'And the young of both sexes who are currently living in this Castle are no exceptions,' the Dowager added crisply. 'Take Lucy. Such a very short while ago the gel was enmeshed in her first London season. What a superlative season it was! Then there is Stephanie. That child is no longer compelled to live the life of a nun! The amnesty has effectively drawn the most virulent poisons from the label "Suffragette".[1]

'For a few weeks longer—until she begins to show, it would not be wrong for Petula to take part either. Then of course there are the gels in the immediate neighbourhood, all of them bereft of the gaieties it is only right and proper that they should enjoy!' Thus they justified their ploy to each other.

'Some of our young convalescents are quite up to dancin' a little too,' nodded the Countess. 'They are a charmin' lot of boys . . . some of the best regiments . . . all of good family . . . perfectly suitable material.'

'Exactly, so all we need is a gramophone and some, er, records. We can use the Music Room, the parquet is perfect for dancin', the proportions more than ample for, say twenty-four couples. So now I think we need Palliser.' She shook the little bell at her elbow. Palliser the Dowager's personal maid, sour-faced as ever, materialised with a celerity which indicated that she had been listening outside the door.

'You rang, miladi?'

'Yes, Palliser, I did. Pray have the goodness to take a message

[1] See Book 2, *Shadows Over Castle Rising*.

from me to the tutor, Mr Sissingham. Tell him I wish to know immediately whom I should approach in London for the very best and most up-to-date gramophone.'

Palliser's eyebrows rose alarmingly, however she merely bobbed, repeated the message and scuttled away. Even so: '*Now* what's afoot?' she speculated as she climbed towards the schoolroom. When she returned with the information, the Countess was no longer there. Palliser delivered her message and withdrew to the next room, leaving the door ajar. Then she crouched down on the other side and prepared to enjoy a little more eavesdropping.

Making a small grimace at her son's warning which was pasted above the telephone the Dowager wound the handle of the instrument, clapped the receiver to her ear and waited for the sound of Sawby's voice. When it came she spoke,

'Ah, Sawby, pray find the telephone number in London of Messrs Chappell. Yes two "p"s and two "l"s ... they sell music, what? Oh, Bond Street, I believe ... and then connect me. Thank you.'

She replaced the receiver and began making a list. After a short pause the bell rang and she found herself in contact with her objective.

'Do you sell gramophones, if you please? ... You do, very good. Yes I want you to supply me with the very best that is available. Yes. My name is Aynthorp, the Dowager Lady Aynthorp ... Castle Rising ... Essex ... now can I obtain records of dance music from you too...?'

Eleven minutes elapsed before she replaced the receiver once again by which time she knew that the only fashionable dances were the Tango, and the Waltz ... and murmuring, 'What in the world is the Tango?' she turned to find Palliser at her elbow.

'Good gracious, Palliser, I had no idea you were still here!'

'If you have no further need for me my lady, might I take some of your gowns to the ironing room?' Palliser murmured meekly.

The Dowager was still hock deep in her ploy, 'Oh yes,' she said absently, 'run along do, I thought you had gone long ago ... now where was I?'

Palliser fled, scuttling towards the servants' quarters pregnant with the news and anxious to impart it over a tisane in the Steward's Room, where she could crow a little over the remainder of the upper servants. All about her clocks were tinkling, chiming . . . sounding the hour of eleven.

Before she could do more than slip inside a trifle breathlessly, seat herself and accept her tisane from chef who rose to pour it for his compatriot there was a scratch on the door.

'Come in,' called Sawby a trifle wearily. Agnes the third kitchen maid poked a dishevelled head around the opening and disclosed a somewhat smudged countenance.

'Begging your pardon, Mr Sawby,' she said nervously, 'but Richard's aunt, Mrs Simms, is in the 'all. She wants ter see you. Says it's urgent like.'

'Oh drat!' exclaimed Mrs Parsons, 'wen you've only jest set down; and after the nasty shock as you 'as already took this morning.' Then to Agnes crossly, 'Carnt the pore man 'ave five minnits peace and quiet?'

Sawby had already taken down his coat and was shrugging into it. 'It's all right,' he assured the others, 'it's probably some very slight matter. I shall be back in a few moments I dare say. Just pop a saucer over my cup, Pansy. He turned to the waiting girl, 'Show Mrs Simms to a seat by the fire, then *go and wash your face my girl.* You are supposed to be a kitchen maid in an exalted household not a chimney sweep!'

But his return was far from speedy. A few minutes elapsed. Suddenly his voice shouted from the hall 'Pansy!'

She jumped up and ran out leaving the door open behind her. The rest of the senior servants stared out as if they had suddenly looked upon Medusa's head. They saw a weeping woman in a rusty black coat and dress huddled in Mrs Parsons' chair. Sawby was bending over her. As his wife came running to his aid they all heard him saying, 'It's Richard, our Richard the footman. As next of kin Mrs Simms had a telegram this morning. He's killed he is. Now please help me with Mrs Simms.'

Mrs Parsons shrieked. This brought them all to life and they poured from the room. Mutely Sawby held out to them the dreaded telegram, then shook his head and turned away.

'*Regret to inform you Lance Corporal Richard Simms killed in action.*'

They all read it while Sawby stood with his back to them staring out at the relentless rain. Presently he passed a slightly unsteady hand across his face and muttered,

'What a terrible day. I only hope I never live to see another like it.'

But the day was not yet over.

Gyles' attempt to reach his wife had finally drawn her from the Housekeeper's Room; but by the time he had broken the news to her and asked her to pass it on to the rest of their womenfolk, Plum, the head poultry woman and two of their farmers were waiting for him. When he had dealt with their tales of damage and destruction, handed them over to Sir Charles and then told them all of George's death it was past eleven o'clock. He came back into the Great Hall only to find Sawby waiting for him once again. One glance at the man's face was enough. Gyles' mouth tautened.

'What now, Sawby?'

'Below stairs this time my lord.'

'Who?'

'That nice young footman of ours, my lord, Richard, Richard Simms. I have his aunt below. She lives entirely alone so she brought the telegram to us seeking a bit of comfort poor soul.'

Gyles moved abruptly.

'Come into the library,' he said over his shoulder. Once there he went to the tray of drinks which as usual stood on the big round library table where they had once unwrapped the Talisman.[2] Then, picking up the brandy decanter he poured two stiff drinks, handed one to his butler and said, 'Drink that it may help you a little.'

Sawby took the glass gratefully. 'Thank you, my lord . . . most thoughtful . . .'

They drank slowly, in silence, each busy with their own thoughts. At length, 'What can we do for the poor woman?' Gyles asked wearily.

Sawby hesitated. 'You see, my lord, she lives entirely alone. There is a friend of hers, another widow, who lives in Upper Aynthorp. They went to Dame School together. I thought that perhaps if we could have permission to send someone to fetch Widow Betsy, as all the village folk call her, and then come back and collect Richard's aunt she would not feel quite so badly. What she needs now is someone else. That boy was the apple of her eye.'

[2] See Book 1, *The Lormes of Castle Rising.*

Gyles nodded impatiently, 'No need to ask. See to it, and Sawby, be good enough to do anything else you see fit without waiting to obtain permission. I rely on your judgement absolutely.'

The master of Castle Rising stood for a long time beside the old library table. His thoughts were not pleasant. For, if this war lasted, as he was already assured it would do for between three and four years, just how many times he asked himself was the same scene to be re-enacted?

So thinking he moved and went heavily away.

Somehow the day dragged on. Somehow everyone rallied, even if they moved about their duties with shoulders which seemed to droop with the weight of shared sorrows.

When luncheon was served the older women came to it wearing black. The younger ones wore their nursing uniforms with black armbands as did the men who had also assumed black ties.

The Bishop said grace then they all sat down and began the farce of pushing chef's creations around their plates. Only the Bishop did justice to them. At length temporarily sated, he opened his mouth to speak instead of stoke. Clearing his throat he began,

'Ahem . . . if, er, everyone is in accord I propose a brief service in the chapel at six o'clock tonight. Then we can all offer up our prayers for the souls of those two gallant young men,' he paused, looked across at his sister, 'perhaps, Marguerite, you would be good enough to see to the flowers and candles?'

She nodded. Bishop Alaric sketched the sign of the cross over his enormous frontage and looked expectantly round for pudding.

Christine choked but closed her lips tightly and said nothing. Gyles doggedly resumed his reports on the damage done by the gales, supported by Charles Danement; but presently even they flagged. After a long silence Charles asked,

'What have you done about those Rolls of Honour, Gyles?'

'Commissioned them weeks ago,' Gyles shook his head at the proffered puddings, 'no thank you Wilkes I will wait for coffee.' He resumed, 'There was a letter today telling me they were ready for despatch tomorrow, so I telephoned . . . to . . . er . . . give them the first three names, Stephen, George and our footman Richard. I told them to put them all on each Roll, then to despatch one and keep the other for me. Thus I have ensured the least possible delay... should... should there be more names to add. I also considered on reflection that all names should be together. It is more fittin'.'

There was another lengthy silence during which Christine caught her husband's glance, read what she wanted, rose and took the women away.

The three men resumed their seats. The Bishop promptly fell asleep and began to snore quite gently but on a deep note which reminded both his listeners of the sound of drums. It made an obbligato to the theme of the relentless rain still lashing at the window panes.

'Much more of this and m'y river will flood. There are men out watching.' Gyles chafed.

'And my reaches,' Charles Danement added, 'there's a nasty bit of erosion already in the reach between m'y lowest water meadow and the bridge at the entrance to Pleched village. Pet and I drove over to Messing afterwards, that reach of yours was in danger there and you've two meadows under water already, so I put a team of volunteers to sandbaggin'. I think we should take another look and see if we can estimate how far the damned water will rise by nightfall.'

'Of course,' said Gyles automatically. He reached for a cigar, unbanded and pierced it, pushed the box to Sir Charles then exploded savagely.

'Why must it always be our young men?'

Sir Charles nodded. 'Echo answers "why?" indeed; but it has always been so. Even your Marseillaise stresses it, remember?'

Gyles looked up questioningly, then, 'Oh yes, of course!' and he quoted, ' "come *children* of our country, the day of glory has arrived".'

'And,' stressed Charles, 'death and glory are just another seemingly indivisible twin.' His eyes narrowed. 'My dear chap,' he added bitterly, 'do you not think I too would give my right hand to be out there now instead of my son? I've had a bloody good life all things considered and a fair run; but what's the use? They're simply not entertainin' the idea of fifty-three-year-old fliers, more's the pity.' He sank back into his thoughts again but after a while added, 'At least I can tell you we have advanced a bit.'

Gyles turned to him in astonishment. 'Advanced?' he repeated, 'in what way?'

'We no longer send little drummer boys to be cannon fodder. I shall never forget my Gov'nor tellin' me when I was a cub how a little feller of thirteen died in his arms. At the moment of death the child choked, and tears began to roll down his face. "I'm afraid to die, sir," he whispered, "is it because I am so very young?"... then he just died. What a bloody, bloody indictment!'

Gyles stood up. 'Let's get our legs across a couple of horses,' he said abruptly, 'they're bound to be fresh. We're behavin' like two old women. We'll go to those reaches, possibly lend a hand, a bit of hard sweat will do us a power of good. You cut along and change, I'll send a message to Plum...' and so saying he strode from the room.

The Dowager saw them go down towards the stables, their hacking raincoats flapping in the wind, caps pulled low over their eyes. Resolutely she turned away, determined to keep herself from grieving, in so far as was possible, by occupying herself.

She went to the Music Room where she knew Lucien would be practising at this hour, even as she knew that whatever work Lucy had to complete, she would be found sitting on the big white bearskin rug, listening to her brother.

She opened the doors very softly, put finger to lip as Lucy looked up, slipped into a nearby chair and settled until the boy stopped playing. Sitting there, straightbacked as ever, it seemed that the day had already etched in the lines around her mouth more deeply, as if in fact even the flesh over her beautifully boned face was weary, the eyelids too heavy to open fully. Lucy missed none of this. She felt her own eyes sting with sudden tears, made no attempt to brush them off but just bit her lip in a valiant effort to curb them.

Lucien came to the end of the fugue he played. He swung round on the music stool, exclaimed, 'Grandmama, how lovely to see you,' and quickly came to her side. Then he nuzzled her shoulder consolingly.

'Poor darling,' he whispered. She put up one white, veined hand on which the rings seemed suddenly heavy and rather loose.

'I came to ask a favour,' she said, slipping her fingers through the soft, fair hair, 'but I want you to understand that if the idea is distasteful you can of course refuse.'

'What can I do?' he asked simply.

She put out a hand to Lucy who joined them, sitting at the Dowager's feet. Thus she explained to this most unusual pair, 'I have been thinkin' a great deal about all those young men whom we are tryin' to nurse back to health again. It occurred to me that they would derive immense pleasure from hearing you play to them. I thought, if you were willin', that you could do this at tea time. Would you like that or would you hate it?'

Typically, Lucien replied, 'I should love it. If they didn't rattle their teacups. But where would the piano come from?'

'Mr Prewitt, dear Mr Prewitt. I consulted him. He is very happy to lend us his just until the one I have ordered comes from London.' Again she pressed him, 'But are you quite sure you would not be shy or uncomfortable?'

Lucien smiled down at her, 'I couldn't be,' he answered, 'when I am playing there is only music, at least,' he hesitated, 'Lucy would be there wouldn't she?... I mean ... I might want some music and then Lucy could turn the pages for me couldn't she?'

The corners of the Dowager's weary mouth twitched. 'Oh you two!' she exclaimed, 'well now, Lucy can hardly be said to be part of the curative treatment, but without any doubt her presence could only be considered as beneficial,' she allowed. 'Gracious Lucien you are *towerin'* over me. How you've grown! Well is that settled then?" she looked fondly from one to the other.

'Of course,' they said in chorus.

'There is one thing, Grandmama,' said Lucy hesitantly.

'And what is that?'

'Well you said you always wear elegant dresses because it pleased your patients didn't you?'

'So I did,' the Dowager actually chuckled. 'That, my dear little Lucy, is what is called bein' hoist by my own petard; but by all means put on a pretty frock, though I am bound to admit you look charmin' in that plain blue thing. Now tea will be served as usual at half-past four,' she examined the small jewelled watch which dangled from her dress, 'it is now half-past three. I dare say the piano will have arrived already, so run along and change, then come to my boudoir and I will take you and introduce you.'

Lucy scrambled to her feet, shook out her skirts and said to her brother, 'I'll change now. Meanwhile you can decide what you will play and collect any music you may want. I promise not to be long, you will probably want to try out Mr Prewitt's piano first anyway.'

At four fifteen the trio assembled and made their way towards the Convalescent Home's Rest Room. The Dowager and her sister-in-law had scattered deep armchairs about the room, placing a small table and footstool by each. They had seen to it that a big chimney piece was installed with a wide open hearth below it on which a wood fire burned constantly. One long wall was covered with bookshelves, the rest, papered in a soft pale green, formed a background to gentle Corots.

There were flowers banked on the mantelshelf and more flowers in eighteenth-century porcelain flower pots on every table. It was a warm cheerful room, carefully understated, wisely including only those things which formed a restful background. Lucien and Lucy looked around approvingly. Across one corner, angled to the drawn hangings, stood Mr Prewitt's piano.

Then suddenly the room was filled with young men, some walking with sticks, some with slings supporting one arm and one or two in wheeled chairs brought in by the V.A.D.s. When everyone was settled Lucy seated herself by the piano and carefully spread out her skirts.

There was one among them that afternoon who would say in after years that his whole life changed in the course of an hour while they all sipped tea and listened to Lucien's playing. He chose to stand, leaning on his good shoulder against one end of the mantelshelf, his left arm cradled in a sling. He was both tall and slender but what made him stand out from the rest was the exceptional colour of his hair. He was prematurely grey, the slight, unruly waves tapering to white. This only served to emphasise the fine-drawn youthfulness of the profile he turned to Lucien, for he looked past him to his sister and as he looked Swinburne's lines flashed through his mind, '*I will say no word than a man might say, whose whole life's love goes down in a day, for this could never have been, nor ever till the Gods and the years relent shall be*'.

Lucy was dressed very simply in blue velvet with a spreading skirt which belled out from her small waist. This was further emphasised by an encircling sash of satin ribbons. Her fair curls, brushed by the ever obliging Pearson, were drawn up on the top of her head and secured by a small matching velvet bow. Pearson had stepped back as usual to examine her handiwork and then had drawn out a single curl, laying it to one side against the nape of her neck.

The Dowager looked around her, cleared her throat and then said,

'Gentlemen, may I introduce to you my great-niece The Lady Lucy St-John.' She added sternly, 'you have my great-niece's insistence that *you do not rise please.*'

Lucy reacted perfectly. With just the right touch of shyness she said,

'Good afternoon, everyone. Presently I will hope to learn all your names and meet each one of you properly; but now I think my brother Lucien is waiting to play.' She sped a questioning look at Lucien who nodded and then mimed 'no music'. So Lucy settled back to listen.

If his life had been forfeit should he fail to remember what Lucien played in that hour, then Mr Piers Fournes, a lieutenant in the Fifteenth (The King's) Hussars; twenty-five-year-old veteran of the British Expeditionary Force and the fortunate recipient of a 'Blighty' one month ago, would surely have died.

With his face propped on his good hand, and thus in shadow he gazed at Lucy. The Dowager, now engaged in a game of chess with a stripling who had been buried alive under an eruption of mud blown up by an exploding shell, chose this precise moment to look up. Thereafter, while her opponent deliberated she watched the watcher intently.

Presently she made a soft, 'Tch ... tch ...' to Stephanie, whose day it was for dispensing tea. The girl obediently leaned forward to hear the whispered, 'What, pray, is that silver-haired boy's name?'

She whispered back, 'Piers, Piers Fournes. He is of French descent, British now like Lormes.'

The Dowager nodded, expended one final hiss. 'Find out all you can, then come to me,' and returned a little of her attention to the chessmen. Beneath her deliberations ran a strong thread of secondary thought. 'Smitten, hip and thigh,' thought this astonishing old person, 'never seen anyone take a harder toss'— but then she thought still in Justin Aynthorp's vein, the association of nearly half a century being hard to sever.

'Might not be unsuitable,' she speculated, 'I wonder if he has ever seen her before? The boy is manifestly besotted!' At which point Lucien stopped playing and a spatter of applause broke out. Before he began again the Dowager excused herself to her opponent with the promise of a return; then she walked quietly to where Mr Fournes stood.

She began a little under-cover chatter with him, speaking in French which brought a flush of pleasure to his pale face. He replied eagerly. 'Well,' thought the old schemer complacently, 'his accent is impeccable anyway.' At length he could stand it no longer. He bent to the Dowager and began to stammer out,

'Lady Alicia, would it? . . . I mean, er . . . might I? . . . that is, would it be possible? Oh dear!' and he broke off to run a thin hand across his hair.

'You would like to be presented to my great niece? Is that what you are tryin' to say?' she responded coolly, 'then please just contain your impatience until her brother has finished playin' and I will call her over.'

As Lucien played on, the door opened and Lady Constance looked in. She saw her charges, relaxed and listening; she noted that Stephanie was well in control of herself, if a trifle pink-eyed, and so she withdrew apparently well-satisfied.

The music ceased once more, Lucien stood up, closed the piano and the more active convalescents surged around him. The Dowager heard a diffident, 'I say, that was perfectly splendid. Could you, I mean, would you play some ragtime for us one day as well?'

She caught Lucy's questioning glance. She beckoned, and when Lucy drew level with her she said, 'My dear, Monsieu Fournes would like to be introduced to you.'

Lucy held out a small hand, lifted her eyes and encountered such a blazing fire in eyes as blue as her own that it made her catch her breath. Outwardly, still holding on to her composure she murmured her pleasure, laid her small hand in one which she noted was as long and well-shaped as her Uncle Gyles' and then began to chatter as she had been taught to do. Under this cover she examined the face thinking it like Lucien's for gentleness, like Lormes for the nose; but like only one person whom she had met for the markedly flaring nostrils. By this time reverting to her normal detachment, she remarked, dimpling, 'May I please ask you a question, Mr Fournes?'

'Please, anything you like,' he stammered helplessly enmeshed.

'I wondered if you were a poet? To me you have the face of one and I am trying very hard to recall whom it is you remind me of. Someone I met during my first season?. . . Wait I have it, he *is* a poet I know, at least he is beginning to be but is still at Cambridge, his name is Rupert Brooke.'

Piers Fournes smiled. 'Am I like him?'

'Oh yes, it's a look,' she explained seriously. Then she coloured suddenly, 'now I am being farouche and I apologise!'

'Oh please don't,' he pleaded, 'I want to be a poet one day, but now,' suddenly courage came upon him and scarcely believing he dared, he managed, 'at this moment the summit of my ambition is to obtain permission from you to paint your portrait.'

This both surprised and pleased her. 'What a pretty thing to say!' she exclaimed, 'if I have permission and can make the time —I work these days you know—then it would give me pleasure to sit for you, especially if it would help you to get well quickly.' It was so artless and yet so charmingly said that he stared in astonishment.

'Would you really?' he sounded incredulous.

'Why certainly, but tell me please have you your easel here? brushes and paints, canvas, palette? for if not, my brother paints and would I am confident be happy to supply you with anything he has which you found adequate.'

He assured her quickly, 'I brought everything with me. So your brother paints too?' he sounded as though he were weighing something up, then he went on, 'of course he would. He certainly plays very beautifully. Might I ask his age?'

'Fourteen,' she said. 'Is he not remarkable?' His eyelids flickered,

'Indeed so, and you are, I would say, seventeen?'

'Oh no,' she laughed, 'I am eighteen and a half.'

The Dowager, a watchful listener to this exchange said lightly, 'My great niece has the gift of extreme youth. When she was presented I was actually asked if she was of age for making her come out. Sometimes I have the belief that she is some fairy changeling. Indeed the pair of them could well be so. Come, Lucien, let me introduce you to Mr Fournes.'

Lucien, conscious of his sister's preoccupation had worked his way around to them and now stood at the Dowager's side. As he shook hands, so he experienced a curious tingling, as if the contact conveyed to him a small electric shock. Piers felt it too.

This awareness added to a sudden fear that what he felt was visible. He said hurriedly,

'I have been hearing that you paint. I would very much like to see some of your work, that is unless you detest showing it.'

Lucien regarded him gravely. 'With some people I do,' he agreed, 'should you like me to bring some tomorrow afternoon?'

Lucy felt very happy suddenly. Lucien clearly approved of this poet-person with the silvery hair. For thus and thus only had his personality impinged her. If Lucien liked him then they could all be friends. She said eagerly, 'We will look at some together this evening, Mr Fournes, and make a selection for tomorrow.'

Piers Fournes put one hand up and pulled at his tie. These two! They were overwhelming. Again he felt the small electric shock, this time of fear at the first intrusion of that inclusive 'we'.

They went on chatting, the brother and sister finishing sentences for each other, corroborating, linking, the young man forcing himself to come to terms with what they revealed to him quite unconsciously.

Later, when they had gone he crossed to the windows, drew back one heavy hanging and looked out at the angry night. 'No way', he told himself watching the wind-bent branches, the scutters of leaves along the faint illuminations which seeped from curtain sides to fall on the old stone terraces, could he otherwise take even a sip from her cup, and no way could he ever again contemplate full measure from that of any other girl or woman. He was caught in a dream made manifest by the simple fact that *au fond* they were three of a kind, possessing a recognition of each other and an immense attraction one to the other. Both these facts brooked no questioning; not even of the shattering truth that the boy too was almost as close-drawn into the mesh of these shared emotions. Piers Fournes looked out at the night and let the fatal question surge in his mind. 'Then what am I? Ye Gods what then *am* I?' and he shivered as he stood.

The night was vicious. Water dripped from the flying buttresses, ran from the gutters and drummed down upon the leaves from the stripped branches which the winds had ravished. These lay like soggy carpets over the dormant bulbs. Then the rain paused. In this pause a solitary rook flapped struggling to its nest in the topmost branches of an elm. A mournful owl hooted—a despairing sound. The black sky showed not a single eye, even the stars were failing to penetrate. From time to time dripping figures bent by the winds scurried to their cottages; others fled to the Castle from the stables, dashing from stalls with sacking clutched across their shoulders; and more men and women thrust their way homewards, with here a lantern swinging from one half-frozen hand, their boots squelching as they hastened for warmth and shelter.

Inside all was bright enough. Lights sparkled, fires blazed, but the same heaviness made the light and warmth seem spurious.

Mrs Parsons, huddled beside the crackling stove, rubbed her cold hands together and complained, 'I'm chilled to the marrer! even afore this fire wen I should be warm as toast wot with all that baking.'

They were all the same. To crown discomfort, Pansy complained of another of her headaches. She actually snapped at chef who watched her in astonishment as she marched away holding her head. Little Boots came lumbering in with yet another hob of coke for the insatiable maws of the giant ranges. Inadvertently he trod on chef's toe, '*Crétin!*' chef screamed in pain, '*imbécile!*' and even Boots, instead of apologising, dumped the hod and marched off in dudgeon to grumble and mutter to himself in his cupboard sanctuary under the back stairs.

Presiding over this scene of gloom and despondency were two small photographs, newly installed on the mantelshelf. Somehow Mademoiselle Palliser had managed to obtain one of Mr George, and Spurling, who had played coachman to poor little Mrs Simms, had returned clutching one of their late footman. Now, draped with scraps of black crèpe and with a bowl of white flowers cadged from Sawbridge and arranged between them the two 'likenesses' stared down. Nor was this atmosphere confined to below stairs.

Primrose de Lorme, her embroidery idle in her lap sat staring into the fire remembering. Her letter to Canada lay stamped and waiting for Wilkes to collect it. Scrumpled sheets in the waste paper basket were eloquent of the difficulty she had found in writing it. 'How' she thought despairingly, 'does one find words which offer any solace to a beloved brother on the death of his eldest son?'

John de Lorme, at the writing desk, smoking innumerable cigarettes—which he normally regarded with anathema—was scribbling and scrumpling as his wife had done, writing, erasing, pausing, tearing up, beginning all over again.

Petula had already written to Henry who she knew would feel George's death possibly more than any of them. In plain terms Henry had loved George though he would have pooh-poohed anyone who dared tell him so. He would only have mumbled,

'A capital feller an' all that'. . . and 'a good man in a scrap'; hiding his sorrow under a self-defensive screen of what he would call 'suitable' phrases; but Petula knew, not only of the bond between the pair of them but of the strength of this bond, even as she knew how the love of one man for another—the David and Jonathan emotion—such as flowed between James and Ninian, was just about as fine as any which existed. Eventually she made a tremendous effort, wrenched her thoughts away and began dressing for dinner.

Even Pearson brushed and dressed Christine's hair in silence. Only when all was to her liking did she enquire gently, 'The black, my lady?'

Christine nodded. 'The black, Pearson, if you please.'

Upstairs in the nursery where all the remaining children now had tea together, ten-year-old Gilbert Delahaye, whom Nanny had long ago christened, 'Little Mr Moneybags', sat hunched on the window seat. First he thought about what a 'rotten half-term hols', this had turned out to be. Then he, too, began to think about George Newmarket's death and of their late foot-man's too. Unfortunately he voiced his thoughts.

It happened that Nanny came bustling in chiding, 'Now, Master Gilbert, whatever are you doing sitting there all huddled up looking out at such a very narsty night?'

'Thinking,' said Gilbert shortly.

Some evil genius prompted Nanny to continue. 'Thinking indeed, well it's high time you put your young thoughts to mak-ing a visit to your pore father and mother. You've scarcely been near them since you came home!'

'I hate sick people,' said Gilbert coldly, which invoked a tirade. Gilbert waited, slightly bored. When Nanny eventually paused to draw breath he slid from the seat, stood up, brushed an imaginary speck from his knickerbockers and said, 'I'll tell you exactly what I was thinking, that I am going to be a multi-millionaire one day.'

'Stuff and fiddlesticks!' snapped Nanny, 'a multi-millionaire indeed, I don't know where you get such nonsensical ideas from. You're a very silly little boy.'

'Oh no I am not,' he was quite unruffled, 'and when you interrupted me I was thinking what a pity it is that I am too young to profit by what could obviously have been my easiest chance.'

'And what, pray, do you mean by that?' Nanny stared at him.

Gilbert yawned, 'why, anyone who isn't a fool can see there is a most wonderful chance to make a fortune *at this moment*.'

Nanny came closer, anger warring with curiosity in her boot-button eyes.

'And how Mr Moneybags would you say they could do any such thing?' she demanded.

Gilbert regarded her steadily. 'Simply by cornering all the black material. If one man bought up every scrap of it, at the rate we are going now, I reckon he could make up to a million pounds a year while this war lasts. All the women will rush to buy black, and all those black armbands and black ties, why it's a wonderful opportunity!'

For once in her life Nanny was bereft of speech. She could only stare with mingled shock and horror on her old face.

At length through shaking lips, 'Oh merciful God,' she moaned, 'wot 'ave we got this time? Not a boy at all, a monster! To think of all those suffering, weeping women and all them dear, dead boys. How could you think of making money out of their miseries at a time like this?'

Gilbert looked at her contemptuously. 'My dear Nanny,' he said quellingly, 'one should always be practical. You are just being sloppy and sentimental.' And so saying, he strolled out of the room, small hands in pockets.

Nanny just sat down and swayed to and fro with tears rolling down her cheeks. This at length was how Rose found her.

At five minutes to six the servants who had worked with Richard gathered outside the chapel porch. They stood waiting in their outdoor clothes, stamping their feet against the bitter cold. They whispered together as one by one the family appeared.

When Sawby had checked them, counting heads carefully, he led the little domestic procession to their pews at the back. The 'shoveresse' as Mrs Parsons called Gyles' chauffeuse, came in last with Mrs Simms leaning heavily on her arm. Behind her trailed the Widow Betsy also in shabby black.

Up in the organ loft Mr Prewitt played softly. The Bishop stood at the altar, his back turned to his little congregation. On either side of him the flames swayed above the white candles in their sconces. They highlighted the Countess's flowers turning them to china whiteness. She had also massed flowers and candles in each of the embrasures so that the chapel was filled with scent and tiny spears of golden light.

There was a slight rustling as everyone knelt. From the gallery rose Stephanie's voice singing 'The Lord Is My Redeemer'. When she ended Bishop Alaric turned and began to intercede.

'We are gathered together here in Thy house, O Lord, to intercede with Thee. We pray that in Thy infinite mercy and understanding Thou wilt take the souls of our dear departed, George John Newmarket and Richard Simms and lead them to Eternal Life with Thee. They gave the only riches that man may offer up to Thee, by laying down their lives that freedom may live in this dear land and we be saved from the dreadful power of our enemies. Grant that their sacrifice may not be in vain and that their reward may be in heaven with Thee.' He waited for a while and then resumed.

'Bestow upon us we beseech Thee the fortitude to rise above our shared sorrows that we may press forward, spurred by this heroic example, to fight and fight again until an honourable peace enables us all to build a new land fit for heroes to live in. For only by so doing can we offer up to Thee a fitting memorial to our glorious dead.'

Then saying, 'let us pray,' he began the familiar words and the congregation joined in ... 'Our Father who art in heaven hallowed be Thy name. ...'

When, at length they came out Gyles spotted little Mr Prewitt slipping away unobtrusively so he called, 'Mr Prewitt, could you spare me a moment if you please?'

Reluctantly the little man came over to him. 'Good evening, my lord,' he said uneasily, 'I was just hurrying home, now is not the time for me to intrude.'

'Pish, my dear man,' said Gyles, 'are you not one of the family after all these years?'

Mr Prewitt flushed, and murmured something quite unintelligible.

Gyles withdrew the statutory guinea from his pocket and held it out, 'I just wished to thank you for playing for us at such short notice and tell you how much we appreciate it.'

Mr Prewitt stepped back as if he had been stung. 'Oh no, my lord, pray forgive me; but not tonight. Oh dear me no, not tonight!'

Gyles attempted to expostulate but the little music master, suddenly and astonishingly emboldened, closed his lips stubbornly and just stood shaking his head. At length he managed, 'it was my privilege you see ... so very little ... just a widow's mite reely ...' and turning he bolted like any little frightened woodland creature.

Holding Christine's arm carefully, for the path was slippery with fallen leaves, Gyles said, as they walked towards the Castle together, 'That dear little feller must have his fees increased ... such an enormous gift ... from him. ... Would you please be so good as to see he is informed that from now onwards he is to receive two guineas for each music lesson and one and a half guineas each time he plays the organ for us in the chapel?'

Christine nodded. 'Of course, but pray tell me, my love, why now?'

She had been out of earshot during his exchange with the music master. So Gyles recounted the incident. Only then, for the first time that day did Christine break down and cry.

Once inside the Castle she sent for Sawby, gave instructions for a basket of hothouse fruits and a big bunch of flowers to be sent to Mrs Prewitt in the morning. She sat down and wrote a short note while the butler waited. *'Just a small token of our appreciation and esteem. Lord Aynthorp wishes me to inform you that from now onwards Mr Prewitt is to receive two guineas for each music lesson and one and a half guineas each time he plays for us so beautifully in our chapel. Sincerely and gratefully, Christine Aynthorp.'* She folded the note and handed it to Sawby. 'Please pin that to the flowers, Sawby,' she concluded.

After a valiant attempt at dining—which Sawby described as 'a travesty'—they all returned to the Blue Drawing Room.

This was the moment which the Dowager elected as 'suitable' for launching her latest plan upon them all. 'At least, she argued, it would keep their minds occupied.

Gyles heard her out in total silence. The rest held their breath as she concluded,

'Constance, Marguerite and I feel that this load of combined work and sorrow which has fallen upon such young shoulders must be relieved by a little of what your father would have called "divarsion". Small weekly dances in fact, to a gramophone— already ordered—are what we have in mind. It will bring some of the other lonely "gels" we know into our circle and be beneficial to our young convalescents. Nor need it make a great deal of extra work for the servants. We could use the Music Room, which has a pianoforte, so Lucien can play some *valses*. We should only require some cup and a few little sandwiches . . .' even she quailed a little at Gyles' silence, as with down-bent eyes he heard her out. Then he spoke. His words brought every head up in amazement.

'You are to be congratulated,' he told his mother, 'I agree with the scheme wholeheartedly. The only flaw is that you do not go far enough. I, too, have been increasingly aware of tensions building up, and frustrations. I believe now that I am the prime offender. No,' he lifted one hand as if to forestall any interruption, 'please hear me out as I listened to you, Mama.

'Nursin' those boys with love and skill is not enough. Playin' to them in the afternoons, arrangin' little "hops" as I believe such informal dances are now called, is not enough either. We have all been very foolish in our efforts to minimise danger to our treasures and save labour for our staff.

'Even to me, it is all too apparent, when I take time to look back over our immediate past, that the staff are wiltin', fretful, all at sixes and sevens because they no longer have any opportunities for displayin' their not inconsiderable talents.' He looked around him . . . at the Bishop, who had woken with a start at the strength of Gyles' declaration 'you do not go far enough', and stayed awake, registering astonishment and disbelief; at the Dowager into whose eyes was creeping a sparkle Gyles had not seen since the first knowledge of imminent hostilities had quenched it; at his wife, her face alight with tenderness; and at Charles Danement who sat back in his chair, long legs crossed, contemplating the ash on his cigar with the utmost appreciation tinged with amusement.

They all waited. After a brief pause to collect his thoughts, Gyles went on, 'We forget one matter vital to the recovery of our patients. *They are away from home*, and therefore devoid of the warmth of kindred human contacts. Despite all your lavish nursin' attentions they have no one but each other with whom to communicate. I think this is absolutely wrong and it must cease forthwith. We will restore our beautiful White Drawing Room to all its splendour. I will entertain those who are fit enough to a civilised dinner in our proper dining room once a week. Then I will bring them to you and you will assume your prettiest gowns, your jewels, restore yourselves in fact to some semblance of your normal appearances. Then you will *entertain* them. It is for Constance to right any ill-effects thereafter with the help of Jamieson. I propose to begin preparations tomorrow mornin'. I ask one great sacrifice from all of you. No matter what our losses, and God knows they are heavy enough already, there will be no mournin' in this house and no one, absolutely no one will enter the Home in black, nor wear armbands either. *We* do not need the accoutrements of mournin' to mourn our dead. *They* do not need a posse of sombre black crows potterin' among them'—there was an outraged gasp at this but he swept on—'I have been puttin' myself in m'y father's place and askin' m'yself what he would have done had he been here. I think he would have done precisely what I now prescribe. He would have been the life and soul of the party and a dam' sight more good to those young fellers than all the medicines and cossetin'. How say you, Mama?'

The sparkle was well in evidence now.

'I say,' she said softly, 'spoken like your dear Papa. Christine?' The Dowager turned to her daughter-in-law.

The wife of this unpredictable man replied very simply. 'This is what I have been waiting for. I will play my part with alacrity. As for the servants, I think it will be like a tonic to them all and I shall tell them in the morning.'

The doors opened again before anyone else could speak. It was Sawby. Before he could say anything Petula jumped up and kissed her father-in-law, 'Hello, Grumpy' and 'welcome' she whispered so that only he could hear. Gyles saw the tears in her eyes, and clasping one hand he gave it a warm squeeze as he turned in his chair to the butler.

'Yes, Sawby.'

'I am sorry to disturb you, my lord, but there is someone on the telephone who wishes to speak to you. He says he is speaking for Lord Bartonbury. I think the call has come from the House, my lord.'

Gyles jumped up, 'I will come immediately,' then, turning to the others, he said, 'either stay and we will talk this out in detail presently or if I find you gone I will accept that you prefer to think things over and we can re-open the subject in the mornin'.'

Then he followed Sawby from the room.

He took this telephone call in the library. He dismissed Sawby, took up the receiver and said into it, 'This is Lord Aynthorp, to whom am I speakin'?'

'Good evening, Lord Aynthorp,' the voice came back, 'I am his lordship's private secretary, speaking from the House of Lords. His lordship asked me to telephone you some hours ago; but I have had the greatest difficulty in reaching you—due I imagine to the gales . . .'

'Quite so,' said Gyles.

The secretary continued, 'his lordship asked me to explain why he could not wait to speak to you himself. He is already on his way to France.'

'To France!' Gyles interjected.

'Yes, my lord. I am afraid I have some rather bad news for you.'

Gyles answered evenly, 'That is nothin' new today, what is it this time? pray tell me as briefly as you can.'

'Very well,' agreed the other. 'Lord Bartonbury received a telegram this morning to his home in Yorkshire. He and her ladyship were already in London so there was some delay in reaching him. It appears that his eldest son, Lord Steyne, has been severely wounded. Lord Bartonbury has been very busy. The outcome of his activities is that he has obtained the necessary permission to collect Lord Steyne in a special private ambulance. He has a nurse and a qualified driver with him. They sail at midnight and hope to return in two or three days bringing Mr Ralph, er Lord Steyne with them. He wishes you to know that as soon as he can communicate with you he will do so.'

'Where is Lady Bartonbury?' Gyles asked.

'With her mother-in-law, the Dowager Countess. The Dowager is apparently taking the news very badly and Lady Bartonbury is staying with her for the time being.'

'I see,' Gyles hesitated, 'thank you very much for your lucid explanation. I had planned to come to London, but now I shall remain here so that you may contact me at any hour of the day or night. Is that quite understood?'

'It is indeed. You may rest assured I will telephone you immediately I hear anything. May I add my condolences, my lord, and hope things will not turn out to be as bad as any of us may fear at present.'

'Thank you,' said Gyles curtly, 'and good night to you.' He replaced the receiver his thoughts chaotic. 'Three in one day ... Eustace's heir ... and ... if he went? then James who was already rarin' to go and after James, *Lucien*.' Gyles shivered. He sat on by the dying fire while the wind took up its previous theme and howled around the ancient walls in fitting accompaniment to his thoughts.

CHAPTER 5

Flanders Mud

Despite the triple tragedies which had brought them all down, Gyles Aynthorp's sudden decision had given them fresh heart. They had always possessed a resilience which had laid them open on many past occasions to both criticism and misinterpretation; notwithstanding, while theoretically holding breath as they awaited news of Ralph, they flung themselves thankfully into preparations for 'Gyles' plan'.

Before any news filtered through to them as to the progress of the ambulance, Gyles received word from the French Ambassador concerning Chef André's position. This established that the man need not leave England and return to France unless he so wished.

As this news came after the disclosure of Gyles' plan to the domestic staff it was received by André with his familiar shrug and a terse, '*J'y reste milord.*' Having said this André hurried to his desk and set about shaping the first draft of his menu for the projected, all-male dinner party.

Even Mrs Peace was discovered hauling down boxes and opening up crates which she had filled with all the finest of the Castle's napery, having been led to believe that she would have no further need to issue any 'for the duration'. Sawby, meanwhile, busied himself lecturing the footwomen on the intricacies of what he termed 'proper dining' and was actually heard whistling in the silver room.

Then came Doctor Jamieson's welcome announcement that Sinclair was to be allowed downstairs for the first time since his stroke. The doctor further heartened them by stating that some movement had already returned to Sinclair's damaged left side. Admittedly he still dragged his left leg and his left hand was virtually useless but, after asking for and abtaining an eminent second opinion, the doctor told them their mutually agreed expectation was that only a slight limp would remain by the spring and also that the fairly adequate use of Sinclair's left hand might be expected with some confidence.

He and Henrietta now spent most of their time together in their own apartments in the west wing. This, irreverently nick-named by Henry, had become known as 'the Chelsea Pensioners' ', as all the oldest members of the Family were quartered there. These included the now retired Bishop, who was already well into his eighty-fourth year and inclined to remind his relations with a remarkable display of tactlessness—even for him —that he had already lived longer than his late brother Justin.

Henrietta now took a short walk every day in the solicitous care of Stephanie. The girl had never looked better. Certainly she would never be a beauty, nor had she any of the other women's fastidiousness in matters of dress and personal groom-ing, nevertheless, she now looked a healthy and pleasant-faced young woman and had become her parents' joy, instead of as previously, their hair-shirt. Save for these leisurely constitu-tionals Henrietta seemed content to sit with her husband, occasionally stabbing at a piece of *petit point,* sometimes with the additional companionship of Stephanie. The girl would hurry in, flushed and slightly dishevelled. She would pull up the tooled calf pouffe which had become 'her' seat and submit with docility to her mother's attempts at straightening her dress and pushing escaping wisps of hair back under her generally askew head-dress. Beside them in his wheeled chair Sinclair rested close to the fire with a light rug across his knees. He talked incessantly of Stephen and both took a further step towards recovery when Gyles brought to them the reply to his letter to the King's private secretary.

He wrote that His Majesty had directed him to convey his sympathy to all the family in their tragic loss and also at Mr Delahaye's disability. The writer further affirmed that the posthumous investiture could and would be postponed until Mr Delahaye had recovered sufficiently to accept the Distinguished Service Order on his late son's behalf.

Sinclair showed this letter to staff and family alike. He never tired of reading it. He also expressed the fervent hope that, providing he was still alive, he would have the opportunity of meeting and talking to the young man who had followed Stephen on that last reconnaissance flight. He had, as Sinclair now knew, flown immediately behind Stephen so had seen everything. 'Then,' Sinclair would exclaim, 'I can hear from his own lips the story of my son's heroic actions!'

When Gyles heard of this he resolved to make some discreet enquiries of his own. At the back of his mind lay the uneasy anticipation that should there be a meeting it would need to be prefaced by some fairly strenuous vetting by him, lest something be disclosed which could in any way damage Sinclair's pride in his late son's eleventh hour heroics.

This decision taken, on the morning after the storm had finally abated, Gyles hurried off to join Sir Charles on their tour of flood and gale damage inspection. Petula was away shopping for Christmas in London so the two men went alone.

The rain had ceased at last. After three days the wind had dropped too and it was now vital to survey and assess the storm's damage and to set in train the immediate salvage and restoration work.

Later, on the same day, the gramophone and records arrived and were duly uncrated and carried through to the Music Room, where the curiously anachronistic machine, with its huge shining horn, seemed ill-suited to the harpsichord, grand piano and the marble busts of Beethoven, Mozart and Chopin. Nevertheless, as it transpired, the machine and its great horn were there to stay. Later they would be replaced by a still more modern instrument as the Tango and *Valse* were supplanted by curious gyrations to music called the Shimmy, the Two-step and even later, the Charleston.

The Dowager despatched her notes naming the twenty-eighth of November as the date for the first 'small evening of dancing to a gramophone' and more colloquially described by the young of the county as their 'hops'.

Gyles in the meantime declared his chosen date for the first male dinner party. It was to be given on December the second. When giving his orders Gyles included in them instructions to Sawby to serve dinner in the Breakfast Room as usual to the ladies.

In due course both these entertainments received the blessing of Dr Jamieson and the Lady Superintendent—as Constance was styled by the authorities who ordered the overall pattern of their Convalescent Home.

Sitting *à trois* in the Dowager's room sipping at their coffees and tisane after dinner, Constance, the Dowager and the little Countess conferred somewhat hilariously.

'If,' Constance opened the discussion, 'we are to receive the dubious privilege of an official inspection by our Commander-in-Chief on the very day Lord Aynthorp has chosen for his dinner, then I do feel it would be just a trifle foolhardy for us to let our young men sit down to a meal which could guarantee us some fairly stringent questioning as to whether we have not taken leave of our senses.'

The Dowager placidly poured and passed her a cup of coffee, her eyes bright with amusement.

'I do not quite see...' she began, then amended, 'but no matter, pray tell me the meanin' of that observation, for it sounds most provocative.'

'Possibly,' Constance admitted, 'however let me explain. It concerns chef's chosen menu.' Her eyes began to reflect the Dowager's amusement. 'As you know Lady Aynthorp referred both chef and Sawby to Lord Aynthorp, explaining that he and not she would be issuing all instructions for this experiment. Chef promptly got the bit between his teeth. I think Lord Aynthorp's previous order that only home produce could be used for the duration presented itself to him as a challenge. Then, further encouraged by the news that the silver gilt is to be used, and that he has permission to extract both grouse and pheasants from the London hospital and restaurant orders, the whole affair went to his head. He demanded cream from the Guernseys, he obtained permission to take wines for his sauces, he even excavated some of his precious hoard of black truffles and persuaded Sawbridge to supply him with fruits from the stovehouses. Then he arranged to have two calves killed and hung *so that he could extract the sweetbreads!* and so on, *ad infinitum.* In the end he compiled a menu of such excessive richness that it would have laid some of our young men low for days afterwards.'

Her audience were by now chuckling openly.

'Oh dear me!' exclaimed Marguerite. 'What a pretty pickle we should have been in!' she broke off, 'Alicia, did you tell Constance?'

'Tell me what, pray?'

The Dowager's eyes blazed with mischief. 'Well my dear,' she confessed, 'It is really very simple. You see our Commandant-in-Chief just happens to be one of my oldest cronies. In recent years we have sat together with the rest of the fishin' fleet at countless balls sharin' the latest gossip. As a matter of fact I had a letter from her this mornin',' she reached to an adjacent table and rifled through a pile of papers. 'I have it here, she says, "would it be monstrous of me to propose myself as a guest after my official tour is completed? If it would not be a great bore I would dearly love to spend the night with you so that we might indulge ourselves in another lengthy gossip. If this would not inconvenience you greatly—and please do not hesitate to tell me if this is so and I will quite understand—I would find it most agreeable." '

She laid the letter aside. 'Of course,' she added, 'I wrote back immediately. I warned her of the impending dinner, I told her that all the females would be relegated to the Breakfast Room for a "hen" dinner but I urged her to stay if she did not consider we would be altogether too dull for her in such circumstances, and,' here she paused again and began to laugh, 'ha, ha, I actually invited her, ha, ha, ha, to make a small tour of the —ha—ha—kitchens so that she might have the opportunity of seein' and approvin' the dishes chosen for our young convalescents.'

This engulfed them all. Eventually, when they had recovered, after much dabbing with wispy handkerchiefs at streaming eyes, the Dowager asked with some anxiety,

'Constance dear, what shall we do?' To which she replied calmly,

'Nothing, I think. I have already seen chef. It was a slightly *difficile* interview, however, I took him very cautiously.'

'Whatever did you say?'

I managed to persuade him that if we did not moderate the extreme richness of his menu it could well turn out to be both the first and the last of such entertainments. Once he took my point he began scribbling down alterations with astonishing celerity.'

The two 'old naughties' exchanged meaning glances. Then Marguerite said,

'Alicia, I have always suspected that there was a distinct vein of Victoria runnin' through this remarkable young woman. Now I know! Really, Constance, you never cease to amaze me.'

She proceeded to amaze them still further by observing not without a touch of *coquetterie*, 'After all ... chef is a man ...

and so very Gallic . . . it was not quite so hard, shall we say, as if I also had been male.'

After this the fiat went forth that the Breakfast Room dinner which would include the visiting Lady Superintendent would be a replica of the one served in the big dining room. Furthermore instructions were given for the feeding and accommodation of the driver of the visitor's staff car, and lastly, that the Chinese Room must be prepared for the distinguished guest herself.

The effect of his journey to the battlefields of France wrought powerfully upon Eustace Bartonbury.

The evening he received the news, relayed from Yorkshire, that Ralph was seriously wounded he swung all his not inconsiderable guns to bear upon the most eminent of his associates. Brooking no refusals, Eustace steam-rollered his way through the corridors of power. He thrust himself into the presence of the mighty; he wrested sanctions, permits and personnel from them, forcing them to sever the reams of red tape which at times threatened to entangle him, until at length, a mere few hours after he had embarked upon the project which his peers had warned him at the onset was predestined for failure, he had the grim satisfaction of greeting a trained nurse of most outstanding ability, a young driver of considerable skill and, most notable of all, a brand new ambulance which had only just rolled from the assembly lines into the outfitting department and thence to him, in what later turned out to be the fastest time on record.

At length, flanked by his exhausted personal secretary and two other weary young men, co-opted in most peremptory fashion, Eustace stood huddled into a fur-lined overcoat in the small yard of the depot to which the vehicle had just been delivered. As it came to a standstill he directed the packing away of all the additional items which he had deemed necessary to the comfort of his son. Now with every piece of special bedding, every extra pillow, thermos, hamper, hot-water-bottle and fur rug safely stowed, he waved the nurse in, nodded to the driver to climb in and installed himself beside him, clutching the large brandy flask which one of the limp young men thrust into his outstretched hand.

'Right,' he grunted, 'let us begin.'

A small leather case, commandeered from a Special Messenger

was padlocked to his left wrist. This contained all their papers, documents and clearance forms duly signed, countersigned and headed by three hurriedly obtained photographs of the travellers. Last but not least, the case held the document which authorised Lord Bartonbury to collect the person of Second Lieutenant Ralph Steyne, otherwise Lord Steyne, eldest son of the Earl and Countess of Bartonbury.

The ambulance moved slowly out of the small yard, turned left and took the Dover road in a flurry of snowflakes.

It was a silent journey. Eustace was busy with his thoughts. The driver's attention was firmly riveted upon the road, the nurse, immensely conscious of the honour being done to her and quite unruffled by the perilous nature of the expedition sat tranquilly ... knitting. The clicking of her needles impinged on Eustace. He turned and in the sudden light from a passing vehicle saw her illuminated face. She smiled at him. He turned back, moved despite himself by the steadiness of the grey eyes and the compassion in the smile she directed upon him. His protest was stillborn. So the needles clicked on ...

When they came in sight of Dover Castle, etched in charcoal against the falling snow, banded in white where the snow had settled on the battlements, the nurse spoke.

'Lord Bartonbury,'

Eustace turned.

'I only wished to say that I fear that we shall encounter delays ... officials ... documents ... I do not want these to fray your already strained nerves unduly ...'

Eustace made a great effort. He said, his own words coming out jerkily, 'How kind ... pray accept that I will ... er ... contain my ... er, impatience.' He broke off as the ambulance turned into the docks. There they were halted for the first time.

When they were free to move on, he said,

'Nurse, you must both be cold, I suggest you remove the thermos I asked you to lay on the bed. It contains hot soup for which I believe we might all be grateful. At least,' he added somewhat tartly, 'it will give us something to do during the seemingly inevitable delays.'

When at long last they pulled away and the small hospital ship with its destroyer escort began to plough through the choppy sea, a shore clock could be heard dimly by the three who stood on deck. It was striking one a.m.

They made good time until they reached the entrance to Calais harbour. Then the engines stopped, and there began a long and tedious wait until they at last received permission to come alongside. When the ambulance was set down on the quay, dawn was breaking over Calais. From then until the hospital ship with its maximum complement of wounded pulled away once more—seventeen hours later—the rumble of gunfire rolled about them unceasingly.

With the dawn the slight fog lifted, the wearisome paper checking was completed and their cheerful driver was at long last permitted to climb in. He moved off, repeating to himself his last instructions, 'Keep close to the coast road. Head towards Dunkirk. There'll be further instructions for you when you get aloft'. Taking this last to signify the northward coastal route he settled to the last outward lap. Behind him the nurse resumed her knitting.

As he drove, so a thrill of excitement stimulated him even more than the warmth of the soup which he had drunk. He was a conscientious objector. He had refused to engage in any activity in this war which involved him in the possibility of taking life; but he had professed his willingness to render such service as was possible in any life-saving activity. Naturally he had taken a very hard and sometimes bitter road. He had collected his share of white feathers, offered by unthinking women who had nothing better to do than perform this office to any young man in civilian clothes. He had endured scorn, contempt and contumely; so, to find himself in France actually driving to the assistance of a severely wounded man, and to be voluntarily exposed to some danger in so doing was exhilarating. In short he felt himself justified at last for the line he had taken, now that he was being given the opportunity to put his own life at risk without actually endangering that of any other man.

Snow had fallen heavily in the night. The traffic was heavy. Wheels and tyres had already churned up a quagmire of slush and mud. Soon the ambulance began to skid; then came the pot-holes made by stray falling shells. The slush and water which filled them already was fanned out by the vehicles and by the despatch riders on motor-cycles who weaved and bounced between, displaying scant regard for normal traffic rules. They came bucketing round corners, flinging the muck head-high. The ambulance was already encrusted with the stuff. The riders' faces were camouflaged by it beyond identification. It rose to the tarpaulin covers which were drawn close above loaded carts whose civilian leaders, old Belgian peasants, led their horses, plodding along, bent-shouldered, doggedly heading for the battlefields with food for the men in the trenches.

Forming a pathetic border on either side, now slipping to their knees, now supporting one another, the refugees trudged by with their pitiful bundles, only halting to let the streams of traffic through. Then they just stood bent, hopeless, shivering, while the mud fell upon them mercilessly. Once the ambulance was forced into the verge as a line of tooting open-topped double-decker London buses thrust their way through, lurching perilously, packed on the upper deck, down the stairway, on the steps and inside with British Tommies being hurried up to reinforce the changing line of battle. Some of them leaned out as they went by, over advertisements for Fry's Cocoa, Buchanan's Whiskey and Beecham's Pills, shouting at the refugees, '*Sales Boches, sodding 'uns, Vive les Belges...*' This brought the refugees' heads up, some even waved, while the ambulance wheels made a sucking, screeching sound, spinning helplessly for a moment, then won a purchase and somehow lumbered to the crown of the road again when all the buses had gone by.

They pressed on, lurching, bumping, slithering.... They passed what had once been a little wood. Now the blackened remains of trees lifted mute trunks to the dun skies while all about their roots lay bodies heaped like spillikins ... the bodies of the 'glorious' dead.

They slithered through somehow, reached the outskirts of what had once been a village, where now a field, charred and blackened like the tree stumps was no more than an ugly tangle of shell-torn gun carriages, half-submerged in water which filled the larger cavities made by Big Bertha's vomit. From these the noxious smell of rotting corpses rose and spread like marsh gases.

Among the eloquent carnage in the flooded yard of a ruined farmstead, some horses were tethered. Hard by them, up to their knees in water, a handful of Dragoons fished unconcernedly. They were using their lances to spear the stranded fish while, overhead, occasional shells exploded leaving small white puffs which drifted at the wind's caprices.

The driver forced the ambulance forward doggedly. The road

worsened with every bend. Added now to the danger from the
shell-holes was the menace of the frost-hardened ridges slashed
by the wheels of gun-carriages. Over these they rose and fell with
jarring springs.

Eustace sat huddled inside his coat, fighting to choke back
the waves of nausea which engulfed him. Nurse had forsaken
her knitting. She sat, clutching the struts of the stretcher bed
with one hand, and holding a handkerchief over her mouth and
nose with the other. Even the cheerful driver had ceased to smile.
All the while Eustace thought of Ralph, working himself into
a concentrate of fear at the thought of this return journey with a
badly wounded man. He tried to conjecture what this travesty of
a road would do to his son in his condition. Then he made a
desperate effort to drive thought out, *for there was no other
way.*

At the crossroads before the entrance to Dunkirk a hospital
orderly straddled the road on his motor cycle. Seeing the ambulance he dismounted hurriedly. He leant his cycle against the
side of an upturned cart and held out both arms signalling the
driver to stop.

'Lord Bartonbury's ambulance?' he queried hoarsely, thrusting his head inside and addressing the driver. 'Yeh, well then,
chum, you'll 'ave to go on north and stick on this road till you
come to a right fork. Just beyond Ostend you'll find it. Take it
and then quite soon afterwards turn right again. That'll take you
to the outskirts of Nieuwport; but for the love of Christ don't
miss them turns or you'll find yourselves in the loving arms of
the enemy; or at best be caught between both lots of fire. Do as
I say and you'll find the temp. base hospital just after that
second turning. And come up to it carefully. It's a bleeding bog.'
So saying he saluted, added 'an' good luck matey' then he
hurried back to retrieve his motor-cycle.

'Nearly there,' said nurse reassuringly.

'That's right,' echoed the cheerful driver, who was not quite
so cheerful now nor as enthusiastically absorbed in his thrilling
adventure. Over the engine's rumblings came another—that of
guns. This developed quickly into a snarling roar.

They were halted again about a mile farther on, just short of
the first turning to be negotiated; but the orderly had followed
on behind and now came roaring up to explain the mission. Thus
they were released at speed. As the driver let out his clutch so

the orderly revved, wheeled round, waved one hand and went bouncing over the pot-holes in the opposite direction.

They were alone again, and as the driver acknowledged grimly, they were 'coming into the thick of things and no mistake about it!' He gripped the wheel, clenched his teeth and began whistling softly to keep himself company. Just as they came within sight of the second turn a shell shot screaming overhead. It fell to the left of them. As the explosion spurted the inevitable mud and water fountain, so a red core of flame grew from the centre. The ambulance rocked.

Eustace grunted. He and the driver asked simultaneously.

'All right, nurse?'

'Perfectly, thank you,' came the composed voice from the back.

Whistling was out now for the driver. Instead he consoled himself as they jolted, rocked, slithered and bounced, by a monotone of blasphemous invective so startling that even Eustace turned, examined the tense profile and nodded his agreement, for now the road was lined with wounded men. Some lay in the filth. Others sat propped back to back, supporting one another. All were crudely bandaged; but only patches of white showed between mud and blood.

Nurse gave a small, stifled gasp, leaned forward about to speak; but Eustace forestalled her. 'Stop this thing,' he barked. The ambulance halted. 'Now get down and give us a hand with some of those boys.' To nurse he flung, 'How many?' and began to plough his way towards them.

'Seven, I think, of sitting ones,' she answered at his shoulder.

Eustace bent over a man with a bloodied leg bandage,

'Think you can make it to our ambulance if I help?'

'Fink I could run, gov'ner, it's bleedin' 'orrible out 'ere,' the man essayed a grin.

Eustace put one arm round his waist, levered him upwards and together they began the short return, the man hopping on his good leg.

'Wot you doin' in this pleasure resort?' he asked, 'soddin' picnic aint it?'

Behind him the driver and nurse hand-chaired a second man. In five minutes, with two more screaming shell bursts to spur them on they had their seven wounded stowed inside and

Eustace, with blood and mud on his overcoat now, climbed back into the vehicle.

He groped in his coat pocket, produced his flask, passed it back,

'Share that round,' he advised, 'nothing like it to keep out the cold ... only hope there's enough to go round,' and as he spoke so there flashed into his inward sight a picture both ludicrous and macabre in this charnel. He saw himself, in white buckskins and hunting tops, astride Stardust, saw hounds fretting impatiently, heard the Master's voice, felt again his hand go to the pocket of his pink coat, take out a flask, unstopper it, drink from it, heard as he replaced the flask the old, familiar cry 'G ... ooone awaay ... ay ... ay!' as if it were a miraculously coloured cinematograph.

He jerked back to reality as they drove through yet another village. Now with his normal vision his eyes' retinas recorded the empty shells of devastated homes, the littered shell-torn streets, strewn with fallen masonry, the silver line of water betokening what had once been trenches. These had been flooded by the Belgians in one last, desperate attempt to stem the German advance. The Belgians had opened the floodgates, the water poured through inundating the land and, as Eustace heard later, it had drowned no less than four thousand of the enemy.

Eustace suddenly noticed a half-broken signpost flung up by some recent explosion and fallen back into a ditch where it lurched at a tipsy angle, looking like a broken cross. He peered at it curiously. The name was still clear enough to decipher— *Ramscapelle*. The startled driver read the name too.

'Christ sir!' he exclaimed, 'we've taken the wrong turning! I shall have to try and get away.' He yelled back over his shoulder, 'Nurse, tell the boys to hang on I've got to try and turn. I'll be as careful as I can ...'

The sounds of battle had intensified. The rumble of guns had become a snarling thunder. To add to it all, shells came screaming over in quick succession while the ominous rat-tat-tat of machine guns barked around them. They made their turn— somehow. Then they began their lurching, heaving return towards the turning they should not have taken. When they found it, negotiated it, headed onwards to the next turn, they saw a party of Belgian stretcher-bearers running under fire, carrying their wounded towards a once luxurious open F.I.A.T. which waited against the verge. The driver pulled out to pass it. Immediately he saw another in front of it and another and another. Now they could also see that as the stretcher bearers worked their way towards those cars, so troops with fixed bayonets poured across the travesty of a field, while others with hand grenades streamed between pausing to lob their grenades at the enemy just over the hill.

'Here's the rotten turning!' gasped the driver thankfully, and so saying went into a skid. He spun his wheel into it as he had been taught to do. The ambulance slithered alarmingly but the skid continued to develop until the side of the ambulance lurched against the smouldering hedge. As the ambulance hit it so the hedge crackled and tongues of flame sprang up licking, growing until they too began to roar. Very slowly the ambulance began to right herself. 'We're winning,' the driver exulted, 'hang on chaps.' With dreadful slowness the vehicle reached the road's saddle once again . . . and thrust on. Fifty yards down the turning they skidded again; but this one was only slight. It was just enough to bring them cross-ways on. The road's verge ran down steeply and they ran down with it inevitably, as in terrifying slow-motion they slewed again and hit a quagmire which acted faster than any brake could do. They had reached the entrance to the temporary base hospital.

'We've made it, sir,' said the driver quietly. Then he leaned forward, laid his arms on the driving wheel and his head went down.

'Thanks to you,' said Eustace a trifle gruffly; but the driver did not hear him. He was asleep.

Already the nurse was helping the wounded to dismount from the tail of the ambulance. Eustace tried his door. It had jammed when they came into contact with that burning hedge.

Muttering, 'Damn you, open,' he put all his weight against it and it gave. He climbed down stiffly, passed one slightly unsteady hand over his filthy face and stared with total disbelief at the piteous sight which confronted him.

The area was almost covered with stretchers laid down in the mud and muck in the bitter cold of this November morning. As Eustace stared in horror so more orderlies carrying more stretchers came hurrying up to dump their burdens wherever space remained, only to turn at once and run back for more. Between these wounded, what seemed to him like unbelievably young nurses in flimsy cloaks moved with bandages, bent to light cigarettes, to wrap meagre blankets more closely, knelt in the filth to hold cups of water to parched lips, to comfort the dying. All the while the shells howled menacingly overhead, explosions thundered, and the persistent rat-tat-tat-tat of the machine guns formed a monotonous accompaniment.

Over the ground hung a terrible smell, which only the nurse was able to recognise for what it was—the unmistakable stench of gangrenous wounds.

The horrified Eustace did the only thing which came into his mind. He dived into his greatcoat for his cigarette case, and went in among the stretchers offering cigarettes and lighting them; kneeling himself to put them between lips which were both blue with cold and drawn with pain.

'Thanks c-chum,' mumbled one youngster whose teeth were chattering so he could scarcely hold the welcome offering, 'It's so bloody, bloody cold!'

Eustace got up and went back to the ambulance in search of more cigarettes. The Commandant, appearing on the steps saw him between the stretchers and came across.

'Lord Bartonbury?' he queried.

Eustace turned, rose, 'Yes,' he said.

'You have come for your son?'

Eustace nodded, glanced around him again, then he exploded savagely, 'Can't you get these poor bastards under cover?'

The greying official attempted to explain; as if even talking were an effort. 'No, my dear sir, unfortunately we cannot. This is only a temporary base hospital and we are flooded out. We have seriously wounded men inside on stretchers, just lining the corridors. Our surgeons have been operating for eighteen hours now without a break, while neither our nurses nor our doctors have taken off their clothes for three days. He lifted his shoulders eloquently. 'But I can tell you that help is coming.'

'When, for God's sake?'

'Perhaps you passed some London buses on your way here?'

'No they passed us, loaded with Tommies.'

'Ah, good. When they have discharged those urgently needed reinforcements they will come here and take the less dangerously wounded men to a hospital ship,' the Commandant corrected himself, 'to the hospital ship on which I imagine you crossed and the one which will return you with your son.'

Eustace stood, head bent, listening. Then, seemingly a *non sequitur*, he queried abruptly, 'Under whose aegis were the private cars I passed taking in wounded?'

'A private enterprise. Some Belgians who have mustered a volunteer ambulance force—and now—if you will follow me I will take you to your son."

Still Eustace remained, staring at the ground. Then abruptly he said, 'Thank you. I am indebted to you for your information. What one man can do *so can another*. Pray take me to Lord Steyne now.'

With these cryptic words, Eustace made to follow, then seeing the nurse standing waiting he called, 'Nurse, if you please,' and together the little trio disappeared inside leaving the ambulance driver. He sat as before hunched over the driving wheel. He was still fast asleep.

An hour later the first of the London buses slithered in and the work of improvisation began. Planks were ripped out of a tumbled shed and lashed across the seating leaving a narrow passage down the centre on both upper and lower decks through which stretcher bearers struggled, somehow managing to slide their burdens on to the planks and again, lash them as best they could. In two rows, the men were laid out. On to the platform of the bus conductor's area a miniature mobile canteen was being erected from which nurses then dispensed hot drinks and sandwiches. Just before departure the urn and trays were replaced by medical bags, then a nurse and a doctor swung themselves aboard and a ragged cheer went up as the bus lurched and heaved its way back on to the roadway. No sooner had the cheers died away than a second bus lumbered in and the whole performance began all over again.

Their nurse came out pulling a pair of woollen gloves over her hands as she struggled to the ambulance. Then she woke the driver and led him back inside for food. All the while the shells swooped overhead, the cotton wool puffs billowed out and began their drifting, the plumes of soil and flame erupted and the persistent rat-a-tat-tat of the machine guns chattered. Presently even the newcomers became accustomed to it and worked on unheeding.

Inside, in an improvised ward, Ralph was given an injection before being carried out, so mercifully he knew nothing of the struggle which ensued to force the ambulance from the clinging hold of the dreadful mud. The driver sat alone now for Eustace had wedged himself alongside his son with the nurse crouched at Ralph's head and shoulders.

Little was changed on the return journey. The traffic and shells had further ploughed the roadway, the early afternoon thaw had further increased the dangers of skidding. On one of the few straight stretches of road Eustace saw through the open partition between the back and the seat he had occupied during the outward journey, a field which still resembled one. The ambulance had pulled over for a long line of artillery and gun carriages to go by. On their side of the road two army trucks were stationary too, but clearly not because of the artillery. A little clutch of British officers stood chatting idly on the edge of the field inside the rather steep verge. Nearby lay a pile of caps, greatcoats and accoutrements. Their owners were kicking a football about and clearly enjoying the makeshift game. Eustace choked back an involuntary gust of laughter which he knew well enough had less in it of mirth than near-hysteria. He made a small, helpless gesture at the players to the nurse who obediently followed the line of his lifted arm. 'Can you credit it!' he muttered, 'playin' football! They must be stark ravin' mad!'

The nurse smiled at him, her face serene, her grey eyes brimming. 'Oh no, Lord Bartonbury,' she said softly, 'they are not mad. They are English and, of course, they are expressing to each other in their own way their absolute certainty of victory.'

The ambulance jerked into motion once more. Then they passed a procession of Paris taxis whose owner-drivers sat hunched, impassively at the wheels. Troops were packed inside each one, troops were also jammed in beside the driver and hanging on to the doors. One or two intrepid souls were even sprawled across the roofs. The springs groaned, the wheels spun but the taxis went forward, somehow, taking their complement of reinforcements to the line of battle.

As the ambulance came to the Dunkirk cross-roads Ralph opened his eyes and the nurse said quickly, 'Lord Bartonbury your son is conscious.'

Ralph's eyes, swimming through haze into a moment's focus, rested on his father's face as Eustace bent over him oblivious of his own appearance.

'Hello sir,' murmured Ralph vaguely, 'what the devil are you doing here? ... your face is filthy ... good of you to come though ...' then he sank back into unconsciousness.

They came at last to the Calais docks. Much to their shared surprise they were remembered. They found the same men on duty. They heard hoarse voices congratulating them ... asking after the patient; then they were waved straight on, and after what seemed to all three of them to be a remarkably short time they and the precious ambulance were on board again.

When Ralph had been taken below with the nurse in attendance—and they had been asked, 'Please stay away, at least for a while,'—the driver and Eustace decided to remain on deck. Always supposing they could find a square inch in which to sleep both were too keyed up to even attempt it now, so they leaned over the rail instead to watch the embarkation of the first of the London bus loads. As each one drew alongside and began to disgorge its passengers, cheers were raised by the wounded at the first glimpses of the hospital ship with the big white circles and bold red crosses painted amidships on both port and starboard sides.

The work went on. The two men debated the value of offering their services to help but decided against it because of their manifest inexperience and so remained as watchers.

Before long, night came and simultaneously what the old hands described as 'the firework display'. This lit the night sky with massive spillikins composed of searchlight beams. Once two of these crossed and pinioned an enemy aircraft in their lights. Then up streamed the brilliant sparkle of tracer bullets, soaring towards the tiny black object which seemed as harmless as a paper dart. Upwards they ran until suddenly a shaft of flame shot out across the ceiling of night sky. The tiny object seemed in moments to have become a torch which was spun by some giant invisible hand; it turned it over and over in a diminishing spiral until the little black thing exploded and came tumbling towards the sea. Another cheer went up.

Eustace asked, irrelevantly, 'Is that ambulance difficult to drive?'

'No sir,' the driver sounded positive, 'not in ordinary conditions. It's very easy to handle in fact but just a bit tricky at times on the ground we've just covered.'

Eustace nodded, managed haltingly, 'I can never begin to

thank you y'know, for no words of mine could possibly express my gratitude with anything approaching adequacy.'

'That's all right, sir,' the man shuffled his feet in embarrassment, 'I don't mind telling you I volunteered.'

He then explained, pausing as another eruption of sound rendered speech impossible. He ended with a chuckle which was compounded of both relief and slight hysteria, 'I was scared sick once or twice I don't mind telling you, sir.'

Eustace grunted. 'No more than I,' he agreed, 'I was frightened out of m'y wits.'

They became silent again. Then the driver volunteered, 'that nurse sorted me out though. What a woman! Then again, when, er, when we got among them others, the nurses and the wounded in that bloody horrible yard . . .'

'Quite,' Eustace agreed inadequately.

Suddenly the last bus emptied. On the quay side a scruffy figure shouted through a megaphone, 'That's it! Gang plank away!'

The rattle of chains was followed by another sound rising from within the hospital ship. Someone among the wounded began to play a mouth organ. Over the clink and rattle of the chains, over the ground barrage flung up by the shore batteries rose voices singing 'Good-Bye-ee, wipe the tear baby dear from your eye-ee.' To these strains the hospital ship inched her way out into the harbour. Immediately below, Eustace and his companion watched as a powerful lamp poured its light on to the red cross. On the starboard side another sprang up simultaneously, proudly declaring its mission as the ship turned her bows towards Dover.

They were on their way home at last.

Once arrived and winding their way through the maze of Dover's dockland as yet another grey dawn broke, some watching men saw the mud-caked ambulance with its dented fender and its long searing scar of flame blisters. One said to a mate,

'They've 'ad a bleedin' picnic I shouldn't wonder! A lord aint it, sporting old sod,' then spitting hugely he began to trudge towards another day's work.

Once outside, clear at last of officialdom and facing towards their objective, Eustace somewhat surprisingly ordered the driver to stop.

'Now I drive,' he said, preparing to dismount.

The man protested. Eustace told him, 'You said she was light to handle and easy to drive on normal roads. There is in my opinion a limit to any one man's endurance. Come on man, get out. You're droppin' with fatigue. Even my bad drivin' could not be as perilous to any of us, I trust, as you would be if you fell asleep at the wheel.'

Reluctantly the driver climbed down. Eustace crossed to the driving side, waited, then hauled himself up, settled at the wheel and cautiously, with infinite care he drove his son to hospital.

CHAPTER 6

Three of a Kind

What Eustace had done in order to bring Ralph from France, the irrepressible little Dowager proceeded to do in a somewhat less perilous manner, now that her grandson Ralph was back in England.

He was at the Cambridge Hospital at Aldershot while his parents stayed with friends nearby. He had stood the journey well, was operated upon at once and, so said Eustace's private secretary, he would telephone immediately he had any further news. Ralph's life hung in the balance after a grave brain operation, thus the next bulletin.

To occupy herself during this suspense period, the Dowager had recourse to her old ploy of pulling strings. She had made up her mind that Ralph would recover. She was also absolutely determined that he would convalesce at Castle Rising and nowhere else. At the same time, even she had become slightly wary of showing her hand too freely to her eldest son. His outburst of temper and his autocratic decrees were of course perfectly acceptable, no more than to be expected; but such eruptions were wholly unpredictable and the Dowager had, of late, arrived at the unwelcome conclusion that Gyles was becoming unpredictable. Fifty years with Justin had schooled her to the handling of wilful men for he had taken displays of temperament to the outside edges of excess. Even so her instinct now warned her that Gyles was 'becomin' a horse of an entirely different colour', who could not be measured by the same rod as she had applied to her Justin.

'Shootin' about at tangents,' she grumbled to Marguerite, 'jumpin' about like a Jack-in-the-box, blowin' now hot, now cold. At first it was all rein in there and what with cuttin' expenditure to the bone, makin' us all play at campin' in pokey rooms and then on an instant it's a swing round to banquets for our convalescents; takin' the few men we still have workin' for us to bring all back from storage and re-open the drawin' room, dinin' room, re-hang pictures and chandeliers . . . not that I am complainin' about that, but it's unsettlin'.'

'One minute it's reduce menus, spend nothin' on a little appealin' food for our table and then without warnin' it's talkin' high, wide and handsome about makin' a memorable Christmas for these boys who are away from their own hearth and homes. I tell you Marguerite,' she wagged her lorgnette threateningly, 'we must keep our own counsel, so don't you go lettin' any cats out of bags—at least not until that poor boy is safely tucked into one of our beds in his own home.'

Unsympathetically Marguerite pointed out that Castle Rising was not Ralph's home and was snapped at for her pains and told not to be silly—'I was merely speakin' metaphorically as you well know, and besides that,' she added wickedly, 'we do not want the slightest trail to lead back to poor old me in this affair lest it bring Gyles' wrath thunderin' down upon my old head.'

At the end of this peroration she eyed Marguerite crossly, 'What in the world you find to laugh at foxes me, my dear,' she said icily.

'Oh Alicia, how can you say such things, you know perfectly well you can manage Gyles exactly as you do everyone else—a word from him and you proceed just as you wish, you always have done and you always will.'

A gleam appeared in the fine old eyes, 'Well, mebbe,' she admitted grudgingly, 'but I really do have the feelin' it would be sound policy at this juncture to avoid rather than court trouble. Besides,' she added, 'you know how furious Gyles gets when I wheedle m'old beaux . . .'

Thereafter the wheedle process was instigated. The proceedings opened with the Dowager asking her son with disarming gentleness if he thought it would be too unreasonable at this time for Grantham to drive her to London in the Royce.

'You see, my dear, I'm gettin' on,' she told him a trifle sadly.

At this Marguerite choked over her soup and had to be patted on the back and given a glass of water by a solicitous Sawby who was far too observant and experienced to miss what was afoot. As he told Pansy when he next had a quiet word with her, 'Don't ask me what it is but I just know there's something brewing. Maybe his lordship did swallow that "soup gone down the wrong way" story; but not me! And not with her Dowager ladyship nor the Countess neither, I've seen it too often, Pansy my girl, so mark my words it'll come out in the end or my name's not Albert Sawby—which it is.'

For a moment Gyles had looked alarmed. His redoubtable mother had never before been known to cry frailty. It disturbed him. He studied her thoughtfully and decided that, today at any rate she looked exceedingly *small*. He gave his assent immediately.

'Christmas shoppin'?' he queried smiling, 'but of course Mama! If you think you could possibly face the return journey on the same day. I do not fancy any of my womenfolk sleepin' in London at the moment.'

'I think so my dear'—she was all compliance—'if that is what you wish.' As soon as she said this she wondered if she had not done it slightly too brown—so she added,

'I doubt however that I can encompass all I have to do in one day and it might cause me to ask for a further trip...' which was, for once, a perfectly truthful answer although its true content was calculated to deceive.

The pair went together accompanied by Pearson and Palliser whom they would require, they stated, 'to carry parcels'. They were seen off by Gyles who folded a fur rug round his Mama's knees, kissed hands and closed the Royce door after the warning, 'Now take care both of you and do not try to do too much.'

As they bowled between the trees,

'Well we're off,' said the fragile one with complacence, 'and now we shall see.' She proceeded to rummage inside the fur rug. At length she produced a sovereign case, extracted one gold coin and bending forward, she held it between the shoulders of the two maids.

'Take this,' she commanded, 'when we reach London *go away*. Grantham will put you down outside Messrs. Swann and Edgar. Look at the shops, have somethin' to eat in a respectable tea room, and await me at the Carlton Hotel main entrance— you know that Palliser—at five o'clock. I shall not require either of you until then.'

The astonished Palliser lifted a black cotton claw and attached it to the gold.

'Oh miladi!' she exclaimed, 'how very kind, miladi, but what about your parcels?'

'Never you mind about my parcels,' rejoined the Dowager, 'go and enjoy yourselves. Keep your eyes to yourselves, be careful crossing the streets, don't speak to strangers oh, and one other thing,' she laid emphasis here, 'say not one word of this to any other of the servants, now do you both understand that clearly?'

Still more mystified the two women chorused, 'Yes, miladi.'

'Good,' she was satisfied, so she settled to quiet conversation with Marguerite, to which both servants listened avidly. But they learned nothing. As the Dowager would have phrased it, 'little pitchers have long ears' and the two conspirators were most discreet.

London shocked and depressed them. Neither had been there since the end of the last Season. It was all so drab, so sour and so *'lourd'*. The pall of anxiety and fear was palpable.

All the way along the Strand the Royce kept pulling in to the kerb as the tinkle of ambulance bells cleared the way and the red-cross marked vehicles bustled through. At each halt they could see unfamiliar notices in all the shop windows *'ici on parle français'*, which was eloquent of the need for French to be spoken in a London which had become a haven for refugees.

Whole families of them drifted aimlessly along, eyes listless and clothes unfamiliar. Many contained in their midst some figure in hospital blue.

'Hmm,' said Marguerite, 'half these people are Belgian or French.'

'Cela se voit,' retorted her companion, 'they look totally bewildered poor souls, look at them!'

They looked. Later they passed the Carlton Hotel where, at the restaurant entrance cars were drawing up disembarking parties of allied nations. They saw that almost without exception there were wounded among them.

When the maids had been disposed of,

'The War Office if you please, Grantham, take the long way round and go up Piccadilly and then down Constitution Hill, though why,' she added 'they call it a hill has always confounded me!'

Thus they passed Arlington Street where Grantham slowed that they might see their town house once again. It too depressed them. It showed such a lonely, shuttered face, so alien to the wide windows, flower-filled window boxes and elegant striped awning which it had displayed with such panache when they stepped into the Royce for the last time at the end of the London Season.

In St James's Park, going slowly down the Mall they could see that all the seats were occupied by men in hospital blue, while the cars which flowed by them all contained wounded men being given airings in private cars. The pale sunlight also fell on others walking slowly between the bare trees with nurses in attendance.

They slid under Admiralty Arch; they entered Whitehall, they stepped out. Grantham opened and closed doors, watched her charges disappear inside the War Office and began pacing slowly up and down. A contingent of Marines marched past. A grubby terrier trotted up to the Royce and she shooed it away indignantly. Then a gleaming staff car drew to the kerb. Three senior officers stepped out. They too disappeared so the driver came up to the chauffeuse and the two began chatting. An hour passed. When the precious pair re-appeared they seemed considerably more cheerful. She then took them to their jewellers. Again they vanished, this time beneath the Asprey clock. When they re-appeared they were attended by a deferential frock-coated figure who bowed them into the car and handed several small parcels to Grantham.

Their next venue was the chocolate shop of Messrs Charbonnel and Walker where the subsequent parcels were much larger, and larger still after their foray into Buzzards.

'Chef will be delighted,' said Marguerite, settling herself and her furs contentedly. 'Fancy, a whole box of fish biscuits! Christine told me there would be none for the children's parties as Mr Palfrey had sold her his very last box and said there would be no more.'

After a spree in Mappin and Webb it required two young men to bring their parcels to the car. Grantham eyed these, unlocked the boot, saw them safely inside and heard thankfully that she was at last driving them to luncheon. She was beginning to feel hungry.

After they emerged from the Hill Street house where they took luncheon the pair set off for Messrs Washington Tremlett. It was then they drew each other's attention to the plethora of newsboys. These stood on every corner selling countless editions of the evening papers and shouting, 'Latest news from the front . . . all the casualty lists . . . evening pipers . . .'

Twilight came down eventually over the sad city. Gone were

the flashing signs, the brilliant arc light over Piccadilly, instead, mere chinks of light showed behind drawn blinds and in the gloom men and women flitted like wraiths across their line of vision. London had begun to crouch down tiredly under her pall of shadows.

The prevailing sense of desolation darkened the passengers' thoughts too. The spirit of London seemed to have gone away leaving only the shell of what had been so short a time ago all light and brilliance and gaiety.

The Royce began the journey home, weaving now through the empty City buildings which loomed over them sombrely.

They turned into Commercial Road. Dimmed naphtha flares cast some sort of light over the long queues which stood before each stall and the whole road on either hand was flanked at kerb edge by such stalls. The car passengers stared out at the long queues, formed by lines of women with here a soldier or sailor on leave carrying the heavy bags for the shabby, food-seeking housewives.

From one such stall, piled high with small furry objects, a most unpleasant odour exuded. Marguerite asked,

'Pearson, pray what are those things?'

'Trotters, milady, sheep's trotters, they are the cheapest for making stews.'

'Are they so poor?' she marvelled.

'Oh yes, milady . . . besides the shortages . . .'

'What shortages are these?' demanded the Dowager.

'Well, milady,' Pearson spoke gently, as to a child, 'when war came, milk was put on to what they called fixed price, then tea was done the same to and after tea some kinds of fish, bacon and sweets. Once any article is on fixed price it just disappears,' she paused, then added, 'excep' for the privileged few.'

The two listeners thought guiltily of those fish pond biscuits with the jelly and cream inside. They consoled themselves with the added thought that such were not on the shopping list of women like these; nor indeed their boxes of chocolates from Charbonnel et Walker.

Marguerite pressed on, 'What are they buying besides, er, trotters?'

'Well potatoes I expec', they're ever so short already, or may-be rice instead and if they wait long enough they may get an ounce or two of margarine.'

'And what is that, pray?' asked the Dowager.

She was told. She peered out from her nest of furs at the babel and seethe of poorly-clothed, unwashed humanity and murmured, 'it makes one wonder about that thirteenth chair.'

'What thirteenth chair?' Marguerite asked curiously.

'Oh it was only somethin' said to me some time ago now when Justin was alive. He brought a very old friend of his to luncheon, a man who had travelled all his life, mostly in the far east. I think he must have been somethin' of a mystic too. He said to me, "democracy is like the children's game of musical chairs. It only works for so long as there are a dozen chairs for thirteen people. Then while the music plays those thirteen struggle to sustain a position where they can slip into one of the twelve chairs immediately the music ceases...". He added, "my analogy illustrates that unless there is want, need and unemployment to make the underprivileged struggle for survival, *democracy must fail.*" He said something else too that I remember most vividly, "sometimes I wonder if in the days to come *they* will at last become aware of what democracy does for them. Should they ever do so it will be the beginning of the end for some of *us*".'

Marguerite rapped out, 'Pearson, did you hear what her ladyship said?'

'Yes, my lady.'

'Then pray comment upon it. You have a thinkin' head on your shoulders, what do *you* make of those words.'

Pearson moved uneasily. 'You really wish me to comment, miladi?'

'Yes please.'

The words came slowly. 'Well then, miladi, I would just say that to an uneducated woman like me it's the way of the world. There will always be them as have one way of life,' she was clearly picking her way like a domestic Agag, 'and them as has, er, another way of life. It is just up to those of us that has the other way of life to be grateful for what we've got which means I speak for *us*. Our way is so very smooth compared with them pore souls.' She jerked her black-hatted head towards the car windows then she shivered.

Marguerite listened. Then, 'You consider yourself well off, Pearson?'

'Of course, my lady. We has a warm place, good food, fair

employers. We have *places*. If we obey and please why then we know as our places will not be taken from us. So we are the betwixt and betweens as it were.'

'I still do not quite understand.'

'Well, you see, miladi, you spoke of people jostling, struggling to make a way, to earn a few pennies, to keep some sort of roof over their heads. *We* are not of the privileged classes nor ever can be. But neither are we them as plays the musical chairs. That's what I meant by being betwixt and between.'

Two very silent listeners to this philosophy sat beneath their fur rugs and reflected upon the revelations. After some time had elapsed and they were speeding between black hedgerows Pearson spoke again.

'Might I have permission, my lady, to add something to what I said, if you please?'

Marguerite replied, 'Pray do, Pearson, we shall be glad to listen.'

'It's very simple really,' said Pearson diffidently. 'Speaking for myself I would never wish for more. I know when I'm well off; but there's some as feels the urge from time to time to break away ... I say let them see those pore souls as we saw just now. That's what I say. Then let them be thankful for what they've got.' Pearson stopped, hesitated and added bravely, 'you know, miladi, if I may be so bold, the world is a very hard place for women what is poor and has to make their own way. A very hard place indeed.'

Marguerite de Tessedre and Alicia Aynthorp were to remember Pearson's words with somewhat painful clarity in the years ahead.

As the two old ladies stepped from the car and instructed the footwomen as to which parcels were to be conveyed to which of their respective sitting rooms, Gyles and Christine came to welcome them home. They stood in a group in the hall, the servants hovering, while Gyles gave the news of Ralph's continuing steady recovery and then they allowed themselves to be persuaded to take a glass of sherry before going upstairs.

They stood chatting while their maids took off their furs, gloves, and finally hats, and again Gyles and Christine waited while both the old 'naughties' used their long hat-pins to fluff out their hair becomingly, while Gyles looked on amusedly. Finally,

'That will be all, thank you, Palliser, Pearson,' Marguerite said dismissively. The two women bobbed and hurried off while Gyles armed his mother towards the Blue Drawing Room.

'Mark you, Gyles,' said the Dowager, strolling amicably towards their objective, 'I would appreciate bein' allowed to take a light dinner in my rooms tonight. I must own to bein' a trifle fatigued.'

Gyles looked at her curiously once again. He made no comment but gave her her choice, a very small glass of well-chilled dry white apéritif port, and gave a pale dry Amontillado in one of his Papa's copitas to his favourite aunt. Then he spoke.

'Pray tell me, Mama, somethin' about which I am passin' curious. I find you in splendid looks. You seem to have had a highly successful day. In all respects save one you appear to be your normal self. Why then do you evince this unaccountable and mysterious eagerness to obtain *my* acquiescence for anythin'? Accordin' to your usual practice I seem to recall you have always heretofore *simply pleased yourself.*'

She was sipping her port delicately. Over the glass she sparkled at him, 'Reformin' in m'y old age,' she said crisply, 'seekin' to please my dear son.'

'Oh poppycock, Mama!' he exchanged a significant glance over her head with his Christine and added, 'fudge and fiddlesticks, as you yourself would say. It's perfect nonsense. You, Mama, quite clearly, and after a lifetime of experience with your devices, are up to somethin' and merely seekin' to divert my attention from whatever it will turn out to be.'

'Pfui!' said the Dowager, inwardly slightly uneasy. She feared she was being forced into a corner so she brushed him off. Turning to Christine she smiled at her and said, 'Pay no heed to him.' She was rallying fast under the influence of her port, 'he's an ill-mannered boy. You will never believe it my love but I actually obtained from Buzzards . . .' she was off, ably assisted by Marguerite playing chorus and thus managing to create a temporary *impasse*. But Gyles went away with Diana following, absolutely convinced his Mama was plotting some new mischief.

The two cronies dined together in Marguerite's sitting room, watched over by the parrot Boney who interlarded their conversation with croaks of, '*Que tu es bête . . . zut, alors*', and '*not a word to Gyles, remember*'.

The room was, as usual, a small interior garden with glass fern-cases, bowls of bulbs and miniature Bonsai trees—an art little known to anyone who had not visited Japan; but the iris and water lilies in oils had vanished from the looking-glass over-mantel and a new large palm tree, a carefully trimmed standard of white azaleas and another of white Bougainvillaea trained by its owner into a cascade atop its thick, straight stem filled one window from floor level.

When Palliser had cleared away, received the tray of coffee and tisane from Raikes, and set it before them, Constance came in with her list of young men who were deemed well enough to attend both dance and dinner.

'Dr Jamieson has approved the inclusion of Mr Fournes,' she told them sinking gratefully into a deep armchair, 'though he does suspect that young man of malingering.'

'Malingering?' Marguerite repeated, puzzled.

'Yes. Generally speaking we are both delighted with his pro-gress; but we are puzzled over the rather curious fact that ever since, indeed including that first afternoon when Lucien played to them all in the music room, he has run a temperature each night. It seems inexplicable. We have of course checked his lungs. They are completely sound. Every night his temperature is up and in the morning back to normal once again. We have also kept a careful watch on his daily routine. After breakfast he takes a short stroll in the grounds. He then eats a light luncheon with manifest enjoyment, indeed he is even putting on a little weight. Afterwards he rests for an hour before going into the music room to paint Lucy. He never works for long enough there to justify what then happens. It really is worrying.'

During this report the Dowager lay back inspecting the very familiar ceiling as if she had never seen it previously. She now murmured to her ceiling.

'Nevertheless, my dear, I believe I am right in my conjecture that it is the paintin' sessions, or rather the result of them, which lies at the root of your problem.'

'But why?' asked Constance, frowning.

'Because, my dear—as I remember you were not present on that first musical afternoon ... no? I thought not—but I was there throughout.'

Constance replied, 'I looked in, of course, but as all seemed to be progressing according to Hoyle I busied myself elsewhere.'

'Precisely,' still the Dowager stared at the ceiling. 'Had you been there I undertake that you would share my present views. Remember it was I who presented him to Lucy.'

Constance stared.

'He was besotted my dear, even before he met the gel and Lucien seemed uncommon partial to your young man too.'

'Pray continue,' Constance asked.

'I am right am I not in claimin' that the boy had a rather shatterin' experience in France?'

'Perfectly. He is not here solely because of a wounded arm; but chiefly because the powers that be decided that his condition of acute nervous tension would best respond to treatment here, as unless it were to be put to rights he had little chance of being returned to active service.'

'Well then,' the Dowager sounded triumphant, 'surely to such a mind, experiencin' the impact of falling head over heels in love, with, I may add, an intensity such as I have not seen equalled for many a year, would be sufficient to send his temperature soaring?'

'It could be so,' Constance admitted thoughtfully. 'But, are you sure?' she still sounded doubtful.

'We are both very sure,' said Marguerite, 'I too was there, remember. What is even more relevant to us is that we are both rather pleased.'

The Dowager amended, 'We are very pleased indeed. After all with your percipience you cannot have failed to notice that Lucy and Lucien are, er, a slight problem. They always have been.'

'Ah....'

'Moreover the young man is of good family, excellent in fact. He is undeniably personable. I think becomin' silver haired overnight has actually enhanced his romantic appearance. So let me say that I am deliberately fosterin' this. Indeed I will go further and say I am nurturin' it as Meg does her plants and trees.'

This silenced Constance completely. She played for time, rose, held out her emptied cup, waited in silence while Marguerite replenished it, then returned to her chair and sipped reflectively.

'You are, I assume, thinkin' that I have let some cat out of the bag?' the Dowager pressed her.

Constance became careless. 'Oh yes,' she agreed, 'but it's been out of the bag for me for quite a while.'

'Then?' two pairs of eyes regarded her intently.

'I would infinitely prefer to leave it at that,' she said uncomfortably.

'Fustian!' exclaimed the Dowager irritably, 'then I will say it for you. You became aware through that remarkable perception of yours that there existed an unusual rapport and intimacy between that pretty pair.'

'Ye . . . es, possibly.'

'And something else as well perhaps?' the Dowager was not to be put off.

Constance glanced up at the mantelshelf clock, exclaimed, 'for pity's sake, look at the time, I am afraid I must be away to see my charges safely into their beds.'

'And doubtless take their temperatures,' Marguerite said ironically.

Constance rose and crossed to the mantelshelf. She put one slim foot on the fender and stared into the aquamarine and turquoise log flames for several minutes despite her expressed need for urgency.

Whatever she did say to these two she was resolute on one point. There was no way in which she could tell them how she had seen Lucy in a muslin frock running handheld with Lucien across the lawn below her bedroom windows. Nor how at once she had felt a stab of familiarity at so seeing them; nor that she remembered with a shock what it was that was so evocative—a painting of the young Byron hand-fasted with his half-sister! She knew very well how delicate the situation was already. She also knew that in the curious relationship which had developed between herself and this unusual family certain specific responsibilities had developed also. At length she decided upon her compromise.

'I will say this,' she conceded, turning to face them again, 'that boy Fournes paints Lucy for one hour every afternoon. Now you tell me he is deeply in love with her. That may be so. But in my experience such couples are by nature excluding of anyone else, if of course the emotion is a shared one, yet, although I make it my business to slip in on some pretext every day I have never found them alone together. Lucien is always with them, included in their chatter, I would say totally involved as well. And now I really must go, if you will excuse me.'

*   *   *

Lucien was with them even as Constance spoke.

As she had supposed, both Lucy and Lucien were unaware of the existence of any dangers in their new friendship. Had they been asked they would have explained that they had merely discovered someone with whom they found instant rapport and with whom they were very happy to spend their shared leisure. These two shy youngsters were perfectly natural and at ease with Piers. Because of this they were far more self-revealing to him than they would otherwise have been. Piers in fact had them off guard and because this was so he saw a great deal which he would have given all he possessed never to have seen at all.

The brother and sister, he was beginning to realise, merely delighted in his company in a joint reaction which, like every other with them, was shared completely.

Possibly Lucy was flattered that anyone should wish to paint her portrait; but by her very nature she was immune to any other reactions or indeed any strong emotions towards any eligible young men. This, her highly successful but totally abortive London Season had made plain already.

What both Lucy and Lucien found in Piers was really no more than Lucy had found with the Prince, to whom she prattled on about herself and her brother with an artlessness which had both charmed and entertained him, because it was so unusual in his experience. Therefore the girl took it for granted with Piers that he too was just enjoying himself. She genuinely believed that he was no more than pleasurably entertained by the pair of them, and for her part she enjoyed and appreciated his good looks and his poetic and artistic attributes.

In fact Piers Fournes was in torment. First he had seen Lucy and promptly lost his head over her. He had then met her and in that ridiculously brief space of time had found himself deeply in love. Then he had met the brother. In that first encounter with Lucien, such a frightening attraction to him also sprang to life that later, while lying awake re-living every moment of the two encounters, he found himself agonisingly entangled both in his thoughts and his emotions.

Lucy he saw as all sweetness and charm. To him she was the epitome of complete and lovely innocence and a distillation of all he had imagined the perfect girl to be. She was for him the end of all desire; but even as she filled the corridors of his mind and spirit so Lucien's flushed face, Lucien's curls, Lucien's absurdly long-lashed eyes intruded. Once more he experienced the tingle like a small electric shock which had so startled him when he took Lucien's outstretched hand and thus made contact with the boy for the first time. Since that afternoon the trio had spent some time together every day.

The light in the music room proved excellent, so Piers set up his easel there with the Dowager's smiling consent. Lucien had said to Piers persuasively,

'If you could paint in here it would be perfect. Then if I would not bother you I could play while you painted, very softly if you so wished. I have to practise every day so it would give me the perfect excuse for being there too.' He added, 'You see Lucy and I always spend as much time together as we can manage.'

That was the second time the knife had turned. Piers had agreed, naturally, so that thereafter Lucien played softly, breaking off every now and then to listen to Lucy's happy chatter and make small interjections of his own, rather as if, Piers thought desperately, the brother could not bear to be excluded for more than a moment or two.

Piers fears grew. He began to see that in reality the two were one. Fear gripped him as the conviction grew that despite their obvious eagerness for his companionship, their bubbling interest in his thoughts, ideas and aspirations, they neither of them really had any room at all inside the pattern of their lives for him or for anyone else.

Piers knew that soon he would be sent to complete his recovery in his parents' house. Constance had already been at some pains to assure him that rest and fresh air were the only prerequisites now to his complete recovery and these, as she also stressed, were to be found in even greater abundance at his own home than at Castle Rising. Piers, who was devoted to his elderly parents, also knew that the old couple were counting the days until his return; after all he was their only child.

He forced himself to examine what lay ahead. It was at this point of desperation that he made out he was dissatisfied with his portrait of Lucy. He told them both that what he lacked were charcoal sketches of her face from every angle so that he could study these before resuming each painting session. He pointed out that as these were only charcoal sketches he could do them after dark and asked them to find a way for Lucy to give him a little extra time. All this was done simply because he needed as many sketches of Lucy as he could obtain to take with him when he was sent away.

Later he determined to find out more about them both. After considerable reflection he decided that the Dowager, or the Little Countess would be his most likely sources. Both he knew, if only at the onset, would be present at the 'hops' and likewise would be present in the re-opened White Drawing Room both before and after Lord Aynthorp's dinner party. He also resolved to ensure at the first 'hop' that he worked himself into the Dowager's good graces, little suspecting that he was there already and the object of her very special attention—for her own ends.

All the young officers wore mufti, supplied by their families, but none had thought to bring dinner jackets, the decreed rig for the 'hops'. So once the affair was set in motion the footwomen were kept busy despatching telegrams the gist of which was always 'please send informal dress clothes immediately'.

At nine o'clock on November the twenty-eighth, after dining early, twelve of the home's complement strolled towards the music room which had been stripped of all furnishings except for the pianoforte, some small gilt chairs and the newly installed gramophone with its huge and shiny horn. The little Countess had arranged the flowers. She now appeared with Lady Constance, both in elegant *tenue*, wheeling between them an invalid chair for a spectator-participant as they called the young men who were not able to dance. Behind them came Stephanie with another wheeled chair, and the remainder of the V.A.D.s pushed the rest. These they all placed in vantage positions on either side of the wide chimney piece and in little groups in the corners where the girls immediately supplied them with drinks from the buffet table to which Wilkes was putting her finishing touches.

Then in swept the Dowager like a Flagship surrounded by her fleet—of young girls. Introductions were then effected. Lucy slipped in unobtrusively to tend the gramophone. There was the usual, slight hesitancy normal between unfamiliar young and then at a nod from her brother, Lucy put the first tango record on the gramophone.

The Dowager, watching without seeming so to do, an art at which she had immense expertise, saw young Fournes head straight for Lucy and saw her lift a relaxed and smiling face.

She felt herself well-content. Piers was saying, 'I have so much looked forward to asking you if you will dance this first dance with me and now I am doubtful as to whether you will be comfortable with this stupid arm of mine?'

'Why not?' said Lucy, 'look, if I hold your shoulder, like this, and you take my other hand in your strong one I feel sure we shall do famously together, but,' as he obeyed her instructions, 'please, you must promise to tell me at once if you feel the slightest pain from my hand on your shoulder.'

He smiled down at her and, 'searchlights' thought Lucy, who had been studying the war pictures in the *Illustrated London News*, 'that's what his eyes are, blue searchlights'.

Piers shook his head wondering as he did so what she would say if he told her that it could only be the most exquisite pain if she did and infinitely more pleasurable than any pleasure he could experience with any other girl.

Lucien also watched for a while as they began dipping and swaying, after which he crossed to one of the invalid chairs, pulled up a small gilt one and said, 'Please may I come and sit with you?' his interest in the proceedings suspended until Lucy returned.

'Nice gels,' whispered Marguerite to Christine watching herself as one by one they joined the young men in the wheeled chairs and sat beside them in their pretty dresses, chatting and laughing as if the very last thing they wished to do was dance.

'Properly brought up,' Christine whispered back, fanning herself, 'that young Huntingdon seems to be very taken with old Tommy's girl don't you think?'

Without any change of expression Marguerite studied the twirling couple, 'Pretty child,' she pronounced indulgently, 'obviously enjoying herself wouldn't you say?'

The Dowager returned to the object of her first interest. Lucy was now dancing with a young Dragoon. Once again she experienced the familiar twinge of annoyance with the girl who was dealing out to her new partner the identical smiles and the same artless chatter as she had done to Piers previously. It was all just the same as at those fashionable London balls. Lucy never for one moment evinced the slightest particular interest in any one nor indicated that she was even superficially involved.

Christine was thinking the same as she too watched and she began wondering what her mother felt about Lucy's detachment.

Gabrielle was not communicative on the subject of her children, nor to them come to that! Since Eustace had come into the title, she spent less and less time at the Castle and seemed quite content to leave Lucy and Lucien to their aunts and uncles. It was difficult to discover what Gabrielle thought about anything, Christine decided. Of late she seemed to have accepted that Lucien would remain with Mr Sissingham until the time came for him to go to a crammer who would prepare him for Cambridge.

One of the wheeled chair occupants, a curly haired youngster with a very splendid pair of moustaches, had taken gramophone duty from Lucy, who excused herself from her last partner and whispered something to Lucien on the music stool.

He nodded, and obediently began to play a waltz. This was too much, for while Sir Charles had stood decorously enough on the side lines as Constance moved about chatting to those who could not dance, the sound of the 'Blue Danube' proved irresistible. He strode across to her, said formally, 'Lady Constance, may I have the pleasure?' and without more ado put his arm around her waist and twirled her off into the throng.

'Old Tommy's gel,' had disappeared with the Huntingdon boy and was conveniently assumed to be at the buffet.

There was romance in the air. The servants felt it, and went about their duties with bright eyes. Sawby so far forgot himself —when he spied Appelby peeking round a doorway—that he went out into the branching corridor, looked down the central one to make sure no one could see them and actually twirled his wife down the length, saying a trifle breathlessly, as the music stopped, 'It makes me feel young again to see happy people, young people, enjoying themselves.' He patted her on her neat rump, adding 'go along now you must be off to your duties; but I would say confidentially that it's not all spring in that music room that's enjoying themselves, there's a distinct touch of autumn among them!' with which cryptic phrase he straightened his coat and marched back to chivvy the footwomen.

During the course of that evening two people made decisions which were to have far-reaching consequences. The Dowager found herself quite unable to resist popping her meddling fingers into yet another pie by 'havin' a quiet word with young Mr Fournes', and giving him a few gentle prods of encouragement.

For his part, Piers Fournes, strolling back afterwards with his companions, decided that whatever else happened he must write to his mother immediately. He would tell her that he had fallen in love. He would ignore those other conflicting emotions ruthlessly, crush them down if necessary and plead with his mother to write to Lady Aynthorp inviting Lucy for a Friday to Tuesday with them when he was eventually sent home.

Four days later, as Gyles was coming from his office into the great hall, there began such an uproar of tooting and hooting behind the heavy doors that he involuntarily pulled a bell and brought the footwomen hurrying, with Sawby following at more sedate pace in their wake.

'There is someone,' said Gyles irritably, 'who is creatin' an infernal din outside, pray see to it immediately.'

Spurling hurried to the doors. She folded them back. As she did so Gyles' expression changed abruptly. Outside stood the sports Napier with Henry at the wheel, still hooting madly.

As the butler appeared at the top of the wide steps Henry vaulted over the car door with his cap at a scandalous angle, flung his gloves back into the car and came leaping up two steps at a time yelling,

'Hi, Sawby, I've got leave. Where's the flamin' lord?'

Sawby's face creased as,

'Here,' said Gyles quellingly and endeavouring to look severe. All he achieved was a warm smile and, 'My dear chap what a splendid surprise!'

'Ain't it?' Henry grasped his father's hand. 'How are you, sir? you look splendid,' he threw his cap at Sawby, 'and how's married life, Sawby? where's m'y wife?'

'Very happy, sir, thank you,' Sawby beamed, 'and welcome home.' Then, briskly, 'Spurling, pray inform Mrs Henry at once now, hurry girl, hurry.'

It was like old times. Henry and Gyles went arms-linked into the library with Henry shouting back, 'M'bags are under the tonneau cover, Sawby. I left m'y gloves there too, take care of 'em there's a good chap.' Reverting to his father he answered his questions.

'What's the meanin' of this, eh? and why didn't you let us know?'

'I didn't know myself until just over two hours ago. So I

thought I'd save time. I just beat it.' He put one hand to his copper head and began rumpling it as usual. 'It was simply rippin'. The Old Boy was in top hole form this mornin'. Then just after luncheon he asked, "How's yer lovely wife, eh?" so I said "Expectin', sir," and stood waitin' respectfully. He pulled at his whiskers, scowled and then shouted, "Well then!" which didn't give me much. After a pause he added, "There's nothing to do here at present. I'm off, so you'd better take forty-eight hours too. Cut along now and kindly remember to give m'y compliments to Mrs Henry and yer parents"—and that's not all,' Henry looked around the library appreciatively, 'gosh, sir, it's rippin' to be home! Well anyway when I took in some papers for him to sign, he did so, then glowered at me and said, "When you get home give yer family a present from me. You'll only be a damn nuisance here, blunderin' about the War House on yer own. M'y pheasants need decimating. I'm spending Christmas at home so you'd better take seven days over Christmas too. Now get off you young rapscallion before I change my mind . . .'

Henry trailed off, grinned at his father and added, 'So I just cut. The Napier was runnin' like a bird. There was some tick in R.A.S.C. uniform who thought he'ud try conclusions, but I soon showed him a clean pair of heels—just past Epping it was,' he added reminiscently. 'I flashed past a bobby who gave me a peculiar look but I shouted out "got forty-eight hours leave, goin' to France" as I went by and he never blew his whistle. Shockin' swindle but it worked.'

Gyles' eyes were brimming with amusement. 'It was you that was the tick then wasn't it?'

Henry trailed off, grinned at his father and added, 'So I just so,' and started hair rumpling again.

Gyles was busy at the drinks tray, 'Care for a brandy soda?' he asked.

'Yes please, rippin'.' Henry stretched out his hand for the extended glass, raised it and proposed, 'Here's to us, sir, coupled with eternal damnation to the flamin' Hun.'

'Amen to that,' said Gyles fervently.

They sank into two deep chairs only to rise again as Petula opened the door.

'Did you want me?' she began, then she saw the rumpled head and was across the room and into his arms while Gyles bent down and hastily poked the fire.

'How long, darling?' she said breathlessly, putting up a small hand to tidy his unruly hair, 'how long have you?'

'Forty-eight hours,' he mumbled with his lips on her throat. 'You smell gorgeous! ... and then seven days at Christmas.'

'So soon?' she marvelled.

'I think it was because I've only just bin gazetted,' Henry told her. 'Pet, you're lovelier than ever if such were possible, my love.'

They pulled back sharply as a gentle cough sounded in the open doorway.

'Yes, Sawby?' said Gyles turning from the fire which had no need of his attentions anyway.

Sawby hesitated, 'I am sorry to trouble you, my lord'—he looked inordinately pleased, which rather detracted from his words, 'but, er, with Mr Henry's return, what are we to do about dinner tonight?'

'Lay another cover of course,' said Gyles briskly. 'Place Mr Henry opposite me in her ladyship's chair and send Pine to Mr Henry's rooms. Tell him to get out his Lorme Livery and to dress him first. He can attend to me afterwards.'

'Just so, my lord, will there be anything else?'

Gyles appeared to reflect. 'Yes,' he said finally. 'How many cases do we have left of the '08 *Dom Perignon*?'

'Thirty, my lord,' said Sawby without hesitation.

'Then broach that before dinner instead of the champagne I chose. It's high time we all had a glass or two of *Dom Perignon* once again.'

'What's all this, sir?' asked Henry. 'Vintage bubbly ... Lorme Livery ... I thought you'd declared this Austerity Hall for the duration? Are we revertin'?'

Petula chuckled.

'Yes,' said Gyles, looking a trifle complacent. 'Certainly for tonight and possibly at stipulated intervals thereafter, always provided m'cellar and the estates can furnish us with the where-withal. To give it to you in headlines—Pet can fill you in later —we have restored the White Drawin' Room and the Dinin' Room. Tonight you and I play host to sixteen of our young convalescents: delightful bunch they are. Had a pretty bad time too. That reminds me, I'd like you to pay particular attention to a romantical lookin' feller with silver hair. Shock y'know. Name of Piers Fournes. Y'r Grandmother knows all about him.'

Henry had drawn Petula on to the dark red conversation piece during this illuminating speech. Now his son regarded him with a mixture of mingled suspicion and amusement. However, before he could speak and as usual—according to Petula's later comment 'put his foot in it'—he felt a strong warning pressure from her fingers and contented himself with an improvised comment.

'What's it all in aid of?'

'A confidence restorin' and reassurin' exercise,' Gyles told him. 'Both your Uncle Alaric and Sir Charles will join us. Now that you have arrived so fortuitously the table can be divided by the four of us, for I have already seated the two remainin' members of the family amidships left and right.'

Henry nodded, 'Where do you dine, my love?' he enquired a trifle wistfully.

Petula sought to soothe. She told him, 'We all meet in the Drawing Room at seven-thirty. Then *we* go to the Breakfast Room. We, too, have an important guest. The Chief Commandant has been here all day, doing a tour of inspection. Now she dines *entourée des jupes*. It really means that we keep quiet while Grandmama and she revel in one of their biennial gossips. Afterwards we join you all again.'

'Well that's somethin' anyway,' Henry admitted grudgingly. 'Is this a Lady Constance ploy?'

'No,' said Gyles, 'mine. Now cut along there's a good chap. Get a bath, let Pine dress you and then you and Pet can fill in the details until the second gong rings. I'll just mix up a refresher for you. There's nothin' more restorin' than a brandy soda in the bath.'

As the pair left the room Gyles overheard his eldest son's comment. 'Very grandfather wouldn't you say? The old boy's ridin' us all high, wide and handsome aint he?'

Despite himself Gyles was forced to laugh.

Excitement below stairs was mounting too. Chef, bathed in sweat, was revelling in the opportunity to *éclabousser*, once again. Mrs Parsons with a crimson countenance was taking the last of her 'petty pangs' from the roaring stove, and stacking them on wire trays ready for the footwomen to arrange and carry above; while Spurling, who had by now demonstrated her particular flair for arranging fruits, was piling the primrose and gold tazzas and interspersing the nectarines and figs with tiny stephanotis flowers and dark green camellia leaves.

'Nice,' grunted Mrs Parsons, straightening her aching back and surveying the footwoman's handiwork. 'Does us all good this does, don't it, Monsewer André?'

He had gone to his charge cave, however, so did not hear, but presently he returned bearing a *socle* carved from a block of ice to resemble a gondola.

'*Ou sont mes gelées?*' he shrieked. '*Mademoiselle Panssee!*'

'Coming,' called Pansy, tottering from the immense *garde-manger* carrying a tray of what appeared to be pewter balls.

'Bon,' chef smiled, '*maintenant je vous montre,*' so saying he picked up a ball which was hinged at one side. Plunging it for a moment into a bowl of steaming water, he eased back the flange very gently, then, holding it above the gondola he slid a complete ball of pale green wine jelly on to the dish within the ice container. Pansy copied him. The staff crowded round silently. Gradually jelly ball upon jelly ball was laid on to form a glistening pyramid of pink, green, yellow, pale mauve and blue, until the last one was placed upon the summit and poor Pansy began her slow and perilous return towards the charge cave.

'Now remember,' André turned severely upon the second footwoman, 'you come down, you tell me that you are ready, I carry my *socle* to the door of the Dining Room and there give it to Mr Sawby. He will present it to his lordship and then take it back to the sideboard for service.'

Mrs Parsons sat down heavily in 'her' chair. 'I've seen summink in this kitchen in the past but that beat's all, you're a genius Monsieur André that's wot you are.'

'*Bien sûr,*' chef agreed absently, plucking the tail feathers from a dish of pheasants, and re-arranging them more to his liking.

And so it went, with everyone in a mood of the utmost felicity. One by one Sawby beckoned them from the head of the stairs. Then each in turn was allowed to go into the restored Dining Room and stand in wonder before the completed table.

The silver gilt was out. The great table was draped with primrose and white made by the Beauvais nuns. The room was fragrant with the scent of freesias from the gilt scones on the walls and from the gilt and crystal *épergne* which comprised the centrepiece. Sawby had shown the three footwomen how to fold the pale yellow organdie table napkins with the Lorme crest upon each one, into simulated cock pheasants. Each one rose from a gold embossed venetian water glass, a pleated tail proudly stretched down over each rim.

All in all it was the mixture as before and it acted powerfully upon the participants. It caused Henry, when dressed, and with his Petula he went to see the familiar table, to murmur scandalously, 'The old boy might just as well have put finger to nose at the abominable Hun. It's a gesture of defiance!'

'Defiance or challenge,' Petula mused. 'It's very like what Grumpy might have done is it not? A do-your-damndest-we-shall-still-survive gesture. I just keep wondering what Grumpy would have said to your comment.'

'Flayed me,' Henry smiled reminiscently, lapsing into nostalgic mimicry, 'Damme, boy, no Lorme could conceivably make such a confounded vulgar gesture. Sometimes I find you downright disgustin'.'

Petula smiled with immense tenderness. 'Darling Grumpy,' she said softly, 'Oh, Henry, I am so glad he never lived to see this terrible war . . .'

The atmosphere in the Drawing Room was electric too. The Dowager made a splendid entry causing Charles Danement to murmur as he kissed her hand, 'And Solomon in all his glory was not arrayed . . .'

'Pish!' she chided him, nevertheless well pleased. 'Christine looks well does she not?' Sir Charles agreed but his eyes moved on, for Constance had come into the room. He made his way towards her. She smiled at him.

'I think,' he said quietly, 'that even if you frown upon me for it, I must tell you that you are undoubtedly the loveliest woman I have ever seen.'

Surprisingly it silenced her. She bent her head, as if making a decision and then met his eyes for a moment, coloured and almost whispered, 'I . . . am . . . glad.' Then she moved away and became engulfed with her young men.

One said crossly, 'I smell!' he stood looking gloomily around him.

'I beg your pardon?' Constance looked startled.

'I smell of moth balls,' he told her. 'My mother had clearly decided I would not need these again until this war was over.

They did not arrive until this afternoon, I've been hanging out of the window flapping them. But it's no good!'

Petula was going the rounds, introducing her husband. Her serenity was somewhat marred when one apparent stripling said, 'How d'ye do—sir,' and she stared in amazement.

Henry spoke a few easy words then pulled her away and whispered, 'It's all right, he thinks I'm of senior rank—the silly gudgeon!'

'I thought you had begun to look old to that boy,' she sighed, infinitely relieved.

'I say, sir,' said another to Gyles, looking up from a reverent contemplation of the winking bubbles in his glass, 'this is the most top-hole bubbly I have ever drunk. You are doing us all famously.'

Gyles elected to be forthcoming. 'M'father's choice,' he explained. 'He rated Dom Perignon highest of all champagnes. D'you know the story of its origin?'

'No sir, may I hear it?'

The room was filled with scent from the rustling silks and velvets, from the flowers arranged by the little Countess. Sawby and his women moved among them, and when Stephanie came in she was immediately attached by a serious faced young man who she had already learned was a Chaplain, freshly in orders. They sat down together and were soon deep in conversation, an episode which did not pass unnoticed.

'Stands the wind in that quarter do you suppose?' the Dowager murmured to Primrose, relieved for a moment of her attentions to the Commandant-in-Chief by Gyles engaging her in conversation. Primrose looked across.

'Yorkshire family. Deering, or Devening, I'm not quite sure. He's of the cloth. The youngest Chaplain to go with the B.E.F. I fancy.'

'Very nice,' she nodded approvingly, 'and, er, eminently suitable. One can only hope ...'

Then over the buzz of conversation Sawby could be heard from the doors announcing,

'My lady, dinner is served in the Breakfast Room. My lord dinner is served in the Dining Room.'

CHAPTER 7

Errors of Judgement

The next day, neither Petula nor Henry were seen until luncheon, by the family. They emerged, hand in hand, like two children, on to the West Terrace after only a few hours' sleep just as the sun was painting its first pale swathes of gold on to the grey and white sky. Predictably, they headed for the stables and Plum—whom they ran to ground while he was apostrophising a female stable boy on the heinousness of mucking out stalls inadequately. They heard his voice coming out of one where he was bullyragging the unfortunate.

'Dirt's the henemy of 'osses,' he was proclaiming as they crept up to the opened doors and leaned against the lower one, eyes brimming with amusement.

'You 'as ter be thurrer, so jest you set to now and muck that hanimal's 'ome proper. Then git the 'ose, swill down and then sweep the yard—' Then came a slight pause after which they heard what was clearly a final valediction as Plum moved away, 'An' don't spend all day abart it neither, 'cos Mr Enery is 'ome. 'ee'll want ter ride like always and if it aint Mornin' Star my name's not Plumstead wot it is!'

'Hello, Plum,' shouted Henry as the old man rolled into view.

Plum stopped short on splayed out bandy legs. 'Yer might 'ave tole me!' he exclaimed reproachfully, 'standin' there eavesdroppin'.' Then he remembered his manners but forgot the form saying, ' 'ello, Miss Petula, you're a sight fer sore eyes and no mistake, but that young feller there . . .'

Henry leaned over and pushed a gentle fist into the old man's lowest waistcoat button, 'Plum,' he teased, 'I declare you're gettin' fat!'

'Oh no I aint,' snapped the old man indignantly, 'now 'as you come fer a ride or a gossip is wot I want ter know?'

'Gossip first, ride afterwards,' said Petula.

'Ar,' he seemed mollified, 'that's better. Come along er me

then and get yerselves set down. Fer a start I don't 'old nowise with young ladies in your condition, Madam—' he made the word into a reproof, 'caperin' abart on frisky 'osses. As I was sayin' to Mrs P. over breakfuss this very mornin' "it aint right nor proper".'

'How is Mrs Plumstead?' Henry demanded. 'Shut up naggin' us, Plum, and give us the news.'

'News,' he fumbled, dragging out stools from under a work bench, 'news was it you said? well 'orrible, that's wot it is, blee . . . bloomin' 'orrible that's wot. First it's our young man Mister George wot was the happel of my eyes,' he ceased fumbling and instead began scratching about his person to find a handkerchief. Having drawn out a red bandana he 'had a good blow', which appeared to ease his feelings somewhat.

'I carnt believe it,' he resumed, 'and this is only the beginnin' for 'oo knows where it will hend?'

As usual his aspirates went scattering like hens from the wheels of an oncoming cart under the pressure of his emotions.

'Then,' he went on direfully, 'there's our young Richard wot wos our footman. Gorne too! and Mr Ralph lyin' nigh unto death's door.'

'Oh no he aint, isn't,' Petula corrected herself, finding Plum's disordered phraseology somewhat infectious. 'Mr Ralph has turned the corner and is doing very well.'

'Ar,' Plum glowered, 'that's wot *they* say, I never did trust no doctors. You say he's safely rahnd?' He peered at her.

'Really safely,' Petula assured the distressed old man. 'Cross my heart, Plum.'

The repetition of their old nursery swear made Plum's face lift a little. Still,

'No kiddin'?' he persisted.

'No kidding.' Petula went on, 'and Mr Henry has finished his training, he is a lieutenant now. You should see him in his uniform. No more white cap bands, he's the real thing at last.'

'Yers,' the old man sniffed, 'nex' thing we'll know he'll be off to them Froggies and those 'orrible battlefields.'

'Not yet, Plum,' said Henry regretfully, 'm'y General had me up yesterday mornin', said he couldn't promise me any action yet. He only muttered somethin' about a possible tour of inspection in the spring. Told me I'd have to rein in and contain myself in patience.'

'Thank Gord for small mercies,' ejaculated Plum piously, 'now wot the 'ell wos I a doin'? he frowned at them doubtfully. 'Oh yers I remember, lookin' for me Lardy Cake.' Down he went again scrabbling under the work bench. He brought up a pair of branding irons, a broken halter and a tin of liniment. Then he ejaculated triumphantly, 'got it, I knew I 'ad it somewheres.'

Placing the knobbly bundle on his bench, in yet another and happily cleaner bandana, he explained while his old fingers wrestled with the knots. 'Mother made it larst night, baked it this very mornin' just afore I lef' an' she give it ter me sayin', "Now don't go eatin' all of it, it's fer Mr Enery, 'ee wos allus partial ter a bit of Lardy 'ee was". Having revealed 'Mother's confection' Plum dredged up a penknife, wiped the blade on his sleeve and sawed off three wedges. When all had been supplied,

'Ow long 'ave you got?' he asked with his mouth full, ingesting cake like a horse with a length of hay.

Henry told him and was rewarded with a watery smile. After which Plum thrust a horny thumb into his mouth, excavated something and said, 'Them dratted currants! they'm allus gettin' wedged in an 'ole wot I've got in me molars.'

Petula rocked with amusement. 'Plum dear,' she exclaimed, 'you're as good as a tonic!'

'So's 'is news,' nodded Plum, ' 'ee'll 'ave time ter pop off a bit at them pheasants. They're pre-lif-ick this season and that's no lie! 'Is lordship and Sir Charles does wot they can but wot with the Bishop gettin' so fat he can almost rest the gun on his stummick and all you lot off to the wars we carnt keep 'em dahn and,' he added gloomily, 'wot we does bag goes ter Lunnon or them Convalescents!'

'I'll get you a brace,' said Henry, 'before I go back. I promise. Then you and Mrs Plum can have a feast.'

'Ar,' said Plum thoughtfully, chasing another wedged currant with a horny thumb, ' 'ud be nice that would. I'm allus partial to a bit of pheasant I am,' and he sucked his teeth in anticipatory pleasure.

When there was no more Lardy Cake, they wandered out of the harness room and began walking slowly down the line of stabling.

'Come and see summink,' Plum invited, 'foller me.'

He led them down to the last loose box, went in, opened an

obviously new door which had been cut into the back. Then he stepped aside to let them through.

'Eere's the flamin' menaggerie,' he announced, 'get an eyeful er that lot. That young limb Richard rites me every week,' his pride in this was massive, 'ee allus reminds me ter look after 'is hanimals proper. A right dam' nuisance they are too! That ferret of 'is give me a narsty nip only yesterday an you two know as 'ow I'm not partial ter snakes don't yer?'

They nodded.

'Pheasant mebbe, but snakes ugh . . ! Get a load of the fambly' and he waved one arm expansively over the large hollow square of hutches and kennels, runs and improvised pools.

Petula gasped out, 'Does his lordship know about this?'

'O corse ee don't. Think I'm barmy?'

Henry had begun wandering. The vixen eyed him distrustfully and gave him her brush in disdain. The deformed greylag hissed at him and the ferret shot back into the darkness of his home. The grass snake—the awful Marmaduke who had created havoc on their wedding day—lay coiled in winter sleep. A hamster was lying contentedly, being seethed over by her young.

'Where did he get 'em all from?' Henry demanded.

'Well it's like this,' Plum scratched his thinning poll, 'Esmerelda there—she's the greylag wot 'issed at yer, she broke a wing and wen that young limb er Satan found 'er it 'ad set all deformed like and she couldn't fly. So she 'ad to 'ave an 'ome! That there vixen got 'er paw in a trap she did. Master Richard nursed 'er like she was a babby. She never bit 'im even wen she was in pain. Corse it's healed now. I carnt do nothink with 'er but ee walks 'er when 'ees 'ome. Puts 'er on a lead like a bloomin' dawg! an' she trots beside 'im like she thort she wos one! Talkin' of dawgs, 'ave you seen our lot? Battersea Dogs' 'Ome wouldn't look at 'em. You should a seen 'em wen they come . . .' he ambled towards a large railed and netted enclosure. A bouncing, yapping, barking miscellany flung themselves at the wire, a terrier which was far too long in the legs; two old hounds, a sheep dog with half an ear and a pair of beagles who were only just recognisable as such.

'That little lot is salvidge too. I 'as ter feed 'em a course, and them soddin' rabbits wot breeds like white mice anyways, and it's not like it wos wen 'ee was little. I carnt get away with pinchin' them for the pot and tellin' 'im they've gorne away so we multiply like 'undreds and farsands.' Plum slumped down on an upturned bucket and hollered.

A stable lad poked her face over a loose box door, 'Yes, Mr Plum'—she sounded nervous.

'Fetch me two more buckets,' he commanded and went on with his tale. 'I 'as ter feed 'em all,' he told them direfully. 'Chef 'elps a course. Ee's wunnerful kind to our hanimals, chef is, which is re-mark-able. You'd never dream it would yer? 'Im bein' a Frenchie an' all that.'

Henry choked. 'But—er—Plum so are we, remember?'

Plum remained unruffled, 'You're only playin' at it,' he said grandly, 'you don't count,' which effectively closed that line of talk.

Then the buckets appeared and were sat upon.

'The stable lads lend an 'and too,' Plum explained, 'they better 'ad or I'd trounce 'em—and the kennel maids too, though they feel let dahn goin' ter the village with them ragamuffins,' he jerked his head towards the dogs. 'They was 'orrible when ee fahnd 'em. Torn, bleedin', 'arf starved, down ter skin and bone, but 'ee nursed 'em, 'ee's got magick in them little 'ands of 'is.'

'But there'll be the devil to pay when your father finds out,' Petula protested looking at Henry in consternation.

'Nah,' said Plum scornfully, ' 'ee'll get 'is own way will Master Richard. See ef 'ee don't 'Ee allus tells us 'ee'll spend 'is life with hanimals wen 'ee grows up. 'Ee uses a funny word. I never 'eard it afore, but it's somethin' ter do with catchin' and protectin' rare hanimals wot is gettin' shot to 'termination by them jungle 'unters.'

'*Conservation,*' suggested Petula.

'Right,' said Plum, 'you're heddicated you are, and a blessin' it must be ter you. Mark my words, madam, 'ee'll do it too ef 'ee sets 'is mind to it. Wot I do mind 'owever is them creepie crawlies of 'is. They gimme the wiggles! Beetles in matchboxes; hairywigs in little tins with 'oles in; and sentypeeds; grr ... an wot do yer think 'ee did larst summer?' Plum asked Petula with a malevolent glower.

'I ... cannot ... imagine,' Petula admitted weakly.

'Fahnd a wassipies nest. Wanted me ter git it fer 'im. Wen I put me foot dahn 'ee said as 'ee'd mannidge on 'is own. So I just tole 'im straight aht, I said, "nah you young warmint, jest you git that there wassipies nest and I'll open all these doors and let your 'ole bloomin' mennagerie go. And wots more I'll do it in the dark of night wen you're abed. So let me 'ear no more about wassipies nests". I scared 'im orf proper I did.' He ended complacently. 'Ar, that I did.'

The stable clock was chiming ten o'clock when they finally separated.

The lovely clip-clop of hooves on the cobblestones drew them from Plum's unending narrative but even so they did not escape without another ruction. It came when Morning Star and Easter Star were led out for them by two stable lads. Plum shouted, ' 'Old you 'ard, Mrs Enery,' and trotted off, reappearing with a small step ladder. This Petula eyed with incredulity.

'Plum,' she protested, guessing his intention, 'you put me in the saddle for the first time when I was three! What in the world are you doing with that?' she gestured with her crop at the offending object.

'Up this way,' he commanded, 'and slowly does it. We've got ter be careful now we're not warranted empty any more.'

Petula's mouth set mutinously. She flung a despairing glance at Henry, who was up and watching with one hand to his mouth. He just shook his head at her helplessly.

She stamped her foot, 'I will not, Plum, and that's an end to it. I simply refuse. You're behaving like an old woman.'

'Old woman is it?' Plum's eyes were blazing, 'you don't seem ter realise wot you got inside yer. Yer a flibberty gibbet that's wot you are. That's the Lorme hair!' he thumbed vaguely in the direction of her stomach.

'Oh yes I do. I'm as at home on a horse as on my two feet now kindly put me up . . .'

They went at it hammer and tongs for a few minutes and then Petula, really crossly swung herself unaided into the saddle and in an entirely different voice leaned down and wheedled, 'Please, Plum, be reasonable. I really am very careful.'

'Well see you are then,' he snapped, after which he turned and ambled back inside muttering valedictions to himself on 'wimmen in pod wot shakes their unborn babbies abaht like they was bottles er coff mixture'.

After luncheon, Petula shooed Henry off to talk to his father while she attended to her work. Promising to be as quick as possible she watched father, son and Diana turn towards Gyles' office and then hurried away.

Henry lounged around the big, wide-windowed room for a while, studying the old maps then wandered back to sit down facing his father at the long refectory table.

Gyles put on a pipe, pushed the old pewter tobacco jar across to Henry and invited him to 'take a fill'. Working gently, he began by talking of estate matter, gradually edging round to information concerning the convalescent home.

This prompted Henry to remark, 'I must admit they're as nice a bunch as I would ever wish to meet. Do you fancy, sir, that there is somethin' in the wind between young Stephanie and that clergyman wallah?'

'Young William Devening?'

'Yes, I hear he's been a Chaplain—out there.'

'He was,' Gyles agreed, 'the youngest with the B.E.F., due for a gong I believe. He was caught tendin' a dying man and was wounded, but he stayed with the chap and havin' done his Chaplain duty he decided the man might be saved, so he brought him in and then collapsed. Stephanie you say? Well frankly I had not noticed. I will ask your mother.' Then very casually he put his question, 'Did you have any time to talk to that silver haired youngster, Fournes, Piers Fournes?'

Henry nodded, answering between puffs as his pipe began to draw. 'Spent quite a bit of time with him actually. He's certainly strikin' lookin'. I got the impression he was still under some kind of strain though. He seemed to be holdin' himself on a pretty tight rein.'

'What did you make of him?' Gyles persisted.

Henry frowned. 'Well, he's very easy to talk to actually; but if you really want to know I don't think he's quite my type. Wants to be a poet as far as I could gather, paints too and I would also fancy he's a bit bookish. Isn't he an only child?'

'Yes.'

'Well that explains it I should think but,' up flew the tell-tale hand to his head and he began rumpling. After a pause he added, 'I understand he's keen on Lucy.'

'Well?'

Henry looked steadily at his father. 'Well then, I think the first thing I should want to know is this. *Is Lucy keen on him?* She never has shown any particular leanin' towards any young man as far as I can recollect. Certainly she swep' through the London Season as an outstandin' belle, had dozens of them danglin'; but she emerged seemingly heart-whole ... kind of disinterested. Is she still?'

Gyles shrugged. 'Your Grandmother seems to fancy thcy will make a match of it.'

'Does she indeed?' Henry sounded surprised. 'What's his background, sir?'

'Admirable, originally Norman like ourselves. There was a Fournes at Agincourt and also in King William's train.'

'Then,' Henry raised a questioning eyebrow, 'what's all the doubt about?'

Gyles hesitated. 'I wanted you to tell me,' he hedged, 'your instinct is pretty sound.'

Henry fidgeted uneasily. He began, 'You don't think ... oh no ... of course not.' Then he returned to his hair rumpling.

'Leave your hair alone,' said Gyles quietly, 'you might just as well own there's somethin' or you wouldn't be doin' that!'

Henry grinned ruefully, then retorted, 'You do the same, sir, only you start polishin' your monocle.'

'*Touché*,' Gyles nodded, 'even as your youngest brother stands with his legs straddled when he's in a corner.'

'I've noticed.'

Gyles made a further attempt. 'We were not discussin' our self-revealin' gestures, but Piers Fournes.'

'Yessir,' Henry sounded uncomfortable.

'Well?'

'Oh nothin', really, except, could he, do you think he might just be a trifle on the effeminate side?'

'If he is,' Gyles mused, 'I am persuaded he is unaware of it himself,' he paused, 'Or is he? Dammit!' he erupted suddenly. 'I'm out of my depth with this kind of thing.'

'Me too, sir, but it wouldn't make any sense would it? You say the feller's head over ears potty about Lucy.'

His father remained silent so Henry went on, 'I mean, a chap cannot be interested to that extent in a pretty girl and also be effeminate.'

'No,' said Gyles abruptly, 'though I'm bound to acknowledge there are precedents or if you prefer, exceptions.'

Henry sat up with a start. 'Oh for God's sake, sir, if you're thinkin' what I'm thinkin' ... I mean ... it's not relevant ... is it? It's got nothin' to do with . . .' he trailed off, hugely embarrassed.

'Mr Fournes or Mr Wilde?' the question came from a face heavy with distaste. 'As I recall that poet, playwright, some say genius, married and got a son.'

Henry stood up abruptly, 'Then kick the feller out of the Castle here and now,' he said violently. 'If for one instant you believe . . .'

'I do . . . not . . . know,' said Gyles flatly.

They were silent, both occupied with their distasteful thoughts. Suddenly Henry asked,

'What was the name of that chap, an explorer who was a friend of yours sir? the one I mean was somethin' of a mystic.'

'Arthur Winthrop Mallinson,' said Gyles immediately, 'what in the world has he to do with this?'

'I'll tell you,' Henry sat down again and leaned forward across the table. 'You and he, old Charles, young Charles and I were talkin' late one night in the library. Old Charles said he'd met him. I can't remember now how his name cropped up, but Old Charles said he'd met Wilde several times. He described him as fascinatin', and a superb conversationalist. He added that there was just somethin' about him he couldn't quite pin down but the gist of it was that he claimed Wilde made him slightly uncomfortable. I also remember Old Charles qualified this by addin' "only slightly mind you, but it was there". That was when Mr Mallinson made the remark which has stuck in my mind ever since. He just murmured, "when in doubt—yes" and then he deliberately turned the conversation.'

Gyles grunted but said nothing.

'Will you please tell me, sir, when your first flicker of unease sparked off?'

Gyles hesitated, stroked Diana, stared across the room. Then, 'Lucien,' he said finally. 'I happened to be lookin' at Fournes when he was talkin' to the boy. Lucien was chattin' away nineteen to the dozen—and you know how withdrawn he is normally —Fournes was just watchin' him with his eyes down. When he lifted them somethin' flared in those extraordinary eyes . . . Oh, it was probably nothin' and I'm just turnin' into a filthy blackguard in m'y old age!'

'You aint old,' said Henry absently, 'and you certainly aint filthy . . . but I own it does sound a bit surprisin'. Of course,' he added in a burst of candour, 'those two have always been a trifle too wrapped up in each other for my likin'.'

Gyles picked up his paper knife and began playing with it. 'We're not makin' confusion more confounded by draggin' the Byron touch into this conversation are we?' he enquired with a hard edge to his voice.

Henry stared at him, obviously brought up short by this one. Gyles could see him thinking, could practically follow his train of thought in fact, comparing, assessing and finally. . . .

'No,' he said loudly, 'absolutely no, sir.' This seemed to ease him because he then asked in quite a different tone, 'What is happenin' about Lucien anyway?'

Gyles sighed. 'I don't know that either,' he admitted. 'You see I haven't seen hide nor hair of either yer Uncle or yer Aunt since well before Ralph was wounded. I assume from what I have heard that your Uncle is devilish busy with some project. Now he's either at Aldershot or in London, while your Aunt Gabrielle stays with the Lovells so that she can be near to Ralph all the time.

'Before all this there was some talk of havin' another tutor for the boy. Uncle Eustace is absolutely set on Lucien goin' up to Cambridge. At present he just works with Sissingham, practises his pianoforte, or harpsichord, or blows away on a what d'yerma-call it, oh flute, when he isn't paintin' and bein' with Lucy which he is whenever he can contrive it. At this moment the pattern is different because I hear from yer mother that Lucien plays while Fournes paints and Lucy sits for him. Then in the evenings they are together again while Fournes makes charcoal sketches of Lucy and the boy reads poetry to them—he reads rather well I'm told.'

Henry's face registered relief. 'Then that's it,' he exclaimed, 'their bond of common interest is considerable. Paintin', music, poetry, they're three of a kind and Lucien is starved for companionship. All the other kids are away at school, he's lonely so he cottoned on to a kindred spirit. Despite the age difference I think that Fournes, bein' wounded and havin' this shell-shock trouble, finds the friendliness and simplicity of those two just his dish and just what he needs . . . at present. It'll probably turn out to be nothin' more than a storm in a teacup. Fournes will go away soon. Then one of two things will happen, either our pair will forget all about him or else we're wide of the mark all round, in which case we shall be havin' another weddin' in the family. Honestly, sir, I think we're tendin' to get the whole affair out of proper focus.'

Against his better judgement, Gyles let himself be persuaded. The more they talked, the stronger Henry made his case until at length his father rose with a sigh, tapped out his pipe and agreed that perhaps he had let his imagination run away with him. Henry then undertook to hold a watching brief, having been told that it was most unlikely that Piers Fournes would be gone until after Christmas.

Finally Gyles, by now feeling a trifle uncomfortable at having said what he had, asked, 'Feel like a stroll with a gun? We might put up a bird or two if we went through Monk's Wood and came out by Plush village? 'Tanyrate it would spark up an appetite for dinner.'

When they turned into the gun room Diana went berserk. She capered and leaped and then began running round in tight circles of excitement. She fully understood. She also knew that she would be allowed to accompany her Olympians, for she had long ago shown that she possessed a mouth like a retriever for a fallen bird.

Piers Fournes, standing at the French windows of the Music Room, while Lucy changed behind a screen and Lucien played Brahms, saw them cross by the topiary and then disappear across the rose gardens, guns under their arms, the great dog stalking majestically at their heels.

Quite suddenly he knew what he must do.

The next morning he approached Lady Constance and with some diffidence, explaining that he was an experienced shot, asked if it was out of the way for him to offer himself to help decimate the pheasants, which he added, he had heard Lord Aynthorp complaining, were far too prolific.

Thus it was that three days later Piers found himself with his host in the gun room, while both above and below stairs, the household was working itself into the first fine frenzy of Christmas preparations and Mrs Parsons was standing with sleeves rolled back stirring silver horseshoes, lovers-knots, thimbles, hearts and newly minted sixpences into the traditional Christmas pudding mixture.

Before Henry went he promised to 'cut along to the Music Room and have a look at that precious trio'. He did so and told his father that Fournes appeared to have no eyes or ears for anyone but Lucy. He added that he had stayed awhile, 'chattin' idly', and had discovered that Fournes hunted regularly, liked nothing better than a day's fishing in the Wye Valley where his home was, and not only owned a fine string of polo ponies but also played at both Hurlingham and Ranelagh.

His report made, Henry appended to it his own comment.

'What I argue is, sir, that there cannot be much wrong with a chap who spends his leisure properly!'

Later, when Piers, hell-bent on making himself *persona grata* with Lucy's relatives, brought down a couple of left and rights which drew a grunt of admiration from his host, Gyles experienced another twinge of discomfort at the things he had said to his son and from then went out of his way to be charming to the young man.

Later still, a pleasantly worded letter arrived to Christine from Mrs Fournes. She gave it to Gyles to read and he said unhesitatingly,

'Send her. It would do the girl good to get away for a while—always provided that Constance could spare her—the actual time must of course depend upon when Jamieson decides to send him home.'

Christine then took the letter to the Dowager who promptly showed it to Constance, enquiring when she had read it,

'Have you decided yet my dear when you will send Mr Fournes home to complete his convalescence?'

Constance looked down at the letter and thus concealed the twinkle in her eyes.

'When do you think would be the right time?' she countered.

'After Christmas.' The Dowager did not hesitate to use her advantage. 'Do you not think that would be best my dear?' she added, 'for of course the decision must rest with you and Doctor Jamieson.'

Constance nodded. 'Then shall we say after Christmas and before the New Year?' she was just able to maintain her composure.

'As you say, my dear. I shall now inform Christine of course, who must write back immediately and tell Mrs Fournes, proposing Lucy for the Friday to Tuesday immediately following New Year's Eve. Lucy of course can be dealt with later.'

'You anticipate no resistance to all this from her?'

'Certainly not,' said the Dowager firmly, 'Lucy is a well brought up and obedient little gel.'

'I see,' said Constance seeing a great deal of which she said nothing.

'As to the outcome,' the Dowager concluded, 'we can only hope and wait.'

Taking her lead from Gyles, Constance merely added, 'Quite so,' then hastily took her departure so that she might laugh, albeit a trifle wryly, at the Dowager's shameless tactics.

When Lucy was told she murmured, after one quick, upward glance of surprise 'As you wish, Aunt Christine.' Then she folded her hands and waited.

'I am sure you will enjoy yourself very much,' said Christine briskly, 'and it will give you a nice rest and change from all of us.'

'I need no change,' said Lucy quickly.

'Of course you do, my dear. We all need a change from time to time. One of my greatest worries over this awful war is the dullness of everything for you young ones. A change of scene may well bring back the roses to your cheeks, you have been looking quite pale for the past few weeks you know.'

'I am quite all right, thank you,' said Lucy.

'Now run along,' said Christine dismissively, 'and please send Pearson to me for we shall need to go through your wardrobe and perhaps make a trip to London to buy you some pretty dresses.'

Lucy rose obediently, but she said in the same flat voice, 'I have plenty of pretty dresses thank you Aunt Christine. Now if you will please excuse me I have some important papers to complete for Lady Constance.' That was all. Christine sat when the girl had gone feeling that she had just climbed a very steep gradient which had been thickly coated in black treacle. Lucy did this to her, fond as she was of the girl. She felt that behind her pretty manners and her seeming docility there was a steely determination about something which baulked her every time ... it would have helped, she thought wearily, if she knew what the determination was about.

Meanwhile Lucy ran quickly down the corridors on her way back to her books.

That afternoon, heading for the Music Room she ran into Lucien carrying a pile of music. She fell into step beside him,

said, 'Hello, love, I have been looking for you, I've got to go on
a visit.'

'Oh no!' Lucien lifted a crestfallen face, 'wherever are they
sending you?'

'To Mr and Mrs Fournes, when Piers goes back after
Christmas.'

'Oh,' his face changed, 'did they ask me too?'

'Nnno, I don't think so,' she faltered.

'Well he's my friend just as much as yours,' Lucien sounded
very cross. 'Are you sure?'

'I think so, yes, I am sure Aunt Christine would have said if
you had been invited.'

'How beastly it is to be a boy still!' Lucien exclaimed. 'They
wouldn't do this to me if I wasn't in the schoolroom. I bet you
if I had been eighteen they would have asked me.'

Lucy put out a consoling hand. 'Love, when you are eighteen,'
she said consolingly, 'we will always go everywhere together, we
shall make that quite clear to all our friends . . . like . . . like,' her
dimples emerged and she looked at him naughtily, 'like King
Edward did with his lady friends.'

'Oh did he?' Lucien was intrigued. 'Tell, Lucy-Lou, how did
he make that happen?'

'Well,' Lucy said slowly, 'he was the King. So I suppose he
just made one of his, er, gentlemen in attendance tell each hostess
whom he wanted, Mrs Lily Langtry . . . Mrs Keppel . . . whoever it was at the time.'

Lucien nodded approvingly. 'Then we shall too. We may not
be Royalty but we shall be famous so they will have to do what
we say; but oh what a dreadfully long time there is to wait before
we can make it happen!'

Lucy came back to the present with a start.

'Come along, love,' she urged, 'Piers will be waiting for us
and you know how fidgety he gets if he is kept waiting. I'll meet
you in the ironing room afterwards. There's never anyone there
at tea-time. You can make the excuse that Sissy kept you, and I'll
say I had to finish Lady Constance's books. They're done
already,' she added.

Piers Fournes was in a ferment. No one had said a word about
his mother's invitation and he knew it had arrived because he had
received a letter from her telling him so. She also wrote that she
and his father were counting the days now until they had him

with them again. There were also several pages of news concerning his possessions, the dogs, horses, ponies and above all of Mia, his adored King Charles Spaniel which she had given him last Christmas. Only to Lucy did he explain the little animal's name.

'It means mine you see and she *is* mine. I wanted to be sure everyone knew this from the start. Oh she is such a darling, Lucy. She goes everywhere with me, sleeps on my bed, has her own little pillow and trots around at my heels for miles and miles.'

The next time they met he pulled a picture from his pocket and watched as Lucy examined it. When she exclaimed, 'Oh what a sweet little dog. Oh Lucien look, isn't she absolutely adorable?' Piers knew what he would give Lucy for a Christmas present. Besides, as he told himself when lying thinking about it all after 'lights out' in the home, 'it will remind her of me when I am sent away . . .'

This problem of how to obtain a puppy occupied him for a day or two. Then he heard that his friend the Dowager was proposing another trip to London.

Having by this time made contact with a kennels who were willing to deliver the desired puppy to any given address in London, Piers lay in wait for the Dowager. He encountered her returning from the chapel, asked if he might stroll back with her, to which she assented graciously and then having made a few trivial conversational gambits he plunged into his tale.

He explained about Mia, he said, 'I want to get the puppy here from London and keep it secretly until Christmas morning. Would such a gift meet with your approval?'

This might have been calculated to appeal to the Dowager. She pooh-poohed any notion that the Family either individually or collectively could disapprove and straightway offered to act as puppy escort.

'Even then,' said Piers anxiously, 'despite your great kindness, I should be hard put to find a place for the little thing. I could not keep him in my quarters. Such a thing would outrage Lady Constance, and very rightly so.'

'Ah,' said the Dowager, 'but I have a solution to that too.' She was once again enjoying herself immensely. 'We will take your puppy to Plum and then you can visit it, him, her?—' she broke off, 'pray what is the sex of this animal?'

'He,' said Piers wholly delighted at the success of his idea.

'Plum will then bring him to you on Christmas mornin'. I happen to know you will all be asked to Christmas dinner and to participate in the tree ceremony. There is a small gift for every one of you too. Then you can fully enjoy the delight of givin' your basket—I will prime Gyles so that the parcel is taken early from behind the tree—and you shall see it bestowed upon Lucy in your presence. Oh it's all quite delightful and most divertin'.'

'But, er, forgive me,' Piers faltered, 'who is this Plum, can you tell me?'

'Oh how foolish of me, Plum, my dear, is our coachman. His proper name is Plumstead and he is unique. He treats some of us, nay all of us at one time or another, with a familiarity which would not be endured for an instant from anyone else. But he is special, as you will see for yourself.' Again she broke off to suggest, 'would it fatigue you unduly if we retraced our steps and then came back again in order that I can give you some idea of whom you are to meet?'

'I should like nothing more,' Piers told her truthfully turning those penetrating blue eyes upon her.

They turned about. Christine from a window above saw them walking together and smiled approvingly.

The Dowager set about explaining Plum. When she came to the grass snake story, and told how Marmaduke had escaped from Richard's blouse during the marriage of Petula and Henry,[1] Piers laughed delightedly, and when she actually told him of her Justin's[2] death and the part Plum played, he gripped the frail old arm and looked away, unable to speak for a while.

The Dowager talked on, until she came to the revelation that she knew all about Plum's secret menagerie which he had caused to be built for Richard's cast-aways as indeed she had always known about everyone's secrets both during her own reign and after her subsequent widowhood and relegation to her present Dowager status.

Piers became so animated and excited and looked so pleasing to her old eyes that she was prompted to suggest,

'Why should you not meet me at the stables tomorrow mornin'? I can then introduce our inestimable Plum to you. He is a great character and of course besotted over all the Lormes.'

'Aren't we all,' said Piers gently.

[1] See *Shadows Over Castle Rising*.
[2] See *The Lormes of Castle Rising*.

'Flatterer!' she exclaimed. 'Well then, that is settled. Nothin' easier. You take your mornin' stroll as usual. I will also take a stroll. We will meet, accidentally of course, under the stable clock at, shall we say ten thirty?'

'I will be there,' Piers promised. 'I do not know how to thank you, not only for your great kindness to me but,' he looked away, 'for honouring me with such confidences as you have just done.'

This pleased too, but all she said was, 'Well then run along or Lady Constance will be wonderin' what in the world has happened to you ... *à demain n'est-ce pas?*'

He bent over her hand, replied formally in the same tongue and then obediently left her.

The two conspirators kept their rendezvous. The Dowager excavated Plum from his harness room and introduced him.

When she had disclosed the full nature of their call Plum clapped hand to head and groaned, 'OmiGawd!'

'Just so,' said the Dowager serenely.

Plum recovered,

'I beg your pardon, my lady; but any more han ...' he broke off in consternation, poised as he was over the abyss of revelation.

She bested him of course.

'You were sayin', Plum, that another animal on top of all the ones you are takin' care of so splendidly for Master Richard would prove too much. Am I not correct?'

Plum collapsed and eyed her as if she were a witch on whose broomstick he would be required to ride at any moment now. Out came the grubby red bandana handkerchief. He mopped his forehead, while Piers watched, missing nothing, revelling in the exchange with all the appreciation of a connoisseur sipping a very fine wine.

Plum caught his eyes over the handkerchief. 'She's special, sir,' he croaked, 'allus was'—then to his persecutor, 'though 'ow you ever found out, my lady, beats me ...'

'Oh surely not? was it not you who instigated the phrase which is now in common usage?'

'Wot phrase?' Plum muttered.

'You called it as I remember "havin' a finger in every pie" did you not? well now I and Mr Fournes require just a little assistance from you over this particular pie. It is one which will give Lady Lucy much pleasure on Christmas day.'

Plum scratched his poll.

'Kin I take little dawg home alonger me?' he bargained, 'then 'ee could sleep with me and the missus and will not be lonely like, 'sides,' he reflected, 'ee'll be company for Mrs P. during the day an' only a perishin' nuisance 'ere. It's that ruddy duck, you see, sir,' he appealed to Piers.

'A greylag goose with a broken wing,' the Dowager interpreted in a soft aside.

'Wot don't you know?' asked Plum, despairingly.

'Very little,' agreed the Dowager. 'Oh by the way, how is the vixen?'

'A warmint like 'er owner,' snapped Plum.

All the while Piers stood watching the pair of them, alternately convulsed and fascinated by this extraordinary exchange. Finally. when all was settled precisely as the Dowager had intended Piers armed her back towards the terrace.

'Plum's gorgeous,' he told her, 'as you so rightly said, quite a character too. Can I ... er ... that is to say ... well, one does not tip the Plums of this world; but I would like to give him some little token of my gratitude.'

She nodded approvingly. 'One does not tip,' she agreed, 'not for a thing like this at all events. He is doin' you a favour and as such he would be hurt if you attempted to offer him payment. I, of course,' she chuckled 'was merely exertin' the charmin' art of blackmail. Now just let me think for a moment, yes I do know what you can give. Plum loves tankards. My late nephew, George Newmarket, who was killed recently, brought him tankards from the most unlikely places. Oh jam tarts!' she interjected crossly, using her favourite 'swear', 'I had forgotten, you are incarcerated!'

'I may be,' Piers acknowledged, 'but even so this can be arranged quite easily I fancy.'

He was by now flattered silly by these *intime* exchanges from the great lady whom he now supported on his good arm. He realised well enough that she was not prodigal with her favours, so, entirely on her own account, he felt himself deeply honoured.

Aloud he said, 'My Pater had the same hobby, years and years ago. When I was last at home he was forever grumbling that they were now a nuisance. He claimed they took up too much room in his study, so I can easily ask him to send me some. I shall tell him the reason and I can undertake he will be happy to subscribe. Then perhaps you would further honour me by making the final selection?'

Having obtained her assent they parted, entering the Castle through different doors. The Dowager went to the Countess in her boudoir and there remarked, 'The more I see of that young man the more I approve. He has grace, charm and a delightful manner with old women. There is somethin' of the courtier in him too. All in all I incline to the view that Lucy is most fortunate in havin' engaged his interest, I believe Marguerite that they will do famously together. We simply must pull it off, my dear.'

At long last the Dowager was showing the first chink in her armour of perspicacity. Her judgements were famous, her intuition startling, yet, in this instance she floundered. Possibly she was as dazzled, as others would be throughout his life, by Piers' appearance, manner and what she acknowledged was his great charm. Yet, even so, she above all others, knowing what she did of charm and its consequences should never have allowed herself to succumb to it at this late day.

As for Piers, he was elated. When Doctor Jamieson saw him that evening he spent some time talking with him in his room. Finally he pulled at his beard and pronounced judgement.

'Mr Fournes,' said he thoughtfully, 'you are in my opinion a fraud and I am very satisfied with your condition. A few more weeks of remedial exercises and that arm of yours will be as good as ever. As to your general state of health, this now seems excellent. Lady Constance has however expressed the wish that we keep you here until after Christmas. Then you will go home and await a summons from a medical board. Only they can ultimately decide what becomes of you. I trust you will enjoy the rest of your stay with us.' And so saying he bade his patient good night and left him.

Piers lay back on the bed. He began to think. He went on thinking. Up went his temperature again, and after a sleepless night he was requested to spend the next day in bed.

CHAPTER 8

An Unusual Talent

Once again it was the Dowager who made the first contribution to the Family's proposed invention of good news from Rosalind.

The two fragile old schemers, she and the little Countess, debated the matter in some depth before determining their plan of action. With this settled, they turned their attention to the compilation of a letter to County Limerick in Ireland.

On the first night it seemed that the waste paper basket in the Dowager's private sitting room benefited more than they. On the following night they made headway and by eleven o'clock had compiled a letter which they agreed could not fail to find favour—even with Gyles Aynthorp.

The recipient of this extremely confidential document was an Irish spinster called Eugenie O'Mara. She was in her seventies and had retired from society some years ago to live in the small castle in Limerick which she had inherited from her parents. Here she was surrounded by a devoted band of very ancient servants.

Miss O'Mara, when a young girl, had travelled to Dublin with her parents in eighteen fifty-nine to stay with the then Lord Lieutenant at Dublin Castle. The two girls met at a ball and became firm friends. Both were 'belles'. Both were equally at home on ballroom floors and on the hunting fields, indeed it was at an Irish meet that Alicia first met her future husband Justin Aynthorp.

When the visit ended Alicia returned to England to marry Justin and became mistress of Castle Rising. From then until just before Justin's death the friendship between the two girls endured. Eugenie made frequent visits to the Castle and Alicia and her Justin less frequent ones to the O'Mara castle in County Limerick. The only vital difference in the two life patterns was that Eugenie never married. She became engaged to a young Irishman whom she adored. It was a romance much approved by the circles in which they both moved. Then, disastrously, the young man's yacht went down in a terrible storm which had blown up quite suddenly in the Irish sea. The yacht was lost with all hands. Later Eugenie confided to Alicia, 'I shall remain unwed. I prefer that it shall be so, for I could never be content with second best which is all any other man could ever be.'

There was a finality in her words and an understanding between them both which brooked no questioning of this decision. Eugenie remained in society. She went everywhere, travelled widely, was inundated with invitations even in advanced years for her wit was renowned, her looks enduring and, probably most important of all at this present time, she knew everyone, was perennially primed with every scrap of scandal and gossip and because of the bond between them each could confide in the other with complete confidence.

Knowing that Eugenie was now quite unable to travel owing to a hip disability which had so increased in recent years that she was now almost totally confined to a wheeled chair, Alicia wrote her lengthy letter. To this, when all the salient points had been covered at great length the Dowager appended,

'There is no need to stress to you my dear the necessity for secrecy in this matter. Our fears for Henrietta, whom you know so well, have in a sense increased since the news of Stephen's death and posthumous decoration which so amazingly restored her sanity. Our doctor, a most brilliant and perceptive man, has requested we find some logical invention of good news concerning the silly girl.

'My private opinion is that the Knight of Bourne was confident there would be a grand reconciliation with the family and with it some revenue, of which hearsay has it he stands in great need. However, Sinclair's stroke on receiving the telegram announcing their marriage, and his subsequent condition made it incumbent upon Gyles to handle all his affairs for the time being. Gyles' letter to the Knight made it plain that he could expect nothing from any member of the family. He barred him the Castle—"never darken these doors again"—melodramatic stuff! and only left a mere chink open to Rosalind—a reassurance that she could always return home, but heavily underlining the fact that she would only be welcomed alone.

'Consequently, my dear Eugenie, we know nothing. If we

knew what was going on we could at least fabricate upon a foundation of truth.'

The Dowager then penned a further two pages of intimate chatter, and one consisting of hopes for Miss O'Mara's improved condition *et cetera, et cetera.*

Having signed it with her own pet name 'Licia' she laid down her pen and announced, 'This will do Meg, I am convinced of it. Let me show it to Gyles—for that I must do in the circumstances,' she sounded extremely regretful, 'then I can seal it up and despatch it without further delay.'

'When will you beard the lion?' Marguerite asked curiously.

'Now,' the Dowager rose and shook out her skirts. 'I find my eldest son more amenable at night than in the mornin's. I shall probably discover him in the library. He, Charles and Dr Jamieson have fallen into the way of havin' a night cap and a gossip when the Home occupants are all safely abed. Let us hope it is so on this occasion.' And so saying she gathered up the sheets and trotted resolutely towards her objective. Outside the library doors she listened for a moment, heard the sound of voices, put a hand to her hair, generally composed herself for battle then opened the door and went in.

There was no battle. The three men endorsed the letter unhesitatingly, Gyles went so far as to thank his Mama for her astuteness. This caused her to enquire tartly,

'Are you feelin' quite yourself, Gyles? I confess to feelin' a trifle faint at any encouragement from you. You have been a trifle sparing with such of late.' After which she graciously agreed to accept a small *digestif* before retiring.

In the short period between the despatch of the letter to Dublin and Miss O'Mara's elaborately crossed and re-crossed reply, the Family at last learned something of Eustace's activities.

At first he had stayed close to Ralph's bedside with resolution hardening in him. Whether or not Ralph recovered he determined to use his name and influence to take a private ambulance service to France. This he would maintain at his own expense until hostilities were at an end. Sitting beside his son he relived every detail of that nightmare journey. Presently, through thinking about it so much he purged much of the anguish from his mind leaving only the intention to do what he had seen those

Belgians do, in his case as either a requiem to or thanksgiving for his eldest son.

At the end of the first week in December he was told that Ralph's recovery was now assured. He was also warned that the young man's return to health would be a long and gradual process. The eminent specialist, who had been persuaded to make the journey to Aldershot, subsequently received Eustace in his Harley Street consulting rooms and there this prosy, ponderous, frock-coated expert explained as much as he could with a patience which Eustace suspected wryly was accorded more to his title and his influence than to his paternal distress at Ralph's perilous condition.

'I feel it my duty to inform you, Lord Bartonbury, that it is most unlikely that any medical board would pass Lord Steyne as fit for active service again.' The sonorous voice droned away, manifestly enjoying the plethora of titles. It made Eustace wonder if the same would have happened had Lord Steyne merely been Corporal Jones. However . . . the man was off again.

'Now this, I assure you, is in no way intended to imply that Lord Steyne will be in any way permanently incapacitated. Far from it, permit me to say. It is merely that, ah, er, he will indisputably remain highly susceptible to any sudden or violent noise, and, well, shall we say, noise and battlefields are somewhat indivisible?' The specialist shrugged and launched himself on a further peroration. There was a great deal more in this vein, but at length Eustace found himself hand-shaken and ushered from the presence into the fitful sunshine of a December day.

The effect wrought upon him by his journey into France had been a powerful and lasting one. The change in this once highly self-satisfied, complacent man was total. As he walked slowly towards Wigmore Street one thought was paramount, Ralph was safe! He would not be returned to that carnage. As for his own future that was already determined and had been since the ambulance had lurched past that line of private motors from which private persons had debouched to salvage wounded men. He had merely waited to learn what would happen to Ralph, and now he knew. Strolling along, immersed in thought he was even unaware that he still carried his top hat. Realising this abruptly he clapped it on, hailed a passing cabby and directed the man to the War Office.

Once again he was to force his way through the corridors of

power, this time with the assurance that his objective would be gained without much difficulty. Characteristically he had told no one anything, not even Gabrielle—he changed the thought ruefully—'least of all Gabrielle!'

On leaving the War Office he hailed another cabby and this time directed the man to an address in Bloomsbury. The vehicle ground to a halt outside a seedy building which wore a notice pasted to each of the front windows. Eustace glanced at one, told the cabby to wait then mounted the steps and pulled the bell.

Half an hour later he emerged followed by the driver who had taken the ambulance to France. Together, they entered the cab and were driven to Boodles where Eustace ordered and proceeded to enjoy an excellent luncheon. Not so the driver whose name, it now emerged was Frank Stone. His appreciation was considerably dampened by awe at his surroundings.

At length, with his cigar drawing satisfactorily, a brandy warming in the ballon inside his cupped palm, Eustace said eagerly, 'Well, now shall we begin?' so papers were produced by Stone. Later they went into a quiet room with these papers and worked on for a considerable time. Afterwards they went their separate ways, Frank Stone to catch a bus back to Bloomsbury, Eustace to stroll to Hatchards in Piccadilly.

He bought books lavishly. He handed over his card, scribbled a personal message and ordered that both be marked *For Christmas Morning* and sent to Lord Steyne.

He went on to Fortnum and Masons. Again he spent lavishly on luxuries, repeated the card writing and instructions and hurried off to Aspreys. Here he selected a pigskin case with gold fittings which was a dressing and writing case combined. He gave explicit instructions concerning the monogramming, and for the third time directed both to Ralph for Christmas. Apparently satisfied he asked and obtained permission to use the telephone. He rang his chauffeuse, told her where he was, let himself be bowed out, and stood on the pavement waiting, filling in the hiatus by scribbling figures on a small pad and adding them up. They made an impressive total.

That night he stayed at the Ritz, dined very early and alone, passed the time of day with Monsieur Ritz on his way out and re-entering his car was driven to the London Pavilion to see *Hello Everybody*.

He waited in the foyer while a crowd of young Canadians cleared from around the box office. Once settled in his box, he looked down, observing how thickly the audience was spattered with blue and khaki; then the curtain rose and he surrendered himself to a little light entertainment. In the interval an attendant brought him brandy while a cheer went up from the house as photographs of war heroes were imposed upon a make-shift cinematograph screen.

The next morning he was again driven to Frank Stone's Bloomsbury headquarters. Stone took the wheel, the chauffeuse was ordered into the back, and Stone drove the car to Castle Rising.

Meanwhile, Gyles had spent a day in London. He had lunched at his club, drowsed off afterwards and from the depths of his deep chair had woken to hear a voice saying,

'D'you know that Bartonbury's goin' potty? Accordin' to my information the feller spends his time drivin' a private ambulance over a stretch of his estate which he has had transformed into a mock battlefield. Chap must be ravin'!'

Naturally Gyles coughed loudly so heard no more; but even this fragment gave him food for thought on the return journey.

Late that night, after dismissing Pine, Gyles fastened the frogs on his dressing gown and strolled through to Christine's boudoir. Pearson was brushing her hair, but she too received her congé as Gyles appeared. When the door had closed behind her he said, 'I inadvertently eavesdropped this afternoon at m'y club.' He repeated what he had heard and asked, 'What do you make of that?'

Christine tied back her hair with a broad ribbon and reflected. 'Well,' she pronounced, 'of course I do not for one instant imagine that Eustace has taken leave of his senses; but I heard something too. I was talking to Emmy—our Chief Superintendent—on the telephone and she mentioned something. Only in the vaguest terms, though I believe Eustace has a scheme brewing. Whatever it is we shall learn soon enough.' She yawned, 'Oh I'm so sleepy, come to bed my love,' and she refused to discuss the matter further.

So with that Gyles had to be satisfied.

The following morning the Dowager's Christmas tree was erected. Sawbridge had already stood over a band of lady gardeners while they excavated the enormous hole he deemed essential. Then two more of them appeared dragging enormous barrows piled high with well soaked peat while another bespectacled female hauled a hose from the nearest water point. Finally a dray ground very slowly up the drive. As soon as it came to a standstill a small army of villagers—impressed by Sawby—and seemingly materialised by magic—swarmed about it, unfastening the ropes which held the enormous tree securely. Then with Sawbridge exhorting, cautioning, encouraging, this somewhat decrepit, septugenarian labour force, aided by the more stalwart lady gardeners, inserted the roots in their cavity and with much grunting and wheezing clung to stout ropes and thus gradually hauled the tree upright.

As Sawbridge directed the stream of hose water upon the roots so Eustace's car came speeding up. Stone halted her at the foot of the wide steps. Down came Sawby to welcome Eustace and say a place-putting 'good day to you' to Stone. As he was about to direct Stone to the servants' entrance the chauffeuse took his place at the wheel and he simply followed Eustace up the steps with Sawby behind him carrying Eustace's dressing case and looking thoroughly put out at such unorthodox behaviour.

Eustace, long familiar with the snobbery of domestic servants said, as Sawby helped him out of his greatcoat, 'this is Mr Frank Stone, Sawby, whose splendid driving and indifference to hazards brought Lord Steyne safely back to England.'

Sawby's facial barometer made a swift change from 'thundery' to 'set fair'. He bowed. 'An honour to welcome you, sir,' he said, then turning back to Eustace he asked,

'Will you be staying, my lord?'

'Just two nights. You can put Mr Stone into my dressin' room.'

'Very good, my lord. Lord Aynthorp is in the library if you should wish to see him immediately.'

'Oh yes indeed,' said Eustace, then over his shoulder as he began to move towards the library doors he added, 'Come along, Stone. You can give me a bit of moral support. Lord Aynthorp might very possibly erupt!' so saying he grasped the twin handles and went in.

Sawby, after seeing the crested cases and the one rather battered fabric one carried away by Raikes and Spurling, hastened below stairs to regale the senior staff with his titillating tit-bit.

Gyles looked up as his brother-in-law appeared. 'Talk of the devil!' he exclaimed. 'Come on in, old chap, we're parched for news. How's Ralph?'

Eustace effected introductions, accepted a whiskey and soda, sat down and said, 'I have a great deal to tell you, though I am far from certain that you will find it all to your taste.'

In which, as had been done so frequently already, Eustace demonstrated how little he really knew of his wife's brother.

When he had completed his report on Ralph, Eustace drained his glass, declined replenishment and went straight into the story of his project.

He told Gyles something of the conditions he and Stone had encountered and when he came to the return journey and the amateur stretcher bearers, Gyles rose abruptly and went over to the windows. Eustace continued steadily, until he came to the crux, 'Finally, so as not to bore you into the ground, I have my fleet. I have my authorities. We leave for France in ten days' time. It is no use anyone protesting y'know. This is something I have to do. If you had seen it, Gyles, you would understand.'

Gyles swung round.

'Have you your full complement of workers?' he asked very quietly, 'for if not I would very much like to join you.'

Eustace looked so chagrined at Gyles' words that for a moment or two he could not speak. Then,

'I owe you an apology,' he said, 'though why I should under-estimate you as I have done, God only knows.'

Gyles grinned. 'This is very much to m'y taste, dear feller, oh yes, an adventure to be envied. Come on tell me more, you have only given me the mere outlines, go right back to the beginnin' and fill me in.'

After this the three men talked until the dressing gong rumbled at them warningly. Gyles' impossible request had cut through Eustace's reserves while the effect upon Frank Stone was simply to obliterate his awe and natural nervousness and enable him to talk easily.

Finally, 'Nothin,' said Eustace a trifle despondently, 'would delight us more than to have you with us, but y'know, old chap, it simply is not on! With Christine expectin' . . . Henry away . . . this huge place to run . . . I mean, how could you?'

Gyles shook his head, 'Flamin' well out of the question,' he agreed, 'forget it. I was a fool to even mention it. Tell me instead, what is your complement?'

Frank Stone said swiftly, 'Six Triumph motor-cycles, each with a side-car stretcher and a hood—rather like a baby's pram —and waterproof coverings which clip down the whole length; plus two Minerva ambulance cars designed to take five stretchers apiece and four two-stretcher ambulances—twelve to fifteen horsepower F.I.A.T.s.'

'So,' Gyles mused, 'each convoy can pick up twenty-four wounded. What is your manpower?'

'Mostly recruited from Mr Stone's brethren,' Eustace said shortly. 'Go on, Stone, tell Lord Aynthorp.'

Gyles looked at him questioningly. He saw the man flush, then heard, the quiet words,

'I belong to a unit of conscientious objectors who do not object to saving life, only to taking it,' he said in a low voice. 'We have been allowed to offer our services for ambulance driving, but, not, er, not everyone is anxious to take us.'

'So,' injected Eustace, 'I snapped him up. Then I went to his H.Q. and met some of the others. They did me the honour of saying they would all work with me.'

Gyles' eyes were very warm now. 'How splendid,' he said. 'How many of you are there altogether?'

Frank Stone looked at Eustace who took up the tale. 'Four to ride the motor-cycles, four drivers for the two stretcher vans, two for the five stretcher vans, that makes ten doesn't it, Frank?'

'Yes sir,' said Frank. To Gyles he explained, 'Each ambulance needs two stretcher bearers so that makes another twelve whom we have recruited from the non-drivers among us.'

'All conscientious objectors?' asked Gyles visibly impressed.

'Yes, and we have a truck as well to carry the stretcher bearers.'

Gyles exclaimed, 'the press must hear of this! Have I your permission to get on to the newspapers and tell 'em what you're doin'? There's far and away too much dirty work goin' around and too much persecution of these 'conshies' as they are nicknamed.'

'If you think it would help—of course,' said Eustace.

'Are any of you armed?' Gyles then demanded.

'Of course not,' said Eustace, 'but we have our red crosses, huges ones on white circles fixed to the side car outfits and to each side, back and top of each ambulance.'

'Exactly, and that'—Gyles banged on the table top in an

astonishing display of emotion—'if you ask me, which no one does, calls for just as much bravery *if not more* than plungin' at the Hun with a fixed bayonet.'

The young man's face was illuminated. He was quite unable to speak. Gyles looked at him for a moment and then said abruptly, 'This calls for a drink.' He strode to the bell pulled it vigorously and when Sawby came he demanded, 'You know what is the best champagne in my cellar I presume?'

'Of course, my lord.'

'Then chill a bottle instantly and bring it here. I have a toast to drink with these gentlemen damme, bring four glasses. You shall drink to this too. See that below stairs is informed of every detail, his lordship here is about to embark upon a magnificent enterprise and Mr Stone and his friends go with him. Go on man, don't stand there gapin', fetch the champagne!'

Sawby hurried from the room. While he was gone Gyles excused himself, hurried down the corridor to his office, delved in a drawer, wrote out a cheque and returned to the library with it. He found Eustace and Frank Stone discussing the disposition of emergency medical supplies. As he came in he heard Eustace saying, 'There'll cost quite a bit too,' and came in right on cue.

'Here,' he said with a touch of his late father's gruffness, 'is my small contribution towards the things which cost quite a bit,' and he handed his brother-in-law a cheque for five thousand pounds.

Eustace stared at the scrap of paper, 'I say, Gyles' he remonstrated, 'isn't this over generous?'

'Over generous is it?' Gyles' temper was rising beyond the curb of his frustration. 'God's boots, Eustace, is it generous you say? Put it in yer wallet and don't let me hear another word.' He held up a long, admonitory finger, 'And if you have need of anythin' and I mean *anythin'* I shall not hold your life worth tuppence if you go anywhere else for it and fail to come to me. D'you understand?'

'Yes,' said Eustace meekly. 'B'God you're gettin' more like y'father every day!'

Gyles had the grace to grin.

'I'll tell you somethin',' he conceded more mildly, 'I said the other day thank heaven the old man didn't live to see all this; but I'm not so sure. What you chaps are doin' would be very much to his taste and I think I would be hard put to rate it any higher than that.'

'Amen,' said Eustace, then remembering his manners he turned to the bemused Frank Stone and began attempting to describe his late father-in-law.

Christine spent the morning in the parcels room. Once more, as had been done for so many years this had been thoroughly turned out in preparation for her annual parcels wrapping ritual. She was helped by Petula who, like her mother-in-law, was now forced to conceal as best she might the increasing thickness of her figure. Lucy and Rosemary and Claire slipped in from time to time between their Home duties and Anne worked steadily beside her mother. She was home early because her school had broken up before the scheduled time owing to an outbreak of measles among the younger children.

The room presented an appearance mid-way between a Christmas scene and one of the property rooms under the stage at Drury Lane Theatre. Mountains of tissue paper, reels of scarlet, emerald and white ribbons, and bowls brimming with labels and transfers overflowed down the long trestle tables, together with small mountains of presents still to be wrapped and other similar ones of presents completed. The remaining third, originally promised to be 'only a corner', had been taken over by Lucien and Piers and was descended upon in small, sporadic dives by Lucy to suggest, advise, or confer. The trio were engaged upon a ploy which had received the blessings of Constance, Christine and the Dowager. They were modelling a life-sized *crèche* and, in the process, making their persons into a considerable mess. Every time the door opened to admit someone Piers hastily thrust his wounded arm back into its sling. In between he worked with both hands.

Their basic materials were liquid cement and pieces of old flannelette from discarded mattress covers. These they dipped into the cement and then with little squelching sounds shaped and moulded the wet and heavy stuff into the Virgin's and the three Wise Men's robes drawing down the folds and leaving them to harden after which Piers and Lucien would paint them. The basic figures, heads and hands they had made previously in old newspaper papier-mâché and by dint of tremendous wheedling had won permission to bake these grotesque items in Mrs Parsons' oven. She had been heard to declare on going down like a camel to investigate the contents, and discover therein a very lifelike hand, that she 'come all over with the shudders and no mistake!'

The Family was fascinated by the way the trio worked. The ploy was undoubtedly a difficult one and their whole approach was at once impersonal and dedicated. Moreover they worked as if they had been so doing together for years. Piers, shaping and moulding would take a step back, study the line, and perhaps Lucy or possibly Lucien would say 'Too much,' or 'Widen that fold it's too pinched,' or 'Open the flow at the hem you're losing the line' and never did whoever was working contradict the critic. It seemed as if their minds ran along one simple track. There was none of the wrangling and disputing which ordinarily becomes common coinage between young people in such circumstance. It was to some degree uncanny. This gradually impinged upon the watchers, who were confused by it, for their life style wholly precluded them from comprehension. In fact, the sheltered Lucy and Lucien and the rather pampered only child Piers were being, quite naturally, of the theatre at its most esoteric. They could have been Garricks and Farjeons working in a props room at the old Globe in the agglomerate atmosphere of dust, echoes, greasepaint and invention.

Christine sought to rationalise, using those dismissive phrases with which she handled Lucy ordinarily; Petula became slightly awed, sensing the presence of the unusual and remarkable; the little Countess and the Dowager merely exchanged significant nods and glances whose meanings neither fully comprehended.

It had been the same when, on the previous morning the three had taken the limbs they had made and wired them on to the torsos. Then it was again implicit to all three that once the heads were affixed the Virgin would have wires slid and secured down her back so that, as Piers explained patiently, as to children—when asked what in the world was being done—'once the robes go on top we shall be able to fix Her halo to those wires and "from the front" (their instinctive phrase) they will not be seen. The halo will just seem to encircle the Virgin's head without any support.'

Piers painted the faces, while Lucien sculpted a thicker cement paste into the hair on the heads of Joseph, Mary and the three wise men. There were no discussions as to how each stage would be achieved, they just went about it automatically.

When Piers had finished the Virgin's face which he had previously modelled, he turned his head to ask the little Countess a question. She, having paused yet again in her parcel wrapping, was watching entranced as a face of startling purity and beauty emerged from the baked newspaper substance, 'Is she not pure and young, Madame?' he asked. She looked up at him and so caught the almost fanatic light in his eyes.

'*Bien sûr,*' she assured him, sounding rather vague, for she was marvelling inwardly,

'So remarkably like Lucy, he has shown his hand completely!' Which of course he had not.

The work continued.

That night Christine took Gyles into the emptied packing room, showed him the trio's achievements and then quite deliberately wheedled him, a thing she was not wont to do, deeming two old schemers sufficient for one family.

'Gyles love,' she began, 'do you not consider this work of an extremely high quality, setting aside the sheer ingenuity which these three have displayed?'

Gyles was staring at the Virgin, whose plaster and flannelette robe was now all blue folds and faint, fine gold embroideries banding hem and sleeves—Lucien's work.

'Lucy!' he said abruptly. 'Damme it's Lucy with a halo!'

'Is that not natural?' she said gently, 'the boy is deeply in love.'

Gyles made no further comment but stood alternately studying the figures and polishing his monocle; but Christine achieved her objective and won his consent for the old oak cradle which the Dowager had discovered in the attics[1] to be used for the manger. Gyles merely stipulated that it be brought down only at the last moment and that a guard against any possibility of danger by fire be set upon the barn until the cradle was returned to the Museum.

Thereafter the trio were seen no more, for they transferred their figures and themselves to the great barn which was already being prepared for the tenants and villagers' Christmas Supper. After this affair it had been agreed that the entire *crèche* be moved into the chapel to which everyone was invited to bring their children.

The six tree-lifting ancients were already hard at work, heav-

[1] See Book 2, *Shadows Over Castle Rising.*

ing out old farm implements, working besoms above and beneath the rafters and using them to sweep the huge floor. Then they began laying fire bricks in squares at all four corners so that braziers might be set upon them. Thus the heated bricks would disseminate further warmth drawn from the brazier fires. Lucien and Mr Sissingham—inevitably drawn in—first chalked out the *crèche* area. Then he and the boy pulled in the back and angled sides which Lucien and Piers had painted in semblance of old, grained timbers.

When this was done even the ancients stopped atop their ladders, where they were looping the beams with swags made by the children in the schoolroom. From these perilous positions they also hung kissing boughs made by Sawbridge and his wife and huge straw dollies and cornucopias plaited so miraculously by Plum's gnarled fingers in the fastness of his messy old harness room. When at length the famous cradle was laid into 'rehearsal' position and Piers had reluctantly stopped stroking it, Lucy came in with the Babe in her arms. As she knelt in the straw, lovingly wrapped the life-sized doll in its swaddling clothes and laid it in the manger/cradle the old men were so stirred that a great trumpeting sound of nose blowing arose. Lucien called one of them down saying, 'Please, Trumper, will you come down I want to hang my angel in position.'

The trio had moulded the angel's wings over wires, secured them to the spirit figure, then covered them with cement to which, before it hardened, they had laid on layers of white duck's feathers.

'I think,' Lucien said *en passant*, 'that there may still be fleas in those feathers but I hope that they will have the sense to stay where they are.'

With this pious hope he urged 'Sissy' up the vacated ladder and followed him. Together they threw over the wires, attaching them to the beam so that the angel swung out exactly as they had intended. Easing himself backwards down the ladder with more caution than grace—for he detested heights—he called to Piers who was standing below watching intently, 'How does it look, Piers, will it do?' and Piers replied softly, 'Yes, I think it will do rather well.'

They all stood back to examine their handiwork critically. Abruptly Lucy cried out, 'The lamb, we have forgotten the lamb!' and she rushed away. She came back with the plaster lamb in her arms, and for a few moments they all became absorbed in deciding exactly where it should be placed. When they were satisfied and the old men, gathering around them were exclaiming and praising and the air was thick with murmurs of 'Wunnerful' and 'I never seed the like afore', Piers, his eyes still on Lucy, who fussed with the little lamb, felt such a surge of adoration that he turned to the tutor and asked, 'Do you not think Lady Lucy and Master Lucien are two most exceptionally talented people?' To which 'Sissy' almost overcome himself stuttered out, 'I hhave al al always knknknown it MMMr PPiers. Now it ssseems tthere are tthree of yyou!' and this was said with great wistfulness and deliberate self-exclusion.

It was left to Lucien, when the old men had been persuaded to return to their labours to say rather shrilly, 'You know, Lucy-Lou, we three simply must work together one day.'

In the parcels room Petula and Christine were discussing them with the little Countess. They sought to define the essence of this work they had watched them doing *à trois* and eventually it was Petula who came the nearest to what all three were seeking to say. She with her curly head slightly on one side like a bird, and one slim finger to lip as she pondered, finally achieved. 'Those three worked in here as if they had been doing so for many, many years. It was so professional, so impersonal and yet so dedicated and each seemed to accept immediately the rightness of the others' contributions.'

Ultimately, it was Lucy, as they at last turned to leave the barn who broke the rule which she had imposed upon herself since she was tiny to tell nothing, say nothing and keep all hid. Raikes came to the entrance of the barn to tell Lucien his Mama wished to speak to him on the telephone. When he had followed the footwoman Lucy pulled at Piers' good arm and asked him to sit down on the straw with her. Puzzled, he did so and there and then Lucy told him what she and Lucien would do in four years' time and asked if he would work with them to prepare the salon in readiness for Lucien's eighteenth birthday.

The words flowed over him. The soft voice went on and on explaining, outlining, above all revealing not only everything Piers feared but also the finality of the sleeveless errand which had prompted him in all his recent actions concerning her.

What use, he thought in giving her a puppy which would be a reminder of him when he had gone? What use indeed in persuading his mother to invite Lucy for a Friday to Tuesday? What use his having striven so intensely to win the approbation of Gyles Aynthorp, his eldest son and that powerful and fascinating pair the little Dowager and her sister-in-law?

He looked away from her as she prattled away so happily, driving the sword of her incomprehension deeper and deeper with each successive disclosure. He found himself staring at the face which he had modelled and painted. In so far as he was concerned the real Lucy was as remote, impregnable and as impervious as that plaster Virgin in her flowing blue robe—but for an entirely different reason.

Back into his mind came the Swinburne lines which he had recalled when he saw Lucy for the first time, 'for this could never be . . . and never till the Gods and the years relent shall be . . .' A wave of savage hatred swept over him; hatred for the Being who had created him the way he now suspected he was foredoomed to be; hatred for the indissoluble link which the Being had allowed between this brother and sister. Hatred like a flame engulfed him . . . and Lucy prattled on.

'If you do not have to return to that terrible war,' she was saying, plaiting some wisps of straw between her fingers as she spoke, 'then you see, Piers, we could prepare together ready for when Lucien is eighteen, ready for the real beginning.'

'Is that how you see life when you and Lucien can live and work together?' The words were forced out of him.

She nodded. 'Of course,' she said simply, 'we have always felt like that about each other. We have planned everything down to the last detail; but you see you and I could start to make it work. Lucien said it first, don't you remember? Just now he said, 'You know, Lucy-Lou, we three simply must work together one day".' She paused. A sudden doubt shadowed her eyes, 'Piers, dear Piers, wouldn't you like that too? Are we being silly? Oh do tell me. You see we both like you so very, very much. Would you think it a bore to paint lovely things on the walls of our house so that everyone could see them and you would become famous with us? To choose the house and help me furnish it?'

Piers could not reply. With a superhuman effort he just took one of her hands from her lap and lifted it to his lips. It was as if he were saying goodbye to her, for now he knew beyond all possible doubting that Lucy would never marry him and that therefore he would never marry. What lay beyond he dared not even speculate. He only knew that in some way he had known it all from his first encounter with this deadly pair and that now a chill like a paralysis was sweeping over him in waves which threatened to engulf him utterly.

In the ensuing silence they could hear Lucien calling. His voice became louder as he ran towards the barn.

'Lucy ... Lucy-Lou I ... want ... you ...'

She rose at once, shook the straw from her skirts and said hurriedly, 'Dear Piers, it's so nice to know you will help me. Tomorrow I will explain everything to you in detail ...' saying which she ran out calling, 'Coming, darling ... coming.'

Piers sat on in the straw for some time. The tea bell rang in the Home. The young men gathered in the rest room. Rosemary, who was in charge at this hour, thought nothing of Piers' absence. He had become so much a member of the family that she merely assumed he was in the Drawing Room. The Drawing Room occupants assumed he was either in the Home or in the nursery. The nursery thought nothing about it whatever.

By the time the changing bell rang in the Castle, Piers was more than five miles away, unconscious of the growing darkness, unaware even that he was shivering, for he wore no greatcoat having originally set out just to cross from the Castle to the barn. It began to rain. At first he was unaware of this too; but as its intensity increased he become vaguely conscious of his own discomfort. That was when he turned round and began to re-trace his steps. The going became increasingly difficult. He began to stumble in the darkness and the now sheeting rain. From the curve of the saddle back he could not even see the Castle lights, dimmed as they were, nor any from the windows of the farms or cottages.

When he failed to appear for dinner this was reported to Constance who hurried off to his room. On finding it empty she ordered a systematic search of her domain. When this proved fruitless she sent for Sawby; but when he reported that neither he nor any of the other servants had seen Mr Fournes, Constance went to Gyles. He summoned Lucy who told him what she knew. When Gyles began to question her more closely she lifted anxious eyes, coloured furiously and stammered, 'Oh but he seemed very well indeed, we were, er, talking about the future.'

Baulked, but sensing that something was amiss Gyles went to Christine who was in her boudoir with Pearson. Having listened she despatched the girl to request that dinner be held back. This caused a fine eruption in the kitchens. Chef banged about muttering French profanities; Boots scuttled into his hidey-hole, alarmed, and from this fastness peered out like a frightened toad from between some lily leaves. All the while the rain hammered at the windows.

In moments Gyles and Sir Charles were shrouded in hacking raincoats and with caps pulled down were hurrying towards the stables.

Together they eased a pony between the dog cart shafts and were up and away with a bundle of blankets and extra coats covered by a hurriedly snatched tarpaulin. Gyles felt in his pocket to confirm the presence of his brandy flask. Then they were off bowling down the drive with Sir Charles holding a lantern and shouting 'Fournes', 'Piers' . . . as they went.

They thrashed the lanes, quartered the nearby villages, alerted every homeward plodding figure as they went by; but they found no trace of him. After close on an hour they turned through the gates again and as they came to the last bend in the drive Charles' lantern picked up a slight movement. Gyles reined in, Charles jumped down, rayed out his lantern's beam and saw a sodden figure, arms clasped drunkenly about a tree bole as it slid slowly to the ground.

By the time they carried Piers in, dripping and muttering incoherently, Dr Jamieson had arrived. He was standing talking to Constance. He hastened towards them, 'Upstairs and into bed immediately,' he said sharply. 'Lady Constance, please order plenty of hot water bottles to be filled and have some blankets heated so that we can wrap him in them; but first we must strip him and rub him down with alcohol.'

Constance hurried ahead, Gyles and Charles carried Piers between them with Dr Jamieson bringing up the rear ejaculating, 'Why did the young fool want to go out walking at this time of day I should like to know? . . . without an overcoat . . . sheer madness . . . must be out of his mind. We shall be lucky to get away with this without pneumonia.' All the time Piers muttered, fortunately unintelligibly.

When Gyles had relinquished his burden he and Charles returned to the hall where they found Sawby hovering.

'Excuse me, my lord, but when would you like dinner served? the family is in the Drawing Room.'

'Now,' said Gyles brusquely, 'send Pine to Sir Charles and then tell him to come to me. We will join the family later,' and, as he climbed the stairs somewhat wearily he confided to Charles, 'We shall have to keep a much tighter rein on these chaps in future, otherwise we shall have the deuce of a scandal on our hands one of these days.'

Piers' escapade—for so the family regarded it—cast gloom and speculation over the diners. The three vacant places contributed further to their melancholy. Lucy merely played with her food. She was quite incapable of comprehending what had brought this about. When pressed she repeated what she had told Gyles and escaped to Lucien immediately the rest of the women left the Dining Room.

'If you ask me,' said Claire somewhat tartly—though no one had—'I think there is a great deal more to this than meets the eye. I have a strong suspicion Piers proposed to Lucy and was turned down. We all know how highly strung the boy is. Besides, look how Lucy bolted when we left the Dinin' Room. I just wonder where she is now.'

'Not, I think, hanging about outside Piers' door,' said Christine, 'I would imagine you would find her with Lucien and Mr Sissingham in the Common Room.'

Claire just left time for her to finish before saying sharply, 'Well I do not think she cares two straws for that young man, even though some of you are carryin' on as if the engagement was about to be announced.'

This miffed the Dowager and there was a brief verbal hassle between them after which the former rose, very stately, excused herself to Christine and invited little Marguerite to join her.

When the door closed behind them Eustace asked gloomily, 'What's this all about? Could someone explain to me?' He looked across at the Bishop who had already begun to snore and added, 'Deuced bewilderin' I must say—does Alaric have to make such a revoltin' noise?'

Before anyone could answer him Dr Jamieson came in. He crossed to Christine and sat down beside her. 'I thought you would wish to know,' he said, 'that Mr Fournes has a high temperature. His condition could become grave. Therefore with your permission, Lady Aynthorp, I will inform my wife and stay here tonight. I would like to be close at hand.'

What he omitted to tell them was that Piers was delirious. Constance had insisted on staying with him and had already declared her intention of sitting up with him which, in the circumstances, was fortuitous. Except for Dr Jamieson's regular visits she had the young man to herself while Dr Jamieson, refusing offers of a bed, drowsed in an armchair beside the library fire.

By the time a sullen dawn crept furtively over Castle Rising, Piers' mumblings, incoherent though they were had unwittingly fitted the third piece of the puzzle into place for her. She changed hotwater bottles, sponged her patient's face, checked his pulse, drew over the covers each time he flung himself about but these small duties left her ample time for both listening and drawing her conclusions from what she heard. By the time the growing light filtered through the drawn curtains she had made her decision, though the burden of it was to lie heavily upon her in the years ahead. Almost, at one moment she found herself wishing her patient would not recover. Then, flooded with remorse at such a thought she stifled it ashamedly, realising that even if he were to die then some other young man would inevitably supplant him.

Eventually, when Piers seemed to be sleeping, she stood up rather stiffly, crossed to the windows, drew back the heavy folds and looked out. By some ironic twist the scene which presented itself was almost exactly that on which she had looked when Lucien and Lucy ran hand in hand across the lawns from the summer house. Interim experience, she thought sadly, staring out at the rain sodden, leaf strewn grass, merely confirmed her initial reaction to that little scene.

She was not, however, sufficiently sophisticated to recognise the peril in which Lucien stood. Had she done so she might perhaps have spoken, though even so, Piers' revelations were in essence incomprehensible to her. Even if they had been otherwise she would have been in no better case, though any members of a generation as yet unborn would have been able to clarify for her the inescapable fact that whatever she might say and do could not by the very nature of the problem make one iota of difference.

Even so, into her tired mind came a single phrase in which she had always placed her confidence, 'man does what he must at the point where he stands'. She repeated it to herself and found that she was crying. She dashed the tears away angrily and reminded of her responsibilities, turned away from the windows. As she went toward the bed Dr Jamieson came in. When he took Piers' temperature it was down. 'Maybe,' he grunted, 'we shall get away with this after all.'

With the knowledge disseminated through the Castle by the early afternoon that Piers was not in danger, that the fear of pneumonia was unfounded and that he would suffer no more, physically, than a heavy bronchial cold, the atmosphere lightened considerably. It was also agreed that even now it was obvious that Piers would not be sufficiently recovered to return to his home immediately after Christmas. Ergo, Lucy would not be able to visit Mrs Fournes as had been arranged.

Constance had handed her patient over to Rosemary while she bathed and changed. At the same time she wrote a pleasant, reassuring letter to Mrs Fournes preparing her for the fact that her son's return would be delayed.

Christine likewise wrote in the same vein regretting that Lucy's visit would have to be postponed too and expressing the quite sincere wish that the postponement would be brief and quite untruthfully adding that her niece would be greatly disappointed as she was so much looking forward to the visit. Lucy was, in fact well-pleased at the way things had turned out though still puzzled as to why Piers had behaved as he had done. She decided to ask him when he was well enough to receive visitors.

Meanwhile Lucien took himself off to the kitchen garden, sought out Sawbridge, gave him an artless version of the drama and then wheedled the head gardener into supplying him with hothouse flowers of his choice. These he arranged with great care. He also appended a note, pulled the bell and asked Raikes to be kind enough to take it as soon as was convenient to Mr Fournes' room.

The little note said, '*Dear Piers, hurry up and get better, we all miss you very much. Lots of love Lucien*', which did nothing towards helping matters in any direction.

That night, in the Drawing Room after dinner Eustace, who was once again in splendid spirits, obligingly agreed to answer some of the many questions which various members of his wife's family were burning to ask him.

In the course of the evening he passed some of them over to Frank Stone who had been equipped for dining by Pine. This stately character had completely unbent towards him after he had learned of the journey to France from Sawby. Pine had what he referred to as a 'private emergency wardrobe' all of which he kept in perfect condition in some obscure corner of the Castle. It enabled him to supply on demand any missing item of wearing apparel to any male guest who stayed. So far, he had never been defeated. He now produced a dinner jacket which he decided fitted the young man 'passably well'. He even unbent so far as to instruct him with great kindness in the art of tying a bow tie. Thus, wearing Ninian's second-best pair of patent leather pumps, a pair of Gyles' fine black silk socks with hand embroidered clocks which he was very reluctant to relinquish afterwards, and with dress studs from the private store, Gyles' quick glance as young Stone came shyly into the drawing room, confirmed that Pine had done exceeding well.

The family also went out of their way to put Frank Stone at his ease. The Dowager elected to go into dinner upon his arm. She further instructed him, in her own inimitable fashion on how to arm 'an old person like myself' and he, as was intended, became her devoted slave before the fish was on the table.

Thus he was able, after dinner to answer the questions directed to him with no more than a vestige of his initial panic remaining.

Gyles put up an unexpected hare by asking, 'Eustace, old man, where do you berth during operations? I mean, even you and your small brigade will require some locale for food and waterin'.'

Eustace and Stone exchanged glances. Then Eustace asked, 'Shall I take it?' and to the swiftly said, 'Oh yes please, Lord Bartonbury'—a reply which was the result of another little bit of schooling by the Dowager in the matter of forms of address, Eustace, more at peace than he could ever remember, told them.

'It is the most remarkable part of all,' he began. 'I cannot tell you the exact locale for obvious reasons. What I can state is that we shall have more than adequate food and shelter a few miles behind the enemy lines at what has been called The *Entente Cordiale* Hospital. It is in fact a *château* which belongs to someone whom you know socially. It is surrounded by woods, despite being within sound of gunfire all the time. The *Châtelaine* is the instigator of the whole remarkable project, for she has now transformed it into a very fine hospital.

'It has its own brilliantly lit operating theatre, the most up-to-date equipment, instruments, medical supplies, everythin'. It is also entirely financed by the British, staffed with British doctors, nurses, orderlies, organised by an Englishwoman with huge French connections and wholly financed by British money.

'A large proportion of the staff not only give their services but also contribute a weekly sum which is in each case more than anyone would expect to pay Caesar Ritz for food, accommodation and service. There is always this desperate need for funds. In the brief time I spent there, a mere few hours of one day only, I saw a well-known Church of England clergyman washin' up the plates and cutlery in his shirt sleeves and another of his brethren haulin' in the coals. I also saw many women at work who I dare swear had never even dreamed of dressin' themselves without the assistance of their maids. They were down on their knees scrubbin' acres of stone floors or washin' out filthy bandages all with the utmost serenity and good will. I should say that the label of pride, which was Suffragette, as we all now know, will be bestowed upon all women with ruined hands by the time this war is ended. The hospital has been nicknamed by one of France's most eminent generals "The Eden of the French Army".'

At this point Eustace pulled himself up short, realising he was upon the brink of a disclosure which might seem like personal boasting. But it was not to be. Greatly daring, Frank Stone leaned forward in his chair as Eustace ended abruptly. With hands clasped across his knees—to stop them shaking—the young man said quietly,

'What Lord Bartonbury has failed to add is that the wounded are brought to this hospital from the battlefields by Englishmen who have donated ambulances and are helping to drive them themselves and paying as well for other men too old to fight, or men like me, who refuse to take life preferring to save it instead.'

He had gone scarlet as he launched upon this bold revelation. He was white by the end, and in the silence which followed the Dowager behaved most oddly. She rose, so naturally all the men rose too, she said, 'If you will excuse me' and she sailed from the room without further comment save, at the door, the thrown back, 'I shall be returning!'

Christine looked across at Gyles during this little performance lifting her eyebrows questioningly. He gave a nod and this seemed to satisfy her.

In the same abrupt manner little Marguerite, then Lady Constance and then Sir Charles Danement quit the drawing room. Primrose was whispering to her John and after a moment he too rose and left them.

Into the ensuing lull a nervous voice from Stephanie was heard quavering out,

'Please may I ask something, Uncle Eustace?'

Eustace glanced at her, deduced immediately that—to him—the girl was in another of her 'states' so assumed what he imagined to be a soothing tone and said, 'But of course, my dear.'

Stephanie was flushed. She was plaiting and unplaiting her fingers nervously.

'Uncle, please tell me what sustenance there is for your wounded, between the time your stretcher bearers pick them up on the battlefields and when they are delivered to your wonderful hospital?'

Quite taken aback by this Eustace said lamely, 'Why, er, none my dear.'

She pressed her point. 'Yet some might have been lying wounded for a considerable time might they not?'

He nodded, and turned a frowning face to Frank Stone. 'Miss Delahaye raises a very vital point does she not, Frank?' he asked ruefully.

Frank Stone nodded. Stephanie pressed her point. 'Surely it would increase their chances of survival if, once you had got them into your vehicles, they could be given some hot soup or tea with lots of sugar which is so remedial in cases of shock?'

Frank Stone took another little plunge into the fray.

'If I understand correctly, Lord Bartonbury, Miss Delahaye is suggesting that we lack any form of emergency travelling canteen.'

'Yes,' Stephanie cried, hands steady now. 'Please, Uncle Eustace, could I not pay for one? I have a little money of my own and I could think of nothing I would wish to do more than this if you will only agree.'

A murmur ran round the room. Frank Stone rose and crossed to Eustace. He bent down and began speaking to him in a low voice. Meanwhile Sinclair stretched out a thin hand to stroke his daughter's hair as she sat as usual on a low stool beside him.

'What ... a beautiful ... idea ...' he said in his laboured voice, 'Papa ... feels ... very ... proud.'

Henrietta was naturally weeping and mopping while Frank Stone was murmuring to Eustace, 'The one thing which has worried me concerns dying men and their immediate and urgent need of a Chaplain. If one such could be persuaded to accompany us surely he could drive such a vehicle and divide his labours between ministering to the souls of the departing and serving the physical needs of the wounded?'

Before anyone could say more Sir Charles Danement re-entered endeavouring to look nonchalant. 'Forgive me for leavin' so abruptly,' he apologised as he walked past Eustace and slipped him an envelope.

'What the devil ... !' Eustace exclaimed. 'Excuse me everyone, this might be urgent,' and so saying he ripped the envelope, only to withdraw a cheque. In a very short space of time he was the recipient of four such envelopes and found he was quite bereft of speech. This was just as well in the circumstances as Christine decided to take the floor.

'Now that you are all returned,' she said, looking round with somewhat over-bright eyes, 'I wish to say that I think Stephanie has made a very fine suggestion,' she looked across at the girl and said more gently, 'With your permission, my dear, I will repeat the gist of it so that we may all be fully in the picture.'

Stephanie nodded mutely and Christine recounted what had passed during the absence of the four.

Gyles, meanwhile was busily occupied in polishing his monocle. When he eventually replaced it he spoke, 'Christine, my dear, I am inclined to think that Stephanie has only told us a part of what is in her mind.' His glance at the girl was questioning; but this time she shook her head violently and said, 'No, Uncle Gyles—please.'

'Why not tell them?' Gyles pressed, 'you may rest assured that I will support you.'

This brought a startled stare and a stammered, 'How could you possibly know?'

'But I do,' Gyles persisted.

The Dowager rustled her skirts. 'I really do desire,' she said with some asperity, 'that you and Stephanie abstain from talkin' in riddles in the Drawin' Room. It is not courteous, Gyles.'

She was deliberately drawing attention to herself, very probably because out of the corner of her eyes she had seen Eustace ripping open her envelope and was fully conscious that he was staring at her with an expression of incredulity.

'Furthermore,' she added, 'as Nanny taught you all in your nurseries, it is exceedin' ill-bred to stare—Eustace!'

'Oh no!' exclaimed Eustace with some vehemence, 'you are not drawin' me with that lure *Belle Mère*. This,' he waved the cheque at her as if it was a reproof, 'this is out of all reason generous and you are a very wicked, wilful woman.'

She made him a little *moue* and said with great complacence, 'You really cannot refuse me, certainly not for such a cause my dear as your *Entente Cordiale* Hospital, so pray accept it in the spirit in which it was given,' her eyes roved sparklingly around the diners, 'a spirit which seems to have become almost wholesale in the past hour.'

Sir Charles grunted, Christine nodded approvingly and the little Countess spoke.

'What else should you have expected us to do?' she asked. 'Be quiet Eustace and let that money work for the cause.'

Eustace flung out his hands. 'I'm bereft of words,' he told them. 'The good that this will do, and the delight with which it will be received . . . oh dear . . . it is quite overwhelmin'!'

'Then be overwhelmed quietly,' snapped the Dowager, 'and allow Stephanie the chance to tell whatever it is that Gyles is endeavourin' to persuade her to reveal.'

All this had given the girl pause for thought. Her metamorphosis was by now almost complete.

She still retained some of her nervous gestures; but these were no more than remnant reflexes without any real significance. She had matured quite extraordinarily in the past year and was now transformed from a hysterical girl into a force to be reckoned with by the family, no longer a mere embracer of lost causes.

She realised by now that her Uncle Gyles had guessed what she wished to do. She also realised that what he had just said was his endorsement of her intention and his promise of support; but she had at last gained sufficient wisdom to realise that before she said any more it was imperative she take counsel elsewhere as to just how much she might say. So, although by this time visibly quivering, she gripped her hands together and said rather pathetically:

'Please, everyone, no more tonight. If you really do think well of my suggestion then give me until tomorrow morning to tell you what else I have in mind, but please I beg you not to press me further now. I am only so glad you are not against what I have already said. Tomorrow I really will explain,' saying which she jumped up and ran towards the doors leaving them opened behind her. Frank Stone rose to close them.

A babble of talk erupted immediately. Everyone except Gyles and Constance seemed to have something important to say. Under this cover the two looked at each other, then Constance just gave Gyles a little nod, much as Christine had done earlier. After which she too excused herself on the grounds of urgent duties in the Home.

As she passed Gyles' chair she murmured, 'After "rounds" I will come to the library,' and was gone.

She walked through the long corridors to the Home where, in twos and threes the more active convalescents were drifting towards their rooms. She glanced into the rest room to find only two remaining, the wounded Chaplain and Stephanie. Their chairs were drawn close and they were deep in conversation. She left them; but once she had checked temperature charts, separated a small conclave in one bedroom, shooed the culprits to their respective rooms and seen that every reluctant young man had drunk his hot milk, she went softly to Piers' door, turned the handle without sound and slipped inside.

Piers was asleep. Dr Jamieson had been to see him again at six o'clock and had expressed his satisfaction in his patient's physical condition. 'Let him sleep as much as possible,' he had advised, 'keep him on a very light diet for the next twenty-four hours and by then he should be able to eat normally. We shall then only have his mental state to tackle.' When the door was safely closed behind them he had given the Lady Superintendent what Nanny would have called 'an old-fashioned look' and asked,

'Have you any clue, Lady Constance, as to what brought on this troublesome business?'

Constance had prepared herself for the question so was able to furnish him such part of the truth as she felt able to disclose.

'I think,' she said slowly, 'we can put it all down to an affair of the heart, Doctor. From what Mr Fournes said when he was delirious last night I conclude that he made some definite approach to Lady Lucy and was given the kind of answer which made him temporarily distraught.'

The beard was stroked reflectively. Dr Jamieson opened his mouth to speak again but she forestalled him.

'I think,' she added, 'that it would not be within my territory to say more. If Mr Fournes decides to confide in me further when he is once more in full possession of his faculties I will of course inform you immediately.' And with that he had to be satisfied.

She was thinking about this exchange as she stood beside the sleeping figure on the bed. She was exhausted, moreover she felt that in her present state she could not trust herself to stay awake throughout another night. Then Piers moved restlessly, turned over in the bed and she heard him mutter 'Lucien . . .'

This cemented her resolve to instruct whoever was on night duty to visit him every half hour but not to sit with him.

After adjusting the bedside lamp so that it tipped further towards the fireplace and left the sleeping figure in complete shade, she went out just in time to see Rosemary coming towards her. With finger to lip she closed the door, gestured to Rosemary to follow and when they were out of earshot gave her instructions. Only then did she feel free to return to Stephanie and her companion.

The pair were still talking only now they were also holding hands. Constance coughed warningly and went in saying, 'And now, my dears, you must forgive me for interrupting you but it is past lights out for you Mr Devening and I feel that you really should conclude whatever you are discussing in the morning.'

Stephanie turned a flushed face to her. The expression in her eyes confirmed everything to Constance.

She smiled at them gently. Then she asked, 'I am right, my dears, am I not, in my conjectures?'

'Oh yes,' said Stephanie breathlessly. 'So can we just tell you and then we promise we will stop?'

Constance promptly sat down in the nearest chair and said, 'Please do.'

Half an hour later she walked into the library. As usual she found the expected quartet sunk into deep armchairs before the chimney piece. They drew a chair for her and when she had accepted a drink and settled herself, she deliberately plunged in.

'Are you by any chance discussing Stephanie?'

'Naturally'—from Gyles.

Dr Jamieson removed the pipe for which he had asked and obtained permission and contributed his mite.

'If anyone had forecast that the girl I examined when she was brought from Holloway would ever turn out like this I would have given them the lie direct.'

Constance nodded, quite unsurprised.

'Lord Bartonbury, do you intend accepting her suggestion?'

'Oh yes,' said Eustace without hesitation, 'I think she is absolutely right. I am just a little out of sorts with myself for not havin' thought of it sooner and of course Stephanie cannot be allowed to pay!'

Again Constance nodded, then flung in her little bombshell.

'You all realise I suppose that she wishes to come with you?'

'Impossible!' exclaimed Eustace. 'A gently-natured girl flung into that carnage—quite unthinkable!'

Constance raised an eyebrow at this. 'According to what you told us this evening, your hospital is filled with gently nurtured females of assorted ages,' she reminded him.

'Stephanie is rising twenty-one,' Gyles added, 'and now let me ask a question, has anyone the right to stop her? It was her idea.'

'What I would like to know,' Sir Charles leaned forward, 'is whether in Jamieson's opinion the lass is stable enough?'

All heads swung to the Doctor who sat pulling at his beard and clearly considering his reply. At length,

'As you have phrased it, this is not a fair question,' he said surprisingly, 'you are asking it without being in full possession of the facts.'

'What facts?' Sir Charles looked bewildered.

'Well now,' Jamieson looked questioningly at Constance, 'if I could persuade Lady Constance to complete her revelation, I do believe that it would put an entirely different complexion on the matter.'

'What have you been up to, Constance?' Charles asked looking both relieved and curious.

'Me? My dear Charles, absolutely nothing. I have been the repository for certain confidences which I am now debating upon in order to decide whether or not I have any right to disclose them.'

'Oh no,' Gyles cut in, 'for, Constance dear, if you do not then I shall, for I think the time has come.'

'You know too?' demanded Charles.

'Yes,' said Gyles 'I know and what's more I dam' well approve. Sorry, Constance.'

'And so do I,' said she smilingly. 'So then I will tell you. In the morning if I am not very much mistaken that young Chaplain Mr Devening will be requesting an audience with Mr Delahaye to ask him formally and correctly if he may have his permission to marry Stephanie. The pair are deeply in love. They want to go to France with you, Lord Bartonbury—but together if such a thing can be arranged—and what is more they wish to marry before they leave.

'I have just left them. They both convinced me that they know quite clearly that they are volunteering to put their lives at risk, as he has done already. This is what they want. In the circumstances I think it is what they should be allowed to do; but they will only do so as man and wife. Dear me, they made me feel very old and very touched I might as well confess. They even quoted, "Whither thou goest" ... so I say to you in all seriousness, who are any of you to stop them at such a time and in such circumstances?'

After this they began weighing the pros and cons. Dr Jamieson was at some pains to point out that the matter was not wholly in their hands. He explained that the young man had made an admirable recovery; that he was due to be discharged any day now. Then, as he was attached, as he reminded them, he would then have to ascertain whether or not it could be possible for him to be re-drafted to Eustace's voluntary ambulance unit. Even when this hurdle had been surmounted, it soon became clear that the pair could not be released and married, nor the van purchased and equipped by the time Eustace's party left for France in a few days' time. There was a further obstacle here in that Christmas was almost upon them and would bring inevitable delays over both personal contacts and the van's arrangements.

The group talked on for a very long time. Ultimately it was agreed that nothing more should either be said or done until the young couple were formally engaged. Then, it was decided that they could follow on; they could make a suitable rendezvous with Frank Stone and he could convey them to the Hospital. On this note the matter was left and when at length Gyles closed the library doors behind him and went to his own quarters he found Christine asleep, so could not even debate the matter with her until the morning.

CHAPTER 9

A Letter from Limerick

While the children made paper chains and the very small ones laboured over their Christmas presents: wibbly-sewn pen-wipers, multi-coloured paper spills, and pomanders studded with tipsy-angled cloves; Nanny talked to Rose and rocked herself before the guard-protected fire in the day nursery.

Nanny was only the titular head of her nursery world now, wielding precious little save authority and leaving all the work to her newly-promoted, Assistant Nanny Rose, and to Rose's underling, the new nursemaid Dorothy, youngest daughter of Peak the Carpenter.

Nanny dismissed her inactivities rather grandly under the heading 'saving meself for the new babies' and she rocked away, not unlike a stout spider with over-bright, beady eyes and buttoned boots.

There was much going on. All of it provided her with absorbing food for thought. She stodged away omnivorously, ingesting every stray snippet of gossip, sending these tasty morsels down moistened with the saliva of her famed intuition and regurgitating the resultant predictions over the wide-eyed Rose. It all emerged under one or other of those famous banners of hers, 'Me corns is pricking again', and 'Nanny knows'.

Nanny really did know an astonishing amount. She was not unlike a lowly Dowager in this respect for she too had her finger in every pie within her reach, though in the Dowager's case, she being both privileged and exceedingly mobile, it was comparatively easy to deduce most of her sources of information.

For her part, Nanny just sat, or seemed so to do, while somehow or other information filtered to her. She knew now that something was afoot over Stephanie.

During the days when she suspected the girl intended to be a nun she had done her utmost to awake normalcy in the then distorted attitudes of her early adolescence, for she regarded any such withdrawal from real living as totally un-natural, viewed segregation in a nunnery with the utmost horror and repugnance and said so loud and clear.

Once she had witnessed the remarkable changes wrought in Stephanie in the aftermath of her abortive suffragism, Nanny began to thaw towards her and, automatically, to pry with greater interest. Having once written Stephanie off her books in terms of food for speculation, she returned to what was, after all, providing her with singularly appetising morsels. Even before the Drawing Room company suspected, or the library assembly knew, Nanny had put her twos and twos together and from them, with uncanny perception, had arrived at the correct conclusions. She told Rose, rocking furiously, that she fully expected that there young Mr Harry Devening was courting Stephanie and was likely to be accepted. Nanny predicted marriage, she expected it and currently rocked in anticipation of the event.

She caused Rose to do some hard thinking on her own account when she also informed her that there was something brewing over 'that there wicked Rosalind too'.

'How could she possibly know?' Rose marvelled, well aware that with Palliser and Nanny at permanent daggers drawn and Pearson 'like a n'oyster', both these likely sources of information were closed. Yet Nanny predicted, and placing her trust in her seismographic feet, insisted that 'Summat's up'.

She went so far as to declare her conviction that the delinquent would be back at Castle Rising before long and she added, 'A fat lot of good that will do for anyone, for if it's off with her blooming Knight, then it's the most foolishest thing I ever thought on to bring a bolter like Miss Rosalind back here at a time like this. Just as sure as God made little apples she'll be casting them blue eyes around and she'll fix herself on to one of them shoals of young men what's swarmin' everywhere.'

Nanny had no objections to exaggerating in order to make a point, yet distortions admitted, it was a version of what was very likely to occur.

She added darkly, 'It was obvious to anyone with a grain of sense in 'em that it was all doomed to failure once 'is lordship set 'is face against letting that Knight have any money. That's wot 'ee was after from the start and no complaining natcherally that a be-auti-ful young girl went along with the brass.'

This was followed by a gargantuan sniff in which was compounded contempt for the Knight, pity for the family and the ingrained revulsion of her kind for what she saw as a future scarlet woman. Before she let go of this subject she warned Rose that whatever 'come about', as like as not Rosalind would be with child by the time she 'up and bolted from that 'orridsounding Ireland'—as undoubtedly she would be doing ere very long. Nanny entertained the healthiest dislike of every nation other than her own—which was Welsh—and the English and the French. She evinced the scorn and total incomprehension characteristic of almost all British persons towards the occupants of the rest of the world.

In between predicting she would bring out her ink pot, her pen, penwiper, a sheet of much-used blotting paper and a writing pad. Then she would labour away at what she called 'me calendar'. This comprised the first six months only of nineteen fifteen. Having completed it she ringed round two dates and showed her handiwork to Rose.

'Forewarned is forearmed,' she declared, 'as my dear father always used to say, and it is my opinion—and wenever 'ave I been wrong, Rose?'—this last was purely rhetorical as Rose knew, wisely withholding any comment, ' 'is lordship got 'er ladyship in the fambly way the night of that Mond Ball. Never you mind 'ow I know, I jest know. So give or take a day or two we should expect 'er to be in 'er labour some time around seven or eight o'clock in the evening of February twenty-sixth,' saying which she thickened the ring around that date, assuring Rose that Doctor Jamieson was but a bent reed in such matters by comparison with her superior knowledge.

After a brief pause for reflection and some absent-minded teeth sucking Nanny ringed a second date the while making similar observations concerning Petula's accouchement, whose date she explained, precluded her from inside knowledge save that conception occurred on the night before war was declared; but first babies were known to be unreliable over their débuts. Here she was indiscreet enough to let slip a revealing phrase.

'Come down late to dinner they did, all flushed and starry-eyed, and their bed in a terrible state, churned up like a brontysaurus had been exercising in it. Mark my words that's wen it 'appened.' She owned her vision was foggy concerning Petula so returned to the subject of Christine. Had she not always started her pains around early evening? With steadily decreasing periods of labour as the arrivals 'popped out more easy in their succession'; but the date she ringed round for Petula still remained as May the fourteenth.

As Nanny anticipated any happy events by expecting the gloomiest eventualities, she made sure each time that all was absolutely ready by the seventh month. Thus she had two whole months clear for checking, nagging, rocking and recalling the most hideous premature births in her experience.

In the meantime the complement under her direct rule consisted only of Rosemary de la Coutray's fat little four-year-old Charles-Louis, and baby Dominique who at only four months was obviously destined to be a beauty and over whom the old woman crooned and boasted until the tiny little object was well on the way to being thoroughly spoilt.

The nursery would remain in this sparsely tenanted state for a further two and a half to three months. Then Christine's baby would turn all topsy turvy. Nursery dementia would then reach its summit in the spring with the arrival of what Plum always referred to as 'the hair'.

During the Christmas holidays, which were now upon them, the seven occupants of the schoolroom—all run together for the convenience of the staff in general and Rose in particular—would contribute colour and quasi-activity to Nanny, each in their own particular way.

Anne de Lorme had already been home for ten days. Her brother Richard, Christine's youngest and most exhausting offspring, was back too though scarcely seen within the Castle walls as he spent every possible hour from dawn to dusk with Plum in and around the coach house, and was proving more and more difficult to prise away even for meals and bed-time.

'At least,' Nanny sniffed, 'we is able to avoid the worst of the varmint's shocking 'abits', by which she meant his attachment to the lower species of animal and insect life. Still there remained a sufficiency of dramas concerning the little treasures he secreted about his person. These led, eventually to an inspection. He was required, on pain of extermination of The Lot if he refused, to deliver himself at the schoolroom door and there to wait until a thorough and penetrating search had been conducted. Only when he had been frisked by Raikes—the only member of the staff willing and able to risk encountering squirmers in matchboxes, pockets seething with tangled worms, or even bats drowsing under armpits—was he allowed to enter.

On the other hand, Peter Christian and Priscilla, Major Christian and Mrs Clare's young, caused, few problems to anyone. They were just solid, healthy, biddable children with pretty manners and a strong sense of discipline. Nanny would often hold them up as examples to the rest quoting, 'Speak when you're spoken to, do as you're bid ...' in their favour, following this with a general lambasting of the rest of the brood for not possessing similar virtues.

By rights the same should have been said of Lucien and Gilbert Delahaye as was said of young Peter and Priscilla; but Nanny always went out of her way to find fault with both of them; Gilbert because she accused him of dumb insolence and of being sly and deceitful besides artful and crafty. In truth Nanny was frightened of him, particularly during her mealtime onslaughts when he would sit coldly composed with just a faint sneer on his thin mouth.

Lucien, Nanny regarded as a 'sissy' and never failed to tell him so, with much embroidery upon her theme. Consequently both boys detested her; but while Gilbert's hatred of her was leavened by his contempt, gentle Lucien merely suffered silently although it hurt him deeply when Nanny bullyragged him and heaped scorn upon his down-bent curls.

Out of all this there emerged at length a very curious alliance. Gilbert feared no one but despised many, so, when Nanny emptied vindictive comment over Lucien anent his appearance, character and behaviour, Gilbert fought his battles for him. He lashed out, always quietly, but with a deadliness which left Nanny with heaving bosom and burning cheeks. If she were goaded into taking her last desperate remedy by ordering him out of the room, he would merely pick up his plate—if it happened to contain something he liked but had not yet finished—make Nanny a little bow, which in itself was not unlike a spit in the eye, and stroll out whistling. Nanny could not win with him, so after a while Lucien took less of the brunt because Gilbert would always come to his defence in an oblique but telling way. Lucien spent as little time as possible inside the nursery wing; but whenever he did appear Nanny would shout at him, 'And where have you been this time, sissy-boy?'

Gilbert coached him in his reply so now he would give it

looking at Nanny very straightly, 'With the Dowager, Nanny, pray ask her if you do not believe me,' which she dared not do.

Lucy found out what was going on when Lucien cracked after a particularly vicious drubbing and sobbed out his story in her arms. She determined to take action, for she was little less than Mr Rudyard Kipling's she-bear where Lucien was concerned. She was also shrewd enough to realise that she must handle this matter very cautiously.

So, firstly, she decided that she must take her problem to Piers.

She then waited until the fiat went forth that he was permitted to receive visitors. Straightway she approached Constance again to renew her request to see Piers. Constance gave it very reluctantly. She was uneasy as to what his reaction might be but realised encounters were inevitable.

She was already unhappy about him, although he gave no outward sign that he was in any state of mind which was other than completely normal. Though he seemed outwardly relaxed she had watched over him without seeming so to do beyond her natural interest and involvement as Lady Superintendent, sensing that his outward composure was only a protective façade. He had already apologised both to her and Doctor Jamieson for his self styled 'idiocy'. After this he dealt out the small change of slightly crestfallen ashamedness at having caused so much trouble to so many people. This performance even hoodwinked the Dowager and her sister-in-law; but then she was already, for the first time in her life very wide of the mark where Piers was concerned and besides, possessed no clues concerning what Constance knew.

Somewhere along the line from the time Piers had regained consciousness after that first night's revealing delirium, he had come to terms with himself, his situation and his future relationship with Lucy. Constance mused in the quiet of her own room thinking sadly that, at whatever cost to himself, Piers had overlaid his emotions with a brittle gaiety which was at least temporarily impregnable.

He welcomed visitors, joked with his convalescent companions who drifted in and out; he played chess with the Dowager and, when he was informed that Lucy wished to see him he looked up from a game of patience and said smilingly, 'I was hoping she would come soon. It has been far too long.'

Constance reminded herself that all this massive repression

could only build up to eruption; though whether it would come while he was still with them or remain repressed until after he had left she could not conjecture. Nor, with her decision taken, could she bring herself to confide in Dr Jamieson.

This then was the situation when Lucy visited him for the first time.

Her preoccupation with Lucien and her anxiety for him made the encounter very simple. That it only served to cause Piers even greater pain was at this juncture, strictly his own affair.

She came in smilingly carrying a little basket of petits fours made specially for him by chef. She also bore a message from her Uncle.

'Hello, Piers,' she greeted him, 'how lovely to find you so much better. What a silly you were to go out walking in all that terrible rain!'

'Yes wasn't I,' Piers agreed, accepting the basket and listening with over-bright eyes as she passed on her message.

'Uncle Gyles met me as I came along. Lucy prattled on, he said to tell you he has asked Sawby to bring you a little bottle of that champagne you enjoyed so much at the dinner. He said Lady Constance had given her permission for you to drink it.'

'How ripping of him,' Piers smiled back, 'perhaps I might persuade you to return later and share it with me.'

Thus they exchanged the trivia. Then Constance appeared in the doorway, nodded pleasantly and warned, 'Not too long, Lucy dear, remember that Mr Fournes must not be over excited yet. We all want to get him well enough to share Christmas with us, don't we?' After which she went on her way, well aware of the flush on her patient's face and of those brilliant, over-bright eyes.

Thus forewarned Lucy shed her chatter and came hurriedly to her point—Lucien.

'I shall not be able to stay very long,' she said, 'so, dear Piers, can I please ask your advice and help? Lucien is in trouble.' She did not even wait for his assent, so absorbed was she in her brother's distress. Instead she plunged in to a description of Nanny's behaviour and went straight on to explain that she was quite determined to go to the Dowager. She was not to know that, as Piers listened, so a huge impulse shook him to reach out and protect Lucien himself.

She ended her sad little tale. Piers waited a little until his inward emotion subsided and then said, 'I think that is all you can do with any hope of success. The Dowager has been so kind to me. She has already visited me twice and on the second occasion we played a game of chess together. How would it be if you waited just a little . . .?'

At this Lucy broke in but he overrode her.

'She has already said that when I am allowed up I can visit her in her private sitting room and suggested we play chess again. Wouldn't it be wise to wait until that happens? Then I can support you which just might help.'

Lucy's dismay at the thought of waiting subsided at his words.

'Oh yes,' she breathed thankfully, 'that would indeed help. *Grandmère* has formed a very high opinion of you I know and we really must do something Piers, Nanny is driving Lucien distracted.'

They talked on for a few moments longer and then Constance re-appeared. This time her manner was firmly dismissive, so Lucy rose obediently; but before she could move Piers said, 'Lady Constance, I was telling Lucy that her grandmother has invited me to visit her in her private sitting room to play chess as soon as you allow me to leave this dreary bed, and I was hoping it might be quite soon now.'

'We shall have to ask Dr Jamieson,' Constance hedged, 'why do you not ask him yourself when he visits you this evening? And now Lucy my child I really must take you away. Mr Fournes must rest or he will never be allowed to do anything.'

Three days later Lucy heard from Piers that he was to process under Rosemary's escort, and in a dressing gown, to her Grandmother's rooms that afternoon. She went too. Under her disarmingly gentle appearance she was absolutely determined to ensure a restoration of Lucien's content. Even so she was shrewd enough to realise that she must approach the subject very cautiously.

She knocked on her Grandmother's door with a hammering heart. Opening it on hearing the familiar '*Entrez*', she went in to find Piers and the Dowager setting out their chessmen in two facing chairs by the fire.

'Oh,' she faltered, having taken in the scene, 'have I come at an inconvenient moment, *Grandmère*? I, er, wanted to talk to you about something when you have time for me.'

The Dowager paused, King's pawn in hand, 'Then pray come in, my dear, and stop standing in that opened doorway creating a draught for Piers. Is it a private matter or suitable for a personable young man's ears?'

Lucy obediently closed the door and approached the fire. 'Of course Piers can hear,' she said, 'are you sure you don't mind, Piers?' and she lifted an appealing glance to him.

He had risen of course and now he nodded. She coloured, then stammered out, 'pray sit down then, you should not be standing for me.'

Piers obeyed, settling back in his chair with an air of amused attention to whatever it was she wished to say.

For her part, having won the first round, Lucy gained assurance and settling her skirts thanked him prettily and launched herself upon her perilous venture.

She began by asking the Dowager if she did not consider that Mr Sissingham led a very lonely life. This was a viable opening for, in truth, at this period all tutors and governesses led lonely lives. They were the real betwixt and betweens in any great household, neither lowly enough to participate in life below stairs, nor sufficiently acceptable to take part in family life above them.

Lucy chattered on. She spoke of Miss Maxton who now shared governess duties with 'my friend' Miss Byrne. At least, she reflected aloud, they were old friends so could keep one another company during the long evenings when their duties were ended for the day. Alas poor Mr Sissingham had no one.

Greatly daring, and seeing the spark of interest kindled in her Grandmother's old eyes, she entered upon the crux by the route of some well-thought out prattle about how wise Aunt Christine had been to combine nursery and schoolroom meals in time of war. She was astute enough to show how wholeheartedly she supported the humane principle behind the move to lessen staff's labours. Then, taking a deep breath and throwing a pleading glance at Piers, she summoned the courage to say reflectively,

'The only trouble is *Grandmère*, that both Gilbert and Lucien are so intelligent and so indeed is Anne. Nanny, dear soul, always dominates the conversation at mealtimes, so prefers silence from her children. She discourages any talking, she always did I remember. With the little ones this is good of course, though it is most depressing for Anne, Lucien and Gilbert who want to talk about sensible things; books, music and painting and in Gilbert's case financial matters about which he knows so much for a schoolboy. It is really most instructive and interesting even to me.' Lucy paused for a moment just to make sure she still 'held' her audience, then seeing that she did she plunged on recklessly. 'She calls Lucien "Sissy Boy" and "ort to 'ave been a girl". She only jeers at Gilbert but calls him "Mr Moneybags", which makes him shut up like a clam and eat far less than I think he would in more, er, more responsive company. You know of course that he is far too thin?'

'I did not,' said the Dowager sharply, 'but, my dear Lucy, I shall make a point of doin' so now that you have drawn my attention to this fact.' She leaned forward and patted Lucy's hands. 'Thank you for bein' such a kind brave little gel. It cannot be easy for you to tell us all this. Now, have you discussed these matters with Lucien?'

Lucy, for the first time in her life, lied quite deliberately.

'No, *Grandmère*,' she said 'I, er, did not, er, think it advisable.'

'Good girl,' the Dowager approved. She looked across at Piers. 'Mr Fournes?' she asked, 'Would you consider such an atmosphere suitable for boys in their formative years?'

Piers played up beautifully. 'Well,' he said slowly, seeming to be a shade reluctant, 'of course I am not qualified to judge; but, since you ask, no, of course not!'

He made much of his natural diffidence, and was wheedled to express himself more fully, so eventually added, 'Well, if I may? Thank you, I think things could be made much easier for everyone concerned; for the governesses, the tutor, and those three older children if they were all allowed to have their meals and spend their leisure together in some separate place. Would that be a totally outrageous proposal? No? Well then, if it is a question of saving work for the staff, why not combine them all in one suitable room, which would eliminate trays to the tutor, trays to the governesses and entail having one laid table for them all.'

The two held breath as the Dowager reflected upon this proposal. They dared not even glance at each other now, so studiously looked away. Lucy sat playing with the folds of her out-spread skirts. Piers lifted his head and began studying the great painting of Justin Aynthorp over the mantel. After a while he turned, to find that the Dowager was studying him.

'Is that he?' he asked very gently.

She nodded. 'I was just thinkin' what he would have said to this revelation.'

'And have you reached a conclusion?'

'I have,' her voice was brisk again suddenly. 'He would have have made a tremendous scene, ordered us to make appropriate changes and commanded us to reprimand Nanny—which I may add he would never have done himself. She was the only person in this Castle for whom he had a healthy respect—he was you know a beloved termagant.'

Piers smiled at her, which she never could resist. He was wise enough not to speak.

The Dowager went on, 'Of course Nanny has aged a great deal since my husband left us all four years ago and perhaps these three children are overwhelming to her now.' She looked up again to the painting, as she did so many times a day. 'He was really rather splendid,' she added softly, 'does he give you that impression I wonder?'

'Oh yes—indeed,' said Piers.

Lucy interrupted. 'I'll tell you what he was,' she said, eyes very bright suddenly. 'He was terribly difficult, quick to lose his temper, but scrupulously fair, very loving and generous. Life with him was like living in the core of a whirlwind which comes quite suddenly. Without warning that whirlwind would abruptly become a gentle breeze; but of course,' she smiled reminiscently, 'he would have turned back into that whirlwind person at once if anyone had dared to tell him he was nicer than nice and very special.'

The expression in Piers' eyes would have torn at Constance's heartstrings.

'I understand,' he told Lucy, 'I only wish I had been fortunate enough to meet him.'

If anything had been needed to spur the Dowager on, Lucy's unrehearsed and completely sincere description of her late husband furnished it. She told Piers, 'He would have approved you, I dare undertake, and now, you very nice boy, let us play our game, please. Lucy, be off with you. I enjoy you very much and I am grateful for what has been said but now Piers and I must have our game and then I shall have work to do. All must be very carefully arranged. Lucy you will leave all this to me and of course say nothing to anyone.'

'Yes, *Grandmère*,' Lucy murmured dutifully.

'Then go, my dear, shoo ... run away,' saying which, she resumed the placing of her chessmen in final confirmation of dismissal.

Lucy went. The game was played; Rosemary came to collect Piers and after he had gone the Dowager sat staring into the fire. At length she rose and pulled her bell. When Palliser appeared she ordered her to seek out the little Countess to whom, when she came birdlike into the room, Palliser, closing the doors behind her as bid heard her mistress saying, 'Meg, here's a pretty kettle of fish, Nanny's bullyin' the boys and we must intervene.'

Which, of course, they did.

Presently the fiat went forth from Gyles via Sawby, who conveyed his part of it to the Servants' Hall; and likewise from Christine to Nanny. This latter, was as usual, done with the particular blending of tact and firmness which was Christine's *forte*. In this instance she allowed an unusual vein of authority to invest her words. This even Nanny realised. She actually experienced a faint tinge of fear that she had gone too far, which caused her to capitulate with precious little expostulation and thereafter life became much easier for those three instructors and the three older children.

When, for the first time, supper was served in what was to become known as the Common Room, Gyles went so far as to order that a bottle of light claret be taken up so that a glass apiece might be enjoyed by both children and adults.

Later in the evening Gilbert discovered to his elation that both the governesses played chess. He produced his own treasured board and ivory men and there began a life and death battle between himself and Miss Maxton, with Miss Byrne as a contented spectator. Lucien and Mr Sissingham brought out their new secret ploy and set to work in the greatest serenity upon drawings for a fairy story which Lucien had written; while Anne sat completing the embroidery on the needlework bag she was making for her mother's Christmas present.

Then suddenly two smiling faces appeared round the door and, 'May we come in, please?' asked Lucy for herself and Piers.

No sooner had introductions been effected and chairs brought than Lucien cried out, 'What do you think, Lucy-Lou? Uncle Gyles sent us up a bottle of claret. It's all simply marvellous after that beastly schoolroom!'

Lucy and Piers exchanged conspiratorial glances; but before much more was added Piers said, 'We are so happy for you and doubly so if Miss Maxton, Miss Byrne and Mr Sissingham will permit us to visit occasionally. I am supposed to be sketching Lucy now, so I thought if I could obtain your sanction I could do so in here and give myself the added pleasure of your company.'

Thus it was that Christine found them when she 'looked in'. She was not only thanked most touchingly by the seniors of this new Common Room, but also by the young, including even Gilbert which sent her away wondering how in the world she could guard against any future sins of omission, such as this one which she had been able to put right—in time.

December the twentieth was declared an open day for visitors to all the convalescents save Piers Fournes. Because of the Castle's comparative isolation Grantham was required to run a shuttle service to and from the station.

While she was making her first collection of anxious, gift-laden relatives Constance inspected her team. Conspicuous among the V.A.D.s was Stephanie, whose cap and apron were for once spotless though she evinced a marked tendency to fiddle with the former and smooth down the latter, possibly in order to display the small diamond ring on her engagement finger.

The Bishop joined Constance. Together they received their visitors. 'Thus,' as the ever-naughty little Countess Marguerite confided maliciously to her equally naughty sister-in-law, 'adding both weight and the blessing of Holy Writ to our endeavours.'

To this the Dowager retorted promptly. 'More of the former, dear, than the latter I imagine; yet one can suppose that dear Alaric will be at his unctuous best, eh hu! what it is to possess such a mountainous and hypocritical relation!'

On the same day the young Chaplain, Mr Devening, travelled to London to confront his medical board. Before he left Gyles said to him,

'If they pass you, Harry, and your subsequent audience with

your Colonel sets the seal upon this enterprise, my wife and I hope that you will return to spend Christmas with us here *en famille*. If on the other hand the verdict goes against you, the invitation still stands as we shall need to put our heads together over precisely how we shall shape authority towards our ends.'

Quite overcome and somewhat shy still of Gyles' unconscious grandeur, Harry Devening wrung his hand, murmured a fervent if slightly incoherent speech of gratitude and climbed into the Royce beside Grantham. Stephanie was unable to go with him as she was on duty and Constance saw no reason to give her leave of absence for she knew that the young man would be at the Castle for Christmas. So, he spent the time alternately chatting with the chauffeuse and reflecting upon his remarkable good fortune.

He was a simple man. He had spent his orphaned childhood in his uncle's house which had been a very happy one. The uncle sent him to Winchester and on to Oxford and had bought him his first cricket bat when he was only five, having been a friend and admirer of W. G. Grace, besides being no mean cricketer himself. Thus, under his personal tuition the boy's natural flair for all games and for cricket in particular had been given full rein. In fact until the war Harry Devening's main interests had centred around cricket and the Church, with the Church just winning by a short head.

By the time war came Harry was in holy orders. He had seen the war as a kind of grail and was humbly and profoundly grateful that his Almighty had seen fit to let him serve in any capacity whatever. The moment of total dedication had come when he heard Eustace Bartonbury's story. He talked it all over with Stephanie, found she was of precisely the same mind as himself and at this his cup was filled to overflowing. So now he sat, a beatific smile on his rather chubby face, his long legs stretched out, counting his blessings, which to some might have seemed meagre. For once he had forgotten entirely that other goal which had seemed to lie within his reach when he left England with the British Expeditionary Force—for he had been hotly tipped to be selected to bat for England.

He had also obtained Sinclair's blessing with consummate ease the moment he stammered out his request for permission to marry Stephanie, received the dubious blessing of a fond if damp embrace from the inevitably weeping Henrietta and been informed by Niobe that he had made her, 'The happiest future mother-in-law in the world.'

At this point in his reflections Harry found himself at Upper Aynthorp station. He dismounted and surrendered his and all the other vacant places to more visitors to the Home. On the next outward journey the Royce contained the Dowager and Sir Charles who were to travel by train to Epping station, there dismount and complete their journey in Eustace's chauffeuse-driven Daimler which would also, at the end of the day return them to Castle Rising.

The post not having arrived by the time she left, the Dowager had left strict instructions with her sister-in-law, Marguerite, that she was to open, read, and share with Christine, Gyles and Constance any reply which might arrive from Ireland.

Thus it was that no sooner did Sir Charles set foot inside his club that he was informed that the Countess de la Tessedre had telephoned him and would be obliged if he would telephone back to her immediately. When he obtained the connection he thought that she sounded slightly breathless. 'Charles dear' she fluttered, 'the letter came as Alicia supposed it might. I won't bother you with details now but will tell you instead that I feel both of you should spare the time to call on Lizzie Stanhope at Lancaster Gate today.'

'I see,' said Charles, seeing little.

'Well,' Marguerite continued, 'the O'Mara's abigail is there and has news. We have all read the letter and think it wise for you to save time by getting what you can out of the woman. You know Lizzie well enough,' at this point a faint chuckle came down the line. 'I seem to recall you were somewhat *éprise de,* many years ago.' To this Charles only grunted so she ran on, 'The crux is, Charles, can you get hold of Alicia?'

Charles informed her somewhat drily, 'She has done me the honour of consenting to take luncheon with me at the Ritz, together with, as I understand, a highly secret, small animal in a basket—but say nothing to anyone about that if you please.'

'Oh dear! animal?—how intriguing.'

'I trust Caesar Ritz will view the matter in the same light,' said Charles. 'Now I must go Meg or I shall never complete my commitments before luncheon. I will telephone Lizzie and make sure it will be convenient to call. All news tonight, eh?' At length he succeeded in terminating the call. He then delved into his diary, discovered the Lancaster Gate telephone number and found himself entangled in a telephone conversation of even greater length. The Lady Elizabeth would be enchanted, ravished in fact. 'Dear Charles and how was he? How sweet of him to remember his old flirt after all these years;' and so on, until Charles managed to insert the query, 'Have you the O'Mara abigail below stairs, dear Lizzie?'

This brought a changed tone of voice, as 'Have I not!' echoed the lady. 'Such a to do! Poor wretch she is quite put out, all at sixes and sevens in fact. Cook is even now giving her sal volatile. I understand the crossing was tumultuous and the poor creature has only, as she told me "crossed Cork Bridge these past ten years..." and is in all her states. By three o'clock I fancy the poor wretch may be calmer...'

At length this ordeal was over and Charles hurried out again to keep a much overdue appointment.

The gist of the letter, pored over by the four older ones, was difficult to obtain, for Miss O'Mara still crossed and re-crossed her letters. However, it was at length managed—less the pages of personal chatter—and Gyles persuaded 'Sissy' to take it down to his laborious dictation; after which Sissy typed it out on the brand new machine which had been presented to the Common Room.

Miss O'Mara wrote: 'The two counties *seethe* over this marriage. As I am sure you are fully aware *he* has no money. The estate is derelict. He has a man, an erstwhile groom who goes with him everywhere and from what you tell me I imagine it must have been he who acted as go-between when you took the gel to London for her coming out. Now he is butler—of a kind—really a general factotum! He has a handful of village girls to help him, but of proper domestic staff there are none. The place itself is hideously run down, curtains frayed and faded, some fine old furniture which has been innocent of polish since his mother died, plaster falling down and paper peeling from damp walls.

'Society is more lenient here in many ways but in others much more severe. *He* has more male cronies to the place than suitable visitors of both sexes. I have no knowledge as to where he obtains any funds from but certainly there is a great deal of gambling until the small hours and no one knows what she does with her time. Of course they both ride exceeding well even by our standards which as you know are somewhat exigeant. He has clung to the remnants of what was once one of the finest stables in all Ireland and somehow he manages to pay his way with the Hunt. *She* is a beauty and much admired but so very little seen. At first they put up a good front especially when he took her to Dublin; but now I fancy he is at the end of his tether or very near to it. Some say she is expecting, if this is so she still rides like a Jehu which cannot be wise; though I know Mama was in the saddle the day before I was born. By dint of very cautious enquiry, I have obtained the impression that all is far from well between them. This is not altogether surprising if one considers her background. Of late a young Italian has been staying nearby at an Inn which keeps a very good table. I do not think he fancies their hospitality. Be that as it may, the three of them are together all the time, or so runs the *on dit*. The more scurrilous of the gossips say she has taken a fancy to this young foreigner who has a title of some sort, but then you know my dear how profuse these are in Italy and frequently as impoverished as some of our own first families—even supposing he is of such ilk.

'Putting all together at best I may, I should say that your wisest possible tactic would be to infer that you have heard from the gel in some roundabout way, and that she is already aware of her mistake. You could possibly add something to the effect that she misses her home and parents greatly but is too proud to admit defeat. Say if you like that I am the informant. I do not mind at all. Say that you have, as it were a friend at court in me and that I am pledged to keep you informed. Indeed Alicia I do most seriously warn you that they are unquestionably heading for a crisis of some kind. While of course I cannot define its nature in any particular I do promise that if I can I will contrive to have her brought to me if matters do come to a serious head. Then I will contact you again. You know me. You know how jealously and closely I am guarded, so you can have no fears on that score for me. My protection goes without saying, I only wish that I might have more definite knowledge of her physical condition.

'I sent my old abigail to London yesterday. She plays courier for me with some documents of importance. She will also bring with her some gifts, including mine to you; but, my dearest

'Licia, remember she is an illiterate peasant. She goes to her sister who works for Lady Stanhope at Lancaster Gate. The address is attached herewith. Lizzie Stanhope has agreed to let Bridget stay there while she is in London. She will also have her collected from the boat and returned thence under escort. If you could possibly contrive a visit to Lizzie I think I would be happier. Or, if this is beyond the bounds of possibility could not dear Charles be persuaded to fulfil this office for you? Then Bridget could tell either of you in her curiously garbled fashion. I only hope your ear is still attuned and that you will remember to translate 'I will be afther getting it' as signifying as it does in Irish-English that it *has been obtained*!!! Vastly confusing to the uninitiated and I have never succeeded in discovering from whence it derives. *We* do not say so, why must *they*...?'

There was much more in similar vein; but this was decreed unsuitable for the typewriting machine and Mr Sissingham. The letter was ultimately re-folded and placed upon the Dowager's *escritoire*.

Meanwhile the Home's visitors were regaled by a fork luncheon from a buffet set up under the French windows in the Rest Room. Gyles and Christine made a duty appearance and then withdrew to sink thankfully into chairs in the Breakfast Room for their own belated luncheon. The Royce continued its shuttle service throughout the afternoon.

When Eustace's Daimler containing the Dowager and Charles eventually returned it went directly to the stables. Plum came to the car door to receive the basket containing the tiny King Charles Spaniel. He did this with rapture, crooning as he picked it out of the basket and tucked it into his coat, 'Wot a little darlin', now you come er long of Plum and keep warm in 'ere until I get you 'ome ter Ma.' After buttoning the shivering scrap into the warmth of his person he peered in anxiously at the Dowager.

'Wot's ee eat, milady?' he demanded hoarsely.

The Dowager handed out an envelope. 'It is all written down in here,' she assured him, 'I have also arranged with Monsieur André to keep you supplied. If you call at the kitchen door on your way home tonight the puppy's milk and chicken will be waitin' for you. In the mornin' M. André has agreed to send down the food for his luncheon.'

'Mid-day time?' queried Plum.

'Yes,' said the Dowager a trifle impatiently.

'Then it's 'is dinner,' said Plum reprovingly.

She left him crooning to the puppy who clearly found much solace in his stable scented garments, for as the car slid away the tiny face peeped out and the scrap indulged in an orgy of licking.

Gyles came out into the hall to meet them.

The Dowager held up one small, gloved hand. 'Not now Gyles if you please, I am a trifle fatigued and so is Charles. Pray let us rest and change for dinner and then we will come to you in the library.' So saying she swept past him and began to mount the staircase. Behind her Charles gave Gyles a rueful grin. All he said was, 'A tricky affair, see you soon old boy,' and then he too made for the staircase.

Gyles looked after them frustratedly. He sensed trouble. It was one of his most distinctive reactions that if there was trouble about anything, in any circumstances and at any time, then he liked to know of it on the instant. He liked to have the cold hard facts given to him with the utmost brevity, agreeing with Lady Macbeth that "if 'twere done then 'twere best done quickly!'

It had been a bad day. The papers were filled with the news of German bombardments in the northern sea-side towns, huge headlines bannered 'Heavy casualties, women and children killed'. Castle Rising had lost another of its young men too— the woodcutter's son who had died of wounds after being taken prisoner. Gyles had encountered the shattered parents as he was returning on foot across the Park. By the time he had handed them over to Christine for strong tea and comfort, Sawby came in with a face like thunder to inform him that Morning Star had damaged a fetlock and his presence was required immediately in the stables. No sooner had he contacted the vet and hurried off to the mare than eldritch shrieks filtered up from below stairs. One of the kitchenmaids had scalded her arm with a kettle of boiling water and was howling like a banshee. When she had been comforted, the shrieks reduced to whimpers and Constance and Dr Jamieson had borne her away for treatment, Raikes sounded the dressing gong. A moment later the Dowager and Charles arrived ...

Swearing softly to himself, Gyles climbed the stairs after them to change.

By the time the Dowager rustled down again the dinner gong

was sounding, so the older members of the family came out of the library and they all went in to dine.

The convention was once more observed although from Andrew to the Bishop they were all immensely curious as to '*l'affaire Rosalind*'. Not by a single flicker of an eyelid would anyone contemplate even mentioning the subject before the servants.

They of course knew a good deal already, conjectured more and by experience out of much practice had managed to construct a fairly clear picture of what was going on, had gone on and was expected to transpire in the not too far distant future; but thus were the conventions observed, with Dowager shaking out her napkin and remarking, 'Well now, let me see what messages I have for you all from Lizzie.' She flung a teasing glance at Charles and added, 'Charles collected his own and was given a somewhat rapturous welcome. After all Lizzie is still a highly eligible *partie*, an elegant widow, not entirely past her prime, with a wide circle of friends and an even wider income at her disposal.'

'Pish, madame,' said Charles, 'you are, I see, in fine fettle and have an instinct to provoke.'

Thus the small coinage of trivia was sustained.

Indiscreetly Christine then asked, 'And how was dear old Bridget?' to be rewarded by a crisp retort from the Dowager, 'old undoubtedly, dear, but also in a high state of dithers. The poor wretch had just experienced a particularly nasty crossin' and was still hock deep in Hail Marys and "Glory be to God I niver see the loike of it afore".'

Her mimicry won a ripple of laughter. After this had subsided Primrose enquired,

'How old is she now?' and Charles conjectured, 'Much the same age as Methuselah you would have thought, my dear, had you seen her today.'

Bishop Alaric pulled down his mouth and asked, 'Are we not verging upon the irreverent with our Biblical and Testamental allusions?' which reproof won him nothing beyond a cold silence into which the little Countess remarked apropos of absolutely nothing, 'Does anyone else feel that it is becoming colder? I fancy we might have a white Christmas after all.'

The Bishop returned to his gorging. When the meal ended, Christine said,

'We will have coffee in the library, please, Sawby,' adding as the man closed the doors, 'and you younger ones can join us for a quick cup and then leave us, we have some important family matters to discuss.'

Lucy excused herself altogether. She went off with Stephanie and Andrew while two of the footwomen helped Sinclair into his wheeled chair and bore him away with Henrietta fussing in his wake. The Bishop was already asleep so they left him and the rest of them went to the library.

Still the *bouche fermée* rule was sustained. Gyles showed Constance some Dulacs he had purchased in London, Marguerite settled with her *petit point* and the rest of the men busied themselves cutting and lighting their cigars.

Only when Christine had finally dismissed the butler did a little babel of questions erupt from them.

The Dowager held up her small, bejewelled hand.

'Shall we not attempt first to give you the bare facts and then let you ask us such questions as arise therefrom?' she enquired.

'If you please, Mama,' Gyles spoke calmly enough but was clearly nearing eruption point.

'Well then,' she leaned back and spoke with her eyes on the fine ceiling. 'That precious rogue and his factotum have quit the Castle and no one knows where they have gone. News of this reached Eugenie O'Mara who promptly ordered her carriage and, with only her coachman and an elderly groom, set out to investigate. What she discovered would have given the average woman of her age a stroke, at least. She merely tackled the problem as you would expect. The plain fact is, the marriage is wrecked. Rosalind has miscarried and was found in bed in a huge unheated room, without food or attendance. The village girls had all fled. There were cattle, in acute discomfort, since no one had milked them, hens starvin' and all the horses gone. The place was literally abandoned, and had Eugenie not arrived, Rosalind might have died. As far as I could ascertain from Bridget when I first saw her none of this was known to her when she set off for England; but shortly after she arrived at Stanhope Gate she was further driven into babbling distraction by the arrival of another servant who was scarcely more lucid; but from whom we did manage to extract some part of what has happened.

'After Eugenie had spoken with the girl—it seems she was

delirious—Eugenie set off with that bad leg of hers down endless corridors until she discovered a huge old kitchen. Here she heated some milk, and went back to Rosalind. She then sent one of her two men for help in the village. He had a terrible time persuadin' anyone to come but in the end he prevailed and by this time Eugenie was found almost prostrate too so they bundled the pair of them into the carriage as best they might and posted back with all speed. I understand the old coachman first put the fear of God into the three villagers, forced them to milk the cattle, wrung a pledge from them with the promise of money to stay and tend the still live creatures, round them up and establish a rota system by which they could be fed and watered until further arrangements could be made. One thing only is clear—the woman who brought the news repeated one message from Eugenie which she had obviously been forced to learn by heart. We are to do nothing until we hear from her. A doctor is in attendance, the girl is not in any danger but it will be some time before she can possibly travel and only when she does will Eugenie wish someone to go over and bring her back here. I have never heard such a terrible tale in all my days. Small wonder both women were distracted. As for Eugenie, Rosalind owes her life to her and I am only fearful to learn at what cost to herself all this has been done.'

'And that scoundrel has vanished without trace?'

'So those women say. It seems there was some gamblin' party and it ended with Rosalind comin' down in her *déshabillé* and beratin' them. Anyway a terrible scene occurred, the men were of course in their cups and the end of it was that Gavin Fitzpatrick said he was sick to death of the whole affair and wished he had never set eyes on Rosalind. She fell into a fit of dreadful weepin', fled to her rooms and there she was when Eugenie found her.'

Gyles had listened to all this in absolute silence. Now he stood up, his face so terrible that Christine clapped a hand across her mouth and shrank back in her chair.

'Charles,' he said very softly, 'when we go over we go together. I think we must run that devil to earth and thrash him within an inch of his life. Do you not agree?'

'Amen to that,' said John, staring white faced from one to the other. 'But what of the girl?'

Gyles turned to him. 'She'll recover,' he said shortly, 'she's

just a silly girl who, heaven bein' willin' has been given a lesson
to last her a lifetime but,' he made an inclusive sweep of his
hand and then brought it down crashing on the library table,
'not ... one ... single ... word ... of ... this is ever to reach
Sinclair or Henrietta. I trust you all understand me. We will
do as we have always done. We will clear up this mess with the
greatest possible discretion so that nothing, I repeat nothing
ever leaks out to harm those unfortunate parents or damage
either Rosalind or us in the eyes of our world. Is that clearly
understood?'

Christine had seen storms before. She had been trained to
them over the years by her explosive father-in-law but now
despite all her past experience she needed every scrap of courage
to dredge up her whispered plea.

'But Gyles,' please, no horsewhipping, no scene with that
man,' and then she used a remarkable phrase for her. 'Let the
dog return to his vomit; but make sure by all you do that none
of the Delahayes are punished any further. They have had
enough.'

'And let him go Scott free!' exclaimed Charles incredulously.
Gyles faced his wife.

'My dear one,' he said, 'remember please that so far but no
farther may woman go with men. We will be discreet, rest
assured; but we shall also bring retribution where it is due.'
He was holding himself in hand pretty well, all things considered. Though, had Henry been present it was a foregone
conclusion that by this time his hair would have been reduced
to chaos by furious rumpling.

As it was Christine closed her lips tightly, rose even so and
prepared to leave the room.

'Are you coming, *Belle-mère*?' she asked with a sigh.

The Dowager nodded, 'I am, my dear, and so is Meg. Come
along, my dear, we have clearly outrun our usefulness.'

'Now, Mama!' exclaimed Gyles goaded.

The Dowager ignored him. Between them the women managed to convey their immense displeasure, together with more
than a modicum of fatigue and manifest regrets that male
domination should dare impose limitations upon them at such
a time.

So successful were they, as they sailed out with Constance
looking straight ahead of her and completely ignoring Sir

Charles' pleading looks, Petula following without a single back-
ward glance at Gyles; that when they had gone the dominant
feeling among their menfolk was of guilt at their behaviour and
too, a measure of sheepishness.

Gyles sank down into one of the deep leather chairs and
unconsciously echoed his Mama's words by exclaiming, 'Well,
Jamieson, here's a fine state of affairs! What in God's name
should we do for the best?'

CHAPTER 10

Christmas, Nineteen Fourteen

The impact of this particular Christmas was very much a matter of attitudes. For the older inhabitants of the Castle it was more painful than joyous, though they too had their moments to remember. In the main their memories were long, so inevitably the shadows cast by them were longer still, bringing with them a nostalgia so powerful that it was at certain moments akin to pain. Christine mused upon this when it was all over and recalled a remark made lightly in her Drawing Room to the effect that every fragment of song holds a mirror to a past moment for someone. She flinched automatically at the use of the word 'mirror'; but acknowledged ruefully that this Christmas resembled a looking glass in which past moments were reflected so vividly that her inmost spirit felt that it was weeping for what had been and might never come again. Over and above this *nostalgie de l'âme* they were all burdened by anxieties for Rosalind.

For the children it was all glorious, from the nine carol, nine lesson services for which the village children crowded into the chapel and watched round-eyed as their companions piped out carols standing before the altar and to the alternated organ playing of Mr Prewitt the music master and Lucien; but the children's greatest moment came when they clustered round the *crèche*, spell-bound, in awed silence until one scrap burst into tears and was carried out wailing, 'I want to hold Baby Jesus. He wouldn't mind, I know.'

Christine promptly intervened. She asked the crimson-faced, chagrined mother to stay until the rest had left. Then she took the child by the hand and led her to the manger. Here she put the Babe into her arms. In a perfectly instinctive gesture the little girl knelt to receive the plaster Babe. When she was eventually led away her shrill little voice was heard proclaiming, 'I've held Jesus, Mam, I've held 'Im.'

Below stairs generally had little time for thought so they got through fairly well with only a couple of characteristic eruptions from Mrs Parsons who finally refused her Christmas pudding on the grounds that it would choke her, she being—as she informed everyone, 'Serrouned by the spirits of our dear departed.'

Pansy ran herself ragged between her own little cottage and her Castle duties but thought it all worth while when Sawby raised his port glass to her in the Servants' Hall and asked the domestic assembly to join him in drinking to, 'The nicest wife any man could ever ask for,' at which, to the astonishment of everyone present, Mrs Parsons said loudly, 'Amen to that' and conjured up a benevolent nod of approval.

The ex-suffragette employees declared they had never before experienced anything like it, not in their whole lives; indeed some of them had never seen a Christmas tree before, let alone received gifts from one—'really new things'—as one marvelled. Their past Christmases had reached peaks when some second-hand toy donated by some obscure do-gooder had come to them via some harassed and penurious curate at hastily got-up parties in broken down East End halls. So they were both dazzled and enraptured.

The nursery and junior schoolroom became thoroughly overexcited. They over-ate and so had to be dosed by Rose with castor oil. Nanny supervised the shuddering intakes. It was left to Richard to chalk up for posterity another awful crime for which he was subsequently hauled up before Papa who gave him a sound walloping and, much worse, told him he was deeply hurt that a son of his could stoop so low as to cause a member of the staff such shame. This nearly reduced the rebel to tears.

'Such a thing,' Mrs Parsons recounted in the Servants' Hall, 'He give pore Nanny(!) a nice white box all tied up with red ribbons. She never noticed the 'oles poked in for air. He writ on a card hisself "With love from Richard" and wot did Nanny find wen she opened it?... why a nant's nest wot was seething through bein' tied up and her apron was all covered in ants and ants was runnin' all over 'er legs and wot is worse that young limb of Satan 'ad stuck some fleas in along of the ants, on some feathers they was, and Nanny was bit all over and 'ad hy-stericks.'

After the walloping and when the door had closed behind his youngest son Gyles threw back his head and laughed. Then he told Henry, who was also hugely amused. When Christine came in to collect the pair of them for luncheon she was shocked, which only made them laugh again until Henry cried out weakly, 'Mama, don't, my sides ache ... ha ha ha,' at which Christine stalked off quite scandalised.

All the convalescents except Piers had 'a rippin' time' and subsequently wrote long, highly-coloured descriptions to their respective homes anent the glories which were Castle Rising Christmas celebrations; while Sir Charles dithered upon the brink of pleading his cause to Constance; but hampered by the painful awareness of the wide gap in their respective ages, lacked the courage to declare himself.

Ninian and James, the 'Inseparables', came at term end from Sandhurst and as usual managed to extract the maximum of pleasure from their leave. The future for them was 'absolutely top-hole', promising them the peak of enjoyment in 'havin' a crack at the Hun'; while the present, with its super-abundance of horses to ride, was naturally perfect. The years had changed nothing for this uncomplicated pair. They roystered around, thundered up and down stairs, wrangled and scuffled precisely as they had done when they were small boys.

Lucy, Stephanie, Petula and Henry, home on his long-anticipated 'seven days', floated through it all with total rapture, able like the Inseparables, with youth's enviable capacity for living in the moment, to wipe war from their minds and live like little frogs splashing about in puddles—in the moment—without a thought for either yesterday or tomorrow. They were unique in this respect for even the young convalescents were aware of the Damoclean sword which hung over all their heads —the constant reminder that their return to the trenches was imminent; while for the ex-suffragette employees there was a bitter sweetness in knowing, or at least thinking they knew, that one day this way of life would end. So their fear was that peace would come too soon.

Lucien simply hated it all. From the moment the basket was produced from behind the Christmas tree and Piers was called out to take it and present it to Lucy, all her attention had been focused upon its content—the tiny white King Charles Spaniel with the absurd brown tips to his ears which she promptly christened 'Mr Silk'. For the first time in his life Lucien took second place, so he simply sulked until on Boxing Day the pup lurched unsteadily towards him as he sprawled upon a rug. He proceeded to lick him all over with an ecstasy of tail-wagging. Wickedly Lucien gathered the scrap into his arms and said, 'I think he likes me best.' Even this Lucy spoiled for him because she cried out, 'How lovely, darling, then we can both love you together,' which made him feel infinitely worse.

In after years Henry and Petula were to look back on this leave as their last really golden time of the war. She went with him when he joined the guns and insisted upon acting as his loader, a duty which she fulfilled with her usual competence. He thought that she had never looked lovelier. Her thickening outline was concealed by a loose, caped coat of golden seal. She wore a matching tam-o'-shanter from which little curls were teased by the wind, this whipped a vivid colour to her cheeks and made her eyes sparkle. So intent was Henry upon this vision that he actually missed an easy left and right and was trounced by Gyles. He just laughed. 'Deuced sorry, sir.' he apologised, 'I was lookin' at m'y wife, don't you think she looks ravishin'?'

Thus challenged Gyles' face softened. 'Enough to throw anyone's aim,' he agreed subsiding.

Henry had always managed to do this to his father. Gyles had more than once reflected upon it and wondered if the results would have been similar, had he done likewise with the redoubtable Justin.

Then, when they went in to Christmas dinner, with the great table extended to accommodate the thirty-eight diners Henry whispered, arming his own wife in—a flagrant rebuttal of his Mama's orders—'I switched place cards, now we can sit together,' at which Petula flung him a shocked glance but squeezed the arm on which her hand rested.

As dinner progressed, two huge turkeys fattened on the estate were carried in by the footwomen under Sawby's watchful eyes. Then tradition was sustained by the entrance of Chef André in spotless whites, his *coq-de-cuisine* set proudly on his head. He removed it, bowed ceremoniously to Christine and then murmured the phrase which had been used for so many previous Christmas dinners.

'With your permission, miladi, I will now exercise my privilege and carve for you.'

The young convalescents, already dazzled by the magnificence of the table setting and the traditional service of punch before the roast in the wonderful old silver gilt Lorme goblets which had known many a mailed hand upon them, were deeply impressed and few of them were not already working away under cover of conversation at the entrancing exercise of memorising every single detail for recounting at future dinner parties or in future messes.

When the covers were drawn finally, and tradition again maintained, Gyles, in his Lorme livery, received the decanters from Sawby and the footwomen placed three foot high spun sugar palm trees in position between the pyramids of hothouse fruits. At the base of these shimmering trees André had massed fruits which he had crystallised himself—*'faute de mieux'* as he had shrugged when he assembled his small masterpieces to the chorused admiration of below stairs personnel.

At long last, having sweated all through dinner, as had all his predecessors in their turn, Richard, the youngest present caught his father's eye. It was his duty to propose the loyal toast. In this first year of war it was a poignant moment.

Gyles gave his son a faint nod. Richard rose as a footwoman drew back his chair. Sawby and the women then froze, hands at their sides as Richard spoke the familiar words.

'By your leave, sir, I will now propose the loyal toast.' He paused fractionally then continued into the silence, 'Ladies and gentlemen pray be upstanding' and finally when the rustle had died away, 'His Majesty The King.'

Having reseated himself, very flushed of face, he cautiously withdrew his toad Humpty from his left hand pocket. Under cover of a corner of his table napkin he managed to inspect him. He was anxious about Humpty, fearing that he might have gripped him too tightly in his last minute panic as he stood up; but he was fine, just blinking a bit in the sudden light so, vastly relieved Richard stuffed him back, gave the pocket a loving pat and helped himself to quite the largest of chef's crystallised apricots from beneath its sugar palm tree.

As if this were not enough, when the port had completed its

first tour Sawby made no attempt to place the cigars at Gyles' side for circulation. He had been warned of what was to come.

Slowly Gyles stood up, raised his glass and looking around the table as though he wished to draw solace from the familiar faces he said very quietly, 'Now if you please I ask you to drink one more toast with me.'

The rustle came again and then the silence into which Gyles then gave them 'Absent Friends', after which even Sawby was compelled to clear his throat. Henrietta was of course weeping copiously.

On Boxing morning Gyles received a telephone call which returned him, grimfaced to his place at the breakfast table. He had heard from a friend that British seaside towns were now being even more heavily bombed by enemy destroyers who lay off Scarborough and killed eighty-seven women and children. Many other northern seaside resorts had suffered too.

It was difficult for the family to envisage such a happening. Brought up as they had been in the aura of certainty which surrounded every English man and woman of privilege at that time that the power of the British bulldog was absolute, it seemed incredible. It was to them, particularly the older ones, as if the sun had suddenly failed to rise leaving them in night's darkness hopelessly trying to perceive the shape of things to come.

Henry took Petula out in his precious motor driving quite slowly over land which would one day belong to him. They went the reverse way to the line which the first Henri de Lorme had taken when he rode into Essex through the great forest where now a broad road cleaved it centrally, and so they came to the river which Henri de Lorme had forded.

Here they climbed out of the car and went to a high rise of the bank where Henry spread a tarpaulin for them to sit on. There were swans preening and cleaning in the shallows. The river was running fast in winter's spate. The sun came out, but it was so pale that Petula was assailed by the fancy that it too had heard the awful news. For a while they sat in silence watching a bustle of waterfowl, a heron who came down and pecked selectively until the pair on the bank made movement, when it took wing and sailed off overhead.

'You're not cold, my love?' he asked her presently.

'Only in my spirit,' Petula told him. 'Not being of your blood I cannot lay claim to prescience; but I am weighted down by fear.'

He took her hand and kissed it, turning the palm over and running his lips across. 'Nothing will happen to us,' he assured her, 'you'll see. We will come back here when it is all over, take up the threads and live our lives out here, together, as Pater and Mama have done.'

She nodded. 'Of course,' she agreed, 'I expect it's only my condition. They all say that women are fanciful when they are carrying children and your son my love is a boisterous young man even now.' She laid a protective palm across her swelling belly, 'I do not think I care for the having of babies,' she confessed a trifle ruefully. 'I am fulfilling a dream but I think it will all be better when the dream makes his appearance.' She looked at him with troubled eyes. 'Do you think me heartless when I say that I look forward so much to the time when I shall have my body to myself again? It does not take kindly to being shared.'

He lay back with his copper head on the damp grass and looked up at the sky. 'I do not think that anything but reasonable. It must be awful to have a thing kicking about inside. Sometimes I also think that the Almighty devised a singularly disagreeable method of bringing children into this world.'

'Oh yes,' she agreed, 'I thought you would understand; but Christine never complains does she?'

'She's had plenty of practice,' Henry grunted watching a sparrow hawk circling over its prey. 'That's the death knell for some wretched field mouse I'll be bound.'

She lay back in the curve of his arm and followed the line of his lifted arm. 'Shall we shout it away then?' she asked.

'It wouldn't be any good. That's the way of the sparrow hawk, he must kill to live. Not like this bloody war, just killing for power.'

He hitched himself on one elbow, rolling over, and looked down on the face which was raised to his—'Have I ever tried to tell you how exquisite you are or how terribly much I love you?'

She made a warm little gurgle, like a contented bird. 'Many times, my love,' she told him, 'but please tell me again.'

He lowered his head, her lips parted and all thought of war ceased to exist for them both.

That evening they strolled hand in hand through the corridors and along the picture gallery looking at Henry's forebears as they idled down the great length.

'One day,' Henry said, rumpling his hair, 'our eldest son will be here too and his eldest son and on and on . . .

When she started to speak he stopped her, fearful of what she might say, for the atavistic streak which had run like a silver thread through so many Lormes was working now and he had a childish instinct that what she said might possibly come true and he felt he could not bear it if she showed that her thoughts were not the same as his own.

At length they strolled on into their own wing and there inspected the nursery. Lightness had returned again as Petula waved a hand about the room with its newly applied nursery rhyme wallpaper. She pointed out little Jack Horners, Bo-Peep's sheep, King's counting piles of gold, the Queen of Hearts contemplating summer's day tarts . . .

There was no cradle in the night nursery as yet, for Petula had insisted their child use the old cradle which was on guarded loan to the *crèche* until Twelfth Night. Instead they spoke of when it would be there, and filled, and how they would come up after dinner and lean over it to study the crumpled little thing inside it as he slept.

Henry told her he had already bought a small Rugger ball with which he would teach his son how to pass from his second birthday onwards. She opened drawers painted pink and blue (just in case) for which the handles had been made in the shape of blue birds. From one she drew out her own christening robe which she showed to him for the first time, explaining that her mother, her grandmother and her great grandmother had all used it for Danement babies and then she returned it to the folds of black tissue paper into which it was folded, 'in case it should turn yellow,' she explained, 'for it is very, very old.'

Then Henry climbed on to the huge rocking horse which Christine had ordered down from the attic. When he first saw it he shouted with delight. 'It's Black Bess, my rocking horse!' he cried, pushing the saddle so that it rocked back and forth with a little jingling of bells.

Later sitting down in the old buttoned nursing chair which Petula had also brought from the Manor she told him seriously. 'I want my baby to know me better than Nanny. Whenever possible I intend that he shall sleep here with me instead of with her. I do not intend to tell her yet, but if she is to look after him during the day then he must associate me with what I regard as the most important part—night time when lots and lots of little things can make a very little boy lose confidence. I can remember waking up in the night nursery at home, although Daddy says "ridiculous" for I was not yet two; but I can remember even so. I yelled and yelled and I became more and more afraid. When Nanny did come in she was cross because she had been eating her supper and to this day I associate a cross bustling, don't-bother-me-sort of voice with darkness and bad dreams.'

It was all trifling. It was all hackneyed to anyone but themselves; to them it was as new and tender and sweet as was their parting three days later—a little like tearing out their hearts. Yet had they known it there was still a little time left before they were to face their long separation.

Then it was all over; the present-giving—at which of course no one had been left out—the admiration of the *crèche* which Gyles had insisted was brought into the great hall after the midnight service on Christmas Eve; the 'hop' on the evening after Boxing night, with Stephanie and her Harry holding hands on the staircase and being encircled under the mistletoe.

Gyles hurried off to London the next morning laden with small parcels to give to Eustace and his team at their send off. Last minute delays had held up their original departure date but on January the second Eustace tucked in the skirts of his fur-lined overcoat and climbed into his seat beside Frank Stone in the first ambulance. The *cortège* moved off with cheerful faces and shining eyes.

The news of Ralph was all good. He was making steady progress and Eustace further reported that any day now a decision would be taken as to which convalescent home he would be sent to.

Gyles returned home with the glad news for Stephanie and Harry that their Mobile Canteen would be completed by January the seventeenth.

There was, however no news from Ireland of any kind whatever. The Dowager and the little Countess fussed considerably in the privacy of their own rooms and Henrietta's anxious eyes were a danger signal to all of them. Somehow, she had become suspicious and had begun harping on the theme of, 'When Sinclair has been to the Palace we shall go over and see for ourselves. If my girl is fretting for her parents it is only right and proper so to do.'

Dr Jamicson counselled agreement, apparent compliance and kept a sharp eye on his patient lest her defences showed any sign of being breached.

Chef André set to work immediately after Christmas on the making and decorating of a wedding cake. There was nothing more deplorable to him than the fact that it had to be baked within a few days of eating it. He disliked rich, black plum cake intensely and was wont to mutter some very rude French comments concerning such. Instead he made a light Genoese, layering it alternately with crushed meringues with a delicate, liqueur flavoured *Crème Frangipane* and a mixture of crushed macaroons sieved, preserved peaches and apricot brandy. He made fondant icing, lifted up great panels of it after rolling it out like pastry-paste and draping it over each of the completed tiers, pleating the sides with consummate skill and then perching tiny apricot coloured birds between the pleatings.

Finally he massed the topmost tier with a spray of edible flowers in *Crème au Beurre Anglaise*; but he shaded this first, so that as he piped the petals they emerged pale at their outer edges and dark at centre, following his theme of apricot since Stephanie had declared she did not want a conventional white wedding cake.

When all was assembled André began making sugar ribbons, a plaited sugar basket handle and sugar leaves, pulling the sugar out with his bare fingers, despite the intense heat, and shaping little Stars of Bethlehem and little half-opened rosebuds which he entwined in the tall, arched handle. At length all was done. He inserted the two prongs he had left for driving the handle into the cake and put it in his *garde-manger* where in turn the staff were permitted to inspect it and exclaim over it.

Mrs Peace produced a flounced chiffon tablecloth in shaded pale lemon to apricot which she flung over a circular table so that the flounces draped themselves beautifully.

While all this was going on below stairs—fitted in as best might be done between their already heavy schedule—Stephanie, Christine and Henrietta went to London in the Royce to concentrate a labour of several months into one day for the assembling of what Stephanie somewhat euphemistically called 'my trousseau'.

Gyles had given Christine *carte blanche*, insisting she cover all expenditures.

In the event all this turned out to be the most modest spending spree in the Castle's lavish history. Dull items like stout boots, waterproof capes, navy serge dresses, white aprons with red crosses on them and organdie squares folded across into triangles to display the small red crosses on them too, took up a goodly part of their allotted time; but finally Christine managed to lure mother and daughter into Bradleys where a little more serious spending was done.

The date for the wedding was fixed for the fifteenth. The couple were adamant that they would have no conventional honeymoon. They wished to take their mobile canteen to Paris where Gyles had arranged for them to spend three nights with some French cousins who had refused to quit Paris. Then everything the bride and groom desired could be achieved. They wished to attend services at both *Notre Dame* Cathedral and the *Sacré Coeur*. Finally before they left, they explained, they would have time to take Communion at the English Church. After all this they would head for their chosen work, Eustace and the hospital.

Bishop Alaric was for once stirred by the absolute dedication of this young couple. At their request he celebrated Communion for them on the morning of their wedding. This brought forth a somewhat startling request from the occupants of the Convalescent Home. It was stammered out by their chosen envoy who managed to put across that all of them wished to join the Family at Mass, 'if this would not be regarded as an unwarrantable intrusion?'

Christine was sitting with Gyles in his old office when the emissary presented himself. The result was a foregone conclusion, had the envoy but known; for as Christine confessed to Gyles when they were once more alone, 'I have never in my whole life found it so hard to restrain tears, darling. It was so touching.'

Gyles for his part failed to achieve any answer. He merely

rose, crossed to the windows, fell to polishing his monocle feverishly and all he at length achieved was a rather curt-sounding, 'Capital fellers, eh?' but Christine seemed content.

Even the day blessed them. The pale winter sun shone with surprising brilliance upon the small procession which made its way back for breakfast after Communion. The crisp snow crunched under their feet. The Park spread out a white and sparkling carpet of it from which the old trees soared. The stuff was feathered with the claw-marks of a thousand birds. It wound in echelons between the boles. Marguerite de Tessedre had scattered crumbs from a huge bag sent up by Chef André so that while the humans celebrated the Sacrament the hungry birds feasted.

Luncheon was brief. Stephanie slipped away quite soon and then Piers came in somewhat shyly with a sheaf of envelopes containing the wedding service order, which a local printer had put together in a hurry and Piers had embellished the covers in the style of old missals. Then one by one the family produced cheques which Henrietta took from them. The pair had insisted they have no wedding presents. Therefore, as Gyles declared in private conclave, 'we will give them cheques that these may form a small security against the day when, God willing, Harry will accept some peace-time living—as likely as not from what I have seen of the feller, in some impoverished slum!'

That was the moment when the Dowager deftly dipped her oar into the for once tranquil waters of family life. Until now she had been so conspicuously quiet that several among them wondered if she were ill.

She began, 'Gyles, my son,' an opening calculated to strike horror into the recipient, who knew his Mama all too well.

'Yes, Mama,' said very warily.

'Is not the living of Upper Aynthorp in your bestowal?'

'You know very well that it is, Mama.'

'And is not Mr Romary comin' close upon his retirement age?'

'You know that too, Mama.'

She levelled her lorgnette in his direction; 'Pray bear with me,' she requested with some hauteur, 'I merely strive to clear the rubble from my way before submitting a suggestion to the master of Castle Rising.' She began tapping one foot on the parquet to emphasise that she was not at all pleased.

'Oh spare me the irony, Mama dear,' Gyles pleaded.

'Don't be impertinent, dear,' she snapped, 'it ill becomes you.'

The Drawing Room assembly giggled under its breath and listened avidly.

'Then, my dear son,' she sat back, snapping the lorgnette closed, 'it has occurred to me that it would be a most felicitous idea for you to bestow that living upon dear Harry—for when this dreadful war is ended. At least we could keep our eyes on that pair, ensure they had enough to eat and did not actually give away the clothes from their backs to some sad mendicant?'

Gyles left her waiting an unconscionable time for his reply. One or two of the family suspected he was searching for a flaw in the suggestion. Clearly he found none for at long last, after this conspicuous hiatus he said abruptly, 'Yes indeed I think it would.' He then rose, approached the redoubtable one, kissed the top of her head and left all speechless by saying, 'Thank you for a truly brilliant suggestion, I am only sorry I failed to think of it myself. It shall be carried through forthwith, Mama, though I am bound to warn you of a hackneyed old proverb. I can bestow the living on Harry but whether any of us can persuade him to take it is a matter for considerable conjecture.'

When Harry and Stephanie had been pronounced man and wife, and despatched to the station in the Royce the family turned back inside the Castle to relax and enjoy what looked like a remarkably peaceful period for them all. Instead, two letters arrived in Gyles' post. One carried an American postmark, the other an Irish one. Gyles ripped the Irish letter open with some haste and read the brief words on the single sheet of writing paper.

Dear Gyles,

Will you please send someone to collect Rosalind. I have it on very good authority that he is still in Dublin. He has been heard boasting at the gaming tables that I am looking after his wife for a while but that he will be collecting her soon. This must not happen. Her health is reasonably good now so have no qualms about the journey. If you cannot come yourself and

I do imagine in these terrible times that you will be burdened
heavily, try to persuade Charles to come in your stead.
With all my love to all at Castle Rising and
in indecent but necessary haste,
ever yours,
Eugenie.

Gyles reflected, thinking that perhaps he would go himself,
though he had looked forward to a few days of quiet. While he
debated his eyes fell on the letter marked Texas, U.S.A. He
turned the envelope over; being schooled in the ways of
Americans. Sure enough the name and address were plainly
written on the flap.

Gyles stared. The name meant nothing at all to him. He had
never heard of Hiram S. Blenkinsop of that he was convinced. In
an offhand way he ripped this envelope open too, drew out a
single sheet of very thin writing paper and began to read.

Dear Lord Aynthorp,
In all probability you have never heard of me, nor of my
little girl and it has taken me some time to write this letter.
However I have gotten around to it at last. I am coming to
England just as soon as I can secure reasonable accommo-
dation on a ship. This is by no means easy but I believe I may
fix things very shortly. When I arrive I ask you if you will be
so very gracious as to give me a short appointment. I shall
hire a car as soon as I land so can drive down. My chauffour,
who is British, assures me he has driven his late employer
Lord Carnaby many times to your ancestral home so knows
the way. He comes across the little old herring pond with me.
You may wonder what in the world this is all about but I
undertake to put you fully in the picture as soon as I can see
you. I can say that the matter is a delicate one; but is very far
from bad news. I have reservations at a hotel called Ritz in
Piccadilly so will call you from there the very moment I make
base, in the hope that you will be so very kind as to see me.
If you can believe the word of a total stranger—I reiterate
that there is nothing for you to fret about nor worry either
but; well, you will understand when we meet.

Gyles frowned. Who the devil was Hiram S. Blenkinsop?
What in God's name was the 'delicate matter' which had to

remain unexplained? He wasted a number of minutes in frustrating, infuriating speculations then, with temper rising, he took up the offending piece of paper again and read the post script.

So that you may have some assurance of my bona fides I append the name of my Bank in England and the manager's name. He is my British financial advisor. He has already been briefed to answer any questions about me.

When Gyles read the name of this financial advisor—none other than a very senior official at the Bank of England, and a man with whom he had been at the School—he telephoned him, gave his name and was put through. After fairly lengthy preliminaries, he was able to come to the crux of the matter.

He began: 'I understand "Fluff",—for such was the nickname of this eminent member of banking circles, due to his habit of fluffing certain easy shots when playing Squash for the School and then retrieving his repute by some brilliant stroke or other—'that you have a business contact in the United States of America, Texas to be precise, who says you will vouch for him. He has asked to see me and I've never heard of the feller—name of Blenkinsop.'

'Then you should have done,' said 'Fluff' disapprovingly, 'he's the feller who, if anyone does, will put all our chaps in the air in far finer planes than they are havin' churned out for them at present.'

'I see,' said Gyles, seeing precisely nothing. 'But what about the chap's probity? background . . .'

The voice came back with a touch of asperity. 'He is a multi-millionaire if that's what you wish to know. He is a bit of a rough diamond but a good chap who hauled himself up by his braces. Like every other millionaire it's a mystery as to how he made his first ten thousand but nothin' in his current huge dealings on international markets leads one to suppose they are not absolutely A.1 at Lloyds.'

'I see,' said Gyles again. 'Wonder what he wants with me. Says it isn't bad news but is reluctant to tell me anythin' until we meet.'

'Well then, meet,' said Fluff. 'He won't eat asparagus with a pair of tongs I can assure you. He's been around y'know. He may get in a bit of a mess with English titles, sorry old boy,

French/English too; but he dines with me at m'y club and I rather like him. Oh! and one more thing.'

'Yes?' said Gyles eagerly.

'He has the most ravishin' daughter, called Sue Ellen. Her mother died when she was small. He's never remarried. Gel's a massive great heiress, does that help? Perhaps that chap's danglin' for one of your crop of sons . . .'

There was nothing more to be gleaned from Fluff! Gyles replaced the receiver feeling more exasperated than ever. Meanwhile there was the matter of Rosalind to settle.

As if on cue, Lady Constance walked in holding yet another letter.

Gyles' mouth quivered. 'What's yours?' he enquired, and by his tone Constance realised that something was amiss.

'Have you other letters then?' she enquired settling herself in a chair facing his.

'Yes,' said Gyles, 'demmed mysterious, muddlin' business I call it. Please read the wretched thing and give me your opinion.' He handed Mr Blenkinsop's letter to her and she scanned the lines, examined the signature and studied the postmark before commenting.

'He's nervous,' she pronounced, 'and for some reason which we cannot conjecture he is terribly, terribly anxious not to put a foot wrong with you. Of course,' she glanced up, 'that could be your reputation rather than you as an individual.'

'Ha!' Gyles snorted, 'and if it's not trouble as he insists why should the idiot be nervous of anythin'? Whatever it is it clearly don't concern me.'

Constance was re-reading. 'Have you spoken to the man at the Bank?' she then asked.

'Just finished. Knew the feller, he was a pal at the School. He gives him a thoroughly clean bill of health, acknowledges he is a bit at sea with titles but knows his knives and forks.'

She smiled into his scowling face. 'You will of course, after that write to him and agree to see him?'

'Why should I?' Gyles looked stubborn, not to say mulish.

'Curiosity. We should all die of nervous apoplexy if you did not. And now may I please trespass on your time to give you my news?'

He softened at this, asked for and obtained permission to smoke a cigar and when this was drawing satisfactorily, Con-

stance began by saying, 'This,' and she flapped her envelope
at him, 'informs me that Second Lieutenant Lord Steyne will
be drafted to us for his convalescence as from January the
nineteenth, which is if I am not mistaken tomorrow.'

Gyles stared. 'What a remarkable coincidence and how fortuitous, my dear Constance, I am sure we shall all rejoice that
he will be in your care.'

She coloured a little at this and then dropped her eyelids to
screen the twinkle of disbelief aroused by his words. All she said
was, 'Yes, isn't it?' and 'I, too, am pleased of course,' adding,
'I thought you might cheer the family by telling them at dinner
tonight.'

Automatically Gyles mused, '*Devant les domestiques*? well
why not! Yes with your permission I will do just that. Now tell
me,' his voice changed, 'have you a few moments to spare for
my other problem letter?'

She stretched out her hand with a slight smile and took the
paper from him. When she had read it she exclaimed, 'Oh, but
surely, Charles should be asked to go?' She made a question
of it. 'As I understand it, he knows Miss O'Mara very well
indeed and also the old servants. It would be far wiser to ask
him than to even contemplate going yourself. Consider the
consequences if you were exposed to what just might possibly
develop into a scandal, if, as seems very probable, That Man
should elect to appear on the scene.'

Gyles frowned. 'Then on what possible grounds could I
justify exposin' Charles?' he retorted.

'On the grounds that Charles is far less likely to attract unwelcome attention than Lord Aynthorp of Castle Rising,' she
said quietly.

Gyles continued to frown. 'I shall first have to consult him
and put your point to him you will agree?'

'Oh yes, but when you do so, if you will be so kind as to
also put to him what I have said, I think very fairly, then I
imagine he will not hesitate. And now if you will excuse me I
really should be returning to my patients.'

Gyles crossed with her to the door, closed it behind her and
returned to his chair where he sat staring at his desk. After
considerable inward debate he decided that he would at least
ask Charles Danement if he would undertake the Irish trip for

the family; but before he was able to do so Raikes appeared in the doorway, saying

'A telegram has just come for you, my lord.'

Gyles regarded the extended salver with immense distaste, but took the envelope, dismissed the woman and laid it down, unopened.

'What now?' he thought eyeing the envelope with something akin to dread.

It was almost implicit at this time that telegrams heralded bad news. Indeed it was general practice now for private persons to avoid sending them as the mere sight of one screamed warning of official sources and news of someone either missing, wounded or dead.

The door opened and Charles Danement walked in. Gyles looked up at him blankly.

'This damned thing has just arrived,' he said bleakly.

Charles drew himself a chair, grunted as he sat down and then said very quietly, 'Better get it over then, it may not be too serious.'

Gyles' mouth twisted. 'Yes, of course you're right,' he agreed reluctantly.

The sound of paper being torn seemed over-loud in the quiet room, as did the crackle as Gyles unfolded the flimsy enclosure.

'No one is missing, wounded or dead,' he said flatly. 'Here, you'd better read it, that thrice damned trouble maker of a girl should have been drowned at birth. Ye Gods the Delahayes are tricky customers!' He drew a handkerchief from his sleeve and unobtrusively wiped the sweat from his hands.

The telegram was in fact from Miss O'Mara. It said '*Bird flown, suspectedly with companion. See my first letter to Marguerite for name. Previously proposed visit pointless. Profound regrets. Writing. Eugenie.*'

Suddenly they were both galvanised into action. They hurried from the room with Diana padding in pursuit. They took the great staircase two steps at a time, watched by the astonished Sawby. They ran down the corridor leading to Marguerite's boudoir and met her coming out.

'Really, Gyles,' said she disapprovingly as they pulled up short, 'I thought it was a herd of elephants stampeding.'

'Never mind that,' said Gyles somewhat breathlessly, 'have you Eugenie O'Mara's first letter?'

Marguerite stared. 'Of course not, Alicia has it, my dear, it was addressed to her—remember? But pray . . .'

Gyles dipped into his pocket, produced the crumpled paper, thrusting it at her,

'Read that, *Tante* Meg, and let us go to Mama.'

She scanned the words, let out a small gasp, and then the three of them turned and went as fast as they could to the Dowager's private sitting room. Marguerite opened the door disclosing her sister-in-law lying on her chaise longue reading.

The Dowager lifted her lorgnette and looked affronted.

'My dear Marguerite,' she observed quellingly, 'have you taken leave of your senses? Charles, Gyles, what is the meanin' of this stampede?'

The little Countess was so breathless that she just shook her head and sank into the nearest chair. It was left to Gyles to apologise, explain and excuse both himself and Charles.

Then she made comment, rising as she did so and setting aside her book.

'How . . . predictable,' she observed with great calm. She then crossed to her desk.

'I'm sorry, Mama,' Gyles said again, 'but the sooner we know the sooner we can set about trackin' them down.'

For answer the Dowager rummaged about ejaculating 'Tch . . . tch,' as she did so and then exclaiming, 'Ah! here it is, now please all of you sit down and compose yourselves, and Gyles give Charles and yourself some brandy from that tantalus, it will do you both good.' She retrieved her lorgnette and began scanning the pages. 'Here it is, now listen carefully . . .' and reseating herself she read from the crossed and re-crossed pages.

' " . . . *by dint of very cautious enquiry I have obtained the impression that all is far from well between them*" . . . um umum . . . "*of late a young Italian has been staying nearby*" . . . oh, then there's a bit about the Inn . . . yes . . . yes . . . ah, now we have it . . . "*the more scurrilous of the gossips say she has taken a fancy to this young foreigner who has a title of some sort, but then you know my dear how profuse these are in Italy and frequently as impoverished as some of our first families— even supposing he is of such ilk*" . . .' She lowered the papers defeatedly. 'No name, my dears! I think we had better send a telegraph message back to Eugenie sayin' somethin' of the nature of "Name Please, none in letter. Profoundest sympathies and gratitude".' She paused, eyeing the trio with a distinct gleam.

'It is no use you huntin' for a needle in a haystack,' she resumed. 'Have to have a name, at least then we can turn the young scallywag up in Gotha, I have one here.'

'So have I, in the library,' said Gyles with mounting fury. 'It will take time, Mama, and time is not what we have to spare.' He sat forward in his chair, hands cupped around the ballon, Diana settled to sleep over his shoes.

The Dowager replied, 'Let us be reasonable. That young trollop has clearly been gone with the precious Italian for more than a single night so the damage is done anyway. You really do have only one person to consider now and that is Henrietta. The girl is beyond savin'. Even supposin' you retrieved her and persuaded her to see reason the thing is bound to get out. Accordin' to this letter,' she tapped at the pages she still held, 'the county was seethin' months ago. You can be sure they're on to this too, so no one else would ever marry her. She is a soiled dove now and there is no hope of retrievin' her. And that,' she concluded, 'is my considered opinion.'

Gyles stared at his Mama incredulously. 'You mean we should let her go?'

'Of course,' snapped the Dowager. 'Now let me think a moment, yes I have it, Meg correct me if I am wrong; but as I recall the last time we had a bolter in this family was in the seventeen fifties,' she loosed an unseemly chuckle. 'She was a Marguerite too,' she added wickedly, 'and she cost the then head of the family a pretty penny in tryin' to hush things up. Never did the slightest bit of good. In the end she bolted to New Orleans with the son of a Frenchman who had settled there and thus faded conveniently out of the picture. As I also recall she passed herself from hand to hand at least half a dozen times before she finally settled down in America. Once a bolter always a bolter in my opinion. If you ask me what you should do, my reply would be nothin', except clear your minds and bend them towards workin' out some feasible tale with which to fob off poor Henrietta and Sinclair.' She paused, and let the enormity of Rosalind's behaviour present itself fully.

'I say,' she added to her dumbfounded audience, 'that we are all well rid of her. We suffered considerably less than the family did on the last occasion. First she is respectably married, or so far as we know she is, to a respectable and ancient Irish title—never mind what the wretch was really like—and now she shows considerable promise of slippin' into oblivion. Oh yes, we've been extremely fortunate and should bend all our ingenuities towards fabricatin' an acceptable tarradiddle for the luckless Delahayes.'

There was a great deal more in this vein, with the Dowager confessing in mid-invective that she, 'never did like trollops unless they were both witty and charmin' and Rosalind has proved herself to be nothing but a fool. With her beauty she could have got anyone. First she throws herself away on a roué twice her age; then she gets neatly out of the fryin' pan into the fire with some young good-for-nothin' Italian and like as not he is also impoverished to boot.'

At which point Gyles suddenly threw back his head and laughed.

The Dowager glared at him affronted; but Gyles went on laughing at the sheer relief brought by his outrageous Mama's words.

'You know,' he said, sobering at last, 'you have made me feel very much better. You are of course quite impossible, most unseemly in your attitude, but wholly refreshin', aint she, Charles?'

Gyles turned to his old friend and was greatly comforted to find he too was convulsed. For a moment the pair were off again until Christine's appearance brought them both to their feet and their senses and the conclave sobered and bent their minds towards a solution of the Henrietta problem.

It was eventually agreed that the best policy would be to bend the truth. Surprisingly it was Christine who proposed this. She sat, somewhat awkwardly now for she was less than two months from her time and beyond any hope of concealing her condition. She had already handed over the reins to Petula who seemed to be taking her less advanced pregnancy very lightly and who welcomed any added responsibilities which gave her less time in which to be lonely.

After Gyles had told his wife what Rosalind had done, which she accepted without surprise, she sat back and let the discussion rampage from one unlikely proposal to the next. Then, speaking very quietly she intervened.

'The first thing we must accept,' she said, rather as if thinking aloud, 'is that Rosalind has gone and no one has any idea as to her whereabouts. It would therefore be utterly wrong for us to continue with the fable that the girl is missing her mother and wanting a reconciliation. That way I fear may lead to nothing but disaster in the end. Incidentally, has anyone any idea where she might go?' she broke off and looked at the others questioningly.

'Not much scope,' said Gyles, 'remember there's a war on. Remember too that even if her companion wants to take the girl to Italy, he is goin' to find himself hard put to do so. How would they go? Across France? By sea round the Spanish coast and along the Mediterranean? He would find it extremely difficult. Nor do I imagine that precious pair would consider stayin' in Ireland. If you ask me I would say there is only one way they can go—always supposin' they have the money and can get berths on a ship.'

'America?' asked Charles.

'Of course.'

Christine took over once again. 'That is what I think and therefore I suggest we tell Hetty and Sinclair that the Knight has taken her there. It would be the nearest we could get to the truth. It might be possible even to elaborate a little, to say that Eugénie had gleaned the information in her usual fashion, that the Castle had been closed up and left to a caretaker, which *is* the truth and that in Eugénie's opinion there has been a turn for the better in the marriage and that he has had a lucrative offer from . . . well the best suggestion I can make is from a wealthy American who has a famous stud and wants the Knight's experience in buyin' and breedin' with the intent to expand very lavishly.'

They thought about this and then Charles commented. 'Feasible, practical, non-committal; because even if more trouble starts up in some way we cannot envisage at present, we can always blame Eugénie who has given us *carte blanche* for sayin' whatever is most helpful. What do you think, Gyles?'

'I like it,' said Gyles, 'but I think we should first have a talk with Jamieson. If he assures us this will not distress Henrietta unduly, then I for one can think of nothin' better. Mama?'

'Most sensible,' she agreed briskly. She added with a twinkle of pure mischief, 'Better have a talk to Jamieson when the four of you converge in the library.' Thus disclosing that once again there was no small coinage of family behaviour that escaped her careful scrutiny.

Irritated as he was by the whole affair, with the matter of Mr Blenkinsop niggling at the back of his mind, the gradually accumulating accounts in his office which had already confirmed his rightness in assuming that prices would rise alarmingly in all directions, Gyles rose saying, almost peevishly, 'Really, Mama, the espionage and counter espionage with which you indulge yourself passes all comprehension.' Adding thereafter his usual exit line when thoroughly put out, 'And now if you will excuse me . . .' He began moving towards the door.

'I will, and speed your departure with a scrap of fortuitous advice,' the Dowager riposted, clearly determined to have the last word. 'Stop worrying your head about it, my dear son, and reconcile yourself to the inevitable,' after which she winked at Marguerite and Christine shook her head at her reprovingly.

Nothing more was heard of Rosalind or her husband for some time. Instead, the family became engrossed in an entirely different matter and even decisions concerning Henrietta were set aside. It all began with one of those devastating fireside chats for which the Dowager was now famous or infamous according to the opinions of the family; she elected, when alone with her sister-in-law and Constance, to warn the latter that her grandson Ralph would be sent to the Castle to convalesce so she thought Constance should be forewarned.

By this time Constance was inured to such disclosures. She was however curious as to exactly how this one had been arranged, and said so, her golden brown eyes bright with amusement.

'We fixed it,' she was told, 'Meg and I went to London and paid calls upon some of our old beaux. The rest was easy; but,' the Dowager paused and managed to achieve an expression of tremulous old age as she appended, 'I beg of you, dear, do not disclose any of this to my son Gyles. Like his dear father his temper is so unpredictable and I do not feel quite up to a scene.'

Constance choked back laughter and, no mean feat on her part either, managed to look serious. 'Of course not,' she nodded reassuringly, 'I know you were only thinking of Lord Steyne's welfare and am very flattered that you elected to put him under my care. As a matter of fact I have already received official confirmation.'

This brought about some affectionate hand-patting and an added scrap of advice, nicely disguised. The Dowager said, 'It all works out very well, for Ralph is to be sent to us on or after the sixteenth of January which gives you ample time to put young Mr Fournes' vacated room to rights, does it not?'

Constance could not resist enquiring, 'And when is his departure scheduled?'

Unabashed the Dowager thought a moment, counted on her fingers and then said, 'In time to be out of the way for Stephanie's weddin'. I should say about the eighth or ninth, do you not agree?'

She did so, wondering what would have happened if she had chosen to do otherwise. In any event she had no mind to raise objections since she was very anxious to send Piers home before he reached breaking point. So, once her 'audience' was over she hurried away towards the Home determined to settle the matter once and for all.

Piers was not in his room, nor was he in the Rest Room with the others; but she eventually discovered him in the Music Room alone. He was dismantling his easel and getting his sketches together. As she came in, he straightened up and said apologetically, 'I was just sorting out my sketches. The portrait is finished. I do not think I can do any more to it. It must stand now as it is. Would you care to see it?'

'There is nothing I would like more,' Constance assured him, wishing for the thousandth time that she could do something to help him, and accepting that any move from her could only increase his distress.

He replaced the pegs in the easel, lifted a canvas from the music stool against which it leaned and then stood back.

'Lady Lucy St John,' he said, making a small gesture towards the portrait, 'aged eighteen.'

Then he walked back from the portrait to where she stood and together they looked at Lady Lucy. She looked out of the canvas; but not at them. Her eyes were on something beyond them. Constance moved to the left a little. Still the eyes looked past her. She moved again, this time to the right.

Then Piers said, 'Wherever you move her eyes will look past

you. That is Lucy.' And the wealth of sadness in the young voice made her eyes sting.

He had caught and captured all the indifference which so frustrated Christine; yet he had achieved an overall serenity in the painted face which was that of a woman much older in years than the girl who had sat for him so willingly. The likeness was startling; but the talent lay beyond mere likeness. Whether he had striven for it or not Piers Fournes had achieved the peak of every portrait painter's desire. He had penetrated behind the face and given to it the spirit of the sitter.

Constance found herself saying, 'One day you will be world famous, even so I am inclined to think that no matter what fame you achieve, nor how many fine portraits you paint, you will never capture more completely the essence of any sitter than you have done little Lucy.' She wanted to cry out, 'why if you could see all this and paint it were you not sufficiently forewarned to save yourself so much unnecessary pain?' It was then that Piers showed his hand a little for the first and only time in his life.

He said, very slowly, as if the words were being forced out of him, 'What the painter sees cannot always be transmitted to his own inner consciousness; even though he may be fortunate enough to express it on canvas.' After a long pause he then added, 'I have only one regret.'

Constance waited, scarcely daring to breathe.

'I wish,' he said, 'that I had been able to paint Lucien too. Then I just might have understood—more easily.'

Constance walked over to the chimney piece and held her hands out to the bright fire. Despite it the room had become very cold and involuntarily she shivered. 'I think,' she told him gently, 'it is better that you did not.' She swung round, 'Do you not agree, Mr Fournes?' This she asked him meeting those extraordinary eyes whose brilliance she now saw held a certain blindness in their depth.

Piers merely nodded. Then he began taking down the painting. Presently he put it into its travelling case. 'There is something else,' he said.

Again she waited.

'I just want to thank you for your great patience and kindness to me. What is that phrase? Oh yes I have it, "above and beyond the call of duty", I am very grateful to you.'

Immediately he had said this Constance saw, as clearly as if he had been in motley and had suddenly replaced his mask, the face he had decided to present slip over the vulnerable one which he had shown to her for a few moments and then she knew that there was nothing more to be said, at least not by him.

She took a deep breath. 'I am,' she said striving for lightness to match his own and failing to achieve it, 'deeply interested in all my patients; but more so perhaps than is usual for me in you. I would like you to know that I have acquired a mantle of discretion over the years and that, bearing this in mind, should you ever wish to, er, discuss a problem with me you may be assured of my absolute confidence.'

For a moment he stared at her and she met his gaze and held it steadily. Then she heard him sigh, 'I shall remember that,' he said, 'thank you, and for my part if I should ever wish to confide—er, my, er—problem I can think of no one in whom I could do so with greater confidence.' She thought she heard him add, 'but there are things better left unsaid—always', but was by no means sure of this.

Then Lucy and Lucien came running in and the mask slipped firmly into place again. Six days later Piers left.

When Lucy heard that Piers was leaving she once again tackled the Dowager. She saw in his departure a wonderful opportunity for her to make the first essential move towards her ultimate freedom. So off she went and after careful opening gambits came to the point. She explained that she was beginning to feel the constraint of life at the Castle after all the wonderful gaieties of her first Season.With this her Grandmother wholeheartedly agreed, regretting that there was little that could be done about it while the war lasted.

'Oh but there is, *Grandmère*,' Lucy exclaimed, 'you see I have my own money now as you know and I so very much want to buy a motor and be taught to drive it. It would mean I could drive myself over to little dances in other people's houses. Everyone is giving them but I am reluctant to ask for a Castle car, it would all be so much easier if I had my own.'

In this vein she prattled on, deliberately itemising as her reasons for owning a motor car, only those things of which both the Dowager and Christine would approve.

When she saw that the Dowager had taken the bait she then

ventured, 'I thought perhaps, if only to make the departure easier for poor Piers, that if I took Violet with me I could travel up to London with them both and then take Violet with me to visit motor showrooms as I believe they are called. Then I could choose one for myself.'

The Dowager 'dear deared', a little and exclaimed, 'How one forgets you are no longer a child! Well, I for one see nothing wrong in what you ask; but we shall have to obtain your Aunt Christine's permission, shall we not?'

Lucy agreed, all compliance, and then set about some further manoeuvring so as to persuade her Grandmother to do the necessary asking.

Having achieved this objective too, she trotted off to Lucien and together they hatched up the real plot for the furtherance of their own intentions.

CHAPTER II

A Day in London

Without waiting for the results of her interview with the Dowager, Lucy wrote two letters.

The first was to a famous Mayfair Estate Agents whose name and address she had carefully recorded during her time at the Family's Arlington Street town house.

She informed Messrs Knight, Frank and Rutley that she would be in London on January the ninth and would call on them. She requested them to have ready for her the fullest possible particulars of such, not less than three-floored houses in the vicinity of Berkeley Square as they had available for purchase, adding that she was not interested in ones for rental only. She added, 'I should like to inspect these on the ninth, if you please'. She wound up rather grandly, 'I prefer that you do not reply; but merely have all ready to await my arrival'. She then attached one of the calling cards which Christine ordered and Smythsons engraved for her. Finally she laid the sealed, stamped envelope aside to give to Raikes.

Her next letter proved more difficult. Lucy made several drafts before she and Lucien were satisfied. This one was addressed to Miss Lavinia Poole, 17 Tina Gardens, South Kensington. Miss Poole was the very experienced and much sought after social secretary whom Christine had been fortunate enough to engage at the onset of the last London Season. Lucy and she were already regular correspondents. Lucy began it with deliberate intent, by sending Miss Poole a charmingly worded letter in which she thanked the woman for her great help and many kindnesses 'when I was a shy debutante'. This evoked instant response from what was in fact, as Lucy had suspected, a very lonely woman. The correspondence flourished. She sent Miss Poole a Christmas card signing herself and for Lucien and writing on the card, 'and my brother who is hoping to have the pleasure of meeting you one day'.

Further letters revealed that Miss Poole's social work had been sadly curtailed by the war and that she was far from happy in her present employment. On went Lucy's letters, full of such family news as she guessed would be of interest to the recipient. In short, she laid down her lines with all the skill she could muster. This, as is so often the case with seemingly gentle little girls, was formidable in one so very young, whose life had also been completely sheltered.

Now that the time had come to use Miss Poole, albeit kindly, Lucy felt confident she had brought the unsuspecting woman to the point where she was ripe for exploitation.

She now wrote that she had obtained both her Aunt's and the Dowager Lady Aynthorp's permission to travel to London on the morning of the ninth in the company of her little maid Violet—whom Miss Poole doubtless remembered—and also with a young ex-convalescent of whom the family much approved and who would be returning to his home on the evening of the same day. She was very careful to supply Piers' full name and sufficient of his background for Miss Poole to check on his family and antecedents. She had studied her very carefully and knew this was what she would do. Christine had also exclaimed on one occasion 'that woman is a walking Almanach de Gotha, Who's Who and Debrett!' which helped Lucy to this conclusion.

She wrote on, telling her now that Mr Fournes would take her to luncheon at the Carlton to meet his Mama and that both would be so pleased if she could obtain sufficient leave of absence from her employers to join them. She instructed, 'If you can come, we suggest one thirty. If you give your name you will be brought straight to our table.'

All this was pure fabrication. Firstly Lucy knew that Piers had expressly asked his Mama to stay at home as he had what he termed a boring regimental commitment to fulfil in London; but as no one else at the Castle knew any of it, or that Piers planned on taking her to luncheon in a public restaurant, she was certain there was little fear of their being found out. Even if they were, her explanation was prepared. She would say that they accidentally encountered Miss Poole and that Piers had very kindly asked her to luncheon, realising that without this fortuitous encounter it would have been most improper to take a young unmarried girl without a chaperone and anyway Violet, she would point out, was scarcely up to a luncheon in the fashionable Carlton. She would of course explain to Miss Poole that Mrs Fournes had been unable to come at the last moment.

Thus did the biddable, conformable little Lucy prepare in depth for her day in London. She would merely install Violet in some suitable café and order the girl to await her return there.

This left only one stiff hurdle to negotiate and this she and Lucien now proceeded to discuss. She had already learned from a casual observation made by her Uncle Gyles anent some distant cousin's inheritance, that although she or anyone else under twenty-one could obtain control of monies willed to them, it was highly improbable that she would be able to complete the secret purchase of a London house without being faced with some very awkward questions about parental assent; all due to the tiresome laws pertaining to minors. Not for one moment, Lucy thought crossly, could she hope to delude the Estate Agents that she was over twenty-one. The perils of her appearing to be even younger than she actually was precluded this absolutely. Therefore there was only one way she could achieve her objective, Piers must be asked to buy the house for her and then to hand it back after her twenty-first birthday.

The eighteen-year-old girl and the fourteen-year-old boy weighed up the pros and cons, estimating their chances of Piers' agreement to their plan. 'Because,' as Lucy pointed out regretfully, 'it does mean deceiving the family and most of all deceiving *Grandmère*. Piers admires her greatly as she does him I fancy.'

Sprawled on the rug before the fire in the Music Room with Mr Silk, the King Charles puppy, composing his paws for sleep between them, Lucien stared gravely at his sister's anxious little face before saying, with quite astonishing confidence, 'I think Piers likes me even better. *Grandmère* is a wonderful person; but we three are rather special to each other. I mean, after all, Piers is going to work with us, isn't he?'

'Yes,' Lucy stared back, 'but it is still worrying. Ever since he got so very wet and then was ill I think he has changed, to me, I mean. He has shut up inside himself in some way that I cannot put into words—even to you.'

'I don't care,' Lucien exclaimed sounding really rather pleased. 'Anyway I think you're only imagining things. Piers will choose us, you see if he doesn't. Don't you think, Lucy-Lou, that I should go and find him now and ask him to come in here? If what you say is right about money and all that horrid legal bit which I do not understand at all, then what Piers does is more important than anything else, isn't it?'

Lucy nodded, 'Oh yes,' she agreed, clearly not giving him her full attention.

'Well then,' Lucien scrambled up, 'I'll go now. We will get it over before anyone comes and drags us away.'

Lucy stayed sitting on the rug. Mr Silk raised a drowsy little head and moved. He flopped the front half of himself over Lucy's knees asking to be stroked. She bent over to kiss him, then began stroking, all the while staring into the fire and trying to explain to herself what had suddenly become different in their shared relationships.

Lucien returned chattering, laughing and dragging Piers by one hand. 'We want you,' Lucy heard him saying, 'we want to talk to you very importantly indeed . . . Lucy-Lou, here he is. It's just as well I hurried, he was packing and tonight he dines with the family and I shall not be there.'

'More's the pity,' said Piers, rumpling the boy's head. 'Now what's all this about? may I sit down beside you Lucy? Isn't it sad to think we shall not be able to do this again for nearly four years!'

Lucy looked at him rather strangely. 'You do want to work with us then?' she asked rather flatly.

'But of course, I don't know quite in what capacity though because I certainly do not want to be a *couturier, c'est pas mon métier ma p'tite.*'

Piers had himself well in hand and spoke lightly. Lucy on the other hand was still very diffident, 'it's not so much working with us as being with us that matters;' she explained haltingly. 'Letting our ideas touch off the kind of understanding they did while we were doing that *crèche*. Of course you don't want to be a *couturier*, that's Lucien's work! I think I see you as a kind of *counsellor*,' she emphasised the word, 'looking very distinguished, fascinating people and having hundreds of commissions for painting our clients' portraits. Uncle Gyles says you will be a great and famous portrait painter—*sans doute*. I am also hoping very hard, oh so very hard, Piers dear, that you will advise and help me now. The responsibility of decorating a whole house and furnishing it would be altogether too much without you. You see I want everything to be ready and perfect for Lucien on his eighteenth birthday; that is everything except his salon and work rooms and all that part. We even thought though that if you could possibly make some sketches for him, we could actually do the salon once he had approved everything. You have such a feeling for line and colours, I know I shouldn't go wrong with you to advise me.'

'Do you indeed?' Piers stared in genuine amazement. 'And how do you propose setting about finding this house, buying it, all I assume under the rose? How on earth do you plan to keep it all from the family?'

'That's where you come in, dear Piers,' Lucien spoke before his sister had even formulated a reply. 'You see, we can trust you.'

'Oh God!' Piers exclaimed, 'Sorry, Lucy, but really! you two! I just wonder if you have any idea what you look like at this moment, sitting on that damned rug just asking to be painted.'

'What do we look like?' Lucien demanded curiously.

'I'll tell you.' He joined them, turning over on to his stomach, stretching out his long legs and propping himself on his elbows.

'You look like a couple of beautiful children planning some childish escapade.' Despite himself Piers laughed.

'It's not a childish esca-whatever-you-called-it, it's the most important thing in both our lives!'

'I know,' Piers acknowledged, 'that's why it's so funny.'

'How can you laugh at us,' Lucy reproached him. Piers stopped abruptly, rolled over on to his back, put his arms behind his head and began staring at the ceiling.

'You both drive me distracted,' he complained, 'because you are you; and because I must have some kind of protective colouring, like a wild animal when it needs concealment. Otherwise I think I should go stark, raving mad.'

Relief flooded Lucy's face. 'So that was the difference!' she cried, 'What did you call it? Oh yes, "protective colouring"; but, you big silly, don't you see that is just something else we share! We use protective colouring all the time, don't we, Lucien?'

The boy nodded; his eyes were fixed on Piers.

'Yes I realise that,' Piers acknowledged.

'And all the time,' Lucy marvelled, 'I was thinking that you didn't want to be with us anymore. Oh I am so glad!'

For one lunatic moment Piers speculated on what they would

do if he told them the whole truth as he saw it. All this was becoming unbearable. Then he quelled his impossible urge and instead sat up linked his hands around his knees and ordered, 'Now just you listen to me very carefully and I will see if I can possibly explain. For a start I love you both very dearly, although we have only known each other for such a short time. If anything I have done leads you to believe otherwise I am more sorry than I can say. Now then. I came here to recover from a war wound and what was called "shock". Well I did, but in the course of my stay here the pair of you have afflicted me with another kind of "shock" from which I do not think I shall ever recover. Sometimes, when I am alone in my room at night I wonder how I can possibly manage when I leave here with only a few sketches of you to pin on to the walls of my room at home, or to carry with me wherever I go. Oh no, I didn't need those sketches for your portrait, I needed them for me, my dears. So, if you think you are unhappy because you have nearly four years to wait for the fulfilment of your shared dream, just ask yourselves, *what about Piers?* Can you not get it into those two fair heads that I also have a four-year sentence to serve? As to what you now want from me, well half a loaf is always better than no bread, so of course I will help you in any way I can. You only have to ask; but before you do please stop behaving like a couple of babes in a wood. Wake up and begin to face facts!

'In case it has entirely escaped your notice there is a war on, a bloody, terrible war and I'm in it right up to my neck. In a few weeks' time I shall go before a Medical Board. What they decide not only determines my immediate future but also whether I am to have any future at all.' Piers made a small, inward turning gesture with his hands. 'I, my little darlings, am a mere subaltern in His Majesty's Forces. Has no one even told you that the life of a subaltern like me in this war is estimated at roughly ten days in the fighting line?'

Two faces turned white and became pinched with horror.

'I never knew...' Lucy faltered, 'Oh Piers, I never realised...!'

'Well,' Piers replied, 'it does make the point does it not that I cannot be relied upon to serve you for very long?'

Lucien was crying quietly now. He just sat there with the tears falling on to the white rug. Piers put up one hand to his breast pocket, took out his cigarette case, and after several attempts succeeded in lighting a cigarette. Lucy was murmuring to Lucien, 'Hush, my darling, Piers won't go. It will be all right. He is just trying to make us understand that he too is not his own master any more than either of us are—yet.'

At this Lucien looked up and asked, 'Piers, you will find a way, won't you? You must find a way and please may I borrow a hanky?'

Piers pulled one from his sleeve and dropped it on to the boy's outstretched hand.

'Have a good blow while you're about it,' he advised, 'then when you are ready you had better tell me exactly what it is that you want to do, because the tea bell went some minutes ago and someone's bound to come chasing after us very soon now'

Lucien blew rather loudly, caught Piers' eyes and managed a rather wavery, shamefaced smile. He followed up with another sniff and then said, 'All right, but really it's Lucy this time who needs your help, so she'd better tell you herself.'

The night before he left Castle Rising Piers dined with the family. Now that he had burned his boats he felt much better, though he was genuinely ashamed that Lucy's predicament forced him to deceive these people who had been so immensely kind to him. Time and again, in little pauses between conversation he found himself trying to envisage their several reactions to the whole affair when it became known, as it had to, in four years' time. He knew already that he would not be blamed; but this if anything made him feel worse.

Lucy had explained to him that when Lucien announced he was leaving and presented the house, the salon and his career as a *fait accompli*, she would tell them that she had only rented until such time as she came of age and could purchase their establishment without let or hindrance. Nevertheless he was both determined to do what he had been asked and filled with remorse for his own shoddy double dealing. As a result he drank more than usual and on this account, coupled with a particularly high flush which made him look feverish, caused Constance to watch him anxiously during dinner.

When the women had gone, and the men moved closer together at the large table Piers attempted to thank Gyles Aynthorp. Gyles pooh-poohed this lightly then asked him what he hoped would result from his Medical Board and Piers found himself committed to a promise to sending a telegram when he knew the results.

Then Gyles said, re-circulating the port, 'With a talent like yours, I find myself wishin' you need not be put at risk again; but I suppose like all you chaps you're champin' to get back.'

'I'm afraid so, sir,' Piers replied automatically.

Gyles merely nodded. 'That reminds me,' he observed, 'I would like you to know how much we all appreciate your portrait of little Lucy, and I would like to ask you if you would consider paintin' the pair of them together—for the long gallery?'

Piers looked at him in amazement. 'But sir . . .' he stammered, 'the Gallery's full of great painters . . .'

'Quite so,' Gyles agreed, 'I just happen to think you will not disgrace 'em. How do you feel about it? You could come and stay here, we should be delighted to have you, at any time; or if you preferred we could send the children down to you.' He broke off and exclaimed, 'I really must stop callin' Lucy a child. She has a Season behind her already and is quite grown up, she only looks so absurdly young . . .'

'I agree, sir,' Piers smiled, inwardly in a turmoil at the honour which had been done to him and positively loathing the course he had chosen to take.

'Well think about it anyway,' said Gyles. 'I'll show Lucy's portrait around a bit to see if I can get an expert opinion on it. Then I will write you and let you know what an expert says I should fee you. Hate talkin' money though. Whatever you say would be perfectly acceptable.'

'Oh no, sir, I think your suggestion far better, after all it is my first serious portrait, I'm a mere tyro,' Piers stammered.

Then Gyles said 'merely fiddle faddle' and immediately after the familiar words, 'Shall we go into the Drawin' Room? Other members of this family will want to have a word with you and I understand you are leavin' pretty early in the mornin' . . .' And thus it ended.

The trio were duly delivered at Lower Aynthorp Station in ample time to catch the 8.45 a.m. fast train to London. Violet, in her best black, entered a private railway carriage for the first time in her life. She sat, overwhelmed by her good fortune and seemingly struck dumb throughout the entire journey while Lucy prattled away, carefully steering clear of any perilous topics.

At ten forty-five their taxi creaked to a halt outside the Estate Agents' offices. Piers told the cabby, 'Please wait,' while Lucy, leaving Violet inside said to her, 'Just sit here quietly, the driver will look after you,' and vanished inside with Piers.

She sent in her name and was ushered into the presence of a suave, grey-haired man. He took one look at Piers and immediately formed the conclusion that the two were engaged or at least about to be engaged, a development neither of the conspirators had envisaged; but one which, as it transpired made everything very much easier. Piers introduced himself, explained that Lady Lucy would of course choose the house but that the purchase would be made by him and was rewarded by a positive barrage of 'just so, just so' and a kindly, knowing look, which very nearly brought on another bout of laughter. Piers suddenly realised what the grey-haired man was thinking and the irony of it made him smile wryly.

Sheaves of particulars were then produced and after scanning them Lucy said,

'I think that, as Mr Fournes and I have a luncheon engagement with his mother, it might be as well to take these with us and return this afternoon when we have narrowed down our choice a little. I would just like to know now which of these houses can be seen today.'

'All of them, your ladyship,' her ladyship was told. 'If you would permit me, I had intended showing you round myself.'

Her ladyship promptly bestowed her most ravishing smile upon him and murmured, 'That would be most satisfactory, how very kind,' rose, gathered up the papers, which she then handed to Piers, and took her leave.

By the time Piers put Lucy and her maid back into their railway carriage Lucy was the proud owner of a sixteen-horse Darracq for which she delightedly wrote out a cheque for three hundred and ninety-five pounds.

The parting between them was simple in the extreme. Piers handed her a small parcel, lifted her gloved hand to his lips, murmured very softly, '*A bientôt ma p'tite et Dieu vous garde,*' as the whistle blew. Above the clanging of the doors he heard Lucy calling, 'We will write to you soon, but remember to tele-graph when you know about that wretched board . . .'

Then she leaned over the open window and waved to him, while he stood, one hand lifted until she was out of sight.

That evening he telephoned to his parents to let them know he had been unavoidably detained and could not be with them until the following day. Then quietly and systematically he sat drinking in his club until the Hall Porter was summoned to carry him to bed.

Grantham met Lucy at Little Aynthorp station. She was sur-prised when the girl insisted on sitting in front with her.

'I want to talk to you, Grantham,' Lucy said firmly, 'and if I may do so without interfering with your driving, this gives me an excellent opportunity.'

When they were through the village Lucy began, 'I have bought a car, Grantham, do you think you could teach me to drive?'

'Certainly, my lady,' said Grantham, highly delighted both at the news and at receiving such a palatable titbit with which to regale her fellow workers. 'May I enquire what make of car?'

Lucy told her, ending, 'I have a photograph of it which I will show you when we reach the Castle. I will also ask his lord-ship if you may give me lessons of course. Presently I shall need to engage a chauffeuse. Would you I wonder know of any such person? It must be a woman whom Lady Aynthorp will approve as a chaperone for me as well, otherwise I know I shall never be permitted to go wherever I wish.'

Grantham hedged.

'I think I might well know just the person you require,' she admitted, 'but before I say anything I would like to write to her, just to make sure that she is free. She is a great friend of mine. During the suffragette troubles she worked under Lady Constance who called her "my rock of strength". I know her ladyship would speak for her.'

'How lovely!' Lucy exclaimed, 'Of course write to her, tonight if you can because I shall need someone to drive me while I am learning. You see I particularly wish to return to London very soon. I decided that I must also learn about the workings of a motor, so I have already arranged with the young man who sold me mine, to take lessons with a person whom he called "a mechanic".' Thus she prattled on until they turned into the drive and drew up before the entrance.

Then she produced the promised photograph which was duly exclaimed over. Moreover Grantham made some obviously informed comments concerning its general excellence, the lightness of something she called the 'clutch'; the efficiency of the 'braking system' and the car's splendid capacity for 'holding the road', all of which was so much Greek to Lucy; but all as she had been told previously by her young salesman.

Then Sawby came out and was duly shown the picture which he also admired. As Lucy dismounted she said, 'let me know through Mr Sawby, Grantham, when you have found out about your friend, won't you? And thank you very much indeed, I am immensely grateful.' After which she hurried in and went straightway to find Lucien.

To him in the warm privacy of the laundry room she confided rapturously,

'Everything worked out simply wonderfully, darling. I have all the details about a great many houses here and as soon as we have decided which ones are most suitable I have arranged to return and inspect them with a nice old man from the Estate Agents.'

'How will you manage that?' Lucien's expression was dubious.

'Nothing could be easier, my pet. I have arranged to have lessons in understanding the workings of a motor.' She ran through the details of this and then said, 'So you see I can go to London as often as I like because they will never bother to check on whether I am really with the mechanic person. At least every other time I can go off and see houses and eventually choose one for Piers to buy. We have three months before his medical board so that should give us ample time and then of course it all depends on what happens to him.'

The rumble of the dressing gong brought them back to reality.

'Now I must fly,' she said hastily, 'I want to be very punctual for dinner and be ready to tell them what I want them to hear without getting flustered.'

She rummaged in her bag, produced the house documents, thrust them into his hand and saying, 'Meantime, love, you study those; but for heaven's sake don't let anyone else see them. Now I really must fly.' She hugged him for a moment, said,

'Cheer up, it's coming nearer and nearer,' and then ran off to her rooms where Violet was waiting.

It was only when Violet emptied her handbag and brought the parcel to her that she remembered Piers' gift. Thinking it odd that he had given her a present, yet sent nothing for Lucien, she unwrapped the tissue paper, saw a dark blue box, lifted the clasp and there, lying on the blue velvet interior was a pink jade heart. His card lay underneath. She picked it up and read what he had written.

'*This was mine sweet Lucy. Now it is yours because I fear it is the only one you will accept. Piers.*'

CHAPTER 12

A Present from a German Field Officer

Lucy's first priority on returning to the Castle was to draw a ring round April the sixteenth on her calendar—the date fixed for Piers' Medical Board. She stared at it thoughfully, sitting at her writing desk, pen in hand. Eventually, with a shrug she drew a sheet of writing paper from its rack and wrote in her large rather childish hand '*Piers dear*,' looked back again at the calendar and nibbled the end of her pen. After some thought she decided not to refer directly to the Board in her letter but instead to thank him for the pink jade heart, and for the luncheon at the Carlton and go straight on to tell him about Grantham and how she hoped her friend would prove satisfactory to Christine. She then dealt with the house particulars, explaining that she and Lucien had narrowed their choice down to four of which they had high hopes. She promised to telegraph him as soon as she had her chauffeuse so that they could meet again to choose the house together. She added that she would also need to invite Miss Poole to luncheon again in order to explain how, as soon as she was of age she would set up her own establishment in London and would very much like Miss Poole to be her permanent chaperone. '*I know*,' she wrote, '*that I shall have difficulty in convincing her that I intend to live alone. Even when I do she will still believe the post I offer her is purely temporary. Anyway we have a long time to wait.*

'*I have worked it all out. I shall be nineteen next April. My birthday is the eighth. Lucien was born on February the tenth in nineteen hundred. On April the eighth, nineteen seventeen I can move from here. Lucien will make his break on his eighteenth birthday which will be February the tenth nineteen eighteen. So you see I have exactly two years and eighty-eight days to wait. Lucien, poor love, has four years and thirty-one*

*days before he was free; but if you are safe, which we both
hope and pray you will be, it will all have been worthwhile.'*
She signed *'with love from us both,'* wrote *'Lucy'* underneath
and slid the letter into her blotter for Lucien to sign.

Nursing her secret joyously now that at least a small beginning
had been made, Lucy trotted cheerfully about the Castle, busy
with her book-keeping for the Home and with daily driving
lessons from Grantham.

Her contented appearance did not go unremarked by the
older women of the family. They congratulated themselves on
their wisdom in letting Lucy buy a motor and agreed that it had
been a highly successful move for them to permit such
emancipation.

A week after Lucy's day in London, Grantham sent word by
Sawby that a satisfactory reply had come from her friend whose
name was Elizabeth Jennings. On hearing this Lucy promptly
went down to the Servants' Hall to see Grantham and learned
that Jennings would present herself for an interview on her next
day off. As it transpired, Lucy was working with Constance
when Raikes announced,

'There's an Elizabeth Jennings below stairs, my lady. She says
she is expected.'

Constance looked up from her papers, 'Show her up here,
please, Raikes,' she said turning to Lucy smilingly, 'you don't
mind do you? Jennings worked with me in the old days and I
should very much like to see her again.'

After this the issue became a foregone conclusion. Lucy was
well content to sit back and wait while the two ex-suffragettes
chatted. It gave her time to study the woman and make up her
own mind about her. She noted the neatness of her shabby
clothes, her extreme thinness, her prematurely grey hair and
speculated as to the cause of the scar across one cheek. She felt
an instant sympathy towards her, observed the steadiness of
her rather faded blue eyes and was a little surprised by her
speech which was that of a much more educated woman than
she had expected.

Mentally she re-dressed her in, she thought, a well-cut dark
blue tailor-made, some good shoes and gloves, instead of the
darned cotton ones she wore now. These would, she decided
transform her into someone very suitable indeed to play the part

of a companion. When Constance broke off at last, exclaiming, 'Now I really must leave you with Lady Lucy. If you want me to speak for you and would like the post you can be assured I will do so; in fact,' again she broke off to say to Lucy, 'When you have had time to talk, and if you so wish it I will take Elizabeth to Lady Aynthorp myself. Just send me word in the Rest Room. It is my day for sitting with our young men.' Saying which she rose and left the two together.

Lucy began a little shyly by asking, 'Has Grantham told you exactly what I am hoping to find?'

The faded blue eyes which met hers held a curious expression which Lucy was quite unable to interpret. The pleasant voice replied, 'Grantham said, my lady, that you required a chauffeuse who could also act as your companion, it being unsuitable for a young lady such as yourself to motor about alone.'

'That is so,' Lucy agreed.

'Would it mean, my lady, that I would accompany you when I had driven you to certain places?'

Lucy nodded, 'Like restaurants,' she explained, 'and when I go shopping too. My Aunt, Lady Aynthorp, is emphatic that I must always have an older person with me. You see my mother is moving about a great deal at the moment so I live here—at present.' She added deliberately.

The woman looked at her doubtfully, 'Would I be sufficiently suitable, my lady?'

Lucy nodded vehemently, 'I think you would be very suitable; why do you ask that?'

One of the shabby gloved hands went up to the scarred cheek. 'This,' she said, her voice very low, 'and I'm so shabby, my lady.'

'Oh that!' Lucy exclaimed. 'Of course I should supply you with suitable clothes. You see I should not want you to wear a chauffeuse's uniform. If you are referring to that little scar on your face I think it is rather distinguished. Does it worry you?'

'It ... is ... a ... handicap.'

'Well I do not think so' Lucy was emphatic. 'I understand you have had experience in driving motors?'

The woman looked at her ashamedly, 'I can drive,' she said simply, 'I am driving now—but not a private motor. I am only a driver for a London hospital. I collect and deliver medical supplies. In between I do sometimes get called upon to drive as a relief chauffeuse for some of the medical gentlemen at my hospital. So you might say I have had all round experience of driving different kinds of vehicles.'

'And you do not like your present work I fancy?'

'It's work, my lady,' said Elizabeth Jennings quietly. 'My parents are dead. I am as the saying goes, alone in the world.'

Lucy smiled sympathetically, 'Then do you think that you would prefer to work for me?'

There was a long pause. During the silence Lucy became aware that her applicant was desperately trying to control some very strong emotion. At last the reply came, still in that low, rather toneless voice.

'I can imagine nothing I should like more my lady. I mean, I would be living in would I not? Having a home . . .' she broke off abruptly.

'Why of course,' Lucy sounded surprised, 'if my Aunt, Lady Aynthorp, accepts you—and with Lady Constance to speak for you I imagine that she will do so—you will have a nice room of your own. Then you will share the big sitting room which has been made specially for the women and girls who are replacing the young men who work for us. You know it just occurs to me that some of them may already be known to you for they were all working for the suffragette movement before the Amnesty.'

Elizabeth Jennings' face was transformed. She even achieved a very shy smile.

'It sounds wonderful,' she said a trifle wistfully, as though it were impossible such pleasure could be within her grasp.

'Good,' Lucy decided at this point to be a little brisk, striving also to invest her words with as much authority as she could achieve.

'There is only one other small thing more I should like to say before we go to my Aunt. I want you to understand that you are about to become my confidential/companion-chauffeuse. I am by nature a very private person and although I am so young I like to keep my affairs to myself in every particular. I dislike it very much if *any* of my activities are discussed, even spoken of between other people. It is the most important point, that I can rely on your discretion absolutely in whatever we do and wherever we go together.'

Brilliant blue eyes met faded blue ones resolutely. The older woman gave a slight nod, as if to say she knew very well what her potential employer was saying and fully understood. The nod and what she saw in Elizabeth Jennings' face satisfied Lucy completely, yet she still listened attentively to the answer.

'You can trust me, my lady. You may confide in me and what you tell me will never go any further. My dear mother used to say it was spiritual murder for one to betray a confidence. I never have and I never will, that is one thing about which I *am* confident.'

'Your mother must have been a very nice person,' Lucy was so startled that she spoke like a young girl again.

'She was, my lady.'

Lucy rose, 'And one day you shall tell me about her; but now let us go and see if we can find Lady Constance.'

That night she wrote again to Piers giving him a very full report of the interview. She explained how Elizabeth Jennings had satisfied her Aunt Christine, returned to London and would give her present employers their required one week's notice. Immediately afterwards she could take her letter of authority to the car salerooms, collect the Darracq and drive it to Castle Rising. Lucy also explained how she had written to the 'car shop', as Lucien called it and likewise to the 'house shop'. She ended: *'So, dear Piers, if you write and let me know the name of your club, Jennings and I will collect you there on the morning of the twenty-eighth and then, if you are pleased to invite us to luncheon would you be so kind as to choose somewhere small and quiet? I shall not have outfitted Jennings by this time and a fashionable "dinner shop" like the Carlton would probably embarrass her.'*

Before these events took place Ralph arrived by ambulance and was duly installed in Piers' old room.

By this time Gyles' fiat had gone forth.

'No fuss, no staff to appear, nothin'. I hope you understand me. Lord Steyne has suffered a severe brain injury and needs total rest and quiet. When Lady Constance gives the word one of you can go up each day for just a minute or two. Is that quite clear?'

He was assured that it was.

Ralph was lightly sedated for the ambulance journey lest the sudden noise of motor-cycle or a heavy truck cause him any distress and by the time the vehicle approached the Castle Lady Aynthorp and the little Countess were supervising the laying of extra corridor carpets to deaden the sound of footsteps. The knocker to Ralph's door was already swathed in flannel; as this was red it gave the door a singular appearance but no one seemed to mind although the convalescents found in it some good material for being bawdy.

Peak, in his overalls crouched over one of Lady Constance's up-turned invalid trolleys, fitting large rubber casings over the wheels. After that he nailed down a door-stop over the carpet of Ralph's room so that, in the event of the door flying open, it would break its impact upon rubber. The estate electrician, an extraordinary-looking woman who was replacing yet another man-at-the-front was busily removing the bell and installing a most modern innovation. The planning alone had cost her several sleepless nights, but now she had the trick of it, so that when Ralph pressed the button on his bedside table a strong red light jumped up over the outside of the door and continued to blink on and off until its summons was answered.

'Makes the place look like a brothel!' one curly-haired youngster commented as he strolled past with a crony. 'Damned frustratin' I call it, red lights and no naughty gels, 'taint fair is what I say. Who's the bod?'

He was told, after which he held his tongue.

Ralph was still sleeping when the stretcher-bearers carried him in. Rosemary had asked for and obtained permission to sit with him until he woke so that his first encounter would not be with yet another strange face, of which he had endured a plethora already.

Gabrielle was expected, but then Gabrielle was often expected but so seldom materialised. Truth to tell, she was abysmally bored. She had envisaged coming into the title as the spring board from which she would leap into a giddy whirl of society engagements, instead of which everyone she either knew or hoped to meet was in nurse's uniform and thus their faces appeared in the fashionable magazines. There was no social life as such and Gabrielle now loathed even any mention of her husband's activities.

Rosemary switched on the bed-side light as darkness fell. Then she picked up her knitting and began her gentle click-clicking.

Ralph seemed restless. Once he said thickly, 'Well what *do* you see then?' and then a quick 'Duck you fool duck!' Later he turned over on to his side and shouted 'No I'm not dead though I believe I should be.' He was obviously reliving some experience in the trenches. Rosemary knitted on tranquilly. She was bent on finishing a most elaborate first shawl for Christine's new baby before that highly important person arrived. After this she counted on a further two months, if not three in which to finish the one she planned for Petula's 'hair' as Plum called the awaited baby.

Ralph opened his eyes quite suddenly. Rosemary looked up to see them fixed upon her.

He said, 'Hello, Rosie, how are you?'

She bent over him, 'How are you, old boy, would be more to the point? You're home with us all and here you stay until you can clear a five-barred gate and eat a shooting luncheon.'

Ralph grinned, 'No need to fuss,' he told her, 'I'm all right now. The leeches have done me proud. I understand it was dicey for a while.'

'So I believe,' she replied, deliberately non-committal; 'much more interesting to you now is the fact that from Plum to Grandmother everyone is dying to come and see you. So you must concentrate on eating massively and resting as much as you can or Doctor Jamieson will never allow any of them across this threshold.'

Ralph only grunted and in a few moments was asleep again. He slept for most of the next day too but Constance on peeping in shortly after tea had been served in the Rest Room found him sitting up in bed inspecting the massed baskets of fruit and flowers which had poured in during the day. Having greeted her, he observed somewhat caustically that the room looked like a cross between an Aynthorp Fête and a Funeral Parlour, adding dismissively, 'Too early for fruit anyway and too late for flowers. Take 'em away, please—all of 'em.'

Having disposed of his tributes he then proceeded to do justice to the superb supper which chef sent up with, of course, more flowers and a small card written in his almost equally floriferous handwriting, *'Bienvenu Milord, j'espère que vous seriez robuste encore aussi vite que possible.'* And signed himself with a great flourish, *'respectueusement, André Blanchard.'*

'Very kind,' grunted Ralph, 'often wondered what the feller's name was.'

The nearest he came on that second night to even a very slight indication of what lay in store for his attendants was when, after Dr Jamieson's visit he demanded the huge chest of books which he had brought with him be opened.

'Tonight?' exclaimed the astonished V.A.D. whose name was Valerie Coates and whom Ralph had known since he was in knickerbockers. 'You'll get me shot if the Lady Superintendent finds out.'

'*I've* been shot dear,' Ralph retorted, 'now I require my volume of Dr John Donne's verse. You will find it right on the top. I saw it put there, my lass, so look slippy and chase up a chisel. Then you can prise that lid open while your Lady Superintendent is doing her rounds.'

And thus it was; but the next morning the fun began. No sooner had he finished an astonishingly hearty breakfast than he pressed his bedside button and demanded of the luckless Valerie, 'Chuck all these paintings out, there's a dear girl, I need these walls for more important things, so look slippy Nurse and get someone in here to cart the damned things away.'

'Language please,' said Valerie turning on her heel and rustling off muttering, 'Nurse indeed! I'd like to turn him over and slap his bottom, so there!' but for whom the 'so there', of this unladylike outburst was intended it is doubtful if she knew herself.

Besides, she, like everyone else in the Home had been well-briefed. Within reason Ralph was to be given what he wanted and everyone had strict orders not to do anything which would be likely to cause him irritation. So, in due course the pictures went.

'That's better,' Ralph looked round at the bare walls with approval. 'Now you can pass me that cylinder which is propped up in the corner.'

Having obtained it Ralph began undoing the string. 'Now be a dear girl and get me some drawing pins.' When asked why Ralph retorted, 'You'll soon see, sweet coz, allez, vamoose, skedaddle and get them quickly.'

By noon the walls were covered with war maps of France. All flowers had gone the same way as the paintings, Ralph's bedside table was piled high with crayons, pencils, pens, flags of different colours and small black and red adhesive arrows; whilst books filled the shelves, ran the whole length of the mantelshelf and overflowed in piles against the walls. He also demanded and obtained a superannuated billiards cue with which he directed operations.

When Constance ushered in Dr Jamieson once more, both Rosemary and Valerie were obediently affixing flags and arrows to the various maps so as to give at a glance the exact position of French and British troops, and also those of the enemy.

Across Ralph's knees lay a further map board in the process of assembly. A huge pile of newspapers sat across the spotless white bedcover in company with an only slightly smaller pile of periodicals. A second bedside table had been requisitioned and was now on the opposite side of the bed. This one was piled with files, scribble pads and Army manuals.

Constance paused inside the doorway. Dr Jamieson advanced towards his patient. Constance spoke first, saying, 'You know Lord Steyne this room more closely resembles a conference chamber at some military headquarters than a sick bay in a convalescent home!'

'Yes, doesn't it,' Ralph agreed cheerfully. 'No, up a bit, Rosie, you've put that plumb in the middle of the enemy lines you silly coot.'

'Really, Lord Steyne!' Constance exclaimed, 'I cannot have my nurses addressed as silly coots.'

Ralph grinned. 'Oh yes you can,' he assured her, 'when your patient has grown up with 'em as I have with Rosie and Val.'

Dr Jamieson laughed, 'Well, well,' he said tolerantly, 'we do seem to have made a tolerably successful recovery from the journey, don't we? There is one question I would like to ask you though,' he deliberately kept his tone conversational rather than professional, 'is not that board heavy across your knees?'

'Balsa wood, sir,' said Ralph promptly, 'light as a feather, don't believe in being uncomfortable unnecessarily.' He spoke rather absent-mindedly and continued, 'You know, sir, I am very rapidly comin' to the conclusion that we shall have little change in our positions until either we launch our big spring offensive or the devious Hun anticipates us.'

Dr Jamieson now drew up a chair, Constance was sitting near the door. At a glance from her the two nurses downed drawing pins and vanished. Then the doctor spoke.

'You know,' he said very mildly, 'I should have thought that in the circumstances you would have preferred to forget about the war for the time being and just concentrate on making a good recovery.'

Ralph shook his head. 'My recovery, sir,' he corrected him, 'is concomitant with my return to France. If I had not that incentive, my absolute determination to get back, then I might easily be content to drift. After all I do have my two favourite materials for leisure here, books and paper.'

'Just so,' Jamieson was hoist and dared say no more. He knew only too well that Ralph would never return to France or to any other battlefield and was fully aware that it would be a very long time before he could be told that this was so.

'Well then,' he countered at length, 'so long as you do not tire yourself I see no reason for opposing your chosen activity.'

'Good,' said Ralph. He then went on sticking little flags into position so Jamieson simply bade him good morning and left.

Walking along the corridor with Constance he mused, 'Our young friend said that "good" as if intending to leave me in no doubt that it would be far from good for me or you either if we opposed him. However, for the moment I am content to give him his head and just see what happens.'

Within a week the convalescents' Rest Room had become sadly depleted of young men. One by one they had drifted into Ralph's room to bid him welcome. One sight of the walls and they stayed to talk about the war. Things came to a head when Constance tried the door one morning only to find it immoveable. She rattled the handle, a voice from within shouted, 'Hold on, we'll move,' and a moment later the door was opened from inside disclosing her patient's room looking rather like Beatrix Potter's drawing of 'A Dream of Toaste Cheese'; only it was not mice who were stratified, sprawled, packed against the walls, lounging in chairs but most of the other inmates of her Home. Two were actually sitting on Ralph's bed, a heinous offence at any time.

'Leanin' against the door,' apologised the sinners who had made way for her, 'ever so sorry.' She banished them forthwith; but after a subsequent discussion with Dr Jamieson the pair came to the conclusion that, taking into consideration Ralph's remarkable progress, there was really no reason why he should not be allowed to spend his days in a wheelchair in the Rest Room.

'He will only need a corner for his chair and a couple of trolley tables,' Constance said in a triumph of hope over experience. In the event Ralph spread himself over roughly one quarter of the room. He had all his maps taken down. Then he sent for Peak and cozened the man into producing screens to which the maps could be affixed.

'Stick rollers on 'em, Peak, the screens I mean, then the Ministering Angels can trundle 'em to and fro for me and I can stack my kit on those trolley things.'

'I might have known!' Constance exclaimed ruefully when she saw the results of Ralph's transference. There he sat, resplendent in the brocaded dressing gown sent him by his father, waving his billiards cue and holding forth to the assembled company.

Poor Constance's cup was filled when she observed Gyles, pipe in hand, sitting among the young men as deeply enmeshed in war talk as the rest of them. Nor was Dr Jamieson the slightest comfort—for once.

'It's therapeutic,' he grunted, 'that young feller has an uncanny knack of drawin' the others out. He gets them talkin' about their own experiences which I regard as excellent. It clears their minds. Y'know generation to generation is an admirable prescription sometimes; particularly so in some shock cases. What I now desire to do is to slip in amongst them when they are hard at it. It would, I believe be of tremendous help to both of us if we could hear them talkin' freely among themselves.'

When he did at length achieve this, it constituted an even greater revelation than he had anticipated.

By this time Ralph had become a magnet force which drew the men of the family to him as unerringly as his youthful audiences.

Firstly he assimilated and digested the daily news through the newspapers brought up to him with his breakfast tray. Then, once installed in the Rest Room, he disseminated this among his lazier brethren who lounged about listening contentedly and sending up clouds of smoke from their pipes.

Ralph never showed the slightest flicker of interest in the weekly 'hops', which the rest of them looked forward to with immense pleasure. Nor did he in his Uncle Gyles' dinner parties which had become regular events held once every two weeks and known to the Family as *'les hebdomadaires'*. Certainly, as was somewhat natural with his upbringing, he had an educated palate and an appreciation of fine wines; but the prospect of dining '*en suite*' since the monarch was his own Uncle; and indeed of sharing in the whole, over-familiar ritual, frankly bored him. He preferred one of André's trolley suppers with a war manual or Matthew Paris as his companion.

It therefore became standard practice also for the rest to leave him to his books and supper and then to drift back afterwards and settle down to evenings of 'shop' talk.

One night in early February, Gyles and Charles Danement drifted in with the rest. They were just in time to hear a youngster ask, 'How did you get your packet, Ralph? You listen to all our tales but you have never said anything about your own.'

The two older men saw the abrupt tightening of Ralph's jaw and a quick flash of—to them puzzling—contempt in his eyes as he replied, 'Oh, mine was just a present from a German Field Officer, a charmin' type!' Then after a moment's hesitation he volunteered, 'I'll tell you about it if you like. Though part of it is necessarily second hand.' He paused, clearly marshalling his thoughts and then began, speaking very quietly.

'I and my men were waitin' for a signal to advance. We were standin' in a trench and I happened to hear my orderly sayin' "if you are hit, sir, do remember to sham dead. Otherwise if they get a chance they'll finish you off". Then almost immediately afterwards we got our flash and I ordered a charge. All hell broke loose with the Hun sending over everythin' he'd got, or that's what it seemed like to us on the receivin' end. In fact things began to get rather rough and in the middle of it all I suddenly felt a sharp pain in my left shoulder. I clearly remember seein' my orderly fall and then the next thing I knew was that there was an uncanny silence. 'Tanyrate I started callin' for help. What I did not know was that we had been overrun, the order had been given to retreat and all my yells did was to fetch up a German soldier. I remembered what my orderly had said so I hurriedly feigned dead. What I suppose occurred was that the Hun ranker, seein' I was an officer went off again to fetch one of his. I managed to open my eyes to see the boots ploddin' back through the mud to where a great-coated officer was standin'. At that time I thought my orderly was dead. I closed my eyes pretty sharpish as I saw old greatcoat comin' my way.

I heard him squelchin' up in that awful mud. Then I felt a hand gropin' in my holster. I even felt the hand withdraw my pistol and then the bastard fired at me point blank. That was when I got it in the head. I learned afterwards he was a Commandant Schaffenourg of the Chasseurs of Prague. From here on I only heard all the rest much later from my orderly who wasn't dead at all but merely successfully shammin'. He only got a boot in his ear and managed not to cry out. That bloody bastard of a Hun kept my pistol, stole my field glasses, searched my pockets and took the ten pounds in gold I had on me. All this happened about eleven o'clock in the mornin'. It seems we both lay there until about two thirty when my orderly regained consciousness. I must have come round at the same time because I heard him askin', "Are you dead, sir?" in a rather hoarse voice and I must have muttered somethin', though for the life of me I have never been able to recall what it was because he crawled away. I think he said, "Hang on a bit, sir, and I'll try to find help". The long and the short of it was the splendid feller eventually reached the ruins of a deserted village where he found an abandoned cart with a terrified nag between the shafts which some sod had left tethered and then run away. Believe it or not he dragged himself into it, brought it back to me, hauled me aboard and took me to an emergency Field Hospital where we both were given first aid. Though how the chap ever managed it is a mystery to me; he was wounded and also had that smashed-in ear when the Commandant kicked him.'

Into the long silence which followed Ralph's account a voice from the back of the room said quietly,

'They crucified an Aussie upside down and stuck him in no-man's-land to die. We could see him. He was a first rate chap, attached to our lot, y'know. Then the Hun used him as bait. Their snipers were fiendishly well placed, so much so that every time one of our chaps tried to rescue him they popped him off. Then our Number One called for a volunteer to put the poor bastard out of his agony. A young subaltern of ours who'd won cups at Bisley volunteered. He did it in one and then was sick all over the bloody place.'

Gyles Aynthorp stood up. He did so very quietly but since at any time he commanded attention and sought it now, he drew their eyes unerringly. He went over to the mantel and pulled the bell. Then he said evenly, 'We've all got stories of that ilk. It sometimes does us good to give 'em an airin'. I remember durin' the Boer War, you chaps won't remember much about that one I dare say, but . . .'

Quietly he went on talking, deliberately steering their train of thought from this war to an earlier one. He concluded, knocking out his pipe, 'Y'know that's war. Some play it cleaner than others; but it's a grisly business at the best of times, brings out the very worst in some chaps, gold in others. Now, who'll join me in a drink?'

The female orderly who answered his summons was sent for Sawby. In the interval a freckle-faced young Scot with carroty hair asked, 'Did your orderly get anything for what he did for you, Ralph?'

Ralph nodded. 'Yes. I wrote to m'colonel as soon as I could. Matter of fact I had a letter back only yesterday and my little feller is to be the proud possessor of an M.M. Mark you I think it should have been a D.C.M.'

'*L'homme propose*,' murmured Sir Charles drily. '*Votre colonel dispose*, eh?'

'Exactly so,' Ralph agreed. 'There's one thing y'know that I missed and I'd have given a lot for some first hand experience of it.' He paused, exclaimed, 'What a shockin' sentence! Anyway what I mean is that I never did get a chance to check first hand if there was anythin' in that Angel of Mons and army of spectral archers set of tales, or if anythin' really mysterious ever happened.'

Sawby had appeared. Gyles held up one hand, 'Gentlemen, before you get involved again will you please name your tipple to Sawby and he will send up whatever you require.'

Sawby went the rounds and made his exit.

The instant the door closed behind him a babble broke out. Ralph leaned down, picked up his billiards cue, and rapped it on his chair.

'Gentlemen please. One at a time. I'm deuced sorry, but I get such a splittin' headache in an uproar so just quieten down a bit. Clearly several of you know somethin' of these things first hand, so if you'll just let me run over the preliminaries so that we all have the same factual picture of the battle situation, we can then take your reports in an orderly manner, one at a time, and finally see what sort of picture it all makes.'

Gyles was leaning back again in his chair; but suddenly, at Ralph's words he was struck very forcefully with an idea.

Ralph had them all completely in hand. He was now clearing his 'preliminaries' one by one and they were all content to wait. Something could be made from it Gyles felt convinced. Then he dismissed such thoughts and concentrated on what was being said instead.

Ralph was saying, 'But first let me ask you another entirely different question. Is there anythin' in the tale that's rife about some phantom warriors surgin' to the aid of our hard-pressed armies durin' that retreat from Mons?'

Several hands shot up, but this time no one spoke.

'Right then, thank you very much,' Ralph settled himself more comfortably and began,

'The situation, gentlemen, was that the German army was sweepin' everythin' before them in their advance on Paris until nothin', or so it seemed to everyone both in France and England, could prevent the capture of Paris. Quite suddenly there came a curious change in the whole outlook—which was explained in all sorts of different ways, accordin' to the conceptions of the military situation as seen from the standpoint of innumerable armchair strategists. There was one school of thought which claimed that a great Russian army had come by sea to an English port and, passin' through this country had crossed the Channel —that by the way is probably the origin of the Russians-with-snow-on-their-boots-fantasy. They were supposed to have landed eventually on the French coast and were said to be threatening the German line of retreat. This bubble was, as you know soon burst; but people still continued to ask how it was that the triumphant onward march of that seemingly irresistible German army had suddenly been not only halted but thrown back into disastrous and ignominious retreat. Then came the story published by the *Evening News*, entitled "The Bowmen". This narrated how at a critical point in the retreat of the allies an army of English bowmen with St George at their head was seen marching to the rescue of the retreatin' forces of General Joffre and Sir John French. These struck terror into the Huns.

'It seems, moreover, that while the English claimed the apparition which led those archers was St George, the French claimed it was St Joan, the Scots said it was St Andrew, the Welsh, St David and the Irish—there were enormous numbers of Irish with us at that time—said it was St Patrick. Now who can cast any first hand light on any of those rumours for a start?'

Up went a hand. Ralph said, 'Right, David, you first,' and the young man began.

'First let me speak about the weather which I think was important. It was very hot and very clear and between eight and nine in the evening. We were standing on the edge of a wood, resting in a lull which proved to be very brief indeed. Suddenly the light seemed to intensify which, because of the hour made us look around in surprise and eventually look up. There were no clouds at all. And in this extraordinary, brilliant light, markedly limited to one very bright area, there seemed to be some equally bright objects moving. Simultaneously the German guns opened up and pitched a heavy fall of gunfire screaming over our heads. Then the Hun cavalry appeared over the rise and as we swung round they checked. The horses reared and plunged, the gunfire ceased and after a few dazed moments we saw them turn and gallop back into their own lines in terrible disarray.

'Later in the evening, marvelling at what we had seen both in the sky and in the extraordinary behaviour of the advancing Germans, a runner came up to us with a message. When he had delivered it to me and he was shaking all over like a man with the palsy he asked, "Did you see it, sir?"

'I made a movement to my chaps to shut up and simply said "See what?" He went on, "We all saw it," he sort of chattered the words out. "First there was a sort of yellow mist rising before the Germans as they came on to the top of the hill. They came on like a bleedin' solid wall they did, sir, that was frightening enough and I heard Taffy my mate muttering beside me, "We're goners now and no mistake, chum. No use fighting the whole German race. It's all up with us." The next minute there comes this funny cloud of light and when it clears off the hill there was a tall man with yellow hair, long hair it was, streaming down and golden armour he wore. He was riding a white horse, waving his sword and kind of saying, "Come on, boys, let's put the kybosh on this lot". Of course he never said a single word really. Then before you could say "knife" the Germans had turned and bolted and we was after them fighting like ninety. We had a few scores to settle, sir, and we fair settled 'em. But 'oo was that golden-haired man and wot white horse, I arsk you?" I questioned the man. He said his mates swore it was St George, but the "Frenchies" maintained it was St Michael; I found out later from a French Cavalry officer that *his* men swore it was Joan of Arc they saw brandishing her sword and crying *'tourner . . . tourner . . . avancer mes braves'*, no wonder the Boches fled back down the hill again!" He added, "And I will testify anywhere and at any time to the absolute truth of what I have told you." '

Ralph nodded. 'Anyone confirm David's story?' he asked.

Then it began. Hands shot up and one after another the voices came, 'I can, I saw those Boches turn tail and run, just when we thought we were about to be wiped out'; and another contributed, 'I saw no apparition but I did see that appalling horde of Huns sweeping towards us and suddenly without any warning the cavalry began throwing up their hands in despair while the horses reared, plunged and some fell, bringing others down and then the whole incredible mass of men and horses turned around as best they might, in total disarray and plunged back down the hill. I then turned round, as did many others, and what I saw will stay with me until the day I die—for I did see bowmen, I saw, rank upon rank of them advancing with bows drawn, arrows drawn back and of course there were no bowmen as I realise; but *I saw them* and so did thousands more of us. That's all I can tell you.'

'Not quite,' Ralph's hand went up again, 'James, what did those bowmen look like?'

The boy stared for a moment, nonplussed. Then, 'Oh you mean how big were they? They weren't, they were little men, sort of pigmies compared with us.'

Ralph nodded again. 'Anyone else?' he asked.

As testimony followed testimony, Gyles and the doctor moved slowly towards the door and presently were out in the corridor.

Grunting over his shoulder, 'Library dontcherthink?' Gyles led and Dr Jamieson followed. When Gyles had poured them both a stiff peg and they were comfortably ensconced in deep armchairs Jamieson said, looking down at the winking bubbles in his glass, 'I remarked to Constance that generation to its own generation could sometimes work more successfully than when we tried to achieve similar results. Do you think Ralph would have told us his story had he been alone with us?'

'Not for a moment,' Gyles agreed. 'I merely wonder if you consider it was good for him?'

'Oh yes, I think so. Consider the circumstances. For a start Ralph was not bucking about anything. One of the other chaps asked, and by the way that was revealing too—it is now evident to both of us I imagine that their talk of war has included many of their own stories. I have still to hear any of them and I am very sure Ralph would never have told me in the, er, privacy of his own room—patient to doctor.'

Gyles nodded a trifle impatiently. 'Did that little session prove revealin' to you in any other respect?' he asked quietly.

'Meaning concerning Ralph?'

'Exactly so.'

Jamieson was tugging at his beard. 'I thought,' he admitted, 'that inadvertently we had stumbled upon a possible answer to a problem which I am bound to admit has caused me quite a few headaches already. Before I explain will you answer me something?'

Gyles merely nodded.

'Is there any way in which Lord Steyne's capacity to brief and control could be used outside the battle areas? Is there in fact any form of training, or intelligence in which his avid interest in the war could be used despite the inescapable fact that he can never be allowed on a battlefield again?'

Gyles laughed. 'That thought struck me at approximately mid-way in that telling of tall tales session as I now imagine it did you too. I was already busy thinkin' of whom I could go to about it; whose little strings I could pull.'

The doctor's face lightened, 'It is vital that you try,' he admitted, 'the man cannot be kept in the dark forever and unless we have a sop to Cerberus the results could be, er, rather dangerous.'

Gyles rose and picked up the cigar box. 'I have to go to London in the mornin' as a matter of fact,' he admitted. 'After what happened tonight I had every intention of askin' how you felt and then makin' it my business to do a bit of initial ferretin'. Now I take it that is precisely what you would have me do?'

'It could be the saving of your nephew in my opinion and I am not, as you know, much prone to exaggerations.'

As he finished speaking the door opened to admit Constance and Sir Charles.

'I have just finished putting my charges to bed,' she said, sinking into a chair gratefully. 'They were all fairly excitable and full of some story which Lord Steyne extracted from them, can anyone throw any light on what went on?'

After which, instead of the early night which Gyles had anticipated the great clock in the hall was chiming four when he closed the door on Dr Jamieson and followed the others to bed.

CHAPTER 13

The Price of Love

Gyles Aynthorp was in London when Christine's pains began. He was bound for the dusty offices of Messrs Truslove, Pennyworth and Copthorne where once again, after an absence of almost a year, old Mr Truslove was behind his desk looking even more like an attenuated pelican than before. The old lawyer had been very ill; but, Gyles thought, as he settled in the leather chair which the young Truslove—a slightly less attenuated pelican— drew up for him, that apart from the fact that Truslove *père*'s hair was now quite white, or rather, as Gyles amended in his thoughts, a curious parchment yellow, there was little other change in the old man's appearance.

This was to be the oft-postponed meeting between the family solicitors and their most valued client at which, Gyles hoped, the old Pelican would throw some light at last on the extraordinary way in which these most vigilant of men had allowed themselves to lose touch with the late Stephen Delahaye's illegitimate son. So heinously had this been done that the boy had actually turned up at Harrow and Gyles narrowly missed being forced to invite him to Castle Rising.[1]

Only the war fears of the boy's mama—now the wife of a rich sheep farmer in Australia—which had caused her to take her son away from Harrow to be returned under escort to Australia, had prevented a *dénouement* of the most hideous nature. All this and more flashed through Gyles' mind as he straightened the creases in his trousers and flicked off a speck of imaginary dust from them.

'The fatal Stephen,' he thought regretfully, 'he certainly casts a very long shadow which still to some degree lies across the family despite he has been dead for several months already.'

What Gyles did not know was the real length of that shadow

[1] See Book 2, *Shadows Over Castle Rising*.

which even now, was threatening to loom larger than ever over them all.

He jerked his thoughts back as Mr Truslove opened the proceedings by producing a cut-glass decanter of very pale sherry from his desk drawer and nodding to his son who immediately took down three copitas from a minute wall cupboard.

'You will honour us, Lord Aynthorp? This I trust will please. We, er, we thought it a rather remarkable sherry. It was a gift from a client as you might suppose.'

Gyles expressed his willingness and a glass was poured very carefully with a hand which was no longer quite steady. He had often thought ruefully that there was more than a touch of the high born Chinese about old Truslove. Now, remembering this, he sublimated his desire for information and steeled himself to the ritual preliminaries. These were even longer than usual for when in reply to the enquiry as to Lady Aynthorp's health Gyles revealed that Christine was about to produce yet another child, the old man instantly took up one of the quill pens he still favoured and made a lengthy note observing, in between phrases, 'There will be adjustments then will there not? We must not allow them to become overlooked. Settlements too?' he made the last words a query.

'Of course,' Gyles agreed, 'but then, Mr Truslove, if you will allow me to say so, I think I may leave the draftin' of any such documents in your skilled hands. After all, three generations and more have been handled by your firm and you yourself have taken care of quite a number, have you not?'

'Indeed I have,' the old man looked up and Gyles saw to his astonishment that his eyes were deeply sorrowful. Mr Truslove sighed deeply.

'It will have to be said,' he exclaimed, 'so let us say it at once. My son and I have discussed the matter endlessly since my return to health as you may well imagine and we have finally decided upon the only course open to us.'

'What in the world ...?' Gyles exclaimed; but a parchment-like, mottled old hand was raised, albeit respectfully.

'No, if you please, my lord, let me continue. My son and I, after the disgraceful failure we made over the matter of Mr Stephen Delahaye, feel that it is incumbent upon us as honourable men to offer you not only such explanations as there are and our most heartfelt regrets and apologies; but also our willingness to withdraw completely from the handling of your affairs. If you will instruct us as to who will take our place ...'

Gyles jumped up 'My dear Mr Truslove, I cannot sit here and listen to such chivalrous nonsense. I would never dream of entertainin' such a proposal. Indeed I flatly refuse to allow you to continue. Your family has served mine splendidly and loyally for more than a century. Because there has been a mistake— a single mistake in all those years!—you cannot be allowed to form such a monstrous conclusion. Aynthorps and Trusloves are indissolubly linked down the years by the bonds of the closest trust and loyal integrity; so now I pray you let us have no more of this, for I will not permit it.' Gyles was pacing up and down the very small room during this explosion of wrath and now he came to the rim of the office desk and looked down at the bent heads of both father and son.

'Well?' he asked, still angry but with a distinct softening at the corners of his mouth. 'Well?' he repeated.

There were tears in the pale old eyes when the older Pelican brought up his head very slowly.

'Words fail me ...' he stammered, 'such generosity, such magnanimity ... we do not deserve. ...' he trailed off. 'Oh my dear sir, and you looked so like your dear father!'

'My father,' snapped Gyles, 'would have blown your heads off, both of you, at such a suggestion and do you not forget it. Now may I sit down and may we please resume our conversation? On one condition mark you,' Gyles wagged a long finger, 'that never again is this spoken of between us.'

By now Mr Truslove had regained something of his usual composure. With the nearest he ever came to twinkling, he replied meekly, 'Gladly, my dear sir, oh with the greatest possible pleasure. Is that not so, my son?'

The younger Pelican, who had survived the onslaught by looking from one to the other of these strange protagonists with quick startled glances now achieved, 'Oh, yes, yes indeed, pray be seated yourself, my lord, that is ... er, if you so wish to do.'

Gyles sat down with a thump, crossed his long legs once more and asked almost conversationally, 'How did it happen anyway?'

Before his father could answer the young Pelican came in quickly.

'A letter. When my father collapsed and was taken home by

me in a hansom a letter came from our representative in Australia telling us of the marriage and the husband's declared intention to have his adopted son educated as "an English gentleman". A clerk came in during my absence, saw the letter which the junior had laid on my father's desk, and slipped it into the drawer marked private, which you see there,' a vague wave of the hand indicated the delinquent drawer. 'Of course, it was always understood, no matter what absences there were, unless my father died no one would ever go to that desk. So the letter remained hidden . . .' his voice trailed off like the mouse's tail in Alice and he just sat looking like a dejected bird in a hail storm.

'So simple,' said Gyles compassionately, 'and so very easily done. Well as it happens no harm has come out of it. The woman sent for her son, she withdrew him from Harrow and that is probably the last we shall ever hear of him.'

Mr Truslove shook his head. 'I have already instructed my, er, Australian representative to send all further communications in duplicate, one to my son and one to myself so that both of us shall always receive the most up to date information simultaneously. It could never happen again, thank God.'

After a great many more explanations and exclamations of gratitude, Gyles at length managed to bring the pair of them round to matters in hand. When these were completed Grantham drove him to his club for luncheon. She was driving off aftferwards when a shout caused her to brake and look back. Gyles Aynthorp was standing on the pavement waving his arms. The woman reversed level with him and was astonished by Gyles who wrenched open the car door and said, 'To the Castle, please, Grantham,' as he leapt in. 'I have just received a message from Doctor Jamieson. Her ladyship has, er, that is, er the . . .'

For the first time in her employment Grantham interrupted, 'Is the baby coming, my lord?' she asked him softly.

'Yes, that's it,' Gyles sounded grateful, 'the baby is comin' and I must get back. We can stop somewhere and buy you a sandwich. I am extremely sorry to impose this on you when you should be sittin' down to a meal; but I feel I should return immediately.'

Grantham decided to be brisk.

'I should have been extremely sorry, my lord, had you not,' she told him. 'I have some sandwiches with me anyway as I intended taking the car into St James's Park and feeding the ducks with my crusts.'

'I hate crusts too,' Gyles agreed with a flash of his old composure.

'Then perhaps you will do me the honour of sharing mine, my lord. André always gives me far too many.'

Thus the woman drove and attempted to divert her employer's mind. When they reached Ongar she asked, 'May I stop a moment, please?' obtained permission and went quickly to the boot for her luncheon box. When she returned, she said shyly, 'Would you prefer to drive, my lord? It does tend to keep one's mind occupied. Besides I could then eat my sandwiches and pass some to you to eat while you drive.'

'What an excellent idea,' Gyles jumped out of the car and came round, held the door open for her and almost before she had re-seated herself beside him, the clutch was out and the Rolls purring her way into top gear.

As Grantham said afterwards to a riveted audience below stairs, 'His lordship is a superb driver; but he certainly stretched himself. I think we must have made record time; but I was so concerned for him when he called me back I forgot to look at the dashboard clock.'

Dr Jamieson came running down the steps as Gyles skidded to a halt outside the Castle. He waved Sawby away, only pausing to thank his chauffeuse and then the two men went up the steps together.

'When did she start?' Gyles demanded, 'Is she all right? Are there any complications? For God's sake tell me as quickly as possible.'

'She will be all right,' said Jamieson steadily; 'but I would prefer that she fought her battle without seeing your anxious face. She had her first pain about four hours ago. I want you to come into your own library, down a stiff drink and then sit as quietly as you can while I return to her. Constance is of course with her now. Nanny is hovering like a boiling kettle outside the door and is livid with me that I will not admit her; your cousin Rosemary is standing by and there is no reason for any undue fears. I just thought you would like to know. You can rest assured I will come in to you as often as I possibly can and if there are any complications I give you my word you will be told immediately.'

He then left Gyles, wondering as he did so if he should not have mentioned under the heading 'complications' the fact that his patient was showing signs of somewhat excessive exhaustion already.

He had only gone five minutes when the Dowager swept down the staircase, crossed the hall and went into the library. Gyles rose automatically as his mother appeared and stood looking at her with an expression in his eyes which she had hoped never to see in the son she loved so deeply.

She said, 'Pray pour me a small drink, my son, and then let us talk if you please.'

Gyles obeyed her in silence. He put the drink down on a table beside her and then said harshly, 'There is nothin' to talk about, Mama, we can only wait. If only there was something I could do to help her. She is no longer a young woman and I hold myself to blame for ever puttin' her in such a situation at her age . . .'

'Pfui!' exclaimed the Dowager. 'She is a healthy woman, young for her age and she has been extremely careful. Besides which,' she added drily, 'it takes two let me remind you, to make a contract. Such things happen when people remain in love. When the flame still burns there is no reason to extinguish it. No one has to my knowledge warned you that it should be put out. Or have they?'

Gyles was staring into the fire. 'Never,' he answered, 'as soon as we knew I took her to Greenough. He went over her most carefully. I saw him afterwards. I can even remember precisely what he said.'

The Dowager waited expectantly.

'He said, "Lady Aynthorp is in splendid condition. There should be no reason to suppose hers will not be a perfectly normal birth as indeed all the others have been. I prescribe plenty of rest, moderate exercise and ask you to bring her to me again in three months' time".'

'Well you did, didn't you?'

Gyles nodded.

'Then why are you in all your states?' she pressed, 'it is thoroughly out of character. Is there something behind it? For if so I would wish to know and hope that you will tell me.'

Gyles shook his head, 'Only fear,' he admitted, 'only fear, Mama.'

'And that I can understand.' After saying this she seemed to be rallying her forces and it was some time before she spoke again. Then she said very slowly, 'Let me look back for you at my life, my wonderful life with your father and see if I can reassure you. When we were married your father carried me across the threshold and in so doin' carried me into a supremely happy life. We were as one. He was the most splendid person I ever knew. He, I believe, thought the same of me. So the glorious years went by. At last we began to age. Then came the first tiny twinges of fear. When one is young one does not stop to ask of oneself "what would I do without him?" The possibility is too remote for such conjecture; but as the years' tally grows greater the canker of fear begins to fret one. At first it happens only infrequently, one wakes in the night; there beside one sleeps one's darling. One listens to the breathin', imagines it stops and sees the awful chasm of separation opening up. It strikes cold terror. Then the years increase and you begin to think "How can I have been so supremely fortunate? Surely my time must be runnin' out? No one can expect unbroken happiness to last forever"; these things you tell yourself and I knew I had had so much. So surely, I argued, soon now one of us will have to go and the other be left—only half a person at best, for when two grow more and more closely to each other they become a single entity—and if one goes—well there is nothin' left but just a weary waitin'. And now, my son, you are experiencin' those fears at just about the same age as we when they first beset us both. They grow, alas, until in old age you fear to let each other out of sight lest something happen . . . It is the price of love, my son; but it is still not in any way a true premonition of imminent disaster. I lived with my fears for many many years—yours are only just beginnin'.'

Gyles rose slowly and went to the tiny figure sitting rigidly straight-backed in the large chair. He bent over her and put his lips to her hair. 'Thank you, Mama,' he said, 'I shall not forget that whatever happens it is just the price of love.'

Constance went to them at four o'clock. They were sitting side by side now, talking quietly. She greeted them cheerfully, saying, 'Your wife is doing very well Gyles and is very brave. It should not be long now, and here is Sawby with some of André's excellent coffee. He has also made us some delicious-looking sandwiches—put the tray here if you please, Sawby—thank you —then I can pour for all three of us, it will hurt André's feelings dreadfully if we do not eat some of them.'

The Dowager took one and said smiling approvingly, 'Dear Constance how good you are to us.' Then with a great effort she managed to eat a mouthful.

Gyles shook his head. 'No sandwiches thank you; but if I might have a cup of coffee? Black if you please.'

At this point the door opened again and in came Charles this time.

'Hope I'm not intrudin'?' he too managed a smile, 'thought perhaps I could take a turn with the expectant father. What are you goin' to call this one, Gyles?'

Gyles stared at him unseeingly for a moment.

'Call it?' he repeated.

'Really, Gyles!' the Dowager exclaimed, 'Christine does not bear "its", we are askin' you your imminent son or daughter's chosen names.'

With a visible effort Gyles wrenched his mind from its obsession.

He said vaguely, 'We were always sure it would be a boy again and we finally decided on Rupert Gyles if it were...' he told them. 'I cannot for the life of me remember what Christine asked me to approve if it were a girl. Constance, when will Jamieson be down again? He promised to look in from time to time.'

'He sent me instead,' said Constance promptly, 'bringing an Aynthorp into the world is a great responsibility. He asked me to tell you he is quite satisfied.'

The Dowager shot her a sharp glance, raised an eyebrow at her and received a faint shake of the head. Presently Constance went away only to be replaced by the little Countess Marguerite who trotted in saying, 'I have been lookin' for you everywhere, Alicia. Everyone else is sittin' in the Drawin' Room lookin' at their hands; Petula, Alaric, Hetty, Sinclair, no one seems to realise there is work to be done. Rosie has asked me to stop her tomatoes for her as she is up there with Christine so I only dropped in for a moment. Would you care to take a turn with me, Gyles dear, and get a breath of fresh air?'

'What a happy thought,' said the Dowager mendaciously.

'Sorry, *Tante* Marguerite,' Gyles apologised, 'I prefer to stay here. Jamieson might come down.'

He was leaning against the mantel staring into the fire. Glances were exchanged between the sisters-in-law, then shoulders were shrugged and Marguerite gave up.

'Then I will drop in again when I've finished those dratted tomatoes,' she informed them, and trotted off to perform her chore.

By seven o'clock Nanny and Rose had dragged the old woman's rocking chair down the corridors to Christine's door where Nanny climbed in. She sat there rocking furiously, muttering under her breath and making cats' cradles with her restless fingers. She did this for an hour, refusing to budge and listening avidly. Just after eight she heard an anguished cry, then silence descended once more. A few minutes later another sound brought her to her little buttoned boots. This time it was unmistakable.

'She's done it!' exclaimed Nanny, starting back as the door opened and Dr Jamieson strode out in his shirt-sleeves. He pushed the woman aside, ran down the corridor and pelted down the staircase. Then he opened the library door, said round the doorway, 'A boy, Lord Aynthorp, a fine boy,' sounding a trifle out of breath, 'but I must go back to your wife she is somewhat exhausted. I will send for you as soon as possible.'

Gyles was on his feet, 'But I want to see my wife!' he exclaimed.

Jamieson hesitated, 'She's had a bad time,' he admitted reluctantly, 'a very bad time. I would prefer you did not see her for a while if you will please bear with me. She must rest and if, as I hope, she will sleep soon you can see her when she wakes up.'

'But is she all right?' Gyles almost shouted.

'*If* she sleeps,' he answered, 'I think she will pull round all right. And perhaps it would do no harm if I sent for you when that happens.'

But it was not all right. By eleven o'clock, Jamieson had telephoned Mr Greenough who after listening to what he had to say promptly assured him he would come at once.

A dreadful hush then descended upon the Castle. Sawby ordered all the staff into bedroom slippers, and they shuffled about, refusing to go to their beds. Gyles sat on in the library with his mother who flatly refused to leave him. Mr Greenough arrived just before one o'clock. He was taken straight to Christine and so the night dragged on. Neither he nor Dr Jamieson left the bedroom. Constance and Rosemary moved in and out but neither had anything to say. Eventually a chill, dun-coloured dawn broke without any further news being vouchsafed to anyone. Just before seven o'clock the library door opened softly and Constance looked in.

'Doctor Jamieson says will you come up now please, Gyles. He asks me to tell you he and Mr Greenough think Christine has turned the corner. . .'

But she finished her sentence to herself. The master of Castle Rising had brushed past her in mid-sentence and taking the stairs two at a time was pelting towards his wife's bedroom.

The sun was shining now and there was a tang of spring in the air. Christine was sleping once more. Mr Greenough had gone and a weary Dr Jamieson was unrolling his shirt sleeves and re-placing the cufflinks from his pocket. Gyles stood beside Christine looking down at her. Her hair was spread out over the pillows. She looked not only white and spent; but also in some curiously contradictory manner, extremely young.

'Never again,' he thought, 'never, never again.'

As if he read his thoughts Dr Jamieson completed replacing his cufflinks, shrugged himself into his jacket and came to the far side of the bed.

'You must bear in mind,' he said very quietly, 'that it was a near thing. Never again must your wife be allowed to embark upon motherhood or I cannot answer for the consequences.'

'Can you now?' Gyles whispered back.

Jamieson nodded. 'All she needs now is rest and quiet; but I am bound to admit, now that it's all over, that it was a very near thing.'

Rosemary opened the door noiselessly before any more could be said. She tip-toed into the room.

'Sleeping?' she whispered.

'Safe and sleeping,' said Gyles thankfully. 'Now I can inspect my last son properly.'

As if on cue Rupert Gyles began to yell. Rosemary hurried to the cradle, gathered up the baby and started to soothe him. The instant the new-born felt her arms around him he stopped yelling and opened his eyes.

'You wicked, wilful little devil,' whispered Rosemary, 'Come outside, Gyles, I want to take him to Nanny anyway. She's boiling over with rage and fatigue.'

She led him out into the corridor and there, with the winter sun lighting the windows put the scrap into his father's arms. Gyles held him tightly, looking down at the minute face and putting one long finger into his tiny fist. The baby grasped it firmly.

'Well what do you think of him?' Rosemary's eyes were shining.

Gyles said marvelling, 'He's a strong little blighter. Rosie, he's got the hair even now,' and gently detaching his finger he stroked the reddish down on the pulsating head. 'That will be copper-coloured for a pony!'

'He's got the Aynthorp temper too,' Rosemary added. 'The moment you put him down he yells. The moment you pick him up he settles again. Shoals ahead Gyles!'

His father grinned ruefully, 'Blood will out,' he reminded her, 'come on let's both take him to Nanny or the old termagant will burst a blood vessel.'

They turned and went slowly towards the nursery wing. On the way Petula came round a corner, tears in her eyes.

'Oh may I hold him for a moment, please!' She begged, holding out her arms over the swelling which no dressmaker's skill could now conceal, 'to think I have three more months to wait. Isn't he absolutely wonderful!'

There was a sound behind them. They all turned to see Nanny standing in the nursery wing doorway her eyes sharp with rage.

'Give that baby to me, Madam, if you please,' she said bustling up like an agitated water-beetle, 'pore little mite, only just born and bandied about from hand to hand. I never thought to see the like of it, and me, excluded! Wot has had more babies than could be counted. There my pretty,' this to the sleeping baby, 'got the Lorme 'air 'e 'as and likewise the Lorme temper I'll be bound. . . .'

Gyles escaped from them with a murmured excuse. He went down the stairs, out of the Castle and he took the path to their chapel. The door was ajar, so he pushed it open and entered. A tiny figure was already kneeling in prayer. He went on in, walking very carefully, entered the same pew and joined his Mama thinking only as he knelt of the Dowager's words to him and wondering how he could possibly find the words of his own with which to express his gratitude to his Creator for withholding, this time, the ultimate price of love.

Two days later Petula asked for and obtained baby Rupert, explaining,

'I must take him to Plum, please, Nanny, Plum has not seen him.' And this even Nanny did not gainsay. She fussed a bit, she exhorted Petula, she uttered grim warnings about 'keepin' 'im well wrapped up', but Petula had her way in the end and took her precious bundle to the stables, calling out as she came to the harness room door,

'Plum, Plum, I've brought you the baby to see.'

Plum came shooting out on his little bandy legs. He paused a moment, wiped the back of his hand across his mouth, thus removing what looked suspiciously like some froth from a glass of ale, then,

'Bring 'im in 'ere,' he commanded, 'sit dahn'—he drew out the usual rickety stool, and when chuckling, Petula obeyed him, the old man ordered, holding out his arms, 'now give 'im 'ere and let's 'ave a proper hinspectshun.' Over the baby's shawl-swathed head he looked across and enquired anxiously, 'Is 'ee sahnd in wind an' limb?' he challenged. Petula assured him on this point, her eyes brimming with laughter.

'Got the 'air, aint 'ee?' and then a spate of baby-talk poured from him as he crooned over 'Master Rupert'.

When the excitement had abated somewhat he gave Petula a curious glance, 'A harmful er trouble that's wot I'm 'olding! Make no mistake ee'll 'av 'em all in a kilter afore 'ee's much older.' Then to the baby—'Yes, my lovey, you'm a proper war-mint or ole Plum's very wide er the mark.'

He sat down on his own stool and unceremoniously plonked the 'warmint' face downwards on his knees and began rubbing the tiny back approvingly.

'Master Richard 'ull be a picknick compared with this one I'll promise yer,' he observed sucking his teeth.

'Do you really think so, Plum?' Petula was choked with laughter, struggling to achieve sufficient gravity. 'I wonder what you'll think of mine when he comes.'

'The hair!' Plum exclaimed, 'wot can you expec' with you two as 'is pa and ma? 'Ee'll be another 'andful but some'ow,' he gazed reflectively at the top of the baby's head, 'I think this'll be a holy terrer jest you mark my words. Nex' thing we'll 'ave to look out for a nice little pony for 'im ter ride. I'll 'ave 'im in the saddle as soon as 'ee's parst two I will, the same with yourn,' he added balefully, 'so look slippy and give us another to school like wot we did both you and Mister 'Enery. Wen's yourn comin'?'

Petula told him, 'Somewhere around the first week in May.'

'Blimey!' he ejaculated, 'we're goin' ter 'ave our 'ands full and no mistake. Wen can the missus see this lot?' He indicated the baby with a horny thumb, 'Proper took ter Plum 'ee 'as, gorne ter sleep nice and peaceful. I'm rather partial to babbies,' he admitted superfluously, 'and so's the missus. So wen 'ull it be?'

Petula smiled very warmly. 'Ask Mrs Plum if she will be so good as to come over this evening and then I'll take her up to the nursery, Nanny or no Nanny. After all, Plum, you and she are special.'

CHAPTER 14

An Unexpected Volte-Face

By the time March had stormed in, exhausted her traditional ill-humour and settled to her annual ploy of dappling the countryside with daffodils, studding the banks with primroses and generally stirring up the blood with an intoxication of spring scents, Christine was strong enough to stroll on Gyles' arm each afternoon. These tranquil hours bound them more closely together than ever before, chiefly because they both knew now how close they had been to separation.

The baby Rupert merely increased in weight, slept soundly, yelled piercingly and was pronounced the healthiest and most contented of the whole brood—always provided he had his own way in everything. Rupert Justin in fact possessed not only the famous Lorme hair, but also the equally famous Lorme temper as he managed to establish within a few hours of his arrival which had so nearly been made at the expense of his Mama's life.

Sinclair and Henrietta in this comparatively tranquil lull between dramas also improved daily and presently Dr Jamieson declared that in his considered opinion this was largely due, not only to Stephen's fortuitous demise with honour; but also to the regular flow of letters maintained by Stephanie, her husband and Eustace. Of necessity these gave no clue as to their whereabouts, except that all the Family knew by the nature of their mission that they were at all times in close proximity to the fighting line; but even so, clearly revelling in their work, enthusiastic about their associates, they were all three completely confident in both their own survival and the eventual victory over the enemy. As the weeks passed Henrietta's *petit point* bag became filled to the brim with these letters which she read and re-read not only to herself but to anyone prepared to listen. She put on weight and for the first time in years regained some of her good looks, developed a healthy colour and, most remark-

able of all showed a cheerful countenance to her world; until
Constance expressed her private opinion to both Countess Marguerite and the Dowager that she very much doubted if even
bad news concerning the foolish Rosalind could cause her any
great set-back. Dr Jamieson, being approached concerning this,
was non-committal; but even he began to feel at length that
Henrietta was 'a changed woman'.

In this same lull Henry came roaring up the drive to spend a
further Friday to Tuesday with his Petula. Having made cautious
enquiries of his own he took this opportunity to warn her that
any day now his General might elect to make his threatened
tour of the front line; but he assured her with the utmost
cheerfulness he could guarantee she need have absolutely no
fears. In defence of this assertion he was at some pains to point
out with good reason that after the autocratic and terrifying
front-line escapades of the Prince of Wales, even 'brass hats' were
shepherded and safeguarded as never before and as he would be
in attendance upon his own particular one he would be "as safe
as if I were in m'y bed with you, love', mentally appending the
rueful rider, 'and more's the pity I aint!' In so doing he was
bending the truth slightly, for although in principle his words
were accurate, he omitted to tell Petula that the General had
also said, 'no need to look so crestfallen, young feller me lad.
IF you behave yerself I might consider askin' for you to see
something of the front line—send yer on a night reconnaissance
or some such comparatively harmless ploy'.

Anyway Petula accepted what he told her with, at least, outward tranquillity. They talked mostly of the future; of the
Castle's rehabilitation and restoration which would be needed
'when this damned war is over'; of the Museum and its re-open-
ing and re-developing into a profitable venture. He even suggested a number of hare-brained schemes and a few extremely
sound ones for the future advancement of Lorme fortunes;
while both seemed to have come to terms with the plain fact
that such happy ploys lay a very long way into the future.

Meanwhile Lucy trotted about, always busy when she was at
the Castle and clearly happier than anyone could remember
her being before. Her blue eyes shone, she sang little snatches
as she hurried this way and that and when she and Elizabeth
went off in the shining Darracq she waved gaily to Lucein at
his window and to anyone else who happened to be looking.

She had no pangs of conscience to trouble her. Hers was a mind so singly and totally absorbed with her one unshakeable purpose that there was no room for any other emotion.

As the weeks passed she attained such a standard of driving proficiency that Elizabeth as she preferred to call the woman, was content to relinquish the wheel to her and let her drive not only, as at first, in the surrounding country lanes but also in London. Once arrived Lucy would off-load Elizabeth at some Museum or Picture Gallery—her expressed preference—equip her with funds for food and drink and then go off alone about her own intoxicating affairs.

By the time March gave way to April and rumours of a great spring offensive were rife Piers had bought the house of their choice. This was one of five storeys, not the three originally mooted. As he pointed out, on one of their many house inspections, 'With the ground floor as a salon and with changing rooms behind for the girls who will display Lucien's creations, you simply must allow yourselves room for future expansion.' This he stressed, and that the first major expenditure would have to be on two lifts, one for Lucy's and Lucien's private use and one behind it to take the staff up and down to the third floor workrooms and the fourth floor stock rooms. The 'in betweens' the first and second floors proved to be ample for the pair's private quarters including a sitting room and bedroom for Miss Poole, an adequate guest suite, and a bedroom for both Elizabeth and Lucy's personal maid. The rest of the domestic staff were to be housed on the otherwise empty fifth floor which would still leave ample room for Piers' anticipated but undefined contingencies.

Lucy meanwhile had asked for permission to take Lucien and Mr Sissingham to meet Piers in London for luncheon. She had explained with all the artlessness she could summon up that her little brother so longed to make some sketches of the Victorian and Edwardian clothes which were on current display in the Victoria and Albert Museum. Sanction was granted.

In fact their meeting with Piers would be without much benefit of either the tutor Sissingham or Elizabeth who were packed off to make the sketches and notes of these costumes for them after luncheon when Piers would hand over the deeds of the house to Lucy's safe keeping. By the time he met the Castle party, Number Two, Halcombe Street, off Berkeley Square was

not only his property, freehold and with permission to trade
therein as a dressmaker and designer; if without sanction for
anything resembling a shop window; but the house itself was
bestowed jointly upon the brother and sister in the will which
Piers' lawyer had drawn up. Also included in Piers' bequests to
them was the not inconsiderable sum of money which he had
inherited when he came of age.

By some means he had managed to spend the past few weeks
in a mental vacuum. He was determined to use it as his sanctuary until authority had passed judgement upon him at the
Medical Board the next day. By so doing he had been able to
shelve all responsibility for his future like a man dunned by
creditors and lacking the wherewithal to meet their demands who
merely shovels the bills into a drawer and like Mr Micawber
waits for 'something to turn up'. Piers waited, shovelling all
responsibility on to Fate who would make the decision and
accepted he would abide by it when he knew which way the dice
had fallen.

This state of suspended animation was not achieved without
toll. He had become extremely thin. His eyes now seemed to
burn with a quite unnatural brilliance. He was also very restless and as the fateful date came nearer he took to climbing out
of his bedroom window when his parents were asleep and wandering about in the darkness. Dawn would find him sprawling
at his father's desk scribbling the verse which he had composed
during these nocturnal wanderings.

On the last morning when he was so engaged a line of Henry
Newbolt came into his head. 'All night long, in a dream un-
troubled by hope. . . .' He repeated it aloud. Then he stood up,
gathered up the pages he had written and looked out over the
gardens his mother and father had made with such love and skill.
One day, if he lived, they would be his. There had been a time
when he had so done and so reflected, sure that when the day
came there would be a woman by his side. But now he knew this
would never happen. Hauling himself out of his cocoon of closed
thought and facing the real truth at last—that Lucy was not
for him, and if not she, then indisputably there would be no
other, he now added a rider, that he was no longer even sure
that he was even sufficiently heterosexual to contend with marriage to anyone. This he now saw was the real meaning for him
of the Newbold phrase, for whether he lived or died he at last

accepted with a mixture of repugnance and excitement the reality; that he was not so made.

Looking out over the fading snowdrops, the trees all hazed with breaking green, the swathes of daffodils and narcissi along the broad walk and the banks of budded tulips, still and erect in that moment when the dawn wind drops and every living thing is silenced and listening, Piers took the first step towards whatever future lay ahead by coming to terms at last with the kind of man he was.

Piers could fairly be said to have drunk his luncheon at the round table at which the four gathered before going on to see the house off Berkeley Square. Lucy and Lucien were in such a state of excitement that they paid little attention. Mr Sissingham on the other hand was so utterly bewildered at the new developments that he ate without tasting, drank to assuage the dryness of his mouth and throat and so emerged from the restaurant slightly tipsy and with his head reeling. Lucien helped him fractionally by squeezing his hand and murmuring softly, 'Darling Sissy, now you know all our secrets because we know we are safe with you'; which the poor wretch's mind absorbed and later gave back to him with awful clarity.

Once inside the house, running from one empty room to the next chattering, exclaiming, the pair were in transports of delight. Seeing them so, unhampered by their usual repressions Piers drew such solace as was possible and presently, having found some small empty crates for them to perch upon, he outlined his suggestions for the Salon.

'I thought dove grey for the walls and paint work and an exactly matching carpet. It will make the room seem even larger than it is. Then I suggest crystal chandeliers and wall brackets and very soft apricot velvets for the curtains, draped swags, and also for buttoned arm chairs and one or two conversation pieces—' he broke off here in order to explain these last to Lucien. 'Then,' he resumed, 'if we can find the right ones, we should have silver grey, Regency looking-glasses, as tall as possible like panels on the walls and the entire hall should be lined with looking glass, including the ceiling, so that grey pedestals with big flower arrangements will be reflected everywhere, making the entrance seem like an indoor garden, and, with crystal chandeliers here too,' he broke off abruptly to glance at his wrist watch, then exclaimed. 'Sissy, I hate to remind you but you simply must make some dress sketches for Lucien to take back, I shall have to call you a cab,' and so saying he hustled the bemused young man out of the Salon and towards the front door.

When he returned he said, 'Sissy will meet Elizabeth outside the V. and A. and bring them both back here but I think we should be waiting for them outside by then.'

They were in fact barely half way through Piers' suggestions for the decoration of their private quarters when he happened to glance out of an upper window to see Lucy's Darracq drawing in to the kerb.

'They're here, my loves, come on we must pelt!' he exclaimed chivvying them down but promising as he did so that *if* everything went well at the Medical Board the next morning then he knew exactly how they could come again and again until all their plans were settled satisfactorily.

His telegram arrived soon after breakfast and was taken by Raikes to Gyles Aynthorp's old office where he was head down amid a sea of papers. It said quite simply, '*Rejected by Board. Discharged as unfit for further service. Will telephone later today. Piers.*'

Gyles rose and went in search of Constance. She passed the news on to Lucy who smiled radiantly and rushed off to tell Lucien.

No sooner had Gyles re-settled to his papers than the telephone rang. He lifted the receiver and heard Sawby's voice saying, 'Mr Fournes wishes to speak to you, my lord.'

The call was a protracted one. When eventually Gyles replaced the receiver on its hook he again rose. This time he sought his wife, to whom he said, 'Piers is off the hook, honourable discharge, he telegraphed me the news as I requested him to do before he left us. Now he asks if Lucy, Lucien and Mr Sissingham can go to his people for the paintin' of that portrait I commissioned. He says if Sissingham went Lucien could continue his studies. His parents are missin' him apparently. I see nothin' against it; but of course I told him I thought you would wish to talk to Mrs Fournes first. Would you feel up to drivin' down? We could motor cross-country and miss all the London traffic. Of course,' he appended hastily, 'Jamieson would have the final word, always supposin' you agreed.'

Christine shrugged her shoulders which Gyles mis-interpreted as dismissing the need to ask anyone, so he said quickly,

'I should feel happier, my love, if Jamieson said it was all right, please.'

She was paying little attention. Her mind was bent on quite a different matter. It seemed to her suddenly that however they schemed and whatever they did it always ended up the same. Lucy came back to Lucien or Lucien to her. There and then Christine decided she had finished with such sleeveless interference; although if challenged she would have hotly denied that a mere slip of a girl could so impose her will on her elders as to win the day. Even so that was what she was accepting now.

She said nothing to Gyles. She merely agreed that if it would set his mind at rest of course she would see Dr Jamieson and abide by what he said. Otherwise she took it for granted that the pair would go and then experienced a slight flicker of curiosity, also concealed, as to whether the listless reaction Lucy had shown last time Mrs Fournes invited her would be evinced once more now that Lucien was to go too. She thought most decidedly not.

Aloud she said, 'I'll tell the children, then I will see about Lucy's clothes and write Mrs Fournes a short note saying we are coming to call on her. When would you like to go?'

They finally settled for the following Friday and Gyles returned to his office to resume his interrupted work.

The next morning as Richard was coming back from the stables for luncheon via the main drive he heard a sound behind him. Turning to see what caused it he was confronted by a somewhat decrepit local taxi lumbering round the bend and loaded with suitcases and portmanteaux. He stood aside to let it pass and plodded in its wake. By the time he reached the front steps a tall, slender figure was standing surrounded by cases while the crimson-faced, elderly driver unfastened the straps which held still more cases in position beside his driving seat.

Richard halted, straddled his legs and stared up at the elegant figure.

'Hello,' he said cheerfully, 'I'm Richard, I know your face but I cannot remember your name. I do beg your pardon.'

'That's all right,' he was told smilingly, 'I've been away a long time so it is not altogether surprising you fail to remember me. I'm your Aunt Priscilla. I've just come from Italy and it was quite an adventure.'

'Will you tell me?' Richard's face sparkled. 'I like adventures.'

Priscilla hesitated, 'Well now, I haven't even seen the Family yet and it will be luncheon time pretty soon. Supposing I come up to the Schoolroom tomorrow at teatime and then I can see Nanny and tell her too?'

'Oh fiddle,' said Richard outrageously, 'Nanny isn't interested in adventures she's a perishing nuisance.'

'Richard,' shrieked Priscilla, scandalised, 'where on earth did you learn such awful words?'

'Plum, Plum cusses wunnerful, shall I tell you some?' he looked up eagerly.

'No thank you,' said Priscilla hurriedly. 'Is that all, Mr Miggs? Well if you would be so good as to pull the bell Sawby will send his footmen to collect them.'

The old cab driver smiled pityingly. 'There beant no footmen now Miss, it's footwimmen. The men is gorne to fight,' he warned her.

Priscilla shook her head as if someone had dealt her a blow, 'No footmen!' she repeated blankly. 'Good heavens!' She dipped into the big tasselled bag which swung from one wrist, then looked at the coins she took from an inner purse as if trying to recall what they signified. The old man toddled up the steps, pulled the bell and toddled down again.

Priscilla held out her hand with the coins on the gloved palm.

'Will that be all right, Mr Miggs?' she asked diffidently, 'I'm out of practice.'

'Fine, thank you, Miss.' Miggs took the coins hurriedly, nervous she might regain memory and delete something from this grandiloquent over-tipping.

Then Sawby appeared and Petula, looking out from an opened window on the first floor saw them both and called down 'Prissy, how divine! coming down, hold on—I'm a bit slower than usual these days,' as her curly head disappeared. Nanny's voice could be heard from farther aloft, 'Master Richard, come upstairs this minnit and wash your hands. Raikes is waiting to inspec' you.'

Richard groaned. 'I'll have to go. That old warmint will only go on yelling if I don't. Now remember, tomorrow at tea-time or I'll give yer a rummagin' dose.' This last, with a clear lapse into Plum language before he took to his heels and fled.

Luncheon was very gay and very sad in about equal ratio. Priscilla recounted her extraordinary passage from Tuscany to Southampton via a weary and uncomfortable journey by train across France to Cherbourg. She made light of the whole business, sending ripples of sympathetic laughter around the table.

'You see,' she explained when she had done, 'I suddenly felt like a traitor out there surrounded by friends and luxury and I simply had to get back and see if I could help in any way. You don't know how absolutely frightful it can be imagining all sorts of terrifying things happening to all of you and not being able to find out. What settled it was a cousin of Francesca and Benito's who suddenly appeared. It turned out you knew him, Gyles, when you were hunting for your fountains.'

Gyles smiled, 'A world and a half away,' he said quietly.

'I dare say,' she nodded sympathetically, 'you must remember him, Gyles, Count Paolo Vincetti, he has an art gallery in Florence, and another in Rome. He helped Henry with his Italian soon after you arrived.'

Interest awoke in Gyles' eyes. 'Oh yes,' he agreed, 'nice feller, brought Henry on splendidly.'

'That's right—no thank you, Sawby, I don't eat puddings.' She caught the Dowager's questioning glance and hurriedly explained, 'It's all the willowy look in Italy you see. Everyone takes vows against eating pasta; they diet like anything and spend hours squashing in their, er,' again she caught the glint in the Dowager's eyes and amended 'their, er, fronts.'

Little Marguerite chuckled, 'Yours does seem to have diminished my dear,' she observed.

Gyles cleared his throat in warning as the servants were still hovering.

'Well anyway, Gyles, I was telling you about Paolo. Just before war broke out he went to Ireland on what he called a Treasure hunt . . .'

Quite deliberately Christine shot the contents of her wine glass across the table, exclaimed, 'Oh dear! how clumsy,' then added as she rose, 'never mind, Sawby, we were just leaving. Priscilla come into the Blue Drawing Room and then we can listen to our heart's content to all your fascinating news.' And suiting action to words she collected eyes. Outside the door she linked arms with Priscilla and steered her in an entirely different direction.

Once safely out of earshot, and glancing behind her to make sure the rest of the women had gone into the Blue Drawing Room, Christine said hurriedly, 'You must forgive me, Prissy, but there are things you do not know about yet. I simply had to cut you short, so now, dear, if you will come up to my room I will try to explain.'

Priscilla complied, but her eyes blazed with comprehension which Christine in her preoccupation wholly failed to observe.

Priscilla chatted on brightly about trivialities until Christine had closed the door of her private sitting room, then she said, speaking much more slowly than was usual for her,

'Christine, it was the word "Ireland" that brought you up short was it not?'

'Yes,' Christine admitted. 'Why?'

'That is precisely why I said it,' Priscilla put her hands to her hair which was dressed in a style hitherto unseen by the family. She strolled across to the looking glass over the mantelshelf where she began correcting some invisible faults in what her reflection gave her back. 'Oh yes,' she said, 'I must admit I had forgotten Aunt Hetty though.'

'You mean,' Christine stared incredulously, 'you mean you know?'

Instead of answering Priscilla abruptly put one arm around her waist and drew her down on to a couch. Then she settled beside her and said, 'Listen now and I will tell you. Paolo appeared quite suddenly at the Palazzo with a girl and a bundle. Both were in a sorry state, woebegone, bedraggled; but through all this her beauty showed clearly enough. Francesca behaved superbly as you might imagine. She exclaimed on seeing them and long before any of the rest of us had gathered our wits, "Oh you poor things. No explanations please. What you both need are hot baths, clean clothes and food." She swept forward, put an arm around Rosalind's shoulder and said gently, "Come with me, my dear, my woman shall maid you and I will see whether I have anything suited to your lovely little face, which you can wear until we have had time to replenish your wardrobe."

'Rosalind shook her head unbelievingly, and then the slow tears began to run down her face. She was simply smothered in dust, well they both were actually and when the tears made streaks she looked anything but lovely. Her hair was down and flowing over her shoulders too and the hem of her frock was all muddied and ragged.

'Francesca was not long gone. When she came back into the room, Paolo looked up at her and said quite simply, "I want to marry her. She is someone else's wife and believe me she has had hell. Thank heavens neither we nor they are Catholics. What a relief we are one of the rare Protestant Italian families. Will you take her under your wing 'Cesca?" '

'What did Francesca say?' whispered Christine.

Priscilla's eyes were very warm. 'She said quite simply "I have done already. Now for pity's sake go and make yourself presentable before Benito returns. Then you can present her properly. By the way what is her name?"

'When Paolo told her I gasped. You remember that house-party I went to in Limerick just before the war?'

Christine nodded mutely.

'Well I met Gavin Fitzpatrick. As a matter of fact he tried his blandishments on me and as you can imagine received short shrift. I heard the devil an' all about that fine fellow I can tell you. But of course I know nothing of your side of any of this. Well anyway Rosalind was finally put to bed after being cleaned up. Then Francesca sent for her doctor who prescribed complete rest for several days. He said she was in an acute state of exhaustion. Later when he learned what had happened in Limerick he bore her off to a clinic and there she was when I left. I may say if it had not been for Paolo I do not think I should ever have reached here alive. He was perfectly splendid. But he is very young, wildly impressionable, a typical Latin and I have no idea whether the pair of them will make a go of it.'

Christine tried to order her thoughts. She had listened appalled to Priscilla's narrative. All her upbringing, all her essential fastidiousness recoiled from what she heard. That a gently born, carefully nurtured girl, a mere eighteen-year-old should run away with a man old enough to be her father was enough to put her beyond the pale according to Christine's standards; but that she could thereafter pass herself 'from hand to hand' in such a wanton manner was past imagining, or condoning either.

As the story unfolded, so her heart hardened. Rosalind, she decided was a bad girl and in so far as Christine's judgement went she would, inevitably, come to a bad end as did all trollops. Thus ran her thought as she sat, head bent looking at her hands. Yet none of it really mattered now. At this juncture, the only vitally important thing was to ensure no further harm could come to Henrietta and 'poor' Sinclair.

She began to speak, taking Priscilla step by step through the events which had brought both parents down. She recounted what Miss O'Mara had written from Ireland and what Sir Charles had learned when he went to visit his old 'flame' and there encountered Miss O'Mara's Abigail.

She ended, 'So you see my dear, we must be extremely careful. Now that you have been warned of the perils so must you. Not one word of this must pass your lips until Gyles has been told and has had time to discuss the matter with Dr Jamieson and Lady Constance.'

'And who pray is she?' enquired Priscilla coolly. 'She is a beauty, *molto bella, sans* any *doute,* but whence comes the lady and what is she doing in this Castle?'

Christine was compelled to begin again, this time relating the complicated story which had been kept from Priscilla last time she was in England.

'Sooo,' was all her companion said, save for, as a mere afterthought, 'Well if you ask *me* she'll end up marrying Charles Danement.'

Christine flushed. 'That,' she said evenly 'is what we all hope. How clever of you, my dear.' Clearly her hackles were up now. She added, 'And now if you will excuse me you will want to unpack anyway and I must see Gyles at once, there is no time to be lost.'

Priscilla took her *congé* calmly, pausing only long enough to say, 'Now, darling, do not take this too seriously. Paolo is handsome, charming and of good family. There is not any great wealth as we know it, but he makes a very good thing out of his art galleries and is not exactly penniless. Rosalind might have done much worse. Is that not a consoling thought?'

Christine made no reply, she merely escorted her to the door and waiting for a moment she then almost ran out herself. She flung open the door of Gyles' office and burst out, 'Gyles, I must talk to you immediately. I have had the shock of my life and I simply do not comprehend how people can behave in such a way!'

Somewhat wearily Gyles laid down his pen once more.

The afternoon's post, fortuitously, brought Sinclair's command to present himself at the Palace to receive his dead son's decoration. Henrietta was already excited over her latest letter from Stephanie who seemed to be enjoying both her husband and their shared work. She read the letter aloud to Sinclair, pausing once to interject, 'I must confess I would be alternately terrified and nauseated by the awful conditions those two are encountering, however,' she then continued reading. When she had done she folded the pages, stuffed them with all the rest of her hoard into her now bulging embroidery bag and looked up startled from this activity at an exclamation from her husband.

'It's ... come!' he exclaimed, waving the letter with his good hand, 'we are both asked, my dear.'

'Oh dear,' said Henrietta despondently, 'whatever shall I wear?'

'Quiet ... elegant ... black,' said Sinclair a trifle sharply, 'only ... mourning would ... be ... suitable surely?'

'Yes I suppose you are right,' Henrietta sounded wistful, 'such a memorable occasion!' but whether this was intended to imply she wished to divest herself of her mourning garments for the 'memorable occasion' or for some other, more obscure reason she did not reveal. Sinclair merely grunted, his mind fully occupied.

'We ... had ... better ... travel ... up ... the ... night ... before ... I ... think. We ... could ... stay ... at ... Browns,' he decided. He was sharply reminded of the last occasion he had stayed there, for Stephanie's arrest, and so lapsed into a little brooding from which he emerged with what seemed like a most singular *non sequitur* to his spouse, who was incapable of reading his thoughts. 'What a happy ending anyway!'

'Sinclair!' exclaimed Henrietta, deeply shocked, 'happy ending indeed. Our eldest son's death!' and this led to a lengthy and tangled disclaimer.

After dinner they all drifted into the Blue Drawing Room. Even Sinclair and Henrietta decided to join them and when Sawby and Raikes had dispensed coffee and tisanes, Ralph walked in and took his place among them. He was by now well enough to spend a great deal of his time with the Family.

At first the conversation was dominated by Priscilla, for all the women were eager for news of their Italian friends. The weight of war lay heavily upon them all. The general acceptance of an imminent spring offensive chilled their thoughts. This, in the case of the women, made them almost greedy for trivia.

Even so, they had come a long way in the nine months which lay behind them and the way of life they had always known before. Though all would have denied it hotly they were still hankering for their old, luxurious ways which, cut off as they were by choice from the gaieties which had previously filled their days, was only to be expected. When they were alone together and despite their new and heavy responsibilities, their talk always turned to what life had been like before and which they had enjoyed so tremendously.

This was what divided them from the men of the family who remained within the Castle. For them there was no room in their minds for nostalgia. Their days were filled to the exclusion of any need for looking back. Their concern now was wholly with stewardship for those who might be fortunte enough to return. It demanded their whole attention. Only three nights ago Gyles had shown Charles Danement and Petula the figures he had listed and the assessments he had made.

He came straight to the point, this essentially quiet man, whose forays into temperamental outbursts were no more than a safety valve from time to time now that the reins of government were in his hands alone. War or peace made no real difference to Gyles Aynthorp's priorities. They were quite simply, his wife, his castle and his sons. Now that Christine was making steady recovery, and his elder sons were beyond his jurisdiction, the whole weight of his mind was directed upon the Castle and its lands.

'There's no point in dodgin' the issue,' he told them heavily, 'we shall have to have more labour, otherwise my lands and yours Charles will both be in a sorry state by the time this war is over.' He rifled through a mass of papers, found the one he sought and laid it in front of him. 'Let me give you one simple example— fallen timber—and on estates like ours timber must fall. This has always been cleared away immediately, sawn into logs for the fires, cracked into kindlin' for lightin' them, trimmed into bean poles, bunched into pea sticks and cut into posts. Now the Home Park is littered with dead wood. All work is fallin' behind schedule despite the willin'ness and the capability of the women who have replaced our men. Look at the hours they're workin'.' He turned the paper round for them to study.

'They have done splendidly, but what is done is simply not enough. Daily capacity falls accordin' to my estimates about twenty-five per cent behind what the men did in roughly an hour a day less. It stands to reason! Where it took four men to manhandle timber it takes six women. Where drays were loaded by eight in a mere half hour, it now takes ten women an hour or more; added to which they're behind with the sowin', and those dear old dodderers are laggin' with their repairs to hen houses, pig styes, barns and stablin'. Men of sixty and more cannot encompass the work done by men under thirty, at least not unless it's brain work and not sheer manual labour. Then take the question of thatchin'; we've one skilled thatcher left for all my cottages which is farcical. I have combed both Upper and Lower Aynthorp and the outlying villages too. It is the same story everywhere. That notice on the doors—"A Man Has Gone From This House To Fight For King and Country", and nothing inside but a parcel of women and gels. And the gels will be gone soon too, into munition factories, on to buses, I tell you we shall have to look farther afield, advertise even, for take on more labour we must or everythin' will run to seed and that is quite unthinkable.' He lapsed into silence.

'Have we exhausted our ex-suffragette potential?' Petula asked, frowning at Gyles' notes.

Neither answered her, so she went on, 'Lucy seemed to have no difficulty in finding a chauffeuse. She asked Grantham and the woman produced one. How would it be if I went down when they were at their evening meal? I could talk to them. Find out who has any contacts we could try. Everyone seems to like them and according to Mrs Peace they dread the war coming to an end. They would like to stay here permanently.'

'At a price,' said Gyles gloomily. 'That is another factor. The cost of livin' is goin' up by leaps and bounds. Heatin' the stove-houses has become a major consideration. I admit that even at present prices it is highly profitable to maintain 'em. That feller Ritz, and Escoffier too pay high for hothouse fruits on which the war profiteers gorge themselves. Wages are shootin' up. With all the labour we employ at present it makes a tidy annual sum I can tell you. Food is rocketin' and it has by no means reached peak prices yet. I estimate that all will have doubled in price before this affair ends. I tell you, Charles, when it does, I'm absolutely determined to go into food conservation. Explore the possibilities, see if there is not some way of keepin' food indefinitely. If only we could find the scientific wallahs who specialise in such things. Oh, it's no use lookin' for 'em now. They're all earnin' high fees in Government employ, "engaged upon essential war work" isn't that the phrase? Which is all academic and has no bearin' on the matters which bay us now,' he added apologetically.

Petula did sound the women and she reported she had only partially succeeded. Names and addresses were contributed, certainly, but she was told after some initial backing and filling that it was unlikely these would bring forth additional labour unless Gyles Aynthorp were prepared to match the monies they were earning currently. On the credit side, and as the women thawed out, they admitted that their endorsement of the living conditions at the Castle, plus the fact that they were so well housed and fed in addition to what they were paid could influence decisions. Eventually Petula sat down to the task of writing to every name given. Then, perforce they had to wait. Meanwhile the backlog of work piled up.

It was of these matters that Gyles brooded as he stretched his long legs in a Drawing Room chair.

Vaguely he realised that the conversation around him had turned from Priscilla's chatter to Sinclair's haltingly told news of the forthcoming Investure. So he relapsed into his brooding, only looking up from a frowning contemplation of his embroidered black velvet slippers as Ralph rose and moved into a chair beside him. Then, rousing himself with an effort he managed a fleeting smile. In the past weeks he had developed a great admiration for this long-headed nephew of his on whom he now depended for his daily news of the war's progress. Of late he had made a point of dropping in to see him for his always succinct summary of what news the daily papers contained. Now, as Ralph settled down beside him and Sinclair stammered out his plans for the great occasion, Gyles heard Ralph saying very softly,

'I saw Stephen you know. I ran into him in a Belgian *estaminet.*'

Gyles grunted, then asked dryly, 'How did he seem to you? I would be interested to hear.'

'Unchanged sir, totally and absolutely unchanged. As a matter of fact I lost my temper with him at the finish.'

'Not surprisin'.'

'It was when I asked him if he had any messages for his family.'

'Did you now? What answer did he give you?'

'Said he had none. It was that coupled with the fact that Sinclair and Henrietta were in such a ghastly state that made me boil. He said, now wait a bit, I think I can give you his exact words, he just shrugged his shoulders and said "What's done is done, old boy, best let sleeping dogs lie, no use raking over the coals at this late hour" and I thought of Uncle Sinclair and Aunt Henrietta and saw red.'

'Did you give him the sound dressin' down he needed?'

'No sir, temper doesn't affect me like that, I find myself growing very cold. I just wished him luck as I remember and then pushed off. No, I looked back when I got to the door of the *estaminet* and he was already flirting with the girl who brought our wine.'

'Was that the last you saw of him?'

'Yes sir. The next I heard of him was from "Randy Nelly".'

Gyles looked startled. '*Who?*' he demanded.

'The chap who was with him when he was killed. Good type actually, brilliant flyer but a bit of a lad with girls, hence his nickname.'

Gyles was sitting forward now his face sharp with sudden interest. 'D'you happen to know his, er, proper name?'

'Yes,' said Ralph promptly, 'Second Lieutenant Malcolm G. MacNeill of the Argyll and Sutherland Highlanders, seconded to the R.F.C. and flying reconnaissance with Stephen. He was the only eye witness. I suppose in fact it was his report which got Stephen his decoration. The men who manned the field gun were all wiped out anyway. There was no one else.'

'Thank you very much indeed.' Gyles' face had cleared suddenly. 'I particularly wanted to learn that feller's name because I want to make sure I contact him before Sinclair can do so, always providin' he's still alive and just to make sure he doesn't tell Sinclair anythin' which might distress him.'

'You can forget that, sir,' Ralph sounded uncommonly assured, 'old Randy thought the world of Stephen. They, er, hunted in couples as you might say both when flying and when chasin' skirts.'

Gyles smiled again, 'I can't tell you what a relief it is to learn that,' he said relaxing, 'I have always had a sneakin' unease that somethin' Stephen might have done could throw a long shadow to reach out even from the grave to harm those unfortunate parents of his.'

Ralph hesitated, wondering if he should say anything about Stephen's engagement to the American millionaire's daughter Sue-Ellen; but he thought better of it, deciding to keep his own council. He reasoned to himself that by this time the girl was probably engaged to someone else. In this decision he was heavily influenced by his own growing affection and admiration for his Uncle and his immense pity for Stephen's parents. It was unfortunate that his usually astute instincts failed to run true for at the least he might have been able to soften the blow which lay ahead for all of them.

Instead, feeling that enough was enough of such a distasteful subject he deliberately began talking about the latest developments on the Western Front.

The news was grim anyway, but to a degree encouraging, as he explained. Casualties among the British alone were over a hundred and forty thousand. What they would be after the great spring offensive did not bear thinking about. There had already been fierce action around Neuve Chapelle which had been taken and re-taken in the last few months and now news of it filled columns in every paper.

Hill Sixty was altogether gaining in importance, situated as it was on the crest of the Ypres ridge and thus providing a vital observation post. The German Thirty-ninth division had captured it as far back as December and now on this April eighteenth reverse news was filtering in. It seemed from present reports that the story was an heroic one. Sappers laid their mines with fiendish skill and as the last of these exploded G company of the First Royal West Kents and sappers from the First and Second Home Counties Field Company surged from their trenches and rushed the hill.

In a mere two minutes, 'or so the newspapers tell us' qualified the cautious Ralph, they had overwhelmed the little opposition which remained. The very few survivors of the German garrison were bayoneted. Surprise must have been complete. Only twenty were taken prisoner and the British lost seven men. 'Currently we are or were consolidating their position,' Ralph ended. 'It certainly looks as if things were hotting up nicely. You could call it the prelude to what I see as the first battle for the recovery of Ypres. The Big Shove in fact.'

Gyles stared thoughtfully into the fire. He murmured something which Ralph did not hear so,

'What did you say, sir?' he said.

Gyles turned and looked at him strangely. 'I said,' he repeated, 'that it looks more like Armageddon to me.'

CHAPTER 15

The Courts of Desire

They told Henrietta what Rosalind had done. Acting on Dr Jamieson's advice they chose the evening before Grantham drove the pair to London for the Investiture.

'Catch her mind when it is almost completely absorbed by Stephen and it may possibly make less impact,' he counselled, looking nevertheless extremely anxious and tugging at his beard.

When dinner was over both Henrietta and Sinclair excused themselves and went to their own rooms, there, after a few moments Priscilla and Petula presented themselves, were welcomed warmly and the chosen pair then proceeded to involve themselves in some lengthy fencing in search of an appropriate opening.

After Priscilla had chattered brightly and at some length about her Italian adventures Henrietta made the opening herself. She put down her embroidery, sighed, stared at the fire and then murmured, 'If only we had some hopeful news of my poor Rosalind everything would be so wonderful. With Stephanie such a Changed Girl, the joy of her father's life and mine and dear Stephen's sacrifice and gallantry being recognised by his King ...'

In swept Priscilla. 'I have news of Rosalind,' she said softly, 'though I wondered if I should tell you just before this very sad but even so, marvellous, event.'

Henrietta and Sinclair just stared, so she went on,

'I have seen her, my dears. That marriage was a disaster. She fled with the, er, with an ... er, friend of mine,' thus she somewhat mendaciously avoided styling of the young Count, 'her lastest inamorato' as Priscilla thought privately. Aloud she said,

'She is safe and safely in the hands of the people with whom I have been staying.'

After this it was easy. She was able to recount an admittedly bowdlerised version of Rosalind's arrival in Tuscany, to gloss over the relationship between them and so gild the latest capers of this indisputably soiled dove.

Henrietta shed a few tears, but even this seemed a half-hearted performance. As Dr Jamieson had said, 'her mind was occupied elsewhere'.

Sinclair then created a few awkward moments by asking 'Who . . . is . . . this . . . friend . . . to . . . whom . . . my . . . silly . . . girl . . . is, so . . . indebted?'

Priscilla hesitated, Petula intervened. 'A young man of very good family who happened to meet Rosalind in that dreadful house. He felt so dismayed at her state and indeed at her husband's treatment that he took her away at a time when she might have lost her life had he not so done.' As she spoke she could not fail to hear the feet of Ananias but she pressed on with resolution, 'He has behaved impeccably dear Uncle Sinclair. You are immeasurably in his debt . . . he took her straight to Priscilla and her friends, nothing could have been more splendid . . .' Despite herself Petula felt the shamed colour flooding to her cheeks, but she lied on resolutely, 'and there she is resting now for she is quite exhausted. She has the finest care possible and when she is restored in health, if the geographical position of this war permits, she will contrive to come home to you both.'

As she said afterwards, walking down the corridor from the parents' room, assured before either she or Priscilla left that the couple had swallowed her story completely, 'I felt so ashamed Prissy, I was disgusting, but what else in the circumstances could I do?'

'Nothing,' Priscilla acknowledged gloomily. 'It was all quite dreadful but just supposing that rotter wrote to Sinclair and said something out of turn! We had to make sure neither of them would ever believe a word. Now I feel thoroughly grubby. Oh what a mess! She's another Bolter that lass, I'm sure of it.'

'So are we,' Petula admitted reluctantly. 'What makes girls go like that?'

Priscilla mocked her, 'And you a married woman and expectant mother! Really, Pet!'

'Do not "really, Pet" me, pray, I asked you because I want to know and I have always looked upon you as my friend.'

Priscilla paused at the stair head, put her lovely head to one side and looked at Henry's wife quizzically. 'I am your friend, but as I am nearly one too it is not fair to ask me, darling.'

Petula stared in amazement, 'Nearly what? A Bolter? Oh no, Prissy!'

'Oh yes, Pet,' she retorted, 'didn't you know? Has no whiff of scandal reached your sensitive nostrils? I just abstain from marrying them which is so much wiser and so much more discreet.'

'Oh why, Prissy?' it was a cry wrung from her as she stared disbelievingly. 'Why, Prissy?' she repeated.

'The way I am made, my dear. The famous Daisy was another. Each generation throws up a few. Oh how on earth to explain to you, you sweet innocent that a few women are born with the approach of men to such matters?'

Petula continued to stare. Tremblingly her lips shaped one word 'Sex?'

Priscilla nodded, 'It's an attitude of body and mind,' she said rather roughly, 'sometimes I wonder whether I would have been happier without it; but it's no use wondering is it? What was it that naughty little Richard said when he was reproved for something? Oh yes, I have it, "It is the nature of my beast" even as it is the nature of his beast to love animals far more than any humans and to feel a surge of fury when he encounters anyone being cruel to a bird, an animal, a reptile. What I do, my dear sweet little Pet, is the nature of my beast.' She touched Petula upon the arm, pretending not to notice the girl flinch from her involuntarily. Then she added, 'Come now we must report to the family upon the success of our mission.' So saying she swept towards the drawing room. Petula followed more slowly. She thought herself emancipated, a free thinker, a tolerant woman growing with the century into a wider and more lenient approach to life in all its aspects than any of her Edwardian or Victorian forebears had possessed. Now in one brief exchange it was being brought home to her very forcibly that she was no more evolved from her generation and its accepted shibboleths than had been . . . her mind pounced upon the perfect example— Christine, her mother-in-law.

Later that night, curled up on the window seat in her own sitting room, looking out into the darkness, she realised that she had been both shocked and repulsed by what Priscilla had disclosed so lightly. Idiot phrases like 'fallen woman', and 'no better than she should be' ran through her mind. These at least she rejected scornfully. She found no desire whatsoever to condemn but simply to understand. Yet that self-same pity, which she knew to be a genuine emotion in herself, still contained enough of something else to make her flinch slightly when Prissy touched her just after her horrid revelation. She sat uncomfortably now, her fingers linked over her swollen belly wherein lay her unborn child.

Into her mind came the Box and its contents which she was not supposed to know had been discovered nor seen and reacted from with varying emotions by the male members of the family. Nor was she supposed to have any inkling of what the Casket contained; but she knew and knowing, now found herself wondering what use these ancient Lormes thought such things to be—in reality.

'A chastity belt,' she thought unable to deny the scorn this object invoked in her, 'a useless insanitary, revolting object which could in no circumstances whatever debar any woman so inclined from doing what she wished. Desire at least, if not love, could certainly make a mockery of any chastity belt provided desire was potent enough. There must always have been locksmiths who could be prevailed upon!' So she mused, clear in her own mind that if any mediaeval woman desired to be unfaithful to her lord while he was at the wars she could and would have done so without difficulty. The only guerdon to her chastity, decided this last Lorme bride, comprised her own character and her desires. Then, musing on that window seat while the rest of the Castle slept, Petula de Lorme decided once and for all that for her at least fidelity—that word which formed the lynch pin of the Lorme motto granted those nine hundred years ago by King William to his liege man Henri de Lorme, *'toujours fidèle'* needed no chastity belt to guard it, only each woman's unquestioned choice and, she admitted the word, her limitation of desire to the man she loved *and no one else.*

As she so sat she was swept by a great longing for her darling Grumpy who would have straightened her thoughts and put her on the right track between the Scylla of revulsion and the Charybdis of over-tolerance. The child kicked in her womb and then the idea came to her that perhaps what Grumpy would have said was that there were two kinds of women, mother-women and men-women, and that was the way of the world and therefore when in the world must be accepted, providing that acceptance bred tolerance. This brought her up short for it reminded her of what Grumpy had snorted out in one of his sudden bursts of temper.

'Never forget that tolerance is what we strive to practise at all times to other people; but at the same time never lose sight of the inescapable fact that that same tolerance turns to laxity on the instant if one is fool enough to practise it upon one's self.'

Involuntarily she laughed, partially at relief at that old dictum of his, partially at the sheer fun of his allying such wisdom with his own most intransigent displays of intolerance if anything ran contrary to his own opinions; such laughter eased her mind to some extent so presently she rang for her maid to help her undress.

Even so, long after the light had been put out she lay awake trying to enter into the mind of that other kind of woman and failing so to do, because in every way it was contrary to the nature of her own beast. She was, as she had defined, a mother-woman and so at length she forgot about Priscilla and began dreaming of her future life with Henry when this dreadful war was over and they could come together again, and have many children to warm the corridors of the Castle when the older ones' time came to take the swan's path.[1]

In the morning the two Delahayes set off for London. They spent the night at Browns where they busied themselves during the evening by planning the dinner-party for the following evening which they were giving to numerous other Delahayes in order that Sinclair might show them Stephen's decoration. This would of course be in a private room, all the women would wear black and the occasion as Henry said naughtily over the telephone to Petula 'will be like a funeral meal without benefit of an interment'. He was half-heartedly reproved by his wife who had spent a very bad night and now had a splitting headache. She confided to the receiver that time was dragging terribly and she wished it was all over, meaning not the Delahaye entertainment, but the birth of their child. She added, 'There is so much I want to discuss with you, there have been more "dramas" here.' At which point the General walked into Henry's office so he was compelled to replace the receiver.

The next day was bright, sunny and exceptionally warm for the time of year. Grantham drove the Delahayes to the Palace, decanted them and received her instructions. She was told, 'As

[1] See, *The Lormes of Castle Rising*, Book 1.

Mr Delahaye is temporarily incapacitated you are to wait within these precincts.' Thus she was directed to her place and as she stepped from the Rolls she noticed that a wheeled chair had very thoughtfully been provided for Sinclair. An attendant wheeled him while Henrietta walked by his side through the impressive corridors and out into the great Quadrangle. Here, as the attendant explained, the King had decided to hold his investiture due to the very fine weather. An awning had been erected upon a dais, striped, scollop-edged and centralised before rows and rows of seats for members of the recipients' families. Henrietta was so placed that she was at the nearest point for their return but at the same time extremely well positioned to see everything from the canopied dais where, presently, the King would stand.

Sinclair found himself wheeled off to the head of a single line of chairs set out along one side and with a wide space between it and the main block of seating. There was plenty for him to watch. Photographers were placing their cameras upon tripods, arranging their black cloths and popping in and out of them for all the world like house martins at breeding time. Friends came up and spoke to him, stood chatting by his side until abruptly a rustle went through the entire gathering and the King came out wearing the uniform of a Field Marshal. The gathering rose. The quiet figure stood for a moment and then the ceremony began.

At an obviously pre-arranged signal from one of the equerries on the dais Sinclair was wheeled forward to the left hand side of the ascending ramp which ran down from where the King stood. Suddenly Sinclair gripped his sticks, said something to the attendant, who looked vastly put out by his halting words. Nevertheless, with his aid Sinclair struggled to his feet and leaning on his sticks made his way very slowly on foot towards his monarch. In a few moments more it was all over for him. The King spoke to him at some length, and waited patiently for his replies. Then he bowed low and began shuffling off on the farther side. By the time he reached the ramp end his attendant had scurried round the back to meet him. Sinclair then climbed back into his chair nursing the precious small box and was wheeled back into his original position to watch the remainder of the ceremony.

As the King left the dais Henrietta rose and walked slowly towards her husband. Then they returned the way they had come to find Grantham and the Rolls waiting. Once safely inside,

Grantham moved off and Sinclair opened the small box to show Henrietta what the King had given to him for his son.

He and his wife peered together into the little box. The medal lay on a velvet background—the gold-edged cross enamelled in white, with, in the centre a green enamel laurel wreath with the Imperial Crown in gold. Reverently Sinclair turned it over, so that they could examine the other green enamel laurel wreath and surmounting Royal Cypher. The ribbon from which the cross depended was dark red bordered on either side with dark blue. Sinclair stroked it as if it were a cat and he deriving solace from the texture.

Then with one hand in hers they drove back to Browns by which time Sinclair was in sufficient control of himself to tell his wife what the King had said. For once in recent years, and despite his sorrows and regrets Sinclair was a very happy man.

Constance, Rosemary and Petula were deep in conference. Constance had asked them to come and see her in her tiny office within the Convalescent Home where, when the three had been fitted with some difficulty into the tiny space, she opened the proceedings by saying,

'I hate to impose further responsibility on either of you but I am in something of a quandary. I have to go to London on a matter of urgent personal business. None of the cases we are handling at present are critical in any sense and as I am determined to be here when you have your baby, my dear,' with warm glance at Petula, 'I thought that if you two could hold the fort for me until my return I would go now as it is a matter which has been held back for rather a long time already.'

Rosemary said at once, 'Of course we can manage, but as it is not suitable for Pet to be seen among our young men in her present condition she will have to work in the background and I must take your place. Do you by any chance know for how long you will be away?'

'Three days,' said Constance, watching them both.

'And you have been here how long now?' from Petula.

'Er, nine months I think. I had not really considered the matter.'

'Well then,' Rosemary spoke briskly, 'I suggest you do now and realise that from the very beginning you should have had your breaks like all the rest of us. So please just tell us what we need to know and do not know already and then let Pearson pack for you.'

Constance laughed, 'I had not noticed my time here,' she admitted, 'I love my work and am very happy with you all.'

'Even so,' said Petula warmly, 'what Rosie says is right. You should take a week.'

'Oh no,' said Constance quickly, 'you might . . .'

'Start my pains?' Petula raised an eyebrow, 'I can assure you I have my dates correctly. I know the saying that first babies are notoriously unpunctual either way; but August the third is the relevant date and that brings us, according to, er, to my cycles, to May the third at the earliest and May the eighteenth at the latest. It is now April the twentieth so you have ample time if you leave tomorrow. Time to spare in fact.'

Rosemary put in her oar. 'We have dear Doctor Jamieson to guide us remember. You admit yourself there are no grave cases on our hands. Can we not determine the matter by working out exactly when this lot are due for discharge from here and therefore when there will be a further fresh intake?—we would not fancy handling that alone would we Pet?'

'No,' said Petula very firmly.

'Five at the end of the month,' Constance told them, after a brief scribbling session, 'so five replacements by May first . . .'

'There you are then,' Rosemary sounded triumphant, 'if you go on the twenty-first you will be back on the twenty-eighth ready to give the departing infants your blessings and all that, and fill in their medical reports with Doctor J. and leave yourself with masses of time to get ready for the new lot.'

Constance's face registered a mixture of such combined eagerness and doubt that Petula laughed at her and said teasingly, 'You remind me of a rainbow, rain and sunshine together. You look so doubtful and yet excited, come now 'fess up you do want to go don't you?'

Constance looked down at her hands.

'Yes maybe I do,' she admitted, 'but not at the expense of my voluntarily undertaken responsibilities.'

She looked up as she said this and caught such a look in Petula's eyes that she blushed deeply and in consequence gave the game away to her perspicacious audience. Petula immediately heaved herself to her feet, edged between the other chairs, flung her arms round the Home's matron and said,

'Darling Constance, I could not be more glad and happy and thankful so please do not attempt to hide it from me any more. Rosy here and I will keep your secret we promise, but if you have any doubts concerning how I should feel about it, forget them please. You must remember that I love Daddy very much indeed. Over the years, the very many years since Mummy died, I have done what I could to compensate him for his loneliness. Then you came and something lit up in his face which I had never seen before except when he took my hand and tucked it in the curve of his arm as we walked to the chapel for me to marry Henry; I think radiance best describes it. I cannot think of anything nicer for him or indeed for me—what is more I am quite sure Henry will feel exactly the same except we shall have to get used to having such a young and beautiful parent.'

During this explosion into speech and by some miraculous manoeuvring Rosemary had managed to extricate herself from the small room so that when, at length Constance released Petula and 'had a good blow', so touched was she by the girl's spontaneous outburst, they were both startled to find themselves alone; but there was still much to be said, so they set about saying it at such length that they were again startled to hear the muffled sound of the dressing gong.

After dinner Rosemary announced that Constance had to leave them on urgent business for a few days. She was at pains to point out that the Home's matron had not had one single day of rest in nine months, she was emphatic in assuring everyone that she could cope and tactful enough to add that if she had problems of any kind she could take them to the good Doctor, to Christine or to the Dowager and her sister-in-law the little Countess.

This led to some hilarious volunteering on the part of the little Countess who clapped her hands and exclaimed, 'I have always wanted to wear V.A.D. uniform, now I can dress up during the week Constance is away and take Rosie's place while she assumes the temporary responsibility of Matron.'

'Without any authority to assume such garments?' queried Constance trying to sound severe and failing as her eyes brimmed with laughter.

'Fiddlesticks, it is only just for a week!'

Constance help up an admonitory finger, 'You must promise to take it off at the merest whisper of an official visitor.'

Little Marguerite pouted, prevaricated, but finally agreed and Constance went off to pack leaving them all thankful she was 'taking a few days rest'.

No one other than Gyles knew that Charles Danement had been about a similar errand to him in his old office that afternoon. Nor did any of the family notice the conspiratorial and revealing glance which sped between the pair when Constance announced her intention of leaving them to attend to urgent business. Gyles kept his own counsel, spent ten minutes on the telephone to Cartier's and asked leave of his wife to despatch the most junior footwoman to London the next day to collect 'a small parcel which I do not care to entrust to the postal service'. Permission was obtained without difficulty.

Off went the footwoman, off went Constance and, very quietly and unobtrusively off went Charles too, via a smoke screen 'canter' on one of Gyles' mares whom he arranged should be collected from the Manor later in the day by old Plum. He, when told the matter was secret, began to enjoy himself hugely as was always the case when he was enlisted to conceal some aspect of secret family concerns.

Charles then collected one of his cars from his own erstwhile stablings, packed himself a couple of valises and had a long conference with the married couple who were acting as caretakers for him 'for the duration'.

To them he enquired. 'Do you think you could manage to make up the bed in my bedroom, and to dust and refresh both my dressing room and the boudoir which as you know I have had redecorated very recently? I would like you to put fresh flowers in these rooms too . . .'

In this vein he laid his plans with the couple. They expressed delight in having something interesting to do. So emboldened, he went on to wheedle them into preparing a simple supper on the following evening, 'just a cold bird and a salad'. He undertook to bring back with him from London a basket of fruits, a jar of caviare, some smoked salmon, and a selection of cheeses from Messrs Paxton and Whitfield in Jermyn Street and finally he entrusted a very small box to them which he asked might be set against one of the two covers laid in the library for the *al fresco* supper.

Then he drove himself to London, a cap pulled rakishly over

one eye and whistling as he drove at a speed highly unsuited to his age and dignity.

He called upon the Countess who was Constance's aunt, and after a somewhat vinegary prelude obtained her blessing. 'Though,' she was constrained to observe, 'it is remarkable and fortuitous to me Sir Charles that you are prepared to take a militant suffragette into wedlock. Yours I fancy is an ancient name.'

Charles had flushed at this so he flashed back, 'To which the Lady Constance can only add fresh lustre, Countess, as I am sure you were about to point out' which caused the old beldame to shut her mouth like a rat trap, observe the best part of a minute's silence and then resume speech with a distinct twinkle in her grey eyes.

When Charles had wholly won her round she permitted him to invite her to the wedding. Whereupon she said, 'You may leave the arrangements to me as is only right and proper, did you say St Margaret's, Westminster?'

'No,' Charles replied blandly, 'Caxton Hall Westminster,' and waited for the explosion.

None came. After a pregnant pause she observed, 'I see, a secret marriage. No one to be told?'

'Save only yourself, Countess,' Charles gave her a calculatedly deferential nod.

'I see—hole in the corner affair, eh?'

'No,' said Charles, almost goaded to anger, 'a marriage between May and September in the middle of a World War.'

Thus the old dragon collapsed. 'Very proper,' she decided, swinging round from 'squally' to 'set fair', at a rate which would have smashed a barometer. 'I shall be there. You can come back here to luncheon afterwards and meet some of her relations. Dreary lot. Niminy piminy most of 'em, but I shall force 'em to come. Can we send an announcement to *The Times* afterwards?'

'Can we leave it until the eighteenth?' he temporised, 'no one knows at Castle Rising except Petula, my daughter.'

'Does she approve?'

'She was kind enough to say so to your niece.'

'Then the announcement can wait. Luncheon here then,' she rose, so perforce Charles did also, 'Shall we say one thirty? Yes, well then, my late husband had quite a taste for champagne,

I never touch the stuff, gives me wind, but we'll drink champagne when we return from, dear me what did you call it?'

'Caxton Hall Westminster,' Charles repeated, by now inwardly convulsed. As he turned to go she added one rider,

'I suppose it wouldn't be fittin' to have a guard of honour of the fallen women Constance has helped, No? I rather thought not, more's the pity.' On this line Charles made his exit.

They were married the next day. Charles took his future bride out to dinner at the Ritz and returned her, punctiliously to the Countess in Upper Audley Street for the night. The sun shone for them. Constance in filmy grey with a wide tulle hat massed with pink roses looked as Charles told her, 'Ravishin'.' The members of her family turned up in force for what turned out to be a regal reception for the Countess had worked exceeding fast; but then her rule was law. The florists had done as they were bid and her ballroom looked enchanting. She then proceeded to give the bride a most embarrassingly large jewel case stuffed with family heirlooms; to Charles she gave with a gruff murmur, her late husband's black pearl dress studs, and a cheque of such magnitude that Charles blinked in astonishment. 'When this war's over you'll need a proper honeymoon,' he was told tartly.

Finally, when it was all over, and the old retired Generals, Admirals and decrepit peers and their grandsons had departed, Charles drove his wife by a highly devious route to his old manor house and there, with a chuckle at his own foolishness, lifted her over the threshold.

They remained undiscovered for two days and nights. Then Gyles, leaning from the west window of his picture gallery spotted a light where no light should be—in the double meaning of the terms—for it was forbidden to show guiding lights to German zeppelins and also the rooms, as he knew, was in Charles' own private quarters so he summoned Sawby and together they set out across the fields to the Manor. Here, they thundered upon the door. Charles came down to admit them.

'Oh hell!' exclaimed Gyles, totally crestfallen, 'Dear feller, wouldn't have done it for anythin', thought you had burglars, you never said a word about comin' down here.'

By the time this storm in a teacup had abated and the whole

family had rejoiced at the marriage it became plain to the older women of the Family that Petula was very restless. Christine was the first to notice it. She spoke of it to Gyles who said quite reasonably that all girls were out of their usual balance in the last few weeks before they had their first babies at which Christine regarded him doubtfully and went off to find Rosemary who agreed with her. This did little to help, so presently the current Lady Aynthorp took her anxieties to Claire who was sharing Rosemary's responsibilities in Constance's absence. She found her quite prepared to contribute her mite.

'I think,' she stated firmly, 'that our Pet is fretting for Henry. She is definitely off colour. She will not be persuaded to eat enough to sustain a mouse. She just sits on that window seat in her room and stares out at the park.'

Christine looked defeated.

'What does Doctor Jamieson say?' Rosemary then asked.

'Nothing,' said Christine. 'It might help if we could find out what was going on in our girl's mind. She is normally so level headed, so reliable and steady. I think there must be something besides just her pregnancy to throw her out of kilter in this manner—frankly I don't like it, we must speak to Constance.'

In the chain reaction started by Christine, Claire sought the Dowager. She and the little Countess promised to investigate.

All they got for their pains was a quiet, 'Please do not worry about me I am quite all right really. I am just not hungry but anyway I have eaten so hugely for the past few months that a little loss of appetite is probably restoring the balance and very good for both of us. I shall be fine once my baby is born.'

Little subterfuges like invented needs for carriage drives and invitations to join the old gentlewomen after dinner were brushed aside. Petula stayed by her window seat, displaying the reluctance of a puppy to move in her owner's absence and encompassed by an overwhelming lethargy which made her feel heavy and her body difficult to propel.

Even a council of all women of the family failed to produce either a solution or a remedy. Petula continued to look out over the park, her small hands idle in her lap save when the child in her womb quickened too violently when she would lift one hand and lay it in a little soothing movement across her swollen stomach.

It seemed to the anxious women that her eyes had become

enormous in her now very small, white face. Christine began lobbying for a second opinion as the days went by, but as Dr Jamieson seemed undisturbed she made no headway and as Priscilla remarked, when they sat together in the Blue Drawing Room after dinner, 'Unless we force the issue and literally insist on another medical opinion, Doctor Jamieson will not make a move. Of course he's overworked, with Constance away and an epidemic of colds and bronchitis among the villagers.'

So Christine resumed her pressure on Gyles to do something when Constance returned. By this time he too felt anxious as he went down the corridors towards her office, determined to settle the matter one way or another.

He was too late. No sooner had Constance welcomed him, received his warm and charming congratulations and thanked him for his wedding present than Rosemary rushed in, her face flushed from running through the corridors.

'Pet's started her pains,' she panted breathlessly, 'Nanny's fussing. Pet is very calm; but I would like you to come Constance and when will Doctor Jamieson be here again?'

Constance rose, glanced at the little fob watch which was pinned to her apron and said, 'In half an hour, let me see her now and then I can judge whether we should send for him or not.'

In between her first pains—which appeared to be perfectly normal—Petula went back to her window seat and resumed her dreams. She was pining for Henry, furthermore she had tried to reach him several times only to be told that he had been sent on a small mission for the General and would not be available for a day or two. That was when, in a sudden flash she knew where he had gone. To test her conviction she asked very sweetly if she could possibly speak to the General but was told he too was not available. By that time she was convinced that they had both gone to France, and well aware that Henry hoped to get back before she started having their baby, indeed would very probably be back in a matter of hours, so, stilling the fears which built up despite her resolution to hold them back, she forced herself to think of the future. This was how she had spent all those long hours on the window seat. She had found the present well-nigh unendurable as her time came closer so she projected herself forward into the time when it would all be over. She peopled her dreams with unborn sons. Christine had given her the precedent for this and over the past days Petula had mentally conceived and borne them; one to inherit—the child within her womb—one to be a regular soldier like her cousin Christian, one to inherit her husband's family's inherent instinct for adventure and become perhaps a famous explorer, one to be the finest horseman in Britain.

The corridors of her mind were filled with these future men whom she would bring into the world and see grow into manhood while the years went by for her with Henry at her side. It was a simple dream. In many ways she resembled her father-in-law. Gyles' life revolved around the Castle, his sons and his wife. Now Petula's own forward dream was wholly given up to that self-same Castle when the time came for her to be its chatelaine; and to her husband Henry, copper headed, vital, wholly entrancing to her and to their imagined sons. There was no room anywhere in her dream for daughters. She never envisaged having any, only sons; men who would carry forward their ancient family traditions; sustain the Castle's long history of prosperity despite adversity through the recurring incidence of what the family had come to call their 'runts'. No matter what else the future held in Petula's dream these future menfolk born of her womb would sustain the strength and quality of their line. In the fullness of time they would bring their wives and their children to her as her span of years increased.

The pains came again. Dr Jamieson was now with her, insisting she allow herself to be put to bed so that, as he explained with sweet reason and in tones of great gentleness, 'You can rest properly between your pains and so reserve your strength for your great moment.' That was when Constance came back and the Doctor left them alone. It was a calm, unhurried, confident Constance who shepherded her through the ungainly effort required to bathe; who helped to dry and powder her, who slipped the loose silk gown over her head, fastened the ribbons and helped her climb back into the great old bed upon which so many Lormes had been born. Then Doctor Jamieson examined her once more, after which he kept his own counsel—for he was by no means sure that his growing suspicions were correct.

The day dragged on. When evening came Constance began to experience an unaccountable anxiety which Petula confirmed as she became steadily more exhausted.

Just after midnight the girl drowsed off for a few moments. Constance lifted her small fob watch, examined the tiny jewelled face and calculated. Petula had been in labour now for just over twelve hours. The nurse who stood at her side bent towards her and whispered, 'No sign of the baby yet and if you ask me nor will there be for a very long time yet.'

By four in the morning a sleepless household knew that their darling's life was now at risk. No one from the Dowager to little Boots had anything but love for the slender girl whose strength was ebbing in the great four poster bed. The kitchen maids made endless pots of tea below stairs. Neither Sawby nor his wife returned to their cottage. All the staff sat around talking in whispers. It was all summed up for them by Agnes who whispered, 'Worse'n wot it was with 'er Ladyship . . .'

Upstairs in the Blue Drawing Room Sawby kept taking up fresh trays of coffee. The Castle's womenfolk sat quietly enough, but they were keeping a vigil compared with which the fears they had felt for Christine were as nothing.

The pains were coming more frequently they learned, and also that Constance had sent for Dr Jamieson. When he came she went outside into the corridor to meet him.

'She is too weak,' she told him emphatically, 'you will have to induce the birth. There is something very wrong and I feel we should send for Sir James without any further delay.'

But still he hesitated, standing pulling his beard. Finally he agreed, adding, 'If I scribble down some things I shall need, can you undertake to find someone to go to my house, rouse my wife and get her to put them in a bag and bring them back here as quickly as possible?'

'My husband will go,' said Constance immediately.

'Meanwhile,' he said, 'I will examine Mrs Petula again very thoroughly. Is the Nurse there?'

Constance confirmed this then sped away on her errand. She roused Sir Charles. In moments, he was holding the reins of the Doctor's dog cart and the cart was spanking down the drive at a ferocious pace.

When he returned and trotted up along the drive again first light was breaking. Something made him glance at the Castle's old grey face. He saw with a sickening feeling of fear that there were lights in many of the windows and more leapt up as he looked.

CHAPTER 16

A Taste of War

The two staff cars had already weaved their way through between the heavy eastward traffic and the sentinel plumes of Lombardy poplars which still fringed the roads of France where war had not yet come.

Henry de Lorme sat back comfortably beside his General, a rising excitement making a pulse throb in his neck just below the point where the red tabs of a Staff Officer declared his 'cushy job'.

He forced thought away from both the circumstance in which he had encountered this scornful tag and its unpleasant credibility, compelling it to lie dormant until he was sufficiently free of the rage it sparked in him to reflect upon it with a cleared head, driving his thoughts now along the channels of recollection of the journey which lay behind them. They had spent three days in Paris where turn and turn about the General had released the six members of his staff to put their brief leaves to good account, roystering and drinking vast quantities of champagne. Ahead lay Chantilly and their final climb northwards by a devious pattern of side roads via Compiègne, St Quentin and cross-country to Valenciennes, crossing the main road south of Lille, to their final base just short of Armentières. From there, thought Henry contentedly the 'old boy' would make his tour of inspection prior to the launching of the big Spring offensive. Unless something went very wrong they would be back in England before Petula had her child.

The General sat ramrod straight in the back of the staff car while his personal aide, somewhat cynically defined by his companions as 'O.C. Pink Gin', sat beside him his cap tipped forward in perilous proximity to his Norman nose.

When the news reached him that they were to go so much sooner than expected Henry had telephoned to Dr Jamieson. Together they decided that nothing should be said to Petula, that no compassionate leave should be either solicited or taken and that Henry would, instead, ask for this immediately the trip was over and thus—again 'with any luck' be with his wife by the time her first pains started. Thus musing, a rapped out question from the 'old man' brought him up short.

'Anythin' of interest here, hey?' he enquired as they drove into Chantilly.

'Yessir,' said Henry, shaking himself free of his musings, 'a beautiful *Château* set curiously enough in an English garden and there's a *musée*, er, museum,' he corrected himself hastily remembering his questioner had no French, 'a rather fine church called *l'Eglise de Leu d'Esserent* which is about five kilometres outside the town.'

'Then we'll see the *Château*,' decided the General, 'I always have a taste for lookin' at gardens . . . anythin' else?'

Henry grinned, 'A particularly fine racin' stables, sir . . .'

The General grunted. 'Tell the man *Château* first, then the stables and back on to the road. . . .'

Henry murmured deferentially, carefully concealing a twinkle.

'You know, sir,' he then said, 'there used to be a little place by the canal at the back of the gardens should you wish to, er, inspect it. The last time I was there it was run by a couple called Dubouchard. Madame Dubouchard was an absolutely splendid cook . . .'

The General shot him a glance under bushy eyebrows, 'Oh well then,' he said, himself endeavouring to sound reluctant, 'might as well stop and reconnoitre, hey?'

'As you say, sir.' Well pleased with himself once again, Henry leaned forward and again gave the necessary instructions to the driver. Presently he had the immense satisfaction of being told to order luncheon from Monsieur Dubouchard who came out looking depressed, but brightened considerably at the sight of so many red tabs. Bowing very low he implored them to give themselves the trouble of descending and, in between bows and flourishes, he shouted for a girl to put clean cloths to a table under the shade of a small terrace tressed overhead with bursting wisteria. Then he called to his invisible wife to prepare herself to cook a *déjeuner* of unparalleled excellence.

By this time Henry had also won himself the affectionate soubriquet of 'Froggie' and was kept busy with both justifiable and highly improper requests from his brother officers as to what was the French for 'How much, Mademoiselle?' 'Where's the bog, chum?' and 'How do I tell the feller we haven't got all day?' Eventually a small procession wound itself from the interior of the little restaurant carrying dishes and led by the Patron in a clean apron, his waxed, pointed-tipped whiskers quivering as he set down an enormous array of *pâtés* and *saucisses*.

It was a protracted meal. Under the influence of good wine and food the General became almost benevolent, so it was well into the afternoon when the Patron's daughter stood at her father's side waving a rather sore hand which had been much squeezed surreptitiously and conscious that her small and well rounded behind was throbbing slightly after the exciting pats and pinches it had undergone. Then the two cars vanished in a swirl of dust and the Patron locked up his takings.

It was seven o'clock when the two cars drove through Armentières. Without glancing at their wrist watches the church clock told them so in rather unmelodious chimes.

As they reached a cross roads Henry again leaned forward. 'Take the left hand turn and turn first left again,' he instructed, 'you'll see the four turrets of the *Château* standing out quite clearly on your right. There's a small laneway on the right of the road, take that and it will bring you to the main entrance.'

Five minutes later the car drew up, the driver leaped out, opened the door and stood stiffly to attention as the General dismounted. Henry followed him, pausing to say to the driver quietly, while the old man marched slowly up the steps of a once very splendid small *château*, 'Nip round the back, Jock, and reconnoitre. I fancy you will discover yourself in a smaller courtyard and with what domestic staff remains. Give 'em a grin and you'll find yerself legs under table in two shakes of a duck's tail and with a bottle of wine before you. I'll take care of the other gentlemen and their driver can follow you.'

'Mr Lorme,' thundered the General.

'Coming, sir,' Henry raced up the steps with the rest of the staff following. He was just in time to see the doors folded back by a white whiskered, very old man in a green baize apron with felt slippers on his gnarled feet.

'*Bienvenu, mon Général*,' the old man bowed low, '*M. le Marquis vous attend.*'

'Have to talk to this feller,' growled the General. 'Go on boy you know I don't understand a single dam' word of Frog.'

Henry uncapped, obliged, translated, 'Just follow him, sir, and he'll lead us to your host,' then, looking back he jerked his thumb in the direction the old man was taking and the procession moved forward.

Inwardly Henry was chortling. Once more he would be able to show the old man a thing or two, for this was home from home to him and he was well aware how much they would be at a disadvantage without him. At least so he thought. His pleasure was however very short-lived. They crossed the polished parquet, saw the gilded doors opened revealing what was clearly the salon and . . .

'Ah, there you are,' said the Marquis stepping forward with outstretched hand, 'Welcome, General, come along in, gentlemen, and refresh yourselves after your long journey.'

The General looked relieved, returned the greeting, asked leave to present his staff, did so and ending with, 'M'y personal aide Mr Henry de Lorme.'

The Marquis stared smilingly, 'Lorme! Lorme, what a coincidence! If I am not very much mistaken Mr Lorme you are Gyles Aynthorp's eldest son?'

'Yessir,' stammered Henry, for once taken aback.

'Might have known,' the Marquis nodded, 'that hair.' Then, turning to the General, he explained, 'I dangled that feller's father on m'knee in let me see now . . . dear me m'y memory must be goin'.'

Henry vastly amused by now, essentially at a Frenchman speaking such English and dropping his 'gs' too, said very respectfully,

'My father's risin' fifty-three, sir. . . .'

'Yes that would be it about eighteen sixty. Dear me, how time flies. Now before we do anythin' else, gentlemen, pray be seated, what will you take? Champagne, sherry or, er,' he twinkled, 'pink gin?'

'Pink gin, thank yer,' said the General thankfully.

When they were seated and all save the General held old-fashioned champagne glasses, the Marquis with his long bony legs crossed and one veined hand around the stem of his own glass said smoothly.

'I owe you an explanation, my dear sir. You see I was through Mafeking with this feller's father. He was one of my subalterns.'

'Hope he wasn't as much dam' trouble to you as this chap is to me,' said the General wholly without rancour.

'Oh I say, sir,' Henry protested equally unruffled.

'You nag,' said the General. 'Ever had an aide who nags, Marquis? Well mine does, on and on always pesterin' me to see some action.'

'Aren't we all, sir!' said the others in chorus.

The Marquis' lean face creased affectionately. 'Just like his father!' he exclaimed, 'Why I remember . . .'

The two old men were off and in Henry's opinion would require no further attention for some time so he let them drone on, while he looked about him appreciatively at the furnishing, paintings and carpets, all so reminiscent of his own home.

He was jerked back to reality by the General whom he heard enquiring,

'How is it you haven't cleared out? You're deuced close to the enemy.'

Six pairs of eyes beamed smartly on the Marquis.

'Well now,' he said quietly, 'I think I am too old and too set in my ways. Do not lose sight of the fact that the Prussians were here in eighteen sixty. They behaved themselves reasonably well too. Therefore I see no good reason why they should not again, if we are unfortunate enough to be over-run. Certain of our treasures have been, er, sent to safe custody and we have taken care of our cellars. But they respect blood, y'know, and rank— even now. Furthermore I think we shall hold 'em, 'tanyrate until we begin to drive them back. We must just wait and see.'

The pleasant interlude ended. The Marquis entertained them splendidly. They dined by candlelight at an oval, polished table and for once the General's assorted entourage was content to sit back and listen while the old men spoke of war.

When at length they went to their rooms, each man with his branched candelabra and the flickering flames casting eerie shadows about the corridors lined with huge, carved armoires and old cradles, shadowy portraits and sentinel figures in armour, the sound of the guns was very penetrating. Henry lay back on his bed, arms behind his head and thought about this war and how he must put an end to all the influence and string-pulling and 'bloody mollycoddling', as he thought of it, once Petula had given him the son he knew was coming. There was no room for any doubt in him upon this score and little fear for the girl he loved so deeply, for he knew her to be extremely fit. Much probing of Dr Jamieson had drawn out the same very clearly stated opinion.

These old men, for once Henry lumped his father in with the others, had all seen fierce action in their time, and they had survived. Moreover such experience and survival enabled each one of them to hold their heads high when others talked of war. He stared at a bare patch on the wall from whence a painting had been taken recently, while he, if he did not fight would spend the rest of his days regretting . . .

His mind hardened to this resolution. No bastards were going to fling that insult at him of 'cushy job' any more. Once he got back to England and saw his son safely delivered he would come back. Until then he would play his part dutifully, correctly, but immediately afterwards, he would ask for a transfer, and so resolving he rolled over on to his side and slept.

In the morning the party headed for General Headquarters and the young officers 'hung about chattin'' with a number of baby-faced veterans by whom they were taken to a local *estaminet*. Henry felt his stature diminishing momently in the company of these uniformed schoolboys, many of whom had already been 'over the top', seen fierce action, killed and wounded the enemy. Henry's sense of shame increased and nothing which he saw, nor anything which happened to him in the ensuing five days did anything to lessen it.

Their tours of inspection, when at length these began, included seeing the Fifty-ninth Field Company Royal Engineers, constructing temporary bridges to the North West and East of 'Wipers' as the Tommies called Ypres. They were taken to 'Kitchener's Wood', mute victim of that counter attack by the first Canadian Brigade. This brought Henry and his companions face to face with the grim realities of war. They were told by indifferent speakers of how out of two Canadian battalions only ten officers and a little over four hundred men came back and how, when Lieutenant Colonel Watson of the Tenth Brigade arrived just before dawn, he sent in a company to attack from the left and the entire unit was almost exterminated.

They watched the stretcher-bearers after the resultant retreat, bringing back men who had been victims of early gas attacks and they both saw and smelled the wounded as they went by.

They saw, too, the mud, the rats, and inhaled the dreadful stench of rotting corpses, from which huge rats fled as they approached.

They encountered the realities of what had up till now been 'Artists' Impressions' in the *Illustrated London News* and other glossy magazines, as they ducked under sandbags, drew back gunnybag 'curtains' and entered 'dug-outs' in which men ate and washed, wrote letters home and relaxed by candlelight, sometimes emerging after a night of terrible activity to shave from a mugful of water under the screaming shells.

Worst of all, for Henry anyway, were the men whom they saw standing waistdeep in mud-logged trenches, singing their war songs, cracking their jokes as they did when, as casualties, they were brought to the charnel houses which were advance field dressing stations.

They were sent out by night with their 'nannies', quiet, experienced N.C.O.s who chivvied them out and chivvied them back to safety after hours of crawling on their stomachs in the sludge of no-man's-land, learning, as they had clamoured to do, yet another aspect of the realities of war—by instruction in the repairing of barbed wire entanglements lit by the soaring flares and the occasional eruption of flame from some falling shell. They learned, too, how they must steel themselves to 'freeze' when 'spotted' from the enemy lines, lest by the action of flinging themselves down they drew deadly further attention to themselves from snipers. Officers and men alike showed them the small coinage of their daily lives 'in the front line' and they were chastened.

Once they heard cries coming from some stretcher-bearers. They ran up to help and found they were digging out two riflemen who had been buried by a bursting shell which landed on the parapet in front of them. The men were hauled out at length, dazed, spitting, coughing, mud-drenched from head to foot. Henry and his companions moved quickly aside as a Medical Officer came up, glanced at the pair and sent them back down to the first aid post with one of the orderlies. When one of Henry's companions spoke sympathetically the M.O. retorted, 'Shell shock is an insidious condition. We must show no sympathy. It might encourage a tendency for it to spread. All company commanders are being instructed accordingly.' Then he turned on his heel and walked back the way he had come.

They rode on borrowed motor-cycles through what had once been peaceful little villages and were now reduced to mere twisted, gaping pits and rises of rubble, only identifiable by their names hurriedly scrawled on giant boards.

They joined one night party when they were compelled to wear gas masks rolled up over the tops of their heads under their 'tin hats'. The masks were at least effective against chlorine, but were damp and impregnated with some evil-smelling antidote which raised rashes on their foreheads and itched intolerably. Thus accoutred they hauled gas cylinders up communications trenches for installation in the front line. Inevitably it rained. This made the duck boards slippery as greased poles, causing the cylinders to slither alarmingly, and all the while the little parties swore and stumbled and sweated, paused to scratch and curse and stumbled on again.

Henry returned to be given a steaming mug of cocoa. He experienced an overwhelming longing for a hot bath, which desire he wisely abstained from mentioning; instead he thought of baths and huge white towels as he sipped his cocoa gratefully and fell to wondering what Chef André would have called such stuff . . . and at least this thought made him laugh.

Very gradually the General's staff came to learn the 'drill' which comprised two weeks in the line, one in support and one in reserve for strengthening defences and particularly any barbed wire which had been cut about by previous shelling, when if a light caught them it became a reflex to 'freeze' lest the movement give their position to the enemy.

Then, most macabre of all, on one hot night when Henry was sharing a bottle of wine with two subalterns in their dugout, a third put his head around the supporting wooden prop, leaned in and said, 'They're at it again if you chaps want to listen.'

The others rose immediately so perforce Henry followed. Then the four leaned against a sandbagged emplacement and listened. In between the shells, the tearing rip of flares and the dull thuds of unexploded shells the nightingales were trilling, pouring out magic from their tiny throats, doubtless set off by the sounds of battle.

At last it was over. They said their adieux to the Marquis, they climbed back into the cars which headed towards the coast of France and as they did so the driver 'Jock' muttered under his breath, 'Praise be to God we're goin' back to Blighty!'

Sitting at his old refectory table, with Diana at his side, Henry's father was trying to locate him on the telephone and meeting with no success whatever. Petula was still in labour and the famous gynaecologist Sir James Arbuthnot was climbing into his long underpants at his Harley Street home in London.

When Gyles had been stonewalled for the twentieth time he banged down the receiver and strode from the room. In four minutes flat he was at the wheel of his eldest son's new Bugatti and turning out of the Castle drive towards London. The roads were empty. An occasional sleepy labourer plodding towards his fields as the dawn broke, leaped for the hedge as the great car roared by; but for the most part the car snarled and roared in solitude with Gyles gripping the wheel, his eyes intent on the road ahead, his whole being narrowed down to the task of finding Henry and bringing him home before it was too late. There was no time for self-deception now he knew full well, and he also knew that he would have cheerfully sacrificed his own life to save the girl whom his son loved. Yet her life was now at risk. And as it was he could do nothing, for neither wealth nor power nor influence were of any avail when a woman in labour is racked beyond her strength, until that strength wanes dangerously.

When he reached the General's house in Hyde Park, Gyles leaped over the car door, ran up the steps and banged on the knocker as if to rouse the dead. Presently a sleepy manservant in a dressing gown drew back the bolts, opened the door a chink and...

'I am Lord Aynthorp,' said Gyles in tones which brooked no challenge, 'I wish to speak to her ladyship on the instant. Be good enough to unchain this door. Then leave me. Tell her ladyship this is a matter of life and death...'

The startled man managed a murmured, 'Very good, your lordship.'

'Go, man, go, every second tells,' Gyles thundered, this time he had the grim satisfaction of seeing the man run up the thickly carpeted stairway. He stood waiting.

The General's lady came down that stairway in a remarkably short space of time. She was a tall, slender woman with greying hair, now hanging in two plaits on either side of her velvet wrapper.

'Is it my husband?' she asked, putting out her hands appealingly.

'No it is not,' Gyles took the outstretched hands. 'It is my daughter-in-law. She is in labour and likely to die. She is calling for her husband my eldest son and your husband's personal aide, no one can tell me where they are. CAN YOU . . .?'

Swimming blue eyes met his. 'In time of war?' she half whispered it.

Gyles nodded. 'It is safe enough—to me.'

She shook her head wearily. 'It is no good,' she said, 'they're in France, they are due home today but neither I nor anyone else can tell you where they are at this moment I fear.'

Gyles' face was very white. He passed a slightly unsteady hand over his hair.

'The First Sea Lord?' he made the words into a query.

'Possibly,' she acknowledged. 'Er, shall I telephone him? He and Billy were at school together.'

'Would you?'

She wasted no more words, but put her hand out and led him into a small room on the ground floor. Then she picked up the telephone receiver and at the same time pulled a bell cord. To the receiver she said the number she required adding, 'This is urgent, and official so will you please hurry,' then as she waited, the door opened to admit the manservant once again, now fully dressed.

To him she said, 'Strong black coffee, Perkins, and the General's special brandy as fast as you can bring it, if you please.'

Gyles rose and went to the windows. A milk roundsman was dipping his lidded metal canister into the great metal churn on his hand-pushed barrow and pouring the milk into a large brown jug held by a little maid who stood beside him. A fat old spaniel waddled up to her . . .

Time stood still. Then the General's wife replaced the receiver on its hook and said quickly. 'They are expected to return on the night boat. He will send a signal. Your son will be given a car and driver the moment he lands. The driver will take him straight to your Castle. That is the best I can do I am afraid.'

The silence lay between them like a sword. After a while she removed the receiver from its hook once again and held it out, 'Would you not like to telephone your home and tell them that your son is coming? It . . . might . . . help . . . her.'

He nodded gratefully, gave the number and she waited as the man came in with a silver tray from which rose the aroma of freshly made coffee.

'Castle Rising,' said a familiar voice, 'this is the butler speaking.'

The General's wife rose and in a moment had closed the door softly behind her.

Alone in the room Gyles asked, 'Is her ladyship available, Sawby?'

Back came the voice. 'She is in the Blue Drawing Room with the other ladies of the family, my lord.'

'Then ask her to be good enough to come to the telephone please, Sawby.'

After another pause came Christine's voice. 'Is that you, Gyles?'

'Yes, my darling—now listen carefully. Try to make sure that Petula knows. Is she still all right?'

'Sir James is with her,' came the quiet voice, 'she is still conscious but they are talking of giving her chloroform . . .'

'Then hurry, my love, and I will wait. Let them know and Christine . . .'

'Yes.'

'Tell them Henry is racing to Pet across country from . . .' he lapsed into French and told her the rest. Then he put down the receiver and went to the door. There was no one there, so he returned to the room, looked at the coffee and poured himself a cup if only to give himself something to do. He carried it back to the table and sat down again lifting the receiver to his ear. He sipped the coffee. The General's wife came back fully dressed, took up the decanter and splashed brandy into his cup.

'You shouldn't do that with good brandy you know,' he said automatically.

'Fudge,' said she. 'Drink it and you will feel better able to cope.'

Christine's voice came again. 'Gyles, are you there?'

'Yes.'

'Sir James has told her—he thinks it will help.' He heard her voice crack, heard, 'Come back as soon as you can, my love, but please drive carefully,' then the line went dead and he finished his coffee.

He turned the Bugatti into his own drive as the stable clock struck eight. At the same hour Henry, with a map spread across his knees was coaxing his driver across country towards his home.

CHAPTER 17

'Certum Est Quia Impossibile Est'

The Dowager and the little Countess Marguerite left the family group gathered around the fire which Sawby had chivvied his footwomen into lighting in the library. The rest sat about, with the doors open and held so by their two door stops so that they would be aware instantly of Sir James' arrival... of Henry's return, or of the slightest footfall on the stairs from the room above where Petula was fighting what they now well knew might prove to be a losing battle.

A few moments after Sir Charles came in with Doctor Jamieson's bag and learned that he had already summoned the eminent gynaecologist—whose glossy Rolls Royce was already speeding towards them—first the Dowager and then Countess Marguerite rose and moved from the room. Once clear of the first bend in the great stairway they faced each other, paused and stood panting.

'What now?' whispered Marguerite.

'What indeed, my dear?' the Dowager's resolute old mouth was trembling slightly and a tiny pulse under her left eye was twitching as though it had a life of its own which it was using to protest.

Alicia Aynthorp put a shaking hand to her sister-in-law's fragile arm, 'Let us get our wraps, my dear. There is nothing else we two can do.'

Presently, swathed in furs, they came down again and startled Raikes out of her wits by appearing, with scraps of lace on their heads, in the corridors below stairs,

'Good morning, Raikes,' they each managed in turn, Alicia Aynthorp adding, 'We shall be in the Chapel if we are needed, pray remember.' Then they went on their way, holding on to each other, changed during that long, weary night as they were from the Family's beloved 'two old naughties', their arch conspirators, master schemers and general promoters of a thousand mischiefs; into two very old, frail persons in whose eyes, at long last, lay unmistakable, naked fear.

By the time they reached the terrace garden door through which Henry had led Petula in eighteenth-century dress so that they could show themselves to old Plum in all their finery before joining the Family for the ball at which they became engaged, little Marguerite loosed a little choking sound brought on by recollection, then closed the door resolutely and the pair went down the chapel path beset by their memories. It seemed in retrospect to Justin Aynthorp's widow that both experienced all over again the events of many hours as they moved to the lych-gate. For Marguerite it was a recollection of herself following this self same path in search of sanctuary and solace when her husband Raoul put her aside in order that he might embrace the monastic life.[1] Farther back in her time, she saw herself running down that path, stricken and clutching the flowers she wished to lay upon her father's catafalque. Then, moving sharply forward again in time she saw herself as an old woman, calm with the cold composure which is for some the state of shock, as Christine tumbled out the news of Justin Aynthorp's death. Then, too, Marguerite had hurried away with just such a scrap of black lace flung across her elaborate coiffure, to command Sawbridge, select flowers and make the chapel ready for Justin's lying in state.

For Alicia, Justin's widow, memory took her relentlessly through the stations of her bereavement. She for whom marriage had been a perfect and protracted experience again felt all the agonies of her sudden loss which, with its ending, left her only half a person, as is the law for those who are allowed to know perfect unity. Then Alicia's remembering turned abruptly to when the sun flooded out as she stepped from the crowded chapel to face the bright eyes of the crowds outside, and again in memory she followed Henry and his bride as they paced in youth, beauty and *their* perfect fulfilment between the village children who showered them with rose petals as they went by.

For both these old persons, these painful rememberings were pregnant with Lorme history which like a cinematograph gave them back the past which had been enclosed by these old walls raised by the first Henri de Lorme to settle on Norman-conquered English soil ... sanctuary ... vigils way back to the time

[1] See, *The Lormes of Castle Rising*, Book 1.

of Crusades. They walked with history and their walk was peopled with wraiths of what the old stones had witnessed in their long past. Then into both their minds' agonies came now this newest and most terrible wraith. Were they—they faced the question as they lifted the iron hasp of the Chapel doors and went in—to witness in the immediate future the coming in of yet another catafalque, this time one holding the torn body of a girl?

Together they took tapers from the silver box in which they were stored. Together they moved unsteadily from white candle to white candle in their sconces to send the little gold feathers of flame quivering upwards in symbolic appeal for intervention while there was still time for Him so to do. So at last they knelt. And now, their small, veined hands clasped in supplication they surrendered themselves to prayer.

In moments of crisis the mind, like a wry jester, plays terrible tricks; or so Christine thought as she sat with all her usual outward composure, looking, however, unusually small in the great leather chair, striving with every nerve to sublimate all thought and hold herself in a suspended state of vacuum until ... until, she bilked even now at the mental recognition of what that 'until' might come to signify and bilking, let in the jester who mocked her,

'You should have stopped them. *Belle-mère* should have intervened. Someone should have done something to head them away from the opening of that ancient Thing.'

She shivered. Gyles, standing at the windows staring out blindly at the Home Park chose that moment to turn. Turning he saw the involuntary shiver so caught up a wrap Christine had laid beside her and unfolding it laid it gently across her shoulders. The movement returned her to herself. She looked up. She caught at his hand, said,

'Thank you, my love,' and then clutched the hand more tightly. 'Gyles,' her voice was a trifle hoarse, 'Gyles darling, why did you open the Box?'

If it had been possible Gyles' face would have paled at this, but he was so grey already that there was little visible change save that a shadow seemed to pass across his face. He opened his tight-clenched lips to answer but no sound came.

Again Christine spoke.

'Tell me?' she pressed him. 'Please tell me. I must know now, although I never intended you should ever learn that all we women knew what you had done. *Do you believe that the Box,*[2] *or Casket, held some supernormal power which we loosed to our downfall when you opened it?*'

Gyles sighed, a long drawn out sound as if all breath was being expelled from his body by the power of what her words stirred in him.

'I ... do ... not know,' he answered at last, his voice sounding wooden and emotionless. 'I ... simply ... do ... not ... know.' Abruptly he drew another chair close to hers, put one arm around her shoulders and drew her closer. 'I can tell you though that when you were so desperately ill with Rupert I ...' again he faltered, then forced the words out, 'I wondered then if such a thing could by association and the passing of so many years, acquire an extraneous force. All the logic which I could muster refuted such a thought absolutely; yet it persisted and,' over his grey face spread a rueful smile, 'then when you came back to me and they told me that you were safe I managed to brush it away like a cobweb which entangled in my mind and, God help me, I forgot it.'

'Until now?' her whisper came through stiff lips.

'Until last night,' he amended.

'Then talk to me,' she pleaded, as a child might have asked for comfort having woken on a nightmare and cried out. 'Tell me what you do think. Help me please, Gyles.'

Curiously Gyles used the quotation which had come to Piers Fournes when he was bayed by his peculiar conflict '... "whose whole life's love goes down in a day".' As he spoke now so he gripped the small hands which lay between his own. 'The end of the line. ... if it should happen. Never in the nine hundred odd years that Thing lay cached within its chapel niche has the heir apparent failed to sustain the succession. Never once in our long history has the eldest son not wed and seen his heir before he took the swan's path ... even when he died young.' He broke off again. Then, 'It cannot be that Casket!' he exclaimed. 'I am a modern man, a twentieth-century man. This is no longer an age of witchcraft and superstition. Such thoughts belong at latest to the Middle Ages when witches were burned ...'

[2] See Books 1 and 2, *The Lormes of Castle Rising* and *Shadows Over Castle Rising*.

Christine moved from his embrace. She turned and stared into the heart of the great log fire.

'Yet,' she said slowly, 'we still carry brands for the burning to Puck's Hill, and I dare say, there is not a villager, male or female who does not recount the tale of Puck's home under that hill nor fail to put out gifts to that naughty sprite on All Hallows' Een. Superstition is still with *them* and in some cases their roots are close on as old as ours. Scriveners, Marplots, Bowmans and Drovers. These are names you will presently be having enscribed upon our growing Roll of Honour. What is the derivation of such names?'

She swung round again to him. 'Gyles, were they not so called in their originals because they were scriveners, marplots, bowmen and drovers when this land was young? I believe,' her voice cleared and the words came out strongly, 'I believe,' she repeated, 'that anything can be *invested*—at least I think that is the word—with power through generations of men bending their minds to *think* it so. What was it that Swami said to us when we were together in India? "A native prancing in ardour about a wooden totem pole—if he so prances in a spirit of devotion, self sacrifice, love and service—may well be closer to the Great Unknown than a panoplied priest holding a jewelled cup aloft at some incense-drenched high altar". In all those past generations could we have *invested* power in that Thing and having so done released it upon ourselves by going against the Law we had made sacrosanct through constant usage?'

Again Gyles repeated with a faint note of stubbornness in his voice, 'I do not know, my love, I simply do not know.' He stood up. He began pacing up and down. She had obviously shaken him. As he paced across the Persian rugs to come face to face with a pair of library steps, to turn, re-cross the rugs and turn again at the windows, so he looked back to the events of the five years which lay between them and the tragedy of his father's sudden death. As if it were re-enacting itself in that quiet room where it had happened five years ago he saw his Bishop brother's hand outstretched as the lid was raised from the Box; saw the hand dart back as if stung by a serpent, and saw again the Talisman itself which had lain hid for such a very great span of years at the behest of their ancestress the Lady Mathilde who bestowed it upon her fourth son Henri. He began recalling its journey. How Henri's brother Edouard brought the Thing to England, handing it over crossly, resentfully to his younger brother. Gyles paced on and remembered more. How the King, Henri's chosen liege lord had attended the christening of his firstborn and how his face had become sombre when, after the ceremony and before they went to meat, Henri had shown him the niche that he had ordered his head carpenter to make for it.

Memory recalled for him the scene with the King as it had been written down originally to Henri's dictation by a scrivener in the loneliness of old Henri's advancing years. He had recorded the events of his life, and subsequent de Lormes had rewritten, and eventually translated the original tale put down in clerical Latin.

Henri had beckoned to the seneschal who came forward at his bidding. In his hands he carried a casket. Then turning to the King he had said,

'This, sire, my brother Edouard brought to me from my parents' *château* in Normandy. My mother bade Edouard bring it to me when she was on her deathbed. She spoke words which laid a vital charge upon me concerning both this casket and its contents. I swear upon my life, sire, that I know nothing of the contents. My mother bade my brother, "Charge Henri that he treat the contents of this casket as an heirloom and that he pass the word on thus to his firstborn son". Then on that deathbed she made prophecy saying, "There will be Lormes who put down good roots, bear fruits and seed themselves beyond the limits of my vision while such is carried forward faithfully".

The King leaned forward in his chair, ' 'Tis a strange tale,' he commented. 'One is tempted to enquire if the Lady Mathilde also imposed the injunction that the contents of your casket should remain secret?'

Henri hesitated, then met the King's dark gaze. 'Nay, Sire,' he admitted, ' 'tis naught but my own feeling in the matter; certes, should the opening of it be to your desire then should I do so on the instant!'

The King declined. He remained still, in deep thought for some time then made pronouncement.

'Nay, Henri, let matters rest as your instincts prompt you. Such things are not within your King's authority. *But—as you choose to leave it unopened—see to it that you lay the charge upon your heirs to do likewise and keep the contents secret too. The power of such things cannot be denied and once invoked can never be gainsayed without disastrous consequences.*'

Both Henri de Lorme then and he Gyles now, felt sure at this juncture that the King must have been recalling Harold's oath taken, unknowingly over the Saint's bones and also what that exercise in cheating brought about thereafter.

The familiar words, learned so many years ago when he was a stripling, though almost certainly not in the exact form of the original, yet must contain the essence of what was first said, he reminded himself. They echoed in Gyles' head with persistent reiteration undermining more and more deeply his twentieth-century assertions, until the defences which he had raised against them began to crumble.

Christine watched horrified at what appeared to her to be some soul-searing revelation which had come to her husband as he paced and repaced their library. She saw his struggling with an inner conflict which she could not share and because of it she enmeshed herself with regrets and self-reproaches that she had broached at a time like this anything which caused such terrible struggles in the mind of the man she loved.

Before she could speak the crunching of gravel under tyres sounded through the opened library doors and the great front door which had been opened wide.

Gyles came back to the present dazedly. 'Sir James!' he exclaimed, 'Come, my love, we must go immediately.'

Clearly a watch had been kept above, for even as he crossed the hall Gyles heard Dr Jamieson's voice behind him and together the two men waited as the magnificence which was Sir James came unhurriedly up the steps.

When he had been greeted, Dr Jamieson with a murmured, 'Excuse us, please, Lord Aynthorp,' led the great man away and the two mounted the staircase together followed by the chauffeur with two large Gladstone bags. The murmur of their voices diminished as they disappeared from view. Gyles stood on alone with his returning fears.

Outside Petula's rooms Constance was waiting. Inside, the nurse and Rosemary were bending over the racked girl in the big four poster bed. Dr Jamieson came in and dismissed them summarily, so they went outside to join Constance and stood whispering at a window embrasure.

After about ten minutes the door opened again and Sir James came out looking grim.

Within five minutes the Convalescent Home's senior staff,

brusquely commandeered from their normal duties, were running down the corridors with instructions to prepare the theatre for an immediate operation.

'I will endeavour to perform a Caesarian section,' Sir James told Dr Jamieson brusquely. 'You will do me the service of assisting me, Jamieson? Yes? Good. Have you ever performed this operation or witnessed it in execution?'

'Yes, sir,' he said steadily, 'two years ago, at the Cottage Hospital, Lord Border came down especially . . .'

'Tricky,' said the great man, divesting himself of his coat and pulling a white one from the depths of one of the two Gladstone bags. 'The dangers are so much greater now that she has been so long in labour; by the by I brought one of these for you,' he added tossing a replica coat to him. Then, 'Very tricky,' he said again. 'It's virtually unknown. Only a few have been done successfully. Is the father here?'

The doctor shook his head, explained briefly, ended, 'But I understand he is on his way.'

'Good, then who is the next of kin?'

'Her father.'

'Ask him to be good enough to come here immediately.'

Struggling into his white coat Dr Jamieson turned to Constance. 'Will you please go for me, Lady Constance?' he asked.

'Just a moment, please,' Sir James' voice stayed her. 'Have I not seen you somewhere before, Sister?'

Constance nodded. 'Yes, Sir James, I am or rather I was Constance Cummins.'

'Good Gad!' his eyes were sharp under their bushy eyebrows, 'then you're the gel's stepmother?'

'I am.'

He stared at her piercingly. 'And yet you will assist?'

'If you will have me,' she replied steadily.

'Capital!' he nodded. 'How de do, and may I say I always had a sneakin' admiration for yer heroism, now it seems you will demonstrate it again.' He was busily drawing on a pair of rubber gloves as he spoke. 'Who else have I?'

Constance elected to be grand. 'Madame La Comtesse de la Coutray,' she said a trifle tartly, 'otherwise known in my Home as Sister Rosemary.'

He grunted, despite himself slightly taken aback. Then he came back, 'Can she be relied upon to keep her head?'

'I can vouch for that, Sir James. Let me introduce you.' She beckoned to Rosemary, made the introduction and the great man examined her keenly.

'I understand you have offered to do theatre duty too. Well then, we operate immediately. Pray summon a stretcher without delay. Ah, and tell me, have you a small recovery room?'

Constance answered, 'We have, Sir James.'

He turned to Dr Jamieson, 'Get her down there now. Give her a whiff of chloroform. Then we will anaesthetise her in the theatre. I suggest a mixture of chloroform and ether. . . .' he dropped his voice slightly as he added, 'the old rag and bottle, yes?'

'Just as you say, Sir James.'

Already the stretcher-bearers were coming towards them; but at the same time the surgeon saw the stricken face of Charles Danement as he came round the corner.

'I am Mrs de Lorme's father, Sir James,' he announced, his voice made slightly harsh by his anxiety.

'Quite so, quite so. It's a bad business, my dear sir. You must understand I would not wish to trouble you but I am compelled to ask you, may we do what we can?'

'Oh anything!' it was a cry wrung from him.

'Thank yer. I propose a Caesarian section, know what that means?'

Charles hesitated. 'In layman's terms, yes, but only very vaguely—that you operate and remove the child?'

Sir James nodded. 'Quite so. Now I have to warn you, it is a dangerous attempt. However, I am bound to admit that without it we will lose 'em both.'

Dr Jamieson gave a loud, warning cough.

Sir James swung round, looked at him, frowned then fired out, 'Time is precious, understand. I have to rush my fences, for this I apologise.'

'Thank you,' said Charles.

'Well then, I have to add that we suspect your gel's got twins. We may lose one, we may lose all three but with God's Divine intervention we might just save one or all. Now I ask you again, have I yer permission?'

'Yes,' Charles had himself well in hand by now. 'Just tell me, what chance has she got?'

'Slim,' Sir James grunted, 'and slimmer still for the unborn.

Would do no harm if you said a prayer or two. I always do before I operate. Colleague of mine does too, capital feller called Macadam Eccles . . .'

Charles nodded. 'There is just one more thing.'

'What?'

'Is my daughter still conscious?'

'Barely.'

'If she can hear you will you please tell her again that Henry is coming and urge her please "hold on for Henry".'

Sir James said gruffly, 'Consider it done' then turned on his heel and hurried away. Seconds later, with Constance on one side and Rosemary on the other the stretcher-bearers came out with their burden and they too vanished from the father's view.

When at length Charles went slowly back the way he had come and found himself in the great hall once again a staff car shot up the drive. Henry had come at last; but at this moment the mask was being put over Petula's face while Constance gripped one hand and coaxed, 'Breathe in, my darling, please breathe in. Yes that's splendid . . . and now just once more . . .'

Henry was too late to let Petula know that he had come.

When they had told him, in the library, he remained standing stiffly staring over their heads for what seemed to them an eternity. To the mother this was the greatest agony of all, for she knew that she was helpless. He was beyond her reach. In fact it took him some few minutes to accept their words, which, when their meaning impinged upon him fully brooked no questioning whatever.

He asked them, 'Where is she now?' standing with both hands behind his back as he had stood when bayed by anything as a small boy.

Gyles told him 'In the theatre. Sir James operates, Dr Jamieson assists. Constance and Rosemary are both there too with the anaesthetist whom Sir James brought with him from London—the best I am told.'

'I see,' said Henry woodenly.

The silence in the room became total. They were like three figures hewn from granite, the father, the mother and the eldest son.

Suddenly Henry said, 'We never thought of twins did we? It has never occurred with us. We don't have twins do we?'

'No,' Gyles agreed.

'Then what does Sir Charles say of his line?'

'No twins,' this time Christine spoke.

Gyles was at last aware of the very obvious fact that his son was in an extreme state of shock and for a moment he considered the possibility of hitting him across the face or shaking him violently. Across such thoughts the toneless voice asked 'How long have they been in there?'

Gyles shook his head. 'They have only just gone in.'

Henry was clenching and unclenching those concealed hands as he met the onslaught of fact . . . that his wife would very probably die in their small theatre and in her dying might well take his son—he could not think beyond him—with her . . . out of life as he knew it . . . way out beyond his reach or his imagining.

The nails of one hand bit deep into the back of the other as he stammered out,

'Would Grandfather drive her back to us or would he hold out those strong old hands to lead her away?'

Gyles flashed back, 'Your Grandfather would drive her back with all the force of his, er, somewhat forceful character, you may have no doubt of that. You are so right though in assuming that, wherever she is, he is with her raising merry hell I have no doubt on that other side of life.'

Fractionally Henry's face relaxed. He looked at his father then said with stronger voice, 'That any of us on either side of life could be the cause of breaking our line is unthinkable. That at least holds out some hope for us.'

'I concur,' Gyles cleared his throat with which he seemed to be having some trouble. 'Moreover,' he added, 'I submit that since the power of thought is unparalleled and limitless we should do well to channel ours towards the constructive rather than the, er, other.'

Henry challenged him. 'Can you, sir?'

'For me,' Gyles temporised, 'I hang my shield upon a quotation, one which is very old. It at least summarises how far I believe I am capable of going. It says "for this we truly desire to do *and such desire is parent to achievement*".' He laid special emphasis upon the interpretation.

Henry bent his head as though his father had written the

words at his feet and he now had need to study them. He remained staring down for what seemed to his watchers an agonisingly long time before asking, 'Meanin' the wish is father to the thought?'

'Precisely.'

Henry nodded. 'Yes, I see,' he said at last. 'Thank you sir. I think I will go upstairs now. If I am wanted I will be in our rooms.'

As he disappeared into the Great Hall Christine made an involuntary movement but Gyles restrained her.

'Let him go, my love,' he said gently, 'this is one conflict he must engage alone.'

Christine shivered. 'It seems,' she said forlornly, 'that we are bereft of everything except other men's words.'

He looked at her curiously, 'Of what are you thinking now?'

She began to quote, ' "Your children are not your children. They are the sons and daughters of life's longing for itself. They come through you but not from you. And though they are with you they belong not to you. You may give them your love but not your thoughts. You may house their bodies but not their souls. For their souls dwell in the house of tomorrow, which you cannot visit, even in your dreams".' She ended and sat with her hands quiet in her lap in a pose of resignation.

Gyles then asked her, 'Did he not speak of crime and punishment too?'

'Because of what we said about the Talisman?' she queried.

'Yes.'

'I cannot remember,' she stood up, 'let me see if I can find the book.' She went to the library steps which by some curious accident stood beside the many shelves of verse. She began searching, running one finger with its pale, buffered nail along the books' spines. She climbed a step higher and presently another until with a cry of triumph she drew a slim volume out, sat on the top of the steps and began turning the pages. Then she read the words for which she had been searching to Gyles—the ones which she knew he needed.

' "When one of you falls down, he falls for those behind him, a caution against the stumbling stone. Ay, and he falls for those ahead of him, who, though faster and surer of foot, yet not removed the stumbling stone".' She smiled down at him compassionately her composure wholly restored. 'You see, my darling, we are no further forward in resolving our problem than we were before. You knew I should not follow Henry and I accepted it and then this one among many, many prophets *confirmed* the rightness by his words. That is within universal law. But we do not know about the Talisman and therefore no quote from any prophet can tell us until we have seen and recognised the truth for ourselves. That too is the law.'

The two frightened old persons were still on their knees in the Chapel. After a while, wheezing behind them heralded the lumbering entry of Bishop Alaric who made his way with painful slowness to the great chair which had been placed for him beside the choir stalls—the only one able to accommodate his massive girth.

Priscilla and Claire sat in the recovery room with two of the younger V.A.D.s. Henrietta had drawn a stool close beside her husband's wheel chair where she sat weeping silently while Sinclair stared into the fire.

Below stairs was a shambles of apathetic figures, all their emotion spent through the long night which lay behind them. Sawby sat with his head on his hands on a chair beside the telephone, just listening and waiting. Boots had long ago crawled away with a puckered face to hide his sorrow in his hole below the basement stairs. Chef André's stoves smouldered unreplenished, their coals dimmed down to near extinction while the Frenchman alternately dropped off asleep and sat nodding until his high bonnet crashed over his nose, then waked with a start sat up and began blaspheming in mercifully incomprehensible French.

Mrs Parsons, the arch tragedienne of the Lower Orders was reduced to making cat's cradles with her over-white cook's fingers and twitching her shoulders. Occasionally she muttered to herself; but she, too, was by now unintelligible. Only Mrs Peace that Lady Deadlock of a woman had taken a ruthless grasp upon the housemaids and now stood, in doorway after doorway, grim-lipped and every inch the martinet, as she bullied the torpid women into following their daily routine.

Miss Palliser, long since dismissed by the Dowager with a, 'Go away, woman, and don't come back, your sniffing is unendurable', had taken her sniffs below stairs to the Steward's

Room and there sat facing Pearson who simply stared at nothing in absolute immobility.

Huddled together like sparrows in bad weather the kitchen and scullery maids whispered in the room where they sorted garden produce; while outside in his stovehouses Sawbridge tied up tomato plants as if he were putting dozens of hangmen's nooses about their necks and they the cause of all this tragedy.

Henry marched resolutely to their bedroom. He stood for some time staring at the bed which bore no sign of any stress. Someone, he knew not whom nor spared much thought of it, had come and put clean linen on it and spread a fresh lace cover. The same someone had put fresh flowers in bowls about the room. Even if he had probed, he would not have found that Mrs Peace had done so, by herself, as no one had seen her making the only gesture in her power towards her resolution that the living babes and their mother would return from that theatre.

Henry sat down on the big bed, found it unbearable so stood up, automatically straightening a crease his weight had made on the lace coverlet. Then he went to the door and listened. The Castle was so dreadfully silent. Not a sound came to thaw the pall of fear which was rapidly enveloping him once again. He went through to the Nursery where he and Petula had wandered together and was startled to see Nanny standing near a nursing chair which had been drawn up before the fire. A large brass kettle sang softly on a hob which had been affixed inside the fire guard. The cradle was there too, the tiny hand-embroidered coverlet folded back expectantly. Beside it there was a second to which Nanny was putting the final touches as he went in. Nanny straightened her back, turned, spread down her white apron with steady hands and said to him in a voice fraught with content, 'Now we're ready for her wen she comes back and for the babbies too. I found this bassinet and Raikes carried it in for me. Jest because Number Two is so unexpected we dursn't let either 'im or 'er whichever it proves ter be ketch us unprepared!' After which declaration of faith she sat down in her nursing chair again and eased her buttoned boots on to the fender.

Henry made a stifled sound but no words came.

'I 'ope, Mister Henry,' Nanny then said in her most magisterial tones, 'that you aren't making yourself into a state over this for I can tell you you 'ave no need.' Her sharp little eyes were very bright indeed.

'No . . . need?' Henry stammered, staring at her disbelievingly.

'That's wot I said,' Nanny nodded, 'and that's wot I meant, young man. She may 'ave ter be cut open which is unnachural and crool in my opinion but she'll be back.' After which bland announcement she began a curious kind of rocking—without her rocking chair. With her feet on the fender she did a stiff kind of knees bend, knees straighten, which Henry watched hypnotised.

'Wot's more,' she resumed knees bending and straightening even faster, 'I've never bin wrong! Nanny can see, Nanny can.'

'What can you see now, Nanny?'

'Trouble,' she said tartly. 'Where there's Lormes there's trouble, that's for sure and certain; but not death. Oh dear me no! There's a death coming but it aint your wife's. I carn't promise the earth, nor can Almighty God because that's not wot we're 'ere for. If we was to have everything just the way we wanted we wouldn't be here but in Heaven—' here she loosed a highly critical sounding sniff, adding, 'wherever *that* may turn out to be. The thing with this fambly is that their time is not come yet nor will come for many a long day, you'll see.' After which utterances she seemed to fall asleep although she still went on with her simulated rocking.

The kettle sang, the old woman's boots creaked, above them on the mantel-shelf the clock ticked away. Suddenly she started up, stood for a moment listening and then went rushing out across the bedroom and into the corridor.

Henry heard her calling, 'Mr Henry, jest you come here.'

He raced after her to find her standing with her head cocked, one finger to her lip, and listening tensely.

'I heard it!' she gabbled. 'I did, I say. Now just you listen!'

Henry just stood there beside her the rim of his nostrils white, both hands thrust deep into his pockets to conceal their shaking. Then he heard it too. It was quite unmistakably the cry of a newborn child. Round the corner, carrying her precious burden came the Nurse with something swathed in a foamy shawl.

Henry was unable to move. She came up to them. 'Yes,' she said, her homely face transfigured as she moved a fraction of shawl to disclose a tiny, angry, very red face. 'Saved, living, a dear beautiful, safe perfect little girl, sir,' and she held the little bundle out still cradled in the curve of her outstretched hands.

'Take your little daughter, Mr Henry,' Nanny commanded. 'Take her and give thanks.'

'My ... daughter?' Henry said dazedly, putting out reluctant hands.

'Take her, Nanny,' said the nurse hurriedly, 'I must go back, it's not over yet.'

Nanny did so, crooning and careening over the tiny thing. 'What did Nanny say eh, my pretty? Oh, Mr Henry, she's a beautiful little baby.'

'A ... daughter,' said Henry slowly. 'But what of my wife, Nanny?'

'You heard didn't you? Nurse said, "not over yet". Well if she were gorne she wouldn't say that now would she? Where's your Lorme courage, what's happened to that, may I ask? I'm ashamed of you, you naughty boy,' she nagged with undiminished valiance.

Henry forced himself to look down at the little living thing he had sired. She was such an angry new arrival, resentful of the struggle she had made. As he looked down so the child silenced. Then she opened her blue eyes for one dazzling second. Henry started—he put out one long finger. The minute hand closed over it but the shock was too great. He could not admit the feeling of warmth and tenderness which momently assailed him.

'What about Petula,' he choked, and then, 'A daughter!' and so saying turned away in revulsion. The brightness fled from Nanny's little beady eyes leaving them bereft and cold as pebbles.

'Was this to be the cause of Petula's death?' thought Henry frantically. 'A girl!' The futility assailed him so strongly that even Nanny held her tongue. She just rocked the baby while fixing those pebble-cold eyes on the father.

'Please take my daughter to Lady Aynthorp and his Lordship,' he then said stiffly, as if speech hurt him now. 'After that do with her whatever you know should be done.'

He fled from the room. He went down the corridors, heading blindly in the direction of the theatre. As he reached the recovery room Priscilla came out with another fleecy bundle in her arms. 'Shush,' she said. Henry subsided, staring at the bundle as she then spoke the words he had never thought to hear,

'We have had to fight for him,' she said proudly, 'the poor little mite was almost asphyxiated,' and in her extreme agitation she used her own body to push Henry away along the corridor.

'But your son is alive, Henry, and so is Petula though I must warn you her life hangs on a very fragile thread and you must go away. They are bringing her into the recovery room in a few moments.'

No other birth of an heir to the de Lormes had been received with such sparse rejoicing. When the news filtered through to the Servants' Hall, Raikes leapt to her feet crying, 'The Countess, the Dowager, they are still in the Chapel!' She promptly turned and fled towards it without even pausing to obtain permission from Sawby. He made no move to stop her. He just slumped in his chair as if all the stuffing had been withdrawn from him and he only a rag doll simulation of a butler.

'Let us at least give thanks for an heir,' he said sounding far more severe than he had intended by reason of his repressed emotion.

'But what of their mother I would ask?' came inevitably from Mrs Parsons. Mademoiselle Palliser hastily sketched a reverence, hoisted a rosary from her pocket and began telling the beads the while mumbling appeals to the patron saint of all expectant mothers Saint Gerard.

Upstairs in the new nursery the women were gathering round the two cradles, moving from one to the other, their faces dragged down by their fears for Petula. It fell to the Dowager, when she and her sister-in-law came hurrying in, to ask in the rallying voice of authority, 'Has that boy been examined, Nurse? Is he perfect?'

Nanny shook her head. 'I dursent, my lady,' she confessed, at long last reduced to humility. 'I was afeared.'

'And so am I,' snapped the Dowager, easing her ache with rising asperity. 'So get to it, woman; instantly!'

Before anyone could obey her a steady voice from the doorway said, 'There is no need. I have already examined them both. There is some slight damage to the little boy's left foot, but Sir James assures us all it is only temporary.'

'Is that all?' snapped the Dowager.

Constance hesitated. Then she swept forward to kneel down by the ancient cradle in which the boy had been laid and drew back the enfolding shawl.

'He is sleeping beautifully,' she told them, 'but we shall have to watch his breathing very carefully for a while. There is no need for anxiety, only constant, unbroken attention for the first few days.'

She rose again and the little Countess was the first to observe how exhausted and spent she looked. When she had rearranged her uniform she told them plainly, 'I came to tell you that your daughter-in-law Lady Aynthorp, is now in the recovery room. Sir James wishes to speak to her husband and her father first. I will in the meantime tell you that she will not be out of danger for three or at most four days. The enemy is something called puerperal fever. At present she is too weak to be moved. Rosemary and Doctor Jamieson are with her. I shall relieve them with Claire and Priscilla alternately and when Pet is deemed strong enough she will be brought to her room. No one can remain here of course until Sir James gives permission. Absolutely no one can visit her. Now I must leave you for Sir James wishes to speak to my husband and to Henry immediately.' She glanced across at the Nurse who stood listening attentively.

'You nurse will remain on duty with the twins, with Nanny assisting until such time as your relief comes. I have already summoned her, a woman whom like yourself I have known and worked with for some time and in whom I have implicit trust— like you.' The nurse flushed at this and her eyes shone. Then the Dowager had the last word. She stood up. She looked at Christine and with a little crooked smile she said, 'Payment deferred, my dear,' and so saying made a regal exit.

By nightfall the stream of callers bearing flowers and little notes was undiminished. Carriages bowled up the drive which Sawbridge and Plum had caused to be covered from end to end with straw which effectively deadened the sound of wheels and horses' hooves.

Sawby opened the doors again and again, handed the 'floral tributes' to his attendant footwomen, received the accompanying wafer-folded notes on his silver tray and every so often took them to the Family in the library.

A single reporter reached the front doors, only to encounter Sawby who sent him packing in terms more round than he was wont to employ. After this he sent for Plumstead who bowled himself off like a carriage on his bandy legs to impress more old men. Thereafter the main drive gates and all the lodge gates were manned by septuagenarians who interrogated coachmen, probed chauffeuses and gave short shrift to any who even remotely suggested they might be from newspapers. It was ten o'clock before the last caller went away, after which Gyles came out and gave instructions that no one else was to be admitted until ten o'clock the next morning.

Petula was still in the recovery room. Sir James had been assigned a suite and given the Countess as his telephonist. She put through his calls for him, whisking herself away after each connection had been made with remarkable celerity and returning, once with a cup of Chef André's famous *bouillon*; once with a glass of Gyles' oldest brandy; and once, somewhat diffidently, with a plate of minute sandwiches which she was thankful to find on returning, were not upon their doily-covered plate.

'Capital sandwiches, Countess, thank you very much,' said Sir James cheerfully.

She inclined her head graciously, and risked informing him that food and wine would be served informally in the Breakfast Room in a few moments. If he could bring himself to join the Family it would give them all great comfort.

'Comfort, eh?' he sounded surprised, appeared to examine the word, finally shot out, 'Why comfort?'

'Because,' said little Marguerite with a ragged shred of coquetry beneath the mask of exhaustion which she wore, like all the rest, 'our girl's life is in your hands. You have saved the heir to this name, his sister and, so far, the girl whom we love. Therefore'—the coquetry dropped from her like an unsuitable garment —'our hearts are in pawn to your skill and experience and we would want you to take the greatest possible care of yourself— both for our girl's sake and for your own. You have done so much for us already.'

It was a gallant speech, perhaps not of the quality of which she was generally capable, but he recognised the effort it must have cost her to deliver it so he stood up, took her paper frail right hand and bent over it.

'Then,' he said, 'in the light of your given reasons I have no alternative but to follow you.' So saying he dropped the small hand, offered her his arm instead and together they processed towards the Breakfast Room exchanging the small coinage of conversation, that the one might hold exhaustion and the other responsibility at bay.

Henry did not join them. Only Plum could have told them where he was and presently, when all the gates had been fastened and the old men who had elected to keep watch over them had been supplied with braziers and steaming jugs of cocoa, Plum plodded once more across the park to set the Castle inmates' minds at rest.

He marched into the Servants' Hall, shook his head at their welcome, said tersely, 'Listen ter me ef you please. Then I'm orf 'ome. Ef anyone wonders wot's 'appened to Mister 'Enery 'ee's along er Ma. Ma's got 'im by er fire and wen I left larst he was suppin' a bowl of soup and Ma was givin' 'im a good talking to which is wot 'ee needs. Good night all.' And without further ado he stumped off to begin his long plod home.

When he had been gone for some minutes Sawby came down the staircase, was told and promptly turned around and climbed wearily up them again. He re-entered the Breakfast Room where, the brief meal ended, Gyles, having accepted his guest's admiration of the linenfold panelling, was courteously explaining the portraits which oversaw them. They were all better now, since a stranger was among them and they were consequently bound to holding themselves in leash. Sawby coughed in the doorway.

Gyles turned, murmured, 'Excuse me, Sir James,' said 'Yes, Sawby?' and the butler delivered the message in his own style.

'Plumstead has just called my, lord,' he said stiffly, 'he thought you would wish to know that Mr Henry is with his wife. When he last saw them Mr Henry was taking of some of Mrs Plumstead's soup. Plumstead also asked me to tell you that if he does not return he will be sleeping. Although Mr Henry has not been told so, Plumstead suspects that his wife has put something, er, soporific in that soup.'

Gyles thanked him with quivering lips. Sir James turned his head to conceal a smile. Sawby waited.

'Will that be all, my lady?' he enquired of Christine.

'Yes thank you, Sawby. Pray tell the staff they may all go to bed as early as they wish and try to get some sleep as we shall do presently.'

Doubt was writ large on Sawby's normally impassive face.

So, murmuring as Gyles had done, 'Excuse me, Aynthorp'— Sir James on perceiving this now took it upon himself to reply.

'I have advised it, er, Sawby,' he said with staggering pomposity. 'Pray tell your staff so and tell them also that Mrs de

Lorme has come round from the anaesthetic and is sleeping. She will not be left alone for an instant. If there are any changes you will all be told. And now good night to you.'

Sawby hauled down his flag. He bowed, murmured 'Thank you, sir. My staff will be greatly relieved.'

When he had gone Christine said impulsively, 'That was very kind of you, Sir James. None of them went to bed last night, they are—' she paused, selecting words carefully 'of unsurpassed loyalty and my husband and I have reason to believe they also have great devotion to the family.'

Henry awoke to the smell of frying bacon. He looked around bemusedly. He swung his legs over the couch and rubbed sleep from his eyes. Then up went his hand to his already disordered head. He was in the 'Plums' ' front room. Two old carriage rugs and a plaid one had been laid over him. As realisation came to him so he started up and rushed out following the bacon smell and finding himself in Mrs Plumstead's kitchen.

'Well now, Mister 'Enery,' she greeted him, 'you and Miss ·Petula both 'as 'ad some sleep and all's well at the Castle so far so what about puttin' your 'ead under the pump and then tuckin' into a proper breakfast. Plum's bin gorne a long whiles now. Fust to the Castle were 'ee saw 'is lordship. 'Ee said as 'ow there was no change yet so there's no cause for you to fret and you'll do it stronger,' urged this splendid old creature, 'with a good bit of eggs and bacon inside of yer. I don't h'aspire ter cawfee but I've as good a strong 'ot cup er tea as ever you might wish fer.'

Henry stared at her. Then something inside him began to soften. Slowly he crossed the rag rug and deliberately took the toasting fork from the work-worn hands. Then he put his arms around her and kissed her.

'Bless your loving old heart,' he said, 'of course I will. In fact I think I'm jolly hungry, so just hang on while I freshen up a bit.'

'No one carnt work thet pump and put their 'eads beneath it,' she called after him, 'Go on and I'll come and work it fer yer ... as I does for Pa and 'ee's lef' '*is* pa's razer's out should you fancy a shave ... after you've et.'

CHAPTER 18

Seven Days' Leave

When Sawby reported to the family that Henry was with Plum's wife, Gyles left the Breakfast Room to telephone the General. As he had suspected, the old stickler was still working at the War Office; and having given his name Gyles was put through immediately.

'How's the gel?' came like a bark down the telephone without benefit of preliminaries.

'Hangin' on, sir,' Gyles answered. 'She is safely delivered of twins, a boy and a girl but it will be possibly as much as four days before the mother is out of danger.'

'Then tell your boy to take seven days' compassionate leave and be good enough to keep me informed in the interim,' there was a slight pause, then, 'When did he reach yer?' was rapped out. Gyles duly reported, he heard a faint chuckle and, 'They must have driven like hell!' came from the General. To this he added, 'Don't waste time with me. We can talk later. Pray give my most sincere good wishes and sympathy to yer family. Goodbye.' Click went the receiver. Gyles replaced his. As he walked back to join the Family, Christine was asking, 'Has anyone seen Uncle Alaric?' and as Gyles walked towards his chair the Dowager replied, 'Yes, dear, he came into the Chapel to pray. In fact he seemed so deep in prayer we decided to leave him when Raikes came for us.'

Christine hesitated, then turning to Sir James she explained, 'My Uncle the Bishop is rather elderly. He is also very fond of food, therefore I wonder if we should not send someone to see if he is still there?'

'I'm up,' said Gyles quietly, 'let me go.' He reversed and walked out once more.

He followed the familiar path, lifted the latch and went in. The candles were flickering in their sockets, no more now than tiny stars in the darkness. He groped about unsuccessfully for the recently installed light switch, then began feeling his way along the aisle towards those choir stalls. As he drew nearer to the altar he could just discern the shadowy bulk of his uncle and see that his head was sunk down on his chest. Gyles reached him, stood at his shoulders, said softly, 'Uncle Alaric, sir.'

It drew no response from the huddled bulk. He bent closer, said louder than before,

'Uncle, Uncle Alaric!' Again, failing to obtain any acknow-ledgement he put a tentative hand to the old man's shoulder. The body sagged forward. Gyles grunted, hesitated as the truth penetrated, then slid that exploratory hand down. It touched ice cold fingers. One of the tiny stars went out, and then another, and another ...

'What a splendid way to go,' said Gyles Aynthorp compassionately.

Fumblingly he then made his way towards where he knew the candles were kept in a very old Bible box. Then he moved from sconce to sconce, stumbling, groping, affixing a candle, laying the rest down to reach for his small gold match box. As he made his way slowly along the aisle towards the door, the new-lit candles pointed their clear flames upwards drawing the envelop-ing darkness out into long shadows until it seemed to his over-wrought imagination that other, wraith-like figures developed that they might keep watch over the dead man in the great chair.

That over-wrought imagination began to play tricks with him. He found himself thinking as he closed the Chapel door that Bishop Alaric's life might have been taken in order that Petula's should be spared. A life for a life indeed. The old man had come to the Chapel to intercede for the girl. Could it be that such intercession, made in deep sincerity, from one who was not wholly guiltless of hypocrisy, could be transformed into the willing offering of himself ... as hostage for a young girl? So thinking he went in to tell the family.

Henry was told of his Uncle's death when he returned across the Park after his breakfast with Mrs Plumstead. As Gyles prefaced this news with a report from Sir James that Petula was 'holding her own' and a kindly explanation of his refusal to let Henry see her, Gyles was puzzled by Henry's shocked expression and the bemused silence which followed.

He had listened gratefully when his father told him that Sir

James explained how Petula was sleeping most of the time, though he avoided any reference to sedation, that the gynaecologist very much wished that his patient should not be excited in any way until all fear of the puerperal fever had passed. Henry had grunted, 'Point taken, thanks very much, sir,' and relapsed into that brooding again.

Suddenly he said, 'I shall call my son Justin Charles, sir, with your approval.'

'That would have delighted your Grandfather,' Gyles smiled, 'And your daughter? What will you call her?'

Henry shrugged his shoulders, 'Oh I expect Pet will have ideas about that don't you.' Suddenly he jumped up, 'Holy God!' he exclaimed, 'I have never telephoned m'y General.'

'But I have,' Gyles assured him, 'he has given you seven days' compassionate leave and asked me to report to him daily.'

Except in the library where the two men sat there was a gentle wind of change blowing through the Castle. It was compounded of hope and that resilience which comes from a good night's sleep. Even the funeral could not quite dispel it. Indeed when Sir James appeared down the great staircase with Raikes following behind carrying his bags and other impedimenta, the breeze blew more strongly.

'Sir James is going. Things must be better' . . . thus sang the breeze through the servants' quarters.

Sir James stood on the top of the steps drawing on his gloves. 'Jamieson will keep me informed,' he assured Gyles and Henry. 'I have a vital commitment in London but I, too, will telephone regularly. Rest assured I should not be leaving if I had not complete confidence in both Jamieson and that remarkable Lady Constance.'

Henry could no longer restrain himself. 'And my son's foot?' he blurted out, 'What about my son's foot, sir?' his voice sounded almost shrill.

'These are early days, my dear sir,' Sir James parried blandly, 'have a little confidence and I am sure all will be very well indeed.' So saying and as if to confirm that he at any rate had no more to add, he made his stately descent into his limousine and was driven away. Henry vanished too. Gyles looked for him in the library when he returned but the room was empty. He moved towards his old office. On the way he encountered Lucy whom he greeted with surprise.

'My dear, how nice to see you. I had thought you and Lucien were with Piers having that portrait painted.'

'We were, Uncle Gyles,' said Lucy, 'but it is finished. So when we heard that Petula was so ill we came back. Piers brought us.'

'Is he here now?' Gyles asked frowning slightly.

'Oh no, Uncle, he went immediately. He told us to tell you that he thought you would prefer it so. He said he will bring the painting for you to see, when . . .' she stumbled here, 'when . . . things are quieter for us.'

Gyles' face cleared. He said regretfully, 'This is a sorrowful house for you two young ones to come back to my dear.'

'Oh no, Uncle,' she said again. 'I am to be of use. Aunt Constance has told me that I may relieve the others who sit with Petula all the time. Then they may have food and rest.' The small face lifted to his was immensely grave, 'I do assure you I will be most tremendously careful.'

Gyles put out one hand to touch those fair curls saying, 'I have no doubt of that, my dear; but before you go, I wonder have you seen Henry anywhere?'

Lucy nodded. 'He went up the stairs a moment or two ago. I think,' she dropped her voice confidentially, 'that he has gone to *Tante* Marguerite's rooms. Do you wish me to find him for you?'

Gyles shook his head, 'He could not do better,' he told her, 'but where is Lucien? has he some ploy to occupy him with Mr Sissingham?'

Down went those long lashes. Gyles had an instinct that whereas before he asked this question she had been perfectly natural with him, his last query had imposed some guard upon her, turning her into the likeness of a small castle for whom the alarm had sounded and the drawbridge been raised.

'Yes,' said Lucy non-committally.

'Might one enquire what?'

She had gained her necessary time. Now she lifted her eyes again and said simply, 'He is in the twins' nursery making sketches of them while they are being bathed and put to bed. He wants them to be a surprise for the family.'

Again Gyles had the instinct so familiar to them all that Lucy was only giving him half a truth; but he said nothing and presently continued on his way.

*   *   *

Henry scratched on Countess Marguerite's sitting-room door and in answer to her familiar '*Entrez*' opened the door, revealing both her and the Dowager deep in two chairs by the fire. There was a third one between them, but until he approached he could not see that it contained Lady Constance. He went towards them, drew up a stool and sat down on it beside Marguerite.

'I'm so scared, darling,' he said childishly, leaning his head against the side of her chair.

The three women exchanged glances. Desperately Marguerite sought for guidance, decided she had found it and asked severely,

'What does it do to you?'

Henry looked up, surprised. 'Do to me?' he repeated. 'I dunno,' he rumpled his hair. 'Well, it makes me feel as though I did not belong to myself, did not fit any more, as if the *me*, that is inside had shrunk with it until that *me* is now crouching like a petrified squirrel inside some huge dark cavern.'

'Let us pursue the imagery,' Marguerite pressed him. 'You at least infer that when you are not in a state of fear you do not have this sensation?'

'Of course I do. I mean I do not, oh you know what I am trying to say.'

'That ordinarily the two parts of yourself fit as a glove fits the hand it encloses?'

'Yes.'

'Then,' the tiny figure sat up even more rigidly, 'does it not behove you, or in this case us, to find a way of bringing the two parts into proportion once again? Shall we begin by facing the facts?'

'But what are the facts?'

Marguerite looked at Constance appealingly.

She let the silence lie awhile then responded to that mute appeal. 'The facts are these,' she told him. 'Your wife is very ill. Every hour that passes strengthens her hold on life; but it will be three more days before we can say with any confidence that the real danger has passed. As to your children'—he could not see from where he sat that her hands were gripped tightly together, 'they are alive, safe and well.'

Henry said woodenly, 'And my son's left foot?'

Constance drew a deep breath. Three pairs of eyes were fixed upon her.

'There is the possibility,' she said clearly and deliberately, 'that your son will always have one leg a fraction shorter than the other. If this is so, it will not be enough to debar him a normal, healthy, active life since we are not living in the Middle Ages. Medical science is advancing at tremendous speed due to a great extent to this horrible war. Nor are you impoverished peasants living in some hovel. You have both means and opportunity. Advice can and will be both sought and found. It may well prove to be sound medical judgement that for the first few years of his life the little boy will have a slight limp. I am not sufficiently experienced to tell you whether it would be advantageous or deleterious for him to wear a special shoe in infancy. But whether he does or not he will eventually have one which will enable him to walk normally, and also to have this built in a way that it *will not be visible.* Is this so terrible to contemplate when a few hours ago you stood in danger of loosing both your children and your wife as well?'

'He will not be a cripple then?'

Constance stood up abruptly. To the amazement of all three she bent down and unfastened one small black slipper. 'Am I, Henry?' she demanded. 'No don't stare at me, answer me, please. Have you ever thought of me as a cripple?'

'Nnno, of course not but. . . .'

'But nothing,' Constance said forcefully, 'let me walk for you without my slippers then you may see.' So saying she bent down, removed the other shoe and walked away from the startled trio limping visibly. Across the other side of the room she swung round 'Now pick up my left slipper and examine it, please, Henry. I never walked without a limp until I was fifteen. I know what it was like to be as you said, a cripple. Things had not moved so far forward in my girlhood as they have done now. It was only when my parents were in Switzerland that they met a professor. He eventually asked them if he might be told why I limped. He was the pioneer of such things as he then explained. Eventually he persuaded my parents to have a special shoe made for me. Since then I have moved as I do now and as your son will do whenever the time is right for his growing foot. Now are you satisfied?'

Christine coming through the outer door of the nursery almost cannoned into the flying figure of her eldest son. He pulled up breathlessly, apologised and gripping her arms demanded,

'Mama, can I go in and see my son, can I pick him up?'

Wisely Christine asked no questions, thankful to see at last that he wanted to see his children.

'Most certainly you can,' she said calmly. 'At this moment Lucien is sketching them, Rose is bathing them and Nanny has had her rocking chair brought in so that she can keep her beady eyes on everything.'

The last part of her words were lost to Henry. He had gone to his twins. For the next three days, except when he left them for meals and to follow his Great Uncle Alaric's coffin to its resting place, he spent his time with them. When they slept he nursed them turn and turn about. When he joined the family for meals he fired questions at his father as to when he had had his first Rugger ball, at what age he had first been lifted on to a horse, and on the morning of the fourth day, walking very slowly and carefully he carried the youngest de Lorme, Plum's 'heir', to the stables so that the old coachman could croon over him.

That afternoon, while the women sat behind drawn curtains in the Blue Drawing Room and the men followed the elaborate hearse, in company with the formidable array of clerics who had travelled to Castle Rising to pay their last respects, Constance went into the little Drawing Room to sit with them until the men returned. This was after Alaric's simple will had been read by Truslove *Père* and the clerics and he had been driven to Little Aynthorp Station.

Henry stood restlessly at the tea table while Marguerite poured, as usual. When he had done he said abruptly, 'Mama, will you please excuse me. I promised Nanny I would be back in the nursery by five.'

Constance cleared her throat somewhat loudly.

'Henry dear,' she said, and was rewarded by the warmth of the look he directed to her. 'Could you spare time I wonder before visiting the twins to drop in on Petula? She is waiting to see you, my dear, and Henry, Dr Jamieson asked me to tell you that in his opinion the crisis is over and your wife is doing very well indeed.'

He found her propped up with an immense amount of pillows in their big bed. He crept round the door, saw her, gulped, 'Oh Pet' and then flung himself across the room and into her outstretched arms, all discretion gone.

Some time later Constance, peeping round the door saw her with a baby on each arm and Henry gazing down fatuously at his small family. She closed the door and continued along the corridor towards her patients in the Convalescent Home, wishing passionately that there was even the remotest chance that the size of that little family could ever be increased. She knew only too well, having been present through the Caesarian section that after Sir James had spoken with her husband and Sir Charles had given him absolute freedom to do as he thought best for all three, Sir James had exerted his prerogative by sterilising his patient.

When two indignant nurses had made their way to Petula's rooms and claimed the twins, Henry told Petula what Nanny had said.

'She was the only one,' he marvelled. 'She literally bawled me out. She told me I had no right or reason for my fears. She said —bless her ignorant old heart—that it was sinful to cut you up but that you would not give in. She said there would be a death in the family. She said it would not be you, and what's more the old girl assured me she was never wrong, because her corns told her and they could only be right.'

Petula giggled faintly, said weakly, 'Don't make me laugh, darling, it hurts; but, oh Henry, *her corns*! And then you say Uncle Alaric died in the Chapel praying for me?'

'Yes father found him.'

'It must have been frightful for all of you. But,' she snuggled down deeper into the pillows, suddenly drowsy, 'it's lovely to be so loved and to have twins and . . . to be safe . . . and . . . oh . . . everything.' Her eyelids dropped, her head turned slightly on those pillows and then she slept

When Rosemary came in she shooed him out, saying crossly, 'You've tired her out, you naughty boy. Now go away and don't come back until after dinner.'

For the first time in four days Henry grinned, 'All right, Nursie,' he whispered back, 'see if I care!' and so saying left them both. He began whistling rather tunelessly as he made his way towards the Drawing Room.

Primrose and John de Lorme were there now. Henrietta had wheeled Sinclair in. Raikes and Sawby brought fresh tea, coffee and tisanes. Seeing that all the dishes were empty, they took them below stairs and told the staff, 'More sandwiches, more cakes, more scones, more muffins, they're hungry at last, thank God.'

No sooner had fresh supplies been carried in than Sawby, crossing the hall, heard the sound of tyres on the gravel outside. Saying merely, 'Wait if you please' to Raikes he made his ponderous way to the doors, threw them back and found himself confronted by two people he had never seen before.

When he recounted the event to a spellbound assembly in the Servants' Hall he told them, 'The gentleman looked like Mr Pickwick. He was smiling, friendly, very sure of himself and beside him stood one of the prettiest young ladies it has ever been my pleasure to see. But I was shocked just the same. With the blinds and curtains drawn still and the funeral scarcely over it wasn't right nor proper.'

Sawby was in fact flummoxed for the very first time in his long years as the Lormes' butler. However, struggling for composure he greeted them formally,

'Good afternoon, madam, good afternoon, sir,' and listened to the Pickwickian one's request voiced in the strongest and most unmistakable American accent.

'Is Lord Aynthorp at home? I guess as the head of this illustrious family I should ask for him.' Then he gave his name and that of the pretty girl at his side.

Sawby paled once again recovered himself, bowed as much to conceal emotion as to render courtesy. He managed to say, 'If you will please follow me' then he led them across the hall and into the library.

'Pray be seated,' he said weakly. 'I will inform his lordship immediately.' Then he closed the doors and went reluctantly back to the small Blue Drawing Room.

He entered and stood waiting, miserably.

'Yes, Sawby?' Christine enquired.

'Er, there are callers, my lady.' Sawby told her reluctantly.

'Oh not today!' exclaimed Christine. 'For me?'

'No, my lady,' said Sawby woodenly, 'for his lordship.'

'Who on earth!' Priscilla exclaimed, 'would call today? Today of all days.'

Sawby turned slightly. 'I think they are newly arrived from, er, foreign parts, madam,' he vouchsafed. After this he turned again to face Gyles Aynthorp.

'They wish to see you, my lord. I have shown them into the library.'

'Well who the devil are they?' Gyles demanded irritably.

Sawby took a deep breath, stiffened his already straight back and replied,

'They are a Mr Silas Blenkinsop and his daughter, my lord, whose name the gentleman gave as Mrs Stephen Delahaye.'